The April Dead

Alan Parks

W F HOWES LTD

This large print edition published in 2021 by
W F Howes Ltd
Unit 5, St George's House, Rearsby Business Park,
Gaddesby Lane, Rearsby, Leicester LE7 4YH

1 3 5 7 9 10 8 6 4 2

First published in the United Kingdom in 2021
by Canongate Books Ltd

A CIP catalogue record for this book is available
from the British Library

ISBN 978 1 00404 018 6

Typeset by Palimpsest Book Production Limited,
Falkirk, Stirlingshire

Printed and bound by
T J Books in the UK

In memory of Jean Parks
1933–2020

'Will you bleed for me?'

– James King and The Lone Wolves

'I let him run on, this papier-maché Mephistopheles, and it seemed to me that if I tried I could poke my forefinger through him, and would find nothing inside but a little loose dirt, maybe.'

– Joseph Conrad

12TH APRIL 1974

CHAPTER 1

'Who on earth is going to set off a bomb in Woodlands?' asked McCoy. 'It's the back arse of Glasgow.'

'The IRA?' asked Wattie.

'Maybe,' said McCoy. 'It's Easter Friday I suppose. Not sure blowing up a shitey rented flat in Glasgow is the best way of striking at the British Establishment, not exactly the Houses of Parliament, is it?'

They were standing in the middle of West Princes Street looking up at the blown-out windows and scorched sandstone of what had been the flat at number 43. The flats around had suffered too: cracked windows, torn curtains hanging out, a window box filled with daffodils sitting face down in the middle of the road. McCoy got his fags out and lit one, waved the match out, and dropped it on the wet street.

'How come you know it's rented anyway?' asked Wattie.

'They all are around here, rented or sublet, no rent book, no contract. Half of Glasgow's waifs and strays live in the flats around here.'

3

'You think that's it started? Here I mean?' asked Wattie. 'Bombings?'

McCoy shrugged. 'Hope not but you know what they say. Glasgow is just Belfast without the bombs.'

'Until now that is,' said Wattie.

A shout from one of the firemen and they stepped back onto the pavement as a fire engine attempted a three-point turn in the narrow road. The whole street was a mess of fire engines, hoses, ambulances, police cars, uniforms trying to set up ropes to cordon the area off. The flats around 43 had been evacuated, residents standing in the street looking shocked, dressed in an assortment of different clothes from pyjamas and blanket-covered underwear to a man in a pinstripe suit and socks holding a cat in his arms.

A burly fireman emerged from the close and took his helmet off, sandy hair stuck to his head with sweat. He spat on the ground a couple of times and wandered over.

'It's safe,' he said. 'You can go up now.'

McCoy nodded. 'Any bodies?'

'One,' he said. 'Half of him's all over the walls, other half's burnt to a bloody crisp.'

McCoy's stomach turned over at the thought.

'All yours,' said the fireman and headed off to the reversing fire engine.

'Shite,' said McCoy. 'We're going to have to go up there, aren't we?'

'Yep,' said Wattie. 'You want to throw up now and get it over with?'

4

'Smartarse,' said McCoy, feeling like that was exactly what he wanted to do. 'Maybe we should wait for Faulds? He's on his way.'

'Any other excuses you can think of?' asked Wattie. 'Or is that it?'

McCoy sighed. 'Let's go.'

They ducked past the firemen rolling the hose back onto the wheel and headed into the close. Streams of water running down the stairs, stink of smoke and burnt wood in the air. They trudged up the stairs, making for the top-floor flat and the inevitable gruesome scene.

'You remembering about tonight?' asked Wattie.

'How could I forget it?' said McCoy. 'You keep reminding me every five minutes. I'll be at your dad's at six as instructed.'

'He's booked a Chinese,' said Wattie. 'Down in the town. It's cheap.'

'Great,' said McCoy, making a mental note to eat before he went. A Chinese restaurant in Greenock whose selling point was that it was cheap sounded like a recipe for indigestion at best, food poisoning at worst.

They were at the top landing now. Front door of the flat had been burst open by the firemen, was hanging half on-half off its hinges. McCoy gave it one more go.

'Maybe we should wait for Phyllis Gilroy?' he asked. 'What do we know about bomb casualties? She's the medical examiner after all, she's going to be much more use than you or me.'

Wattie sighed, looked at him. 'Look, if you don't want to go in, it's fine. I'll go.'

'Really?' asked McCoy. 'That would be brill—'

'Aye, and I'll make sure and tell Murray when we get back to the station all about my commanding officer who was too scared to look at a crime scene.'

'You really are becoming a bit of a smartarse, Watson,' said McCoy.

'Learnt from the best. Ready?' asked Wattie and pushed the door aside.

The flat was half normal and half a wet, blackened mess. Smell of smoke was stronger inside, hit them as soon as they went in, catching in the back of their throats. There was another smell under it, something a bit like a Sunday roast. McCoy got a hanky out his pocket, held it over his nose and mouth, didn't do much good. They walked through the hall and into the living room, feet squelching on the sticky mud of ash and water that now covered the carpet.

The living room must have been where the bomb had gone off. The tattered curtains were flapping in the breeze, blowing in and out the missing window frames. The mud was thicker in here as well, covering their shoes. McCoy was following Wattie in, trying to keep behind him so he blocked out the view – he was a good few inches taller than McCoy and a lot broader too. His plan was working fine until Wattie squatted down to pick up a half-melted LP out the mud and suddenly McCoy could see everything.

The bamboo-effect wallpaper by the fireplace looked like someone had splattered red paint all over it. He caught sight of hair and a tooth stuck into it before he managed to look away. On the floor, by what was left of the couch, there was what looked like a pile of burnt clothes. McCoy looked a bit closer, saw the white of a bone sticking out the pile and stepped back, familiar dizziness hitting him.

'Paul McCartney. *Ram*,' said Wattie peering at the label of the warped LP. 'Bloody awful.' He sat it back in the mud. 'Just like that album you made me buy. What was it? Inside Outside? Christ, you all right?' he asked.

McCoy was backed against the far wall, counting his breaths, trying not to pass out. He managed a nod, held his hanky up to his nose again, trying to block the roast beef smell. He looked around the flat, studiously avoiding looking down at the remains of the inhabitant. It looked like every other flat in Woodlands. Faded wallpaper, wee gas burner to cook on, an armchair that was sinking into itself, damp patches on the ceiling and walls. Why would anyone want to blow up a dump like this?

'I'll just go over by the window, get some fresh air,' he said, edging along the wall. Got to the big hole where the window had been and stuck his head out.

'What a mess,' said Wattie. 'There's a bit of his skull embedded in the plaster above the fireplace.'

'That right?' said McCoy, keeping his eyes firmly on the crowd in the street below and trying not to imagine what a bit of skull embedded in a wall looked like.

'I thought you were over all this shite?' said Wattie.

'I thought I was too,' said McCoy. 'Tell you what, I'll have a look around and see if I can find anything with his name on it, eh?'

He caught Wattie shaking his head as he edged back towards the hallway and made his way into the bedroom. It was still intact, bomb next door hadn't made too much difference. Looked like the door had caught fire and been doused, that was about it. An unmade single bed, sleeping bag opened out over it. Wee set of drawers with an ashtray and a copy of *Melody Maker* on it. There was a poster of Black Sabbath on the wall, a couple of pictures of Ferraris above the bed. A young guy living here then.

He opened the drawers, usual array of pants and socks, scud book under a pile of T-shirts. Not many clues, couldn't find anything with a name on it. Opened another drawer. A jumper, pair of 747 jeans. Couple of folded shirts. He closed it and walked over to the window. Glass was gone, took some breaths of fresh air. Down below, a panda car was weaving through the crowd and the parked fire engines. It pulled over as close to the flat as it could get and Hughie Faulds stepped out the back seat. He smoothed himself down, stretched. McCoy didn't blame him, not easy to squash a six-foot-four frame into the back of a Viva. Faulds looked up at the flat, saw McCoy and waved.

McCoy shouted through, 'Faulds is here!'

He sat down on the bed for a minute. Smelt stale, pillowcase was shiny with hair grease. He wasn't quite sure what he was looking for. Just looked like any other rented flat. Noticed there was a suitcase at the side of the drawers. He hauled it onto the bed and opened it up. Just more clothes – three button-down shirts, a tie, pair of baseball boots. He closed it, put it back, walked back through to the living room, took up his position by the window.

'You think they'll be able to get his wallet?' asked McCoy.

Wattie looked at the burnt body, breathed in through his teeth. 'Doubt it. If it was hot enough to do that to him, it'll have been hot enough to burn his wallet into nothing.'

'Probably right,' said McCoy. 'Think we'll leave it to Gilroy to try and find it.'

Broad Belfast accent boomed in: 'How'd you manage to get him up here?'

They turned and Hughie Faulds was standing there, size of him filling up the doorway.

'Wasn't easy,' said Wattie. 'Believe me.'

Faulds grinned, 'Sure it's just a bit of blood and guts, Harry. You must be used to it by now?'

9

'Getting there,' said McCoy, purposely keeping his eyes on the flats across the road. Old man in a cardigan staring back at him. 'This look familiar?' he asked.

'That's why I'm here, is it?' asked Faulds. 'Bloody bomb expert now, am I?'

'Yep,' said McCoy. 'Don't think anyone else on the force has ever seen a bomb site never mind knowing anything about it.'

Faulds barely glanced over at the damage then nodded. 'Seen this scenario more than a few times back in Belfast. This place hasn't been bombed at all.'

'What?' asked McCoy.

Faulds pointed at the pile of clothes by the couch. 'This stupid bugger's blown himself up trying to make one.' He moved closer to the burnt mess, sniffed. 'Almonds? Smell it?'

McCoy shook his head, wasn't taking the hanky off his nose again for anyone.

'A wee bit,' said Wattie. 'Why's that?'

'Means he was using Co-op mix,' said Faulds.

'What?' asked McCoy, getting increasingly lost.

'Called Co-op mix because you can get most of the ingredients for it in your local Co-op. Simple to make and pretty effective. Standard UDA and IRA stuff.'

'You sure?' asked McCoy. 'If one of them is involved we'll be off the hook. It'll go straight to the Special Branch boys. They'll be taking this one over.'

Faulds nodded over at what was left of the body. 'It happens more often than you'd think,' he said. 'Just 'cause it's easy to buy the ingredients they think that's all there is to it, that anyone can do it. Believe me, it's not as easy to make a bomb as these clowns think.'

'You sure that's what it is?' asked Wattie.

Faulds nodded. 'Textbook.' He looked around. 'And besides, why else would a bomb go off in a flat like this? Not exactly a legitimate target, is it?'

McCoy stayed at the wall and watched as Faulds wandered round examining the scene properly. Doing what McCoy should really be doing. Faulds pulled his suit trousers up to his calves and squatted down in front of the body to get a better look.

'Nasty,' he said. 'The bloke must have been right over it when it went off, probably trying to get the detonator connected.' He nodded over at the wall. 'Not sure you're going to get a dental identification either, all looks too fragmented. Half his jaw and teeth are sticking in that wall.'

He stood up, picked up a book that was floating in the sludge by the fireplace. Tried to shake some of the wet mud off, peered at the cover. '*The Life and Death of St Kilda.* You read it?'

McCoy shook his head.

Faulds peeled the front cover back, squinted at the faded ballpoint pen message. 'To Paul. Happy Birthday from Henry.'

11

'Shite,' said McCoy, 'Paul. Could be either side. Protestant or Catholic.'

'What were you hoping for?' asked Faulds. 'Finbar?'

'That would have been good,' said McCoy. 'That or Gary. Don't get many Catholics called Gary.'

Wattie appeared from the hallway, sodden pile of bills and junk mail in his hand. 'They're all different,' he said. Started reading them out. 'Miss E. Fletcher, Thomas Wright, The Occupier, Mr S.A. Bowen, C. Smith. Just goes on and on.'

'Any Pauls?' asked McCoy.

Wattie looked through the pile again. 'A Peter, but no Paul.'

'You done, Faulds?' asked McCoy.

Faulds nodded. 'Can't see anything out the ordinary. Just what you'd expect when a daft bugger doesn't know what he's doing.'

'So if it's Co-op mix, chances are it's paramilitary. You heard much about that in Glasgow?' asked McCoy.

Faulds shook his head. 'Not much. A few lads pretending they're in with the boys, showing off in the pubs. Mostly just fundraising here, maybe somebody hiding out that had to get out of Ireland. I can ask someone back home. See what the story is. Can I get back to Tobago Street now? Do my proper job?'

McCoy nodded. 'We'll come with you,' he said. 'Last thing I want is to be here when Special Branch turn up.'

12

'Or to spend any more time looking at blood splatters,' said Wattie.

'You, Watson,' said McCoy, 'need to shut your trap.'

Faulds grinned. 'He's not wrong though, is he? Must be a bit of a drawback for a detective, being scared of the sight of blood.'

'Not as bad as being a big Irish arsehole. Let's go.'

CHAPTER 2

'Results are back.'

McCoy looked at the doctor. Hadn't really thought that much about it but he was suddenly a bit worried. He'd come in a few weeks ago, sore stomach had finally got the better of him. Was finding it hard to eat, was in pain most of the time. The doctor had sent him to the hospital where he'd drank a pint of chalky stuff then got an X-ray.

'Right,' he said.

The doctor, a miserable-faced Dundonian with a handlebar moustache, took the leg of his glasses out his mouth, put the X-ray down, and looked at him. Smiled.

'It appears, Mr McCoy, that you have a peptic ulcer.'

'A what?' he asked.

'An ulcer in the lining of your stomach. That's what's been causing the pain.'

'Christ,' said McCoy.

'I'd rather you didn't blaspheme,' said the doctor.

'Sorry,' said McCoy, although he wasn't. 'So what do I do now?'

14

'You stop drinking alcohol and smoking cigarettes, you eat plain food, white mainly. Boiled fish, porridge, milk, rice, bread not toast. That sort of thing. If the pain gets bad drink some Pepto-Bismol.'

McCoy was about to say Christ again, managed to stop himself.

'If you stick to that regime the pain should lessen,' said the doctor. 'As a policeman, I imagine you have a stressful occupation, irregular hours, none of that helps. Try and look after yourself. That's the best advice I have. I'm afraid we have no treatment that cures it or really helps very much. All down to you, I'm afraid.'

McCoy stood in the street outside the surgery and lit up. Could still smell the smoke from the flat on his clothes. He was only thirty-two, how had he ended up with a bloody ulcer? Thought that was something fat old men got. He watched as a man came out the off-sales across the street with a clinking plastic bag in his arms, started running for the bus. There was one thing he was sure of though – there was no way he was giving up smoking and drinking, wasn't even a possibility. If that left him with a diet of white food and Pepto-Bismol then so be it. He looked at his watch. Better get going if he was going to get to Greenock. Walked across the street to where he'd parked his car. At least the diagnosis had one upside – it was a perfect excuse not to have to eat rotten Chinese food tonight.

McCoy managed to make it to Wattie's dad's flat just after six and was led by Wattie's dad – Call Me Ken – into a tidy wee living room. Anaglypta wallpaper painted beige and a swirly green carpet, coffee table with a plate of salmon paste sandwiches sitting on it. Three-bar fire blasting out heat. Home sweet home.

Mary, Wattie's girlfriend, was sitting on a leatherette couch by the window, still looking a bit bewildered at what had happened to her. McCoy was a bit surprised too, was more used to seeing her in newsrooms and at crime scenes than sitting on a couch holding a baby's bottle in one hand and a furry koala bear in the other.

'How's you?' asked McCoy, sitting down beside her.

'Exhausted,' said Mary, looking glum. 'And to think I used to complain about working a double shift. All I did was sit at my desk drinking tea and smoking fags. Didn't know I was born. Heard you saw a bombing today?'

Not all of Mary's previous life as a reporter had been submerged into Wee Duggie and his nappies then. Her dress sense certainly hadn't either. She was wearing some kind of short denim skirt with red platform boots and a purple T-shirt that said 'Keep on Trucking' with a picture of a man hitchhiking on it.

McCoy nodded. 'Some arse blew himself up with his own bomb.'

'Special Branch taking it?' asked Mary.

16

McCoy nodded, accepted a drink from Call Me Ken.

'Douglas has just taken the baby next door to see the neighbours,' Call Me Ken said. 'He'll be back in a minute.'

'Don't worry, I see enough of him at work,' said McCoy.

'Was only a matter of time, I suppose,' said Mary. 'Bombs in London, Birmingham, Manchester. Bound to happen here.'

'Looks like it,' said McCoy.

'Great,' said Mary. 'Big story, and here I am stuffing paper hankies down my bra to mop up the leaks and singing Coulter's Candy every five bloody minutes.'

McCoy grinned. 'You wouldn't have it any other way.'

'Oh yes I bloody would. I'd take a full-time nanny any time. Cannae afford it, not unless we win the pools.' She sighed. 'So what else is going on in the big bad world out there?'

'Not much,' said McCoy. 'Got a roasting from Murray yesterday. All your fault.'

'Me?' asked Mary.

'He'd been to Pitt Street and shite rolls downhill. They shout at him, he shouts at me. The *Daily Record*'s on a crusade at the moment. "Our Violent Streets" on the cover and half the bloody pages inside.'

'They do that every couple of years,' said Mary. 'Means they've got no real stories.'

'I know that and you know that,' said McCoy. 'Somebody just needs to let Pitt Street know.'

They looked over as the living-room door opened and Wattie appeared carrying the baby, big smile on his face.

'Told you he'd be delighted,' said McCoy. 'Born to be a daddy.'

'Dad! Get the camera,' said Wattie. 'Want one of the baby and his godfather.'

McCoy got up and Wattie plonked the baby in his arms. Minute he did, it all came flooding back. Was the smell that did it really, baby powder and wool and milk. Didn't think he'd held a baby since Bobby.

'You okay?' asked Mary.

He nodded. Funny thing, he was. Wee Duggie was a bonny wee thing, a tuft of blond hair and sleepy blue eyes. A click and a flash and that was that. Wattie took the baby back, held him up to McCoy's cheek, told him to 'give Uncle Harry a kiss', and the baby obligingly slavered on his cheek.

Wattie looked alarmed, started sniffing. 'No again.' Held the baby's bum up to his nose and sniffed.

'I think he's got a dirty nappy,' said Wattie, attempting to hand him over to Mary on the couch.

'And what's up with you?' asked Mary. 'Your hands stopped working all of a sudden?'

'It's no a man's job, hen,' said Call Me Ken.

That decided it.

'Changing table's next door,' said Mary. 'He's yours as much as mine. Get on with it.'

Wattie mumbled something under his breath and headed for the door as Call Me Ken shook his head.

'You tell him,' said McCoy. 'Angela used to make me do it too.'

'You heard from her?' asked Mary.

'Nope, not for a while, still in America, I think,' said McCoy.

A shout came through from the bedroom. 'Mary! Where's the powder stuff?'

Mary rolled her eyes and got up. 'Lucky her.'

They'd a couple more drinks in the flat, few more photos of Harry holding the changed and now fragrant Wee Duggie trussed up in some outfit Mary's mum had knitted and then Call Me Ken announced it was time to head to the dreaded Chinese.

'You been there?' asked McCoy under his breath.

Mary turned round so Call Me Ken shouldn't see her and mouthed, 'Bloody rotten. For Christ's sake don't eat the pork.'

McCoy nodded. Mary would eat anything. If she thought it was bad there was no way he was even tasting it.

McCoy, Wattie and Call Me Ken stepped out the close. McCoy felt a bit lightheaded as the fresh air hit him, realised he'd drunk a bit more than he'd thought. Wattie's dad's flat was high on a hill behind the town. From up here, you could

19

see way out over the shipyards, and across the Clyde Estuary, distant hills still topped with snow, glowing pink in the dying light.

'God's Own Country,' said Call Me Ken as they started walking down the hill. 'Best view in the world.'

Might've been God's Own Country over the river and in the hills and lochs of Argyll but in Greenock it was anything but. Whole town seemed grey, miserable-faced people hurrying past, all wrapped up against the cold wind coming in from the water. They passed some closed-up shops, wooden boards over the windows covered in graffiti. A group of kids were sitting on an abandoned car with a smashed windscreen, fire going in a metal rubbish bin lighting up the scene. And like Glasgow, there were the inevitable lads on the corners freezing in wee bomber jackets and wide trousers. All pinched faces, all passing fags and cans, all looking for trouble.

As predicted, the Chinese was a dive. Didn't stop everyone getting stuck in though. Wattie's two brothers turned up just as they all arrived. Both looked like Call Me Ken – dark hair, maybe five foot seven. God knows where Wattie had come from. The milkman? James was a joiner, Robby a plumber. Nice enough lads, and boy could they put it away. More pints, spring rolls, ribs, curry, chow mein then double brandies and banana fritters to finish. McCoy picked at everything, pretended it was delicious.

After the dinner they headed to the Imperial, one of Greenock's supposedly nicer bars, a few more of Wattie's pals from school joining them. They sat down at the back, pulled a couple of tables together. Wattie kept asking him every five minutes if he was okay, if he was enjoying himself, as he sank pint after pint bought for him 'to wet the baby's head'. McCoy told him he was having a great time, made sure he didn't see him looking at his watch wondering how soon he could make an exit without being rude.

He was just ordering another round at the bar, kitty glass full of money in his hand, when James sidled up and handed him a wrap of speed. And that was that. Best-laid plans gone in a few lines snorted off the top of the cistern in the gents.

Three hours later he still hadn't left, still wasn't in his bed getting an early night. Instead he was wide awake, standing at the bar of some place called the Rotunda chewing his lip. Maybe wasn't the worst club he'd been in, but it was close. Some basement dive that seemed to be part of the bus station. Club seemed to have been decorated by someone who only bought orange things. Orange paint on the walls, orange carpet, orange plastic lampshades hanging over the bar. That was Greenock for you, the glamour never stopped.

He leaned on the bar watching the barman trying to explain to some wobbling drunk guy in a brown checked suit with the widest lapels McCoy had ever seen, that he'd had enough. Predictably, the drunk guy was having none of it so the argument was on. He watched them and wondered if West Princes Street was really the beginning of something bad. Maybe more bombs were about to start going off in Glasgow. Thought about the guy Paul sitting there, piecing the thing together. Was probably killed instantly, wouldn't even know what had happened to him. Didn't matter what cause you supported, getting blown up for it couldn't be worth it, not for anyone. Supposed the real question they should be asking was who the bomb was intended for, who it was really meant to blast into tiny pieces.

The argument was still going on, had got to the pointing fingers at each other stage. He looked at his watch, just past one. Was getting to that dangerous time of the night. The time when the winchers and the couples and the one-off lumbers had found each other and a lot of guys were starting to realise they weren't going to be one of them. So they'd drink some more and start looking for a way to be offended. A spilt pint, an overheard remark, praise for the wrong football team.

He could see Wattie reflected in the mirror behind the bar. Tie undone, hair all over the place, slumped between his two brothers on the shiny orange vinyl bench along the wall. For a big lad he was useless at holding his drink. Decided he wouldn't miss him if he headed off, he'd see him at work on Monday, assuming Mary didn't batter him black and blue when he got home that was.

McCoy was just about to finish the last of the double Bells he'd kept for the road and to try and quieten the speed down when he felt a tap on his shoulder.

He sighed. He'd almost got away scot-free. Decided to ignore it in the faint hope he'd imagined it. That didn't work, another tap, harder this time. He'd two choices as far as he could see. Get his police badge out and tell the guy not to be daft or try and brazen it out and head for the door. Soon as he opened his mouth he'd have to do one or the other. Glaswegian accent would give him away and that was all an angry and pissed-up Greenock Wide Boy would need to start trouble. He swallowed over the whisky, grimaced and turned around.

'Can I help you, pal?' he said in his least friendly manner.

First thing he noticed was that the guy was smiling, second thing was he had hands like fucking hams. Two big rings on the fingers of the left one.

'Somebody said you were a cop,' he said.

Proper American accent, just like the films. Now that he looked at him it made sense. White teeth, blond crew cut, blue blazer with silver buttons over a pale checked shirt. Looked a bit like Jack Nicklaus. McCoy nodded.

'Can I buy you a drink?' the man said. 'Whisky?'

McCoy nodded again, still not quite sure what was going on.

The guy pointed over to a quiet corner at the back of the club. 'Sit over there,' he said. 'I'll bring it over.' And then he was lost in the scrum at the bar.

McCoy found an empty seat by a wee round table, pulled another one over. Over here, away from the dance floor, 'Do The Bump' had thankfully faded away to a distant background rumble. He got his fags out, lit up, and wondered what the guy wanted. Decided he didn't care that much and was about to make a break for it when he spotted him weaving through the crowd on the dance floor, tin tray with two whiskies and two pints on it. God knows what they fed Americans but whatever it was it must be good stuff, the guy was about as broad as he was tall. He put the tray down on the table. Smiled, pointed at the tray.

'I got you a beer too,' he said. 'Seems like the way they do it here.' He held out his hand to shake. 'Andrew Stewart.'

McCoy shook it, his pale hand disappearing into the massive paw.

'Harry McCoy,' he said, holding up the pint. 'Cheers.'

Stewart sat down, took a slug of the beer, grimaced.

'Sorry,' he said. 'Still can't get used to this beer.' He pointed over at Wattie and his pals. 'I heard one of the guys over there talking, they said you were a cop?' McCoy nodded. 'Great, maybe you can help me. My son's gone missing.'

So that was it. He wanted advice off the clock. McCoy was happy to take his drink but no way was he getting into this, not at this time, and besides he had the perfect excuse. He held his hand up.

'Sorry to interrupt you, Andy, but I'm a Glasgow cop. Means nothing here. You need to speak to the Greenock guys.'

'I already did,' said Stewart. 'Waste of time, they're not interested.'

'Ladies' choice!' shouted the DJ over the beginning of 'Seasons In The Sun'. 'Go get them!'

McCoy waited for him to shut up then asked, 'What age is he? Your son?'

'Twenty-two,' said Stewart. 'He just turned twenty-two a couple of—'

'And how long has he been missing?' McCoy asked.

'Three days,' said Stewart. 'I got here yesterday, went to see them straight off the plane—'

McCoy held his hand up again, determined to cut him off and get going.

'There's your problem,' he said. 'He's an adult, hasn't been missing that long. I'm going to be honest, he's not going to be a priority.' Until they find a body, he thought, but no point going down that road now. 'You might be better off with a private detective?'

'That's what they said.' Stewart dug in his pocket, pulled out a card. 'Recommended a guy called . . .' He peered at the card. 'Bernard Raeburn?'

'Christ!' said McCoy. 'That's the last person you need, he's bloody useless. Let me have a think, there has to be someone better than—'

He looked up and realised Wattie was standing there, swaying back and forward, face grey, eyes half shut.

'I need to go home,' he said. 'I don't feel well and Mary's going to kill me. I'm fucked, Harry, you need to help me.' And with that, he turned his head away and was sick all over the dance floor.

'For fuck sake!' said McCoy, pulling his legs out the way of any splashes. Stewart looked horrified. Wattie wiped his mouth on the sleeve of his suit. Looked miserable.

'I don't feel well,' he said. 'Think it must have been the chow mein.'

The bar staff were looking over, didn't look happy. A heavy-looking guy with rolled-up shirt sleeves revealing 1690 tattoos pushed the bar gate up, started walking towards them.

'Fuck sake, Dougie!' said James, appearing out the dry ice leaking over from the dancefloor. 'You minging bastard!'

McCoy finished his whisky, stood up, put his arm around Wattie, tried to steady him, kept his head facing away from his, had no desire to smell the sick on his breath.

'James, you head the barman off at the post,' he said. 'I'll take this daft bastard home.'

Stewart was still sitting there, pint halfway up to his mouth, shock on his face.

'Sorry, pal, got to go,' McCoy said to him. 'Good luck.' He started trying to guide Wattie towards the door. Shouted over his shoulder, 'Remember! Don't waste your money on Raeburn.'

Stewart nodded and stood up. The barman appeared behind him, pulled his arm and spun him around.

'Hoy! Pal! Was that fucking mess you?'

McCoy left Stewart shaking his head and trying to explain to the barman it was nothing to do with him and shoved Wattie towards the stairs and up to the exit before he was sick again. Chow mein, my arse. Ten bloody pints more like.

13TH APRIL 1974

CHAPTER 3

The alarm clock went off. McCoy reached over, switched it off, and groaned. Seven a.m. Took him a few seconds to remember where he was. Came back to him in a rush. The Sea-View Boarding House in Greenock. He sat up, didn't feel too bad considering it was after two by the time he'd got Wattie and then himself home. Had an idea just how bad Wattie must be feeling, he'd been sick a few more times on the way home. Stupid idiot still insisting that it wasn't due to the drink, it was all the chow mein's fault.

McCoy had eventually managed to half drag, half walk him up the hill then up the stairs. Knocked on the flat door. He was hoping Call Me Ken would answer but no such luck. The front door was yanked open and Mary was standing there in a nightie, Wee Duggie bawling in her arms. Look on her face would have felled a weaker man. Wattie staggered in past her, bumped against the coat stand, and fell face-first onto the carpet. Stayed there quietly snoring while McCoy tried to shush the baby and tell Mary that it wasn't his fault. Honest.

Mary was having none of it. Told him he was a useless prick and he should have known better than to let Wattie get that drunk. McCoy tried to tell her it wasn't him, it was his brothers, but she wasn't listening, too busy trying to shush the baby. She left him at the door, kicked Wattie a sharp one in the side as she passed him on the way back into the bedroom and slammed the door. Wattie just lay there snoring, blissfully unaware of what was going to happen to him in the morning after he woke up and Mary got torn into him properly.

By half seven McCoy was washed and dressed, sports bag in hand, walking down the stairs to the dining room. He could smell bacon and burnt toast. His stomach rumbled, he hadn't really eaten anything last night, but he'd no time for his prescribed porridge. Plan was to stop on the road in a couple of hours, wanted to get going. Cup of coffee and a fag would set him right.

The dining room was a cheery yellow colour, a bright room at the front of the house. Big windows, nice view of the Clyde and the snowy hills across the river. Tables set for breakfast, folded napkins and a wee menu on each one. A couple was sitting down already, middle-aged, dressed like they were going hill-walking, heads bent over a big folded-out Ordnance Survey map. McCoy sat down at a table by the window and ordered a coffee from the young waitress, who, by the look of her, and her grunt of hello, had had as late a night as he had. There was a rack on the wall with the morning papers stacked in it. All the headlines a variation of BOMB and CONFLICT COMES TO SCOTLAND. No heart to read any of them.

He'd just finished his coffee, was stubbing his cigarette out in the *A Souvenir of Dunoon* ashtray, when a Cortina with a CLYDE TAXIS sticker on the door pulled up outside. The back door opened and the American guy from last night stepped out, peered in at the windows. Must be staying here, thought McCoy, immediately trying to work out how he could get away without having to speak to him. Wasn't going to happen though. Stewart saw him through the front windows, waved, big smile on his face. He shoved some notes at the taxi driver, got his bag out the boot and headed for the path up to the house.

McCoy cursed, sat at the table resigned to his fate. A few seconds later the dining-room door opened and Stewart bowled in, waitress and landlady hovering behind him.

'Boy, but you're a hard man to find,' he said. 'Think this is the sixth B&B I've been to. The boys last night couldn't remember which one you were staying in.'

He pointed to the seat opposite McCoy. McCoy nodded and he sat down. Last night's blazer had been replaced by a zip-up jacket, a pair of checked trousers and deck shoes. He really did look like Jack Nicklaus.

'How's your buddy this morning?' Stewart asked. 'Took me a good while to persuade the barman

33

that it wasn't me who'd upchucked all over his floor. He was not a happy man, believe me.'

'Wattie?' said McCoy. 'He'll be fine, nothing a bottle of Irn-Bru and a bacon roll won't cure. Think it's the doing he'll get from the wife that'll be the problem.'

Stewart looked puzzled but nodded anyway.

McCoy stood up, held his hand out to shake. 'Well, it's nice to see you again and good luck with finding your son, but I've got to go, running late already.'

Stewart's face fell. 'What? But I need to talk to you. I've been looking for you all morning. Where are you going?' Held his hands up. 'Sorry, not my business but—'

'Aberdeen,' said McCoy, picking up his bag. 'Got to get going.'

'Aberdeen?' asked Stewart. 'Is that far?'

'Up north,' said McCoy. 'Hundred and fifty miles or so.'

The disappointed look on Stewart's face made McCoy feel a bit guilty, poor guy looked like he'd lost a fiver and found a pound.

'Look, tell you what,' said McCoy. 'If you're in Glasgow in the next few days, look me up. Stewart Street station, it's not far from the city centre, anyone'll tell you how—'

'Can I come with you?' Stewart blurted out. 'Please? Sorry, it's just you spoke more sense in five minutes last night than in three hours with the Greenock cops. You seem to know what—'

'Look pal, it's not a great idea—'

'Please,' said Stewart again. 'He's my only child. He's all I've got left. I've come all this way and I'm hitting a brick wall. I can't—'

And suddenly he had tears in his eyes. He grabbed a napkin off the table, wiped at them. 'Sorry, I don't know what else to do. I thought you could help me. I was counting on it.'

Stewart tried to pull himself together, rubbed at his eyes again. He was a big gruff guy all right, full of confidence like most Yanks, but McCoy felt a bit sorry for him. Whoever he was, he was lost in a country he didn't know, looking for his missing son when nobody cared. Wouldn't kill him to listen to his story, give him some advice.

'Why not,' said McCoy. 'You can keep me company.'

Big grin broke on Stewart's face, he grabbed McCoy's hand, pumped it up and down.

'Thanks, bud. You're a pal. I appreciate it. I'll be no trouble. I promise.'

McCoy peered through the rainy windscreen, saw the sign for Dunblane, four miles to go. Dunblane meant one thing – the Fourways Cafe, traditional stopping spot on the way north. They'd been on the road a couple of hours, made good time, and McCoy's stomach was rumbling again. Time to stop and refuel. He looked over at the passenger seat. Stewart was right, he hadn't been any trouble, mainly because he'd been out for the

35

count for a couple of hours. He was snoring quietly, squashed into the front seat of the Viva. He'd started yawning as soon as he got in the car, told McCoy he hadn't slept a wink all night, jet lag, and he'd been asleep by the time they were over the Kingston Bridge. Slept ever since.

McCoy turned off the roundabout and pulled into the cafe car park, cut the engine. Decided to leave Stewart sleeping, go in and have his breakfast in peace, but just as he was getting out the car Stewart opened his eyes, looked around.

'You fell asleep,' said McCoy.

'Sorry,' said Stewart, sitting up. 'Are we there? Is this Aberdeen?'

'Not by a long shot,' said McCoy. 'C'mon, breakfast time.'

The Fourways was busy, always was. Had to wait a few minutes until the young guy playing at being a waiter cleared a table so they could sit down. McCoy made himself order porridge. Stewart asked for some freshly squeezed orange juice, some pancakes and maple syrup and an order of crispy bacon on the side. Ended up with a roll and sausage, a bacon roll and a can of Fanta. Seemed happy enough with the idea of a 'flat sausage' after he'd had a few bites. 'Sort of like a burger but peppery' was the verdict.

Ten minutes and some small talk about the weather and his flight from America later, McCoy pushed his empty bowl to the side and lit up.

'Okay. Tell me the story,' he said. 'Just start at the beginning.'

Stewart nodded, sank the last of his coffee, grimaced, and began.

'Got a call three days ago, back in the house in Beacon Hill.'

'Beacon Hill?' asked McCoy.

'Boston,' said Stewart. Carried on. 'Said my son Donald had gone AWOL. Hadn't returned to his ship when his shore leave was over.'

'What ship?' asked McCoy. Then realised, should have done earlier. 'He's based at the Holy Loch?'

Stewart nodded. 'Yep.'

The Holy Loch was across the water from Greenock, a huge American naval base built to service their nuclear submarines. You saw the sailors in Greenock sometimes, driving around in the big flashy cars they'd brought with them. A few hundred of them were based there, even had their own schools and bowling alleys and restaurants. Was like a small American town had dropped from the sky onto the banks of the Clyde.

'He's serving on the USS *Canopus*,' continued Stewart. 'Division Officer. Been there for six months or so.'

Something seemed a bit strange to McCoy.

'Hang on, they called you in America after a day of him not coming back?' he asked. 'Is that not a bit quick off the mark? Don't sailors get drunk

37

and come back late a lot? Or have I been watching too many films?'

Stewart shook his head. 'No, you're right. It's not usual procedure. The call was a favour really, a heads-up.'

'Very nice of them,' said McCoy. 'Didn't realise the American Navy was so friendly.'

Stewart sat back. 'To be honest they might not be so friendly to everyone. Let's just say they keep me informed.'

'How come?' asked McCoy.

Stewart looked a bit sheepish. 'Well, I used to be part of them until I retired. Was a captain.'

'That sounds pretty big time,' said McCoy.

'The current commander of the *Canopus* was one of my old lieutenants. Thought I'd want to know. Thought Donny would be back the next day and I could give him a call and blast him. Let him know people were keeping an eye on him so he wouldn't do anything else stupid.'

'But he didn't come back the next day . . .' said McCoy.

'No,' said Stewart, 'he didn't. Nor the next. I got straight on a plane, flew into Prestwick. Hoped he'd be back when I got here.'

'What about his mother, what's she saying?'

'Grace is gone these ten years,' said Stewart. 'Cancer.'

'I'm sorry to hear that,' said McCoy.

Stewart nodded. 'She'd never forgive me if I didn't do everything I could to find him.'

McCoy thought for a minute. 'Not quite sure how to ask this, but is he the kind of boy that goes missing? Gets into trouble?'

Stewart shook his head. 'Not Donny. I used to wish he would sometimes, blow off some steam, get drunk, get laid. He's not that type though, he's a timid boy, quiet, got more so after Grace passed. I wasn't even sure if he was going to make it through basic training but he did. Got posted here, couldn't have been happier.'

McCoy looked out over the grey sky and the rainy car park full of muddy puddles. 'Here?' he asked. 'Really? You telling me this is better than Pearl Harbor?'

'To Donny it is. He stayed with his grandfather when I was overseas and he's been telling him he's Scots all his life, that it's his heritage, that Scotland is his home.'

McCoy looked at him doubtfully.

Stewart held his hands up. 'I know, you don't have to tell me. He's an American born and bred, as American as apple pie, but not according to his grandfather. No, sir. Our family came from Scotland originally, then to Newfoundland then on to Boston. Whalers, then the navy. All of it missed a generation with me. Maybe the fact my dad didn't get anywhere trying to make me Scottish made him try all the harder with Donny. Me? I'd rather be in South Carolina on the back of a swordfish boat, shorts on, sun on my back, beer in my hand. That's where Grace and I

39

went every summer, but Donald fell for the whole thing. Robert the Bruce, clan maps on the wall, even had a Scotland football shirt when he was a boy, couldn't get him to put a Patriots one on for love nor money, and believe me I tried. Hard.'

'And what did the navy say when you got here?' asked McCoy.

Stewart shrugged. 'Not much. Like you said, sailors go AWOL in foreign ports all the time. Told me what I already know. Usually they come back when the money runs out or the woman they've shacked up with gets tired of them.'

'Couldn't that be what's happened to Donald?' asked McCoy. 'Seems the simplest explanation.'

'You know something? If it was I'd be happy,' said Stewart. 'I'd take the worry if I knew he was out having a good time. But it's not Donny. As I said, he's not the adventurous type.' He looked at McCoy. 'That's why I'm worried.'

McCoy stood up. 'I've got tomorrow off. If he doesn't turn up today we'll have an ask about. Then that's me back to work on Monday. Deal?'

Stewart nodded, looked relieved. Went to his pocket and took out a roll of twenties, 'I can pay you, it's not a problem.'

'Put your money away,' said McCoy. 'Don't be daft.' Then thought. 'But if you're feeling generous you can pay for the petrol. We're running low.'

Stewart looked blank.

'Gas,' said McCoy.

Stewart nodded. 'Ah! Glad to.'

They stood up, headed towards the door.

'You know you never said what you're going to Aberdeen for,' said Stewart.

'Just need to pick someone up,' said McCoy. 'A favour.'

Stewart nodded and they stepped out the cafe into the rain and ran to the car. McCoy wasn't lying, he was going pick someone up. Problem was, that someone had no idea he was coming.

CHAPTER 4

Peterhead prison sat on a cliff just outside Aberdeen, overlooking a bay, huge break-water wall stretching out beneath it trying to keep the angry North Sea out. It was a miserable collection of low oblong buildings, painted roughcast, tiny windows, exercise yards covered over with twisted wire ceilings. The wind and the rain howled in from the sea most days, rattling the windows, levelling the trees, leaving warders scuttling across the yards trying to get back inside as soon as they could. Peterhead was where the bad boys got sent from other prisons. The ones that had attacked officers and other prisoners, so wound up and angry and frustrated that they would attack a balloon on a stick given half a chance. They'd get bundled into vans, taken north, taken to a place that even they were scared of.

'We're going to a jail?' asked Stewart as he read the sign and they turned in from the main road.

'Yep,' said McCoy. 'Pal of mine got into a wee bit of bother, nothing serious, gets out today.'

If he was Pinocchio, McCoy thought, his nose would be breaking through the car windscreen by now. Still, what Stewart didn't know wouldn't hurt him. He pulled into the gravel car park, cut the engine, looked out the windscreen at the big gate and the prison behind.

'Hell of a place,' said Stewart. 'Makes the brig at Miramar look homely.'

McCoy looked at his watch. Five to one. Perfect timing. He told Stewart he'd be ten minutes and got out the car. Felt it immediately, the bitter wind blowing in from the sea. It was April down in Glasgow, the signs of spring were coming in. Not up here though, up here it was still winter. He turned the collar of his suit jacket up, stuck his hands in his pockets and headed for the gate. The North Sea, grey and angry, was crashing against the rocks and the wall, sending foam up into the air. Could taste the salt in the atmosphere, feel the cold wind coming in, wondered why anyone would want to live up here.

A few people were waiting outside, looking miserable in the wind and the rain. An elderly couple, a young woman with a wee boy bundled up in an anorak and knitted blue balaclava. McCoy nodded hello and stood beside them, managed to light up after a couple of tries. Realised his stomach wasn't sore for once. Maybe the porridge was a good idea after all.

'No long now, son,' said the elderly man looking at his watch. 'One thing about these bastards, they're always on time. I'll give them that.'

Just as he finished speaking the cut-in door in

the main gate opened and a young man with a skinhead, denim jacket and jeans, bag under his arm, stepped out, grimaced at the cold. The wee boy shouted, 'Daddy!', ran at him and jumped into his arms. Behind him came an older man who waved at the elderly couple and walked towards them. Then nothing. No one else. McCoy swore under his breath. If he'd got the wrong date and had to traipse back up here again he wasn't going to be happy. He waited another minute or so, wiped the spray off his face then turned back toward the car. That's when he heard a familiar voice.

'What the fuck you doing here?'

He turned and Stevie Cooper was stepping out the door, brown paper parcel in hand, big grin on his face.

'Your carriage awaits,' said McCoy, bowing and pointing to the beat-up Viva.

Cooper approached, looked him up and down. Didn't look too impressed. 'You need a new suit,' he said. 'You look a right state.'

'Thanks,' said McCoy. 'Nice to see you too.'

'C'mere,' said Cooper, grinning.

McCoy shook his head. 'Nope.'

'C'mon,' said Cooper. 'I just want to give you a hug. I've missed you.'

'Aye right,' said McCoy, turning to go, but Cooper didn't move, just stood there grinning, arms wide open. McCoy sighed, decided he may as well get it over with. Cooper grabbed him, got

44

his head under his arm, started scrubbing his knuckles on McCoy's head.

'Give up?' he asked.

McCoy tried to say yes but couldn't get the words out, face buried in McCoy's jacket.

'What?' asked Cooper. 'I cannae hear ye!'

McCoy managed a strangled yes and Cooper let him go. He stumbled, fell on the wet gravel. He shook his head. 'How many bloody times?' he said. 'What age are you, Cooper? Nine years old? We're no wee boys any more.'

Cooper held his hand out, pulled him up. 'C'mon,' he said. 'Quit your bloody moaning. Where's the nearest pub?'

McCoy brushed himself off and they started walking across the car park towards the car. Cooper stopped. 'Who's that?' he asked. 'In the car?'

'That,' said McCoy, not quite believing he was saying it, 'that's Andrew Stewart, retired captain of the United States Navy.'

Cooper looked at him. 'You taking the piss?'

'I'll explain later,' said McCoy, opening the car door. 'Now get in, I'm bloody freezing.'

Twenty minutes later Cooper was holding a pint in the corner of some dingy pub called Peep Peeps Bar, of all things. It was down near the docks, the first one they'd come to, would have to do. They were the only ones in it, wasn't surprising given the miserable greeting the landlord had given them and the state of the place. Telly on a shelf on the

45

wall showing the racing with no sound, skinny wee radiators not doing much to ward off the cold. Cooper swallowed half of the pint in one, put it back down on the table. Stewart had offered to go for a stroll to 'let you boys have a chat' and had wandered off into the driving rain of a grey Aberdeen afternoon saying something about looking at the ships in the harbour.

'Christ,' Cooper said wiping his mouth. 'I've been looking forward to that. Got any fags?'

McCoy handed over a packet of Number 10. Looked much the same as he always did, Cooper, a bit paler but much the same. Blond quiff, red zip-up jacket, pair of jeans. Seemed to have put on muscle in the jail, was broader than he'd been before. Must have been exercising.

'So how was it?' asked McCoy. 'Didn't drop your soap in the showers, did you?'

Cooper shrugged. Didn't laugh.

'That it?' asked McCoy. 'You were in for near six months. Something must have happened.'

'You really want to know?' asked Cooper.

McCoy nodded, suddenly not sure that he did.

'Well, get me another pint and I'll tell you,' said Cooper.

McCoy went up to the bar, tried to think what it was about Cooper that seemed different. Realised that he wasn't different at all, he was the same, back to what he was like when he was coming up, before he was a Big Boss cushioned by his troops and his money. The Cooper that had nothing to lose and had no fear. The dangerous Cooper. Made McCoy's journey to Aberdeen all the less likely to succeed. Still, had to try. There was a wee heated glass case on the bar, a couple of dried-up pies sitting in it. Looked like they'd been there for weeks.

'Want one?' asked the landlord, putting the pints down on the bar in front of him.

McCoy shook his head.

'Your loss,' said the landlord, went back to his paper.

McCoy carried the pints back, set them on the table. Cooper had a coin in his hand, twisting over two fingers, foot drumming on the ground. Wound up tight. He took a sip of his pint, started talking. 'The bastards start it in the van up there. Tell you they're waiting for you up in the jail, know all about you, how they're going to kick you to fuck, make sure you can't walk for a week. You fuck with one of us, we'll fuck with you.'

'The officers you mean?'

Cooper nodded. 'I lamped one of the bastards in Barlinnie, that's why I got sent up here. So you get to the jail and they take you along to this cell, right at the end of the corridor so nobody can hear anything, and there's five of them waiting for you. Call themselves the Batter Squad. All of them standing in a cell, coshes and batons out, fucking hard-ons in their trousers and they chuck you in there, lock the door.' He smiled. 'And they batter fuck out you.'

47

'Christ,' said McCoy.

'Started hitting me and hitting me with the batons, got me down, then one of them starts kicking in at my kidneys with his boots. Fought back for a while but it's one against five. Had no chance, did I? Woke up two days later, lying naked in a concrete cell with fucking seawater on the floor and the wind howling in through the bars. Pissed blood for a week, ribs broken, black eyes, the lot.'

Cooper took another slug of his pint, foot still drumming. Looked at McCoy. Smiled. 'Christ, McCoy! Cheer up! Look at your face. You were the one that wanted to know. It was me that got battered, not you. Fuck it, done now. Wasn't so bad once I got put in a proper cell.'

'Must be freezing in there,' said McCoy. 'Right on the coast.'

'Nope,' said Cooper, shaking his head. 'It's bloody boiling.'

'Eh?' said McCoy.

'Three men in a wee cell and a dirty great hot-water pipe going straight through it. Was like a bloody sauna most of the time. Cell stank too. Sweat and farts and piss from three men using one slops bucket.' Cooper sat back, blew a few smoke rings up towards the nicotine-stained ceiling. Watched the racing for a minute. 'So, you gonna tell me why you're really here?' he asked. 'Can't imagine you've driven all this way just to act as a bloody chauffeur.'

McCoy looked at him. Cooper was good at many things but acting coy wasn't one of them. He knew fine well why McCoy was there.

'Aberdeen's a hundred and fifty miles from Glasgow,' said McCoy. 'It's not the other side of the world. You telling me the news doesn't get up here?'

Cooper continued to look determinedly blank, eyes on the TV. McCoy swore under his breath. Was going to have to spell it out. 'Of all the people to get into a drunken fight with on a Saturday night, you managed to get into one with Pat Dixon.'

'Deserved it,' mumbled Cooper.

'Maybe so, but he didn't deserve you going Tonto on the bugger. You punched his face so hard you broke his ocular bone and he lost the sight in one eye. Worth three years away at least for your normal run-of-the-mill villain, but, due to his legal expertise and the giant amount of money you pay him, the esteemed Archie Lomax managed to get it down to a six-month sentence for you to spend in relative comfort in Barlinnie. That was until you, quote, "lamped" some prison officer and ended up in Her Majesty's Prison Peterhead. Want me to go on?'

Cooper shrugged. Kept blowing his smoke rings up into the air, foot still drumming.

McCoy sighed. Why was nothing with Cooper ever easy? Kept going. 'And as you well know, Pat Dixon, while being a nut job of some repute, is nothing compared to his brother Jamsie. That being the same Jamsie Dixon that has been in and out of Barlinnie since he was sixteen. I'm amazed he's no been sent to Carstairs with the rest of the loonies but there you are. Jamsie Dixon, psycho for hire, has now decided you are, and I quote, "fucking dead" because of what you did to his brother.'

'I can handle Jamsie Dixon,' said Cooper. 'He's just another wide boy looking for—'

'No, you can't,' said McCoy. 'No one can. The man's an animal. So much of an animal he's up in the High Court on Wednesday for stabbing some poor bastard seventeen times because he bumped into him in a pub. He also decided to bite the poor fucker's ear off so he could keep it as a souvenir. Upside is Jamsie, not being able to afford a big-time lawyer like you, will be going down for quite a few years. So, all you need to do is stay out of his way and out of Glasgow until then.'

Cooper bristled. 'Why should I?'

'Because I've got enough shite to deal with without you in a feud with the Dixon brothers!' said McCoy. 'Desy only lives in Gateshead. First sign of anything kicking off he'll be back up here like a shot and if he doesn't get you he'll go after Billy or Jumbo and the whole thing'll go on and on.'

'Aye well, Desy can go and fuck himself as well,' said Cooper.

McCoy tried to keep calm, talk quietly. 'All I'm

asking is you keep your head down for five days. Just five days. Check into a hotel here, eat room service, watch TV, wank yourself stupid, whatever, but just stay out of Glasgow until Jamsie goes down. Okay?'

'I've already had six months of wanking myself stupid,' said Cooper grumpily.

'Well, ask the bloody concierge to sort out a visitor then!' said McCoy, exasperated. 'Aberdeen's full of them!' He leant forward. 'I'm serious, Cooper. I've seen what Jamsie Dixon can do to people. It's not fucking nice.'

'How come you're so concerned about me all of a sudden?' asked Cooper. 'Driving all this way just to give me a warning?'

'Wrong way round,' said McCoy. 'It's not you I'm concerned about. It's me. Murray's back and he's not happy. Thinks we've been doing a shite job and he's not wrong, papers are all over it. Headlines. Violence on the streets of our city. Police need to act. All that stuff. The last thing I need is some gang feud spread all over the papers to wind him up even more.'

Soon as McCoy said it he wished he hadn't. Murray was always a red rag to a bull as far as Cooper was concerned.

'So he's back is he then? Big Boss Murray?' he asked.

McCoy nodded.

'So that's you then, back licking his arse, running after him like a bloody puppy.'

51

If Cooper was trying to annoy him he was succeeding. McCoy tried to keep his face straight, not react. Cooper leant forward, face up to his. That look McCoy knew too well appearing in his eyes. The look that meant Cooper was angry. Very angry.

'I'll do whatever the fuck I want to do, McCoy,' he hissed. 'And neither you nor Murray is going to stop me. Got it? If you think I'm going to stay up here hiding like a scared dog off Jamsie bloody Dixon you are very wrong. His stupid arse of a brother started it and I finished it. End of story. If Jamsie Dixon wants to keep things going that's up to him but I'm no shying away from it. He can come ahead any time he wants. Now go and get me another pint.'

There it was, what Cooper always did. McCoy didn't know why he was surprised. He tested you. He didn't want McCoy to get him a pint because he was thirsty. He wanted him to get it because he said so. It was about who was boss, he'd been the same when they were wee boys. All Cooper wanted was loyalty: you were either with him or against him and if McCoy didn't get the pint he would be against him. No way was McCoy standing up to him when he was in a mood like this.

'Stevie, please just let Jamsie be for a few days, keep your head down in Glasgow if you want, but just keep your head down. For me, eh?'

Cooper waggled his empty pint pot in front of him. 'Beer and a whisky and I'll think about it.'

McCoy nodded, took the glass, went back up to the bar. Tried to ignore the knot in his stomach and the feeling that he was back in school, doing what Stevie said so he'd protect him when the bullies and the Christian Brothers came calling. Didn't seem like he'd ever be free of those days.

By the time Stewart came back, Cooper was halfway through his third pint and was in a much better mood. McCoy had done what he wanted him to do, far as he was concerned all was right with the world again. Had even stopped drumming his foot on the floor.

Stewart shook the water off his jacket and sat down. 'Pretty grim out there,' he said. 'You boys want a drink?'

'Coke,' said McCoy. 'I'm driving.'

'Pint,' said Cooper. 'And a double whisky. Malt.'

Stewart trotted off to the bar and McCoy looked at him.

'What?' said Cooper. 'He's a Yank, he'll be loaded. Besides, you're doing him a favour, aren't you?'

'Aye,' said McCoy. 'I am, not you. So go easy.'

Stewart arrived back with the drinks on a tin tray, set them down. 'Harry here said you got into a bar fight?' he said, sitting down.

Cooper nodded, tried not to grin. 'Something like that.'

'Was in a few of them myself in my younger days,' said Stewart. 'On shore leave for a few days, too much drinking in a strange town, it happens.

53

Boys will be boys. So, tell me, what is it you do, Steve?'

McCoy couldn't wait to hear this. 'Yes, Steve,' he said. 'Tell Stewart what it is you do.'

Cooper was having none of it. 'This and that, Andrew,' he said. 'I'm a businessman, fingers in a lot of pies.'

Stewart nodded. McCoy shook his head. 'That right? Well, drink up, Nelson Rockefeller. We need to get in the clapped-out Viva and drive back to Glasgow.'

CHAPTER 5

McCoy drummed on the steering wheel with his fingers. They had stopped by the side of the road for the umpteenth time to let Cooper out to pee. Too many pints back in the pub. All he could see through the rain coming down in sheets was a field full of sad-looking cows huddled together for warmth. Wherever they were, it was bloody miserable. The passenger door swung open and Cooper got in.

'Freezing out there,' he said, blowing on his fingers. 'Not used to it.'

'That's the last bloody time I'm stopping,' said McCoy. 'You're going to have to hold it in next time.'

Cooper ignored him, just lit up and chewed on his thumbnail. McCoy sighed, started the engine and they slid out the lay-by and back onto the road. Football commentary on the radio was droning on in the background, steady back and forwards whump of the windscreen wipers. McCoy was getting tired, scared he was going to fall asleep. Opened the window, took a few deep breaths and rolled it back up.

'What do you think happened to your boy?' asked Cooper out the blue. Hadn't said much to Stewart.

'I don't know,' said Stewart. 'I'm hoping your friend here can help me find out.'

'Aye, well, you've got the right man there. McCoy's an arse as you can tell, but he's a good polis. Good at running about after people. Telling them what's what.'

McCoy made himself say nothing, turned the radio up. Middle of the sports news.

. . . and confirmation today that George Foreman will fight Muhammad Ali on the 24th of September in Zaire in what is being called the Rumble in the Jungle . . .

Stewart whistled. 'Boy, that'll be a fight and a half.'

'You like boxing?' asked McCoy, turning the volume down.

'Could say that,' said Stewart. 'Represented my country at the '48 Olympics.'

Cooper turned round and looked at him. 'Fuck off!'

Stewart nodded, grinned, 'I did. Got beat to shit, but I was there.'

'That's amazing,' said McCoy.

'Well, boxing was a big thing in the navy in those days,' said Stewart. 'They were fanatical about it. All they wanted you to do was beat the army in the annual match. Spent all year training for it. I managed to knock the guy I was paired against out in the fourth, then the Olympics came up. I'd be lying if I said I was good enough to be there but it was just after the war, there weren't so many young guys around, so I got picked. I'd just turned eighteen, got sent to London with the American team, and, boy, that was a shock. The place still had rationing, half the city was rubble, I couldn't wait to get home. Especially after some South African guy knocked the living daylights out of me.'

'So who's going to win then?' asked McCoy. 'Ali or Foreman? Give us your expert answer so I can put all my money on and retire to Barbados.'

Stewart thought for a minute. 'If I was you I'd put my money on Ali. He'll be the underdog, but he's got a good chance. Man's a born fighter. Hates to lose.'

'What you doing tonight, Stewart?' asked Cooper.

'Me?' said Stewart. 'Not much, thought I'd get a hotel room in Glasgow. McCoy here said he'd help me look for Donny tomorrow. Seems nuts to go to Dunoon just to come back.'

Cooper nodded. Smiled. McCoy looked at him, had no idea what Cooper was up to, but could tell by the look on his face he was up to something all right.

Stewart leaned forward, peered through the seats. 'You still on for tomorrow, Harry? That okay?'

McCoy nodded. He'd promised, after all.

'Great! Well, I suppose that's settled,' said

Stewart. 'I'll get a room, meet Harry in the morning.'

They had just passed Stirling, twenty miles to Glasgow, when Cooper finally came out with it. 'You know I said I had a finger in a few pies?' he said. 'One of those pies is boxing. Got an interest in a few fighters, maybe you could come and have a look at them, see what you think.'

Stewart seemed a bit taken aback. 'Sure,' he said. 'Bit rusty, but okay.'

'Great!' said Cooper. 'Then we'll go to the fights, make a night of it. There's a card at Govan Town Hall tonight, wasn't sure I was going to get out in time.'

McCoy couldn't believe what he was hearing. Turned to Cooper. 'Since when did you have boxers?' he asked. 'When did that happen?'

'While ago,' said Cooper. 'Don't have to tell you every bloody thing I do.'

'You coming with us, Harry?' asked Stewart. 'Let me buy you both dinner. Say thanks.'

McCoy was just about to say no, explain he hated boxing, had no intention of seeing someone's blood splattered all over the ring when Cooper spoke up.

'Of course he is,' he said. 'Wants to keep his eagle eye on me, make sure I don't do anything stupid. Don't you, McCoy?'

CHAPTER 6

Cooper's fighters were based in Morrison's Gym on Sydney Street. McCoy pulled the car up outside and yawned. He felt tired and stiff, neck hurt, no wonder, he'd been driving for about nine hours. He shook himself, tried to wake up.

'This is it,' said Cooper, peering out the window. 'Boys should be in there now.'

'Then let's see what you got,' said Stewart. 'You coming, Harry?'

McCoy shook his head. 'Been cooped up in this bloody car all day. Need a bit of fresh air. I'll see you in there in twenty minutes or so.'

Stewart nodded and they got out the car. McCoy lit up. Cooper and Stewart were talking away, Cooper telling him about some light heavyweight in Motherwell he had his eye on. Best pals now.

McCoy left them to it, headed up the road. Didn't really need any fresh air, just didn't want to spend longer in a boxing gym than he had to. He turned into Duke Street just as the rain came on, not much, just a smeary drizzle. Could smell the malty smell of the Tennent's Brewery up the road.

It was that funny time on a Saturday evening when everyone had gone home from the football or shopping in the town and nobody had come back out for the evening yet. Duke Street was quiet, not even much traffic, just the usual rumble of the Corporation buses. Couldn't believe Cooper was now some sort of boxing entrepreneur. Still, if it kept him busy and out the way of Jamsie Dixon it was fine by him. He stopped at a phonebox, opened the door and saw a curly black wire hanging down, no handset at the end, REAL CALTON TONGS sprayed all over the glass. He cursed, let the door go, and looked around. The Shuna was just up the road, corner of John Knox Street. Seemed the best bet. He went in, most of the pub looking up at the football results on the TV, and bought a pint. He took it over to the phone, put his money in and dialled the shop. Got put through to Wattie.

'So you're alive?' asked McCoy.

'Just,' said Wattie. 'Don't know what was worse, the hangover or the doing I got from Mary.'

'All deserved. I had to carry you up the bloody road!' said McCoy.

'Is that how I got home?' asked Wattie. 'I wondered. Never again. Until the next time that is.'

'So what's going on?' asked McCoy.

'Not much,' said Wattie. 'I've spent the afternoon sitting at my desk trying to feel human again.

60

Thomson's been back and forward to the bookies all day and now he's checking his pools. Ah, knew something had happened. Seems like the Special Branch boys are done with that bomb thing already. Were at the flat all day today according to Murray. He went along and saw them.'

'What else did he say?' asked McCoy

'Not much. Just that Special Branch didn't think it was connected with the Irish paramilitaries. Either side.'

'Eh?' said McCoy. 'I don't get it. Who the fuck else is going to be building bombs in Glasgow?'

'Don't know, but apparently the Special Branch boys didnae seem that bothered. Told Murray it was more likely to be some nutter with a grudge against someone who found out too late it's not that easy to build a bomb.'

'A grudge?' asked McCoy. 'Are they taking the piss?'

'Fuck knows,' said Wattie. 'Maybe it's someone who's been sacked or something like that and gone off the deep end. Anyways, they bounced it straight back to us to clear up the mess, tell his next of kin, find out what was going on. Probably just couldn't be arsed looking into it. Where are you anyway?'

McCoy looked around the pub. Beneath a fizzing neon strip illuminating peeling flock wallpaper an old man had his false teeth out and was steadily polishing them with a dirty hanky while he read his paper. Two middle-aged men were propping up the bar, both of them so pissed they could hardly stand. And to top it off a dog had somehow got in and was sniffing about the floor. 'Hell, I think. I'll see you on Monday.'

McCoy hung up, looked at his pint. There seemed to be a film of oil on it, rainbow colours catching the light from the television. Stomach rolled, wasn't sure he could face it. He had just ordered a whisky when he heard a siren, got louder as it passed the pub. Saturday night starting early, he supposed. As he took a sip of his whisky he heard another. Then another. More than just a Saturday night then. He swallowed the whisky down.

Didn't take him long to follow the flashing lights up the hill towards the Cathedral. There were two fire engines and three pandas parked outside by the time he got there, lights spinning, uniforms setting up cordon ropes. Glasgow Cathedral was huge, a great dark building next to the Royal. Stood there, a giant shadow in the dark, Necropolis on a hill behind it. Whatever had happened seemed to have happened inside – two uniforms were standing at the big front door, firemen coming in and out.

He grabbed a uniform and showed him his card. 'What's going on?'

'It's an explosion, sir, inside the Cathedral.'

'An explosion?' asked McCoy. 'What kind of explosion?'

The young uniform looked from side to side as

if someone might be listening in. 'They think it's a bomb, sir, on the altar.'

McCoy swore under his breath. Looked like whoever had been building bombs in West Princes Street had definitely made more than one.

CHAPTER 7

McCoy had never been inside the Cathedral, never had any reason to, so he hadn't realised just how big it was. It seemed to go on for ever, high ceiling, little alcoves off to the side, stained-glass windows and a tile floor that amplified the sound of his shoe heels as he walked up towards the group of people standing at the far end.

'You again?'

He turned and the burly fireman from West Princes Street emerged from the shadows of a pillar.

McCoy nodded. 'Is it—'

'Another bomb?' he said. 'Yep. C'mon.'

They started walking towards the far wall. Now he was closer he could see that a large ornate cross mounted on it was hanging sideways, scorch marks on it and the wall behind.

'It was put on the altar,' said the fireman. 'Didn't do a whole lot of damage, most of the explosion just dissipated in the space. Couple of they embroidered cloth banners caught fire but we got them out pretty quick. Altar is ruined though. All in pieces now.'

As they approached, McCoy could see a minister sitting in one of the front pews, dark suit, dog collar, look of shock on his face. Didn't expect to see the person sitting beside him. DI McCormack held his hand out and they shook.

'Bit out your patch off, isn't it?' asked McCoy.

McCormack nodded. 'Was in the hospital visiting someone when I heard the sirens. Mr Morris here called it in.'

The minister looked up at McCoy. 'I was in the Cathedral House when I heard the bang. Came running. The altar was in pieces, I thought the cross was going to fall too. I called 999 and . . .'

Seemed to run out of words. Just sat there looking bewildered.

McCormack patted him on the shoulder, stood up. 'Want to see?' he asked.

McCoy had no idea what the altar had looked like before but it didn't look good now. Was just a pile of smoking wood and broken marble, wet and dripping from the water the firemen had sprayed it with. The firemen were starting to pack up, pulling down the remnants of a wet and smoking cloth banner from the ceiling,

'Was the place locked up?' asked McCoy.

McCormack shook his head. 'Mr Morris, the minister, can't be sure. Told me he forgets sometimes, asked me not to say.'

McCoy watched the banner fall, land on one of the firemen. His pals started laughing as he struggled to get it off.

'Easter Saturday today,' said McCoy. 'A bomb in a cathedral. Think that's what this is about? Religion?'

McCormack smiled. 'You'd know more about that than me. Don't have much sectarianism in Ballachulish.'

'Just a lot of scared sheep,' said McCoy.

'Something like that,' said McCormack. 'Whatever the motivation was it was more of a protest than anything, I think. Small bomb, nobody injured.'

'Why here though?' asked McCoy.

'That,' said McCormack, 'is for you to find out. I'm off home, not using up any more of my day off on police business.'

McCoy watched him go. Didn't blame him, wasn't his case and it was his day off. He'd have done the same thing. He'd never seen McCormack in any of the polis pubs, always seemed in a world of his own, but McCoy liked him. Knew what he was doing.

He sat down in a pew and tried to think. Why this church? And why on the altar? Maximum disrespect he supposed, the altar was the holiest place in the church. So either the bombers were rabid Catholics with a hatred of Protestantism, or some sort of anti-clerical loonies. Neither seemed to make much sense. He looked up at the wonky cross on the wall. Real question was: was that it? One bomb as a protest, or would there be other bombs in other churches? If whoever was in West Princes Street had made this one, they could easily have made others too.

He stood up, just managed to stop himself crossing himself, and turned to go. Realised Murray was walking up the aisle towards him, hands deep in his sheepskin coat, face like thunder.

'Can you believe it?' he asked. 'A bomb in a place like this? I got married here. It's a disgrace.'

McCoy nodded. Had the feeling his boss was going to take this personally. The last thing he needed.

'Done a bit of damage,' he said.

'So I see,' said Murray, peering at what was left of the altar. 'Bloody vandals.'

'That what you think it is?' asked McCoy.

'Could be.'

'Think vandals would be more likely to spray-paint the place, smash some stuff up. Not sure they're going to build a bomb, to be honest.'

'So who did?' asked Murray, taking his pipe out and sticking it in the corner of his mouth.

'The guy at West Princes Street, I suppose.'

'What for? Why in here?'

McCoy held his hands up in surrender. 'You know as much as I do. Faulds is making some enquiries, seeing if it's a sectarian thing. Hopefully we'll find out a bit more about the bomb-maker, that might tell us something. It was a small bomb, nobody hurt, could be a lot worse.'

'Great,' said Murray. 'Let's not worry about it

then. Just a bloody explosion in Glasgow Cathedral, that's all.'

'That's not what I meant,' said McCoy carefully.

Murray grunted. Put his pipe back in his pocket. 'Need to get to the bottom of it quick. Even if it's just some idiot's idea of a bloody joke or some student protest thing. I don't want any more bombs going off in Glasgow. Hear me?'

McCoy nodded, heart sinking. He was right. Murray was taking it personally.

CHAPTER 8

McCoy's impression of what a boxing gym was like had been gained purely from watching films. *Somebody Up There Likes Me*, *Fat City*, things like that. He looked around. Far as he could see they had been pretty accurate. Morrison's gym was a big room with strip lights and punch bags hanging from the ceiling, foam mats on the floor, dumbbells in metal stands along the wall and an elevated ring in the middle. Walls were covered in framed pictures of boxers, adverts for fights, battered-looking men holding up big belts. There were a couple of young guys in the back warming up, skipping, jabbing and punching the air. Whole place smelled of sweat and that hot ointment people rubbed on sore limbs. All it needed to complete the picture was an old guy in a vest chewing a cigar and Paul Newman with a black eye.

McCoy took a chair off the pile, sat it down over by a big tin ashtray the size of a bin lid by the door and lit up. Could see Stewart and Cooper through the ropes. They were standing watching two skinny guys sparring, pads and

69

helmets on. Stewart was pointing things out, talking to Cooper, demonstrating punches and moves. Cooper looking like he was pretending to understand what he was talking about, nodding every so often.

The guys in the ring were tiny, ribs showing through pale skin, looked more like boys. Must be flyweights or whatever they called them, he supposed. Looked like they needed a good meal and a few days in the sunshine to him. They seemed to spend most of the time trying to avoid each other rather than actually hitting each other, but maybe that was the point. If he was honest, what McCoy knew about boxing you could write on the back of a very small postage stamp.

His mind started drifting off from the sound of the whomps and feet on the canvas. Wattie hadn't made much sense on the phone, probably still half pissed, but one thing was clear, the bombs were back in their court. Looking for Donny Stewart might have to take a back seat for a while. Still, he'd promised to help tomorrow and he couldn't back out now. McCoy wasn't even sure what crime had taken place in West Princes Street. What was blowing yourself up while you built a bomb, exactly? Death by misadventure? Accidental death? Didn't much matter anyway, not like they were going to be charging the guy with anything, just digging his teeth out the wall and sending them back to his mammy.

The real question was how many other bombs the

guy had made. Was the one in the Cathedral the first or the last? And if he had made more, where were they now? Sitting somewhere ready to go off? Maybe he should talk to Faulds again. Even if it was nothing to do with Northern Ireland it was still bomb-making, and he was the only person on the force who seemed to know anything about it.

The bell went and McCoy looked up. The two skinny guys stepped through the ropes and two heavier guys entered the ring, touched gloves and then they started dancing around each other. McCoy finished his cigarette, stubbed it out amongst all the others and wandered over to Stewart and Cooper. He wanted to find out how long they were stuck there, he was starving. Stewart was in full flow, pointing up at the ring.

'This guy's good on his feet, good rotation, hips are good, but he's getting too near the other guy. Needs to take half a step back, it's throwing his whole game off.'

'Think his head needs to be more off-centre too,' said Cooper and Stewart nodded.

'Yep, I spotted that too,' he said.

McCoy was surprised. Maybe Cooper did know something about boxing after all. Wondered what else Cooper had been buying. Had too much cash from the drugs business he needed to get rid of. The accountant was always on at him to spread it about. Far as McCoy remembered he'd a couple of pubs, a few shops and a dodgy disco called

71

Sparkles in Airdrie of all places. Boxers must be the new hobby.

'You hungry, Harry?' Stewart asked, turning from the ring.

McCoy nodded.

'Me too,' said Stewart. 'Steve?'

Cooper didn't take his eyes from the boxers. 'Just one more of them to look at and we're done.'

McCoy sighed, went back to his chair and lit up again. Waited. Stomach killing him.

CHAPTER 9

McCoy looked down at the menu. Not only were there about a hundred different dishes listed but the whole bloody thing was in French. He looked up, Stewart had got a pair of glasses out his top pocket and was examining the wine list while Cooper looked as lost as he did. The Malmaison Restaurant in the Central Hotel. He'd only eaten here once before. Murray's fiftieth and it was a set menu that time, didn't have to choose. Was an impressive place. Chandeliers hung from the ceiling, white tablecloths, plush carpets and the discreet tinkle of glasses and cutlery. The Central was where Stewart had checked in for the night, had asked for a suite at reception. McCoy had no idea how much captains got paid, but it must be a fair bit.

'You boys decided?' asked Stewart, looking over his glasses.

'Just about,' said McCoy, starting to panic. 'What are you having?'

'Thought I'd go for the smoked salmon and then the steak,' said Stewart.

'Sounds good,' said McCoy, closing over his menu.

'That's what I was going to have,' said Cooper, putting his menu back on the table.

Stewart nodded the waiter over. 'Three saumon fumé, three filet de boeuf, medium, some fries for the table and a bottle of the '52 Bordeaux.'

The waiter nodded and scuttled off.

'I called the Holy Loch Base from the room phone,' said Stewart. 'Still no sign of Donny.' He tried to smile but it died on his face.

'He'll be back,' said McCoy. 'He's a grown man, nothing will have happened to him.'

Stewart nodded. Didn't look convinced.

'We'll get on top of it tomorrow. Someone will know something,' said McCoy with more conviction than he felt. 'We'll find him.'

Stewart nodded again, looked a bit happier. 'Thanks for this, Harry. It's appreciated.'

The waiter arrived back with three plates of smoked salmon and put them down with a flourish. Cooper looked at the pale orange fish with horror. He speared a bit with his fork, held it to his nose and sniffed. Put it back and stood up. 'No be a minute,' he said.

McCoy assumed he was heading for the gents but he went the other way. Soon realised why. Billy Weir was standing at the entrance to the restaurant looking round in amazement. Cooper's number two didn't really fit in amongst the suits and long dresses. Not with his leather bomber jacket, feather cut and patched jeans. Cooper hugged him and they went off towards the bar. McCoy shouldn't feel worried, Billy had been in charge while Cooper had been inside, probably just a catch-up, but he was. Had a feeling Cooper was up to something, and that something probably involved Jamsie Dixon.

The wine arrived and Stewart tasted it, nodded, and the waiter filled their glasses.

'You know your way around an expensive restaurant,' said McCoy, taking a sip. The vintage was lost on him, tasted the same as every other glass of wine he'd had. 'Staying in a suite as well. Didn't realise the pay in the navy was so good. Might join up myself.'

Stewart smiled. 'It's not. Money comes from my great-grandfather. Cotton mills.'

'A lot of money?' asked McCoy.

Stewart looked a bit taken aback. 'Well, I suppose you could say so.'

'Sorry,' said McCoy. 'I'm not being nosey. I meant is there enough family money to make it worth kidnapping your son?'

Stewart sat back in his seat. 'Shit. I never thought of that.'

'Is it possible?'

Stewart nodded. 'There's enough all right but Donny wasn't the type to advertise it. Was more ashamed of it than anything else. Thought it was money taken from the workers' backs, as he liked to say. Besides, how would anyone know?'

75

'I assume people knew Donny's your son?' said McCoy.

Stewart nodded.

'Not that difficult to put two and two together,' said McCoy. 'What are the mills called?'

'Stewart's Mills,' said Stewart.

'There you go,' said McCoy.

'But there's been no contact, no ransom demand,' said Stewart.

'Not yet,' said McCoy. 'That Getty boy was all over the news, took them ages to ask for any money. Maybe it's given someone ideas.'

'Christ . . .' Stewart reached into his jacket, pulled out an envelope. 'I brought some pictures of Donny from home, to show people.'

'Good idea,' said McCoy.

Stewart handed him a picture. 'Graduation Day.'

It was a head and shoulders shot of a young man in naval uniform and hat. McCoy tried to see the resemblance but there wasn't much of one – the same sandy-coloured hair, but Donny Stewart had none of his dad's burliness, was tall and thin, looked like a stiff breeze would blow him over. He handed the photo back. Looked up as Cooper appeared in the restaurant doorway, wove his way through the tables towards them, fair few disapproving looks at his jeans and short-sleeved shirt, and sat down.

'What's up with you two?' he asked.

'Nothing,' said McCoy. 'Just having a think about Stewart's missing boy.'

Cooper sat forward, looked at Stewart. 'Look, pal, we'll find him. McCoy's a good polis and I've got contacts all over this city. Contacts on the other side of the tracks if you get my meaning. We'll find him.'

Stewart nodded, held up his glass. 'To you two, God only knows what I'd be doing without you.'

They clinked glasses and Cooper swallowed back most of his glass of wine. 'So,' he said. 'My fighters any good? Or am I wasting my money?'

'You're not wasting all of it,' said Stewart. 'One of them could be the real deal, the middleweight with the black hair. Need to see him in a proper fight situation though. Sparring is sparring, it's how he acts in the ring that matters. Let's see if you've backed a winner.'

'I bloody better have,' said Cooper. 'I paid enough.'

'The guys we saw tonight, is that all of them?' asked Stewart. 'Is there a lot of talent in these . . .'

Stewart and Cooper kept on talking but McCoy had stopped listening. Something had changed. The tinkle of cutlery and glasses had quietened down, no more talking, the room was suddenly still. Looked up and saw why.

Jamsie Dixon, long blond hair, ankle-length leather coat, was moving quickly across the restaurant, heading for Cooper.

'Stevie! Watch!' shouted McCoy.

It was all he managed to get out before Jamsie Dixon was right behind Cooper, open razor in his hand. He swung it down and Cooper twisted away just in time, razor opening up a cut in his arm rather than on his face. Instantly Cooper was up and out his chair. Grabbed the steak knife from the table and turned to confront Dixon. He moved in on him, lunged with the knife. Dixon just managed to jump away, turned and went in with the razor again.

It seemed like time was running in slow motion. McCoy could see the shocked look on the diners' faces, the expression of hate on Dixon's face, Stewart's mouth falling open in surprise and the razor running down Cooper's arm again.

Cooper shouted, 'Fucker!', grabbed Dixon's wrist, managed to pull him off balance, Dixon tried to wrestle out of Cooper's grip but he tripped over the leg of a chair, fell onto the carpet. Cooper quickly stomped down on the hand holding the razor and Dixon screamed, let it go. Cooper knelt over him, held the knife up, ready to bring it down on Dixon's face just as McCoy scrambled round the table and pushed Cooper off.

Cooper fell to the side and the force of his push meant McCoy fell on top of him. That was all Dixon needed. He was up and running for the door, smashing through a dessert trolley and the waiter pushing it on the way. He banged the door open, kept running and was gone.

A couple of seconds of silence before the shouts and the screams and Cooper cursing at him and Stewart asking them if they were all right. McCoy held out a hand to help Cooper up. Blood was all over his shirt and jeans, tried not to look at it. The maître d' appeared out of nowhere asking if anyone was hurt and telling them he was going to phone the police. McCoy dug his wallet out, flashed his police card, told him it was all fine. The maître d' nodded, called over to the station and waiters started swooping in, clearing up the mess. Managed to get things looking back to normal faster than you would think. The maître d' hit the side of a wineglass with a knife a couple of times, managed to get everyone's attention.

'Ladies and gentlemen, I can only apologise for tonight's disturbance. To help us all get back to normal I'd like to announce a stiff whisky on the house for everyone. Thank you!'

A ripple of applause, people laughing, talking again. Suddenly a terrifying situation had become an anecdote they could tell their friends. Whoever the maître d' was, he knew how to run a restaurant. McCoy looked over at Cooper, who was standing off to the side, breathing hard, face like thunder, a waiter trying his best to wrap his arm in some white linen napkins. Stewart asked the maître d' to send the steaks up to the suite with another bottle of wine, pressed a twenty-quid note into his hand.

'Upstairs, boys,' he said. 'Let's leave these guys to clear up.'

Twenty minutes later they were sitting round the table in Stewart's suite. It was at the top of the hotel, windows looking out at the city centre below. Seemed to be about three or four connected rooms, was also about twice the size of McCoy's flat. Cooper was sitting at the table in his skivvies and vest, arms wrapped up in bloodstained napkins, chucking the wine down like nobody's business. McCoy looked up from his half-eaten steak, was about to apologise to Stewart for what happened. Last thing he expected was Stewart looking at him with a big grin on his face.

'You okay?' he asked.

Stewart nodded. 'Something to tell the boys back home.' He held up his glass. 'Cheers!' He turned to Cooper. 'There's some suits and shirts in the closet in the bedroom. We're about the same size, you want to see if you can find one that fits?'

Cooper nodded. Stood up and padded through to the other room in his socks. Stewart watched him go, waited until he was out of earshot, turned to McCoy.

'You want to tell me what went on down there?' he asked.

McCoy shrugged. 'Let's just say Cooper was in prison for more than a bar fight.'

'You mean he's a bad guy?' asked Stewart. 'I don't get it. How come you're a cop and you're pals with someone like that?'

'It's a long story,' said McCoy. 'We go way back.'

'Got it,' said Stewart. 'Well, he's a friend of yours so he's a friend of mine. Take people as they are, that's something the navy taught me. So what happens now?'

'Now we go to the boxing like nothing happened,' said McCoy.

'You sure?' asked Stewart. 'You think he'll still want to go? With all those cuts?'

McCoy nodded. 'Definitely. Show no fear. Don't let anyone know you're hurt. It's how guys like Cooper have to be.'

'Sounds like something we got told at the Citadel,' said Stewart.

'What's the—'

'Not bad if I say so myself,' said Cooper, walking back into the room. He'd a grey suit on, pale blue shirt, looked like they had been fitted on him.

'Very smart,' said Stewart.

'What is this clobber?' asked Cooper, opening the suit jacket and peering at the label. 'Brooks Brothers? Might get some of this myself. They sell it here?'

'Don't think so,' said Stewart.

'Pity, that,' said Cooper, picking up his glass and draining the last of his wine. 'What we waiting for? We've got boxing to go to.'

CHAPTER 10

Govan Town Hall had been built when Govan was quite something. Back when it built ships and sent huge ocean liners off to America every week. When it was the busiest part of Glasgow. It was an ornate red sandstone building that took up a whole corner on Govan Road, meant to impress, show off Govan's importance in the world. These days Govan wasn't as important any more and the town hall was suffering too. Needed a clean, weeds growing out the gutters, couple of broken windows repaired with sellotape and cardboard.

Inside wasn't much better, the vast hall had seen better days. Some of the wallpaper in the foyer was coming away, brown damp patches spotting the ceiling. A boxing ring had been set up in the middle of the main hall, table for the referees beside it, notepads and bottles of water set out. The crowd was in rows of fold-up seats on the floor, red padded ones in the balcony. Looked like a couple of warm-up matches had gone by already, ring was already stained with blood and footprints. McCoy, Stewart and Cooper were shown to their seats by a woman with a torch and an expression that showed exactly what she thought of boxing and the people who had come to watch it. They had just sat down, McCoy already trying to work out how soon he could leave, when Billy Weir appeared at Cooper's shoulder.

'All right, boss?' he asked, taking in the suit. 'You look like a businessman.'

'I am a businessman,' said Cooper. 'Time you got that in your fucking head.'

Billy nodded, did a little salute, moved in close to Cooper, whispered something in his ear. Cooper listened, nodded and went back to showing the programme to Stewart. Billy went to go and McCoy caught his eye, nodded back towards the foyer. Billy nodded back, wandered off.

McCoy waited a minute or so. Stood up. 'I'm off to get some fags, anyone want anything?' he asked.

No response. Both heads still buried in the programme. He shrugged and headed for the exit.

Billy was waiting in the front foyer, standing reading the numbers ballpointed onto the wall by the payphone by the front doors.

'You heard what happened?' asked McCoy.

Billy nodded. 'Fucking mess. That Jamsie Dixon's wired to the moon.'

'I need you to keep Cooper away from him and his mind off it. I don't want him going after him. Dixon'll be in jail in four days. We just have to keep Cooper away from him until then.'

Billy nodded. Didn't look too sure about it. 'It's gonna be hard. He's no in the easiest of moods.'

'You're telling me,' said McCoy. 'What's up with him?'

'Between you and me?' asked Billy. He looked worried, didn't want to be the one telling tales. 'You'll no tell him I said anything?'

McCoy nodded. 'Cross my heart.'

'I don't know for sure but I think it was the prison that set him off. He got me up there last month. I just sat there in the visiting room as he called everybody for everything, practically frothing at the mouth. The warders, the Dixons, anyone. I don't know, seems like he's just really angry at everything and everybody. Remember the old days when he'd been up for a couple of nights on the black bombers, desperate to pick a fight with anyone just so he could batter someone? Like that.'

'Christ,' said McCoy. 'That's all we need. I mean it, Billy, keep him away from Dixon, it's only a few days and then he's out the picture. Maybe he just needs some time out the prison to get back to normal.'

'Maybe,' said Billy. Didn't sound too convinced.

'By the way, what were you whispering in his ear back there?'

'Nothing,' said Billy.

Said it too fast and was too sure about it for McCoy's liking. Was lying through his teeth. Not good. 'Billy, I'm serious,' said McCoy, poking him

84

in the chest with his finger. 'Make this feud stop. The mood he's in he'll do something stupid, something he'll regret.'

Billy did his salute again. 'So you're the boss now too?' he asked.

'Until Jamsie Dixon's put away, yes, I am. Remember that.'

McCoy went back into the hall just as the lights went down and a sweaty-looking guy in a dickie bow and evening suit with a shiny arse stepped into the ring.

'Ladies and gentlemen, welcome back to Govan Town Hall and a night of five bouts. Third bout tonight is a heavyweight match between . . .'

He sat down beside Stewart, wondered how long he was going to be able to suffer. Stomach hurt from the red wine, knew he shouldn't have drunk it but he had and he was paying for it now. The first bout was mercifully bloodless, the two big guys danced around each other for four rounds, an occasional punch thrown. Unlike McCoy, the crowd wasn't happy, boos as they climbed out the ring. Another announcement from shiny arse and two new guys got in. They were fitter, quicker, looked a lot more serious. Bout kicked off and within a couple of minutes one landed a haymaker on the other guy's nose. There was a crack and then the blood spurted out, staining the canvas ring. They were seated so close McCoy could hear it, sounded like rain hitting the pavement. That was his cue to leave.

He stood up. 'I'm going to go, Stewart. I'll see you in the morning, eh?'

Stewart nodded, eyes still on the fighters.

'You all right if I go, Stevie?' McCoy asked.

Cooper nodded, eyes on the ring like Stewart. 'I don't need a bloody babysitter, and before you say it, I'll stay away from Dixon.'

McCoy nodded, headed for the door. Was as good as he was going to get from Cooper. Noticed someone else leaving just in front of him. Johnny Bone, all-round tout and weasel. Be off to tell all and sundry that even after Dixon went for him Cooper was at the boxing, all dressed up in a suit, looking like the cat that got the cream. Just like he was supposed to.

McCoy stepped out onto Govan Road. Was a nice night, spring was definitely here, bit of warmth still in the air. There was something about Cooper all dressed up in Stewart's clothes that was bothering him, just couldn't think what it was. It was at the edge of his thoughts, just out of reach. Decided not to think about it, that was when he normally remembered.

He lit up, started walking down to the rank at Brechin's Bar. Stopped at the crossing to let a car pass, the inside lit up as a guy in the passenger seat struck a match. Wasn't hard to see who it was. Billy Weir. Some guy he didn't recognise driving. Wondered where exactly Billy was off to. Normally he'd be stuck by Cooper's side, be waiting out in the hall for him to leave. But not tonight. Maybe he was just being paranoid. Maybe Cooper had just sent him home because he wasn't in the mood to speak to anyone, least of all Billy.

McCoy hailed a cab, got in. Wasn't in the mood for worrying about Billy or Cooper or the Dixons. He was tired, driven all day, stomach was hurting. All he wanted was a couple of pints in the Victoria then home to smoke a joint, listen to some music and then bed. Had the feeling that looking for Stewart's son tomorrow was going to turn out to be a long day. Just hoped another bomb wouldn't go off in the middle of it.

14TH APRIL 1974

CHAPTER 11

'No.'

'No? Come on, Harry, be a pal. Please?'

McCoy was standing at his door in his pyjama bottoms and vest looking at Wattie's pleading face. 'Wattie, the whole point of you being the point man in a case is that it's you that's in charge. Not me. What am I going to do anyway? Stand there holding your hand?'

Wattie looked like he was going to cry. 'Please, Harry? My head's all over the place. I haven't slept a single night through since the baby came and Murray's in a fuck of a mood, keeps telling me I'm not coming up to scratch. If I bugger this up I'm toast. Just come for an hour, make sure I don't forget anything. Eh?'

McCoy sighed, faced the inevitable and nodded.

'Good man! Get your clothes on quick, I'll be in the car,' said Wattie and disappeared down the stairs before McCoy could change his mind.

Ten minutes later McCoy was lighting his first cigarette of the day, looking out the car window at an empty Glasgow going past. He liked Sunday mornings: the town was always empty, no traffic, just a few buses taking the unlucky few to work.

'So what's the story?' he asked, turning to Wattie. 'Bank robbery? Masked jewel thief?'

'Very funny. A body discovered in a back court this morning. Head bashed in.'

'Lovely,' said McCoy, already dreading seeing it. 'Whereabouts?'

'Shettleston. Just past the Parkhead Forge.'

'Saturday night last night,' said McCoy. 'Bloke that's dead will have been drunk, the bloke that killed him will have been drunk. There'll have been an argument and he won't have realised how hard he hit him. Always the way.'

'Probably,' said Wattie, turning into the Gallowgate.

'You called Gilroy?' asked McCoy.

Wattie nodded. 'All done.'

'Arranged for local uniforms to secure the crime scene?'

Wattie nodded again.

'What do you need me for then?' asked McCoy.

'Because that's the easy bit. It's the other bits that worry me. Besides, what else were you doing today?'

'Lots! I'm busy! Remember that American bloke in the club?'

'Nope,' said Wattie. 'Could have been an elephant in the club, I wouldn't remember it. I was shit-faced by the time we left the Golden Palace. Why?'

'His son's gone missing. I said I'd help him out today, help him look.'

'Good for you, and here was me thinking you'd be lying in your bed all day. You'll only be an hour, tops. Promise.'

'Less,' said McCoy. 'Believe me.'

They turned into Old Shettleston Road, forge on the left, and Shettleston was revealed in all its glory. McCoy didn't know if it was because of the forge but this bit of Glasgow always seemed dirty, tenements black with smoke and soot. Even the pavements looked grimy. They were firmly in the East End now, not McCoy's normal stomping ground. Knew it a bit from his beat days. Walking up and down Shettleston Road on a Friday night wasn't an experience he ever wanted to repeat. Could get wild here. Gangs, pubs on every second corner, gangsters defending their turf. Maybe he was just getting too soft in his old age. This was the Glasgow he started in, should be able to take what it threw at them.

'Just up here, I think,' said Wattie, peering out the window, trying to see a close number. 'Number 779.'

McCoy pointed up ahead. 'That'll be the one with the panda car parked outside then?'

'Ah,' said Wattie, looking sheepish. He drove another couple of hundred yards, pulled in and cut the engine.

'Remember,' said McCoy, 'you're in charge here so you need to seem like you are. Don't faff about, be alert, try and be professional. I'll be there but I'm not going to say anything. Soon as I do they'll all start talking to me. It's natural, I'm the senior officer. Okay?'

Wattie nodded. Looked like a kid on his first day at school.

McCoy clapped his shoulder. 'You'll be fine,' he said with more conviction than he felt. 'Let's go.'

They got out of the car and headed up to the panda. It was sitting with the light on the roof spinning, uniform standing beside it unravelling a rope. As they got closer McCoy realised it was Williams, tall guy from Central.

'Mr McCoy!' said Williams. 'They said you were on holiday today. Did they call you in?'

'No,' said McCoy. 'This is Watson's show, not mine.'

'Through the close?' asked Wattie.

'Yes, out the back by the middens,' said Williams, looking a bit puzzled.

They walked through the dim close, past the stairs, faint smell of piss as always, and stepped out into the light of the back court. Back courts were gardens in posh areas, in places like Shettleston they looked like bomb sites. Rubble everywhere, huge puddles of muddy water, rows of bashed and filthy metal bins. They were the playgrounds for the kids of the flats, no gardens here, just a no man's land of rats, piles of rubbish, abandoned bed frames and broken prams.

'Fuck sake,' said McCoy, looking up. There were

at least twenty people hanging out the back windows of the flats overlooking the back court. Old women with mugs of tea, men in vests smoking, even wee kids. Was like an audience at a Roman amphitheatre watching Christians being eaten by the lions.

Wattie stepped back into the close, shouted, 'Williams, get a bloody tent out here now!'

A distant reply of 'It's on its way, sir.'

Not much they could do about it now. They were just going to have to keep going under the beady eyes of the good people of Shettleston. McCoy didn't really blame them, it was Sunday morning after all, nothing on the telly.

'Hoi, mister,' a boy shouted from one of the windows. 'You're too late! He's dead!'

A ripple of laughter echoed round the back court along with a few tut-tuts.

'Just ignore it,' said McCoy. 'Concentrate on what you're doing.'

Wattie nodded, headed to the body lying on the ground. McCoy let him go, planned to stay as far away as possible. Could see Big Duncan Muir standing off to the side. Thank God for that. Muir had seen more murder scenes than McCoy and Wattie combined. Must be mid-fifties by now, almost time for retirement. Wattie had struck lucky, Muir would keep him right.

'Morning, sir,' he said to Wattie. 'Not a pretty sight, I'm afraid.'

Muir stood aside and suddenly McCoy could

see the very thing he didn't want to. A man was lying on the ground, grey suit black with blood. McCoy made himself look at his face, immediately wished he hadn't. Wasn't much left of his features, face just a red pulpy mess, one eye completely gone, the other swollen shut. His long hair was soaked with blood, hard to tell what colour it was. Nose was flat on his face, looked like someone had pushed it into his skull. The only bit of his face left intact was his mouth: thin lips and small yellow teeth. McCoy looked away quickly.

'Who is he?' asked Wattie. 'Do we know?'

'Not yet, sir. We were waiting for you,' said Muir.

Wattie squatted down by the body, pushed his hand under the man's jacket, fished a wallet out his inside pocket, opened it and started going through it.

'Couple of bookies' lines. Mass card, picture of a wee boy at the seaside and a driver's licence.' He unfolded it, trying to keep his hands free of blood. 'Belonging to one James Dixon, of . . .' He squinted at it. '. . . 779 Old Shettleston Road, Glasgow.'

McCoy's stomach turned over, couldn't believe what he'd just heard. 'What?'

Wattie looked up at him. 'You've gone white as a bloody sheet. You know him?'

McCoy shook his head, needed time to think. 'No, it's just the sight of the blood, you know me. Heard of him though. Thug for hire, works for whoever'll pay him.'

'A right nasty piece of work,' said Muir.

'Well, whoever he is,' said Wattie, 'he's in a right bloody mess. Brick?'

McCoy nodded, tried to keep his mind on what was in front of him. 'That or a hammer maybe, something like that.'

'Who found him?' asked Wattie, looking up at Muir.

'Wifey in the top floor came out this morning, bag for the midden, saw him lying there,' said Muir.

'What time?' asked Wattie.

Muir got his notebook out. 'Back of six. She made a cup of tea, listened to the six o'clock news on the radio then she came down.'

'So it happened some time last night,' said Wattie. 'Need to wait for Miss Gilroy for a proper timing, she's on her way.'

'Last night makes sense,' said McCoy. 'Can't see him being up and at them before six this morning.'

'He got any enemies?' asked Wattie.

McCoy's stomach went again. Pictured Cooper in the restaurant, knife held above his head ready to bring it down on Jamsie Dixon's face.

'As I said, he's a right bad lad,' said Muir. 'Hurts people for a living. Bound to have a good few.'

Wattie stood up. Looked at the licence again, looked up at the flats. 'Flat one/two. Better go up and give whoever he lives with the bad news.'

'I think he's got brothers,' said McCoy, and as he said it he remembered what it was that had bothered him about Cooper wearing Stewart's suit. The thing he had been trying to remember.

''Scuse me, sir.' He turned and Williams was beside him, roll of green canvas under one arm, wooden posts in the other. McCoy stood aside and Williams moved past him, heading for where the body was lying.

McCoy looked at Wattie. 'You okay?'

Wattie nodded. 'I'll inform the next of kin. Medical examiner is on her way. We're setting the tent up, I'll start the uniforms on a door-to-door, see if anyone saw anything.'

'Andy?'

'Fuck!' said Wattie. 'Forgot.' He turned to Muir. 'Can you call in and get Andy the photographer on his way?'

Muir nodded, wandered off, speaking into his walkie talkie.

'One mistake, not too bad,' said McCoy. 'I'm going to go. I'll see you at the shop later.'

Wattie nodded and McCoy left him to it, walked back up the close. Head was full of Cooper. Wasn't a chance anyone else was behind Jamsie Dixon's demise, had to be him, and it looked like the fucker had even managed to rope McCoy in as his alibi. No wonder Cooper had been so keen for him to tag along to the boxing and keep an eye on him.

Wouldn't take even someone as green as Wattie long to find out what had happened at the restaurant last night and put two and two together. Didn't even want to think about what Murray would say

98

when he found out he was the chief suspect's alibi. He was going to bloody kill Cooper. All he'd asked was for him to lie low for a few days and instead he'd got Jamsie Dixon killed, and dropped McCoy right in it.

'Harry?'

He looked up to see Phyllis Gilroy coming down the pavement towards him. Tweed suit, white blouse and trusty leather bag. 'I thought this was young Watson's big break?' she asked, smiling.

'It is,' said McCoy. 'I was just holding his hand for a while. He'll be fine.'

Phyllis looked a bit doubtful.

'Muir's there,' said McCoy. 'Don't need to worry.'

She looked relieved. 'Ah, in that case you're right. So what about you, Harry? Are you on the bomb in West Princes Street?'

'Looks like it. The Cathedral too,' said McCoy. 'Special Branch have batted them back to us. No paramilitary involvement, apparently.'

She smiled again. 'Well, in that case you are the man I need to talk to. You've saved me an extra trip. I did Paul Watt's autopsy last night.'

'So that's his name?' asked McCoy. 'The guy in the flat?'

She nodded. 'Special Branch gave me their report. I've got one for Mr Murray also. Confidential, as they kept telling me with great drama.'

'Anything interesting in it?' asked McCoy.

'In their report?' said Phyllis. 'I don't think I'm giving anything away if I say no. Taciturn to say the least, seems to be a qualification for that particular organisation, but I, however, found something rather interesting.'

'What's that?'

'There was more than one kind of blood all over the scene. Paul Watt is – was – O positive, very common. However, there was a quantity of A negative present too, much rarer. Enough to indicate a wound.'

'Hang on,' said McCoy. 'So there were two people in the flat when the bomb went off?'

'Looks like it. One killed outright, one injured.'

'How badly? Could he have made a run for it?'

'I expect so,' said Gilroy. 'There wasn't a huge amount. If it was a flesh wound, nothing too serious, would still have been ambulatory.'

'Shit,' said McCoy.

'Indeed. Makes things a bit more complicated, I would imagine.' She waited. 'Harry?'

'Sorry, miles away. Do me a favour, Phyllis? Go easy on Wattie? He might need a bit of a helping hand and Murray is watching him like a hawk.'

She nodded. 'First dead body of the day, here I come.'

McCoy watched her disappear into the darkness of the close, lit up, and stood in the street trying to think things through. If he was right, Donny Stewart wasn't quite the timid young man his father thought he was. Far from it.

100

CHAPTER 12

Stewart was waiting outside the Central Hotel entrance when McCoy turned in to Gordon Street. He pulled in by the Corn Exchange pub and pressed the horn. Stewart saw him, waved, hurried over to the car and got in.

'Morning, Harry,' he said. 'You good?'

McCoy nodded. Wondered why Americans always looked so bloody healthy. Even on a Sunday morning.

'So how'd you get on last night?' he asked, putting the car into gear and pulling out.

'Turned out to be quite a night,' said Stewart. 'Steve's guy won, knockout in the second round, so he wanted to celebrate. Went to a couple of pubs in town then ended up going to a casino, of all places. It was just up from here, I think – I was a bit drunk when I walked home. Nice place. You probably know it. Called the . . . hang on . . .' He reached into his jacket, got his wallet out. Pulled out a card. 'Called the Chevalier?'

McCoy nodded. Knew it too well. One of the few legal places in Glasgow you could get a late-night drink. As long as you ordered some food too.

'Smart place. Apparently, some lords or sirs were there. Lord Dunlop, I think Steve said.'

'That right?' said McCoy. 'Be Sir Hugh Fraser he was with then.'

'That's it,' said Stewart.

'How long did you stay?' ask McCoy.

'I left Steve there about one-thirty, he was still going strong. His pal Billy turned up.'

I bet he did, thought McCoy. Came to give him the good news about Jamsie Dixon's demise. He wasn't stupid, Cooper. He now had a cast-iron alibi until the early hours with a fucking polis and a retired navy captain as his witnesses.

Stewart rolled down the window. 'Lovely morning to be going down to the Loch. I called ahead, there's a man called Saunders, a pal of Donny's, he's going to talk to us, see if he can shed any light on things.'

'Great,' said McCoy as he turned into West Princes Street. 'Just need to stop somewhere first.'

'All good,' said Stewart. 'I'm in your capable hands.'

The flat still smelt of smoke, floor still a mud of ash and soggy carpet. McCoy walked through the hall towards the living room, Stewart following behind. Had a quick look at where the body had been before. Now there was just a patch of floorboard surrounded by burnt carpet and ash. Couldn't help himself looking at the wall above the fireplace. Teeth had gone too.

'What happened here?' asked Stewart, looking bewildered.

'A bomb went off and killed the man who was making it. Paul Watt. That name mean anything to you?'

Stewart shook his head, was looking round the flat wide-eyed, trying to take it in.

'Need you to look at some clothes,' said McCoy. 'C'mon.'

He pushed the bedroom door open and they went in, sun slanting through the half-open curtains, bright stripe on the flowery wallpaper and the sleeping bag on the bed. McCoy bent down and pulled up the little suitcase, put it on the bed. He pressed the silver buttons on the locks and they popped open.

Stewart looked at him, looked at the suitcase.

'I think they might be Donny's clothes,' said McCoy. 'Can you have a look?'

Stewart nodded, walked over, opened the case and looked in. He reached in, pulled out a shirt and his face crumpled. He nodded.

'They're Donny's. We went shopping just before he came to Scotland. Bought him some things. He said it was an old man's shop but I was buying so that's where we went.'

'Your suit,' said McCoy. 'The one you gave to Cooper. Brooks Brothers. Took me a while to remember where I'd seen the name. Same label on the shirts.'

Stewart sat on the bed, shirt in his hand. Looked

103

completely lost. 'I don't understand,' he said. 'Why are Donny's clothes here?' Then something dawned, an awful look of pain on his face. Looked up at McCoy. 'Is he dead?'

'Do you know what blood type he is?' asked McCoy.

Stewart nodded. 'A negative. Same as me. The navy always test you, it's on your dog tags. Will be on . . .'

He stopped, looked up at McCoy, and let out a wail. 'Oh Christ, have you found a body? Where is he?'

'I don't think he's dead,' said McCoy. 'But I think he's injured and I think he's in trouble, big trouble. C'mon, let's get out of here, this place stinks.'

They sat on the kerb outside, breathed the fresh air in, sun warm on their shoulders. Could hear the shouts and laughs of some kids playing up the street. McCoy lit up, started to explain.

'A guy called Paul Watt was building a bomb in there, but the thing went up in his face and killed him. He was O positive, his blood was all over the place, but there was other blood there too. A negative blood. Enough to indicate a wound. And as you know, it's pretty rare. With that and the clothes, I think Donny was staying there, was there when the bomb went off, and he ran.'

Stewart looked pained.

'Another one went off yesterday, you probably heard?'

Stewart nodded. 'In a church.'

'Was Donny particularly religious? Anti-religious?' McCoy asked.

'No,' said Stewart. 'Same as me, raised Anglican, but really just for deaths and marriages. We never went to church. I don't get it. A bomb? What for? What does Donny have to do with a bomb?'

'That's what we need to find out,' said McCoy. 'They fingerprint you in the navy?'

'Not back when I enlisted but I'm pretty sure they do now.'

'Okay, so we need to get those and see if we can match it with any in the flat. That way we'll definitely know if Donny was there.'

Stewart leant forward, put his head in his hands. McCoy patted his shoulder. Watched one of the kids bouncing a football, keeping it away from his pal.

'Chances are he's alive,' he said. 'That's the main thing and now we have a way to try and find him.'

Stewart looked up and wiped his eyes with a hanky from his pocket. 'Okay, what do we do now?'

McCoy stood up. 'We go to the Holy Loch and we talk to his pal.'

CHAPTER 13

Stewart didn't say much on the journey to Dunoon. McCoy didn't blame him, he had a lot to think about. He just sat and spun the signet ring on his pinky round and round, looked miles away. Was probably the last thing he expected, his son mixed up with some nutter making a bomb. Whole thing didn't make much sense to McCoy either. He turned the radio on waiting for the news, just in case it had happened again. What he really needed was to get the Special Branch report and find out what Paul Watt's story was. How did he even meet Donny Stewart? And what could they have in common that they'd build a bomb together?

McCoy paid his toll money and drove over the Erskine Bridge, a spindly structure stretching across the Clyde. So high up, there was some view, you could see right down the Clyde Valley, almost to the sea. He tapped Stewart on the shoulder, pointed at the view. He barely looked at it, went back to turning the ring, lost in his thoughts.

'Where are we meeting the pal?' asked McCoy as they drove into Gourock.

Stewart dug a piece of paper out his pocket. 'The Paul Jones, 205 Argyll Street. It's a pub, I think.'

McCoy parked the car and they walked over to the pier. Gourock was Greenock's posher cousin, only a couple of miles from where Wattie's dad lived, but very different. Big houses overlooking the bay, an esplanade, no noisy shipyards here. The sun was shining on the blue sparkling water, green and brown hills in the background. Was like a postcard or the lid of a shortbread tin. This was the Scotland you saw on the TV or in the pictures – the scenery, the roads, the little puffer ships going up and down. Wasn't a Scotland McCoy much cared for. For him the countryside only meant one thing. Children's homes. They were always out of town, mostly in the back arse of nowhere. Had even been in one near Dunoon, just up the road in Kirn. Hadn't been there long, just one weekend when his dad had been arrested again. But sometimes a weekend is long enough and bad enough to last a lifetime. No matter what had happened to Donny Stewart or what his pal might tell them, he wasn't setting foot in Kirn ever again. Never. Funny how he always felt safer on the streets of Glasgow, had done even when he was a boy, even when his dad was at his worst and he hadn't eaten for days, it was still better than a home.

The ferry came into view and they shuffled along towards the end of the pier with the locals and the day-trippers and waited for the passengers to disembark.

'Is it an island?' asked Stewart. 'Dunoon?'

'No,' said McCoy. 'You can drive there but nobody does. You have to go all the way round the houses to get there, takes hours and hours. Everyone gets the ferry – it's not long, ten minutes or so.'

Eventually they got on board and amid shouts and clanging the ferry left the pier. They made their way to the front, McCoy managing to light a cigarette in the shelter of his jacket. Ahead of them, across the river, lay the long strip of Dunoon.

'Pretty place for a base,' said Stewart.

'Think the water's really deep in the Holy Loch, that's why they chose it,' said McCoy. 'Trouble is, soon as World War Three starts the Russians will bomb it and Glasgow will go up in a mushroom cloud.'

Stewart smiled. 'May as well get it over with quick, better than radiation poisoning.'

'True,' said McCoy. 'So when we get there, meet this guy, let me do the talking. Maybe just introduce us and go for a wee walk, get an ice cream, eh?'

'Why's that?' asked Stewart.

'Because this guy's a what, a sailor? Something junior?' asked McCoy.

'A seaman apprentice,' said Stewart. 'About as low as you can get.'

'And you were a captain,' said McCoy. 'You don't think he's going to be a bit intimidated? Clam up a bit?'

'Fair point,' said Stewart. 'Never thought of that.'

Ten minutes later they were disembarking, walking up Argyll Street past the big hotel on the right. The town was mobbed, good weather and the Easter holidays. Kids were everywhere, families, grannies in cardigans sitting on the benches licking ice-cream cones, watching the world go by. Argyll Street was full of souvenir shops, cafes, toy shops with nets of balls, foil windmills and long bamboo poles with nets at the end tied up outside. There was even a fair set up on the green just outside the town. Sounds of pop music and screams of kids on the rides drifting over.

They passed a few sailors in uniform as they made their way up the hill. Even without the uniforms they would have stood out. Like Stewart, they looked like they'd been brought up on something else. They were tall, well built, white teeth, looked like they had come straight off some Midwestern farm. Made the Glasgow day-trippers with their pale skin and bad teeth look like a different species altogether.

Mike Saunders was no different. He was standing outside the Paul Jones in civvies. Jeans, sandshoes and a short-sleeved shirt. Close-cropped dark hair, big smile. He stepped forward to meet them, held out his hand.

'Sir.'

Stewart shook it. 'This is Harry McCoy,' he said. 'Scottish police force.'

McCoy shook his hand. Saunders held it so firmly he was lucky to get it back in one piece.

'Sorry,' said Saunders. 'I didn't think. PJ's is shut on a Sunday.'

'Don't worry,' said McCoy. 'We'll find a cafe. You off to look at the sights?'

Stewart looked at him, puzzled, then realised it was his cue. 'Yep, see you guys later. Good luck.'

They watched him walk up the street and disappear into Woolworths.

'You can breathe out now, son,' said McCoy. 'The Big Boss is gone.' He looked around, spotted a cafe down the street. 'C'mon.'

McPherson's Imperial Tearoom and Cafe looked like the tearoom on the *Titanic*. It was all stained-glass windows, green plants on stands and framed pictures of hills and lochs. They got a table and sat down. Ordered a couple of coffees. Had to be the youngest people in there by about thirty years.

'So, when did you last see Donny?' asked McCoy.

'Don,' he said. 'He hated Donny, that's what his dad calls him.' Saunders smiled. 'And Donny Osmond doesn't help.'

'Got you,' said McCoy.

'Tuesday night,' said Saunders. 'The night he disappeared.'

'What happened?'

'Got the liberty boat, then a taxi into Dunoon. Ended up in PJ's like every other night. Sat at a table drinking.'

An elderly waitress in a black dress and a white lace pinny appeared, put their coffees down on the table. McCoy sipped his, realised if he drank it his stomach would be in agony again, pushed it to the side.

'Was he different in any way? Acting weird?' he asked.

Saunders shook his head. 'Not really. Was the same old Don. We hadn't been out for a while. I'd been on nights so he'd been going out by himself.'

'Where?' asked McCoy.

Saunders shrugged. 'Said he'd met some guys at a different pub one night. Scots guys. Said he'd been hanging out with them. When I asked him where he just smiled, said round and about.'

'You think he was keeping something secret?' asked McCoy.

Saunders shrugged. 'He could have been, but I don't know why.'

'What happened then?'

'Typical night in PJ's. A few other guys came in that we knew, sat at the table, then more guys, then everybody started doing shots, getting rowdy. I kind of lost him in the crowd.'

'And that was the last you saw him?' asked McCoy.

Saunders took a drink of his coffee, shook his

111

head. 'End of the night I was standing outside, trying to get some fresh air, sober up a bit and I saw him. He was sitting in the passenger seat of a car going out of town but it was going the wrong way, not towards the Holy Loch but towards Innellan or whatever that little village is called.'

'What kind of car was it?' asked McCoy.

'I don't really know British cars,' said Saunders. 'But it looked expensive, big. A gold colour.'

'Who was driving?' asked McCoy.

'Didn't see.'

McCoy sat back in his chair. 'Maybe he had a local girlfriend, maybe he's holed up with her.'

'Maybe,' said Saunders. 'But I don't think so, not Don.'

'Why not?' asked McCoy.

Saunders didn't answer, just dug in the sugar with his spoon.

'Were you two more than pals?' asked McCoy.

Still nothing.

'Does his dad know?'

Saunders put the spoon down. 'No one knows because there's nothing to know.' Stood up. 'We done?' he asked.

McCoy nodded and Saunders said goodbye and walked out of the cafe. McCoy tried to work out if he'd touched a nerve or if Saunders was just angry at the implication. Maybe both. He left some coins by his cup and stood up. Wondered if there was anything else Captain Stewart wasn't telling him.

Three hours later they were back in Glasgow. McCoy drew up outside the Central Hotel, took the key out the ignition. Stewart looked at him.

'So what do we do now?' he asked.

'Sorry, pal, it's just going to be me now,' said McCoy. 'I'm back on duty tomorrow and Donny's disappearance is now an official Glasgow Police investigation. Can't have you coming along.'

Stewart looked defeated.

'That's a good thing though,' said McCoy. 'Means we can use all the police resources, people will be actually working on it.'

Stewart nodded.

'You going to stay here?' said McCoy, glancing up at the hotel.

'Think so,' said Stewart. 'Should be here in case you find anything out.'

'Okay,' said McCoy. 'I'll try and keep you informed as much as I can.'

'I'd appreciate that,' said Stewart.

'Investigation starts tomorrow. Anything you want to tell me about Donny now? Off the official record?' asked McCoy.

The question hung in the air for a couple of seconds.

'I've told you everything I can think of,' said Stewart, eyes fixed on the taxi queue ahead. 'If I think of anything else I'll let you know.'

McCoy nodded and Stewart got out the car. McCoy watched him walk back into the hotel. Took out his fags and lit up. Decided to go back to

Dunoon tomorrow night, go to PJ's, get the lay of the land, see if anyone else had seen the mysterious gold car. Turned the engine over. Until then it was time to find out a bit more about Paul Watt and his bomb-making activities.

CHAPTER 14

McCoy pushed the office door open, went in. The shop was quiet, usual Sunday afternoon. All the Saturday night drunks and brawlers safely in the cells until court on Monday morning. Thomson was sitting at his desk, fag in hand, cursing at his typewriter.

'Wattie here?' asked McCoy, sitting down.

'Fucking fucker!' said Thomson, pulling the paper out the typewriter, scrunching it onto a ball and dropping it into the bin beside him. 'No, he's still out at Shettleston, at the Dixon scene, should be back soon.' He looked up. 'What you doing in anyways?'

'Just dropping something off for Murray,' said McCoy.

He waited until Thomson went back to his typing, got up, and pushed the door of Murray's office open. Stink of stale pipe smoke hit him the minute he did. He put a report on the desk, telling Murray that a missing American sailor was now a suspect in the bombings and listing all the details he had about the blood at the site. Looked up, listened. Went round the desk and started rifling through the files on top. Didn't take long to find Special Branch's report. He shoved it under his suit jacket and walked out the shop, told Billy on the front desk he was off to buy fags.

He walked a couple of streets, sat on a wall opposite the flats on Dundasvale Street, and opened the file. A grand total of one sheet of A4 paper. He skimmed it. Paul Watt was a warehouseman, no record, aged seventeen, Protestant, no known connection to any paramilitary organisation, no family members connected either. Conclusion: personally motivated. Domestic police case.

McCoy sat back on the wall, Phyllis Gilroy hadn't been kidding. Even by Special Branch standards, it was a brief report. Seemed to have reached their conclusions very quickly as far as McCoy was concerned, dumping the case back with them. He'd have thought they'd be more interested in someone who was building bombs, but what did he know. Special Branch were a law unto themselves and they weren't going to explain themselves to anyone, least of all a lowly Glasgow detective.

He watched an elderly couple navigate the way up the path to the flats, Grandfare bags and umbrellas weighing them down. Wondered how Wattie was getting on over at Shettleston. Hoped he hadn't fucked it up, Murray would be all over him if he had. Looked at his watch. Enough time to return the file, get home and get something to eat before Wattie turned up.

★　　★　　★

McCoy had just finished his boiled cod and Smash, the whitest and most tasteless meal he'd ever eaten, was about to put the dishes in the sink when there was a knock on the door. He walked through to the hall, pulled the door open.

'Mr Watson, I was awaiting your arr—'

Stopped when he saw the look on Wattie's face. Didn't look happy at all. 'What's up?' he asked.

'So when were you going to tell me?' said Wattie.

'Tell you what?' asked McCoy.

'That your pal Cooper murdered Jamsie Dixon.'

'Ah,' said McCoy. 'So are you coming in? Or are you just going to stand there looking like a kid who's dropped his ice lolly?'

Wattie shook his head, barged past him into the flat, stood by the sink. Looked at him accusingly.

'What's the estimated time of death?' asked McCoy.

'Provisionally?' asked Wattie.

McCoy rolled his eyes.

'Between ten and eleven,' said Wattie. 'Saturday night.'

'Well, in that case he definitely didn't do it,' said McCoy, digging in his jacket hung on the kitchen chair in search of his fags. 'He's got a cast-iron alibi. Was at a boxing match and then a casino. Seen by about a hundred different people, probably.'

'What?' asked Wattie.

'You heard,' said McCoy, lighting up. 'He's in the clear.'

'Fuck,' said Wattie. 'You sure? Just when I thought I'd copped a break that this was going to be an easy one after all.'

'Never is,' said McCoy.

Wattie thought for a minute. 'So he got someone to do it for him?' he said. 'That the story?'

'Think so,' said McCoy. 'No way Cooper is going to let Jamsie Dixon get away with attacking him in broad daylight.' Immediately realised he'd put his foot in it.

'Did he?' asked Wattie. 'When was that and how the fuck do you know?'

Easier to just come clean. 'Because I was there,' said McCoy. 'Malmaison Restaurant. Dixon went for him with a razor then made a run for it.'

'How come you were there?' asked Wattie. Dawned on him. 'You were having your dinner with him, weren't you!'

McCoy nodded.

Wattie let out a whistle. 'Murray is going to go through you like a dose of bloody salts.'

'No, he's not,' said McCoy. 'Because you're not going to tell him and neither am I.'

Wattie grinned, suddenly looked very pleased with himself.

'What you smiling at?' asked McCoy.

'So you're asking me to do you a favour?' he asked. 'Not tell Murray. That the sketch?'

'U-hu . . .' said McCoy warily.

'Good! You can do me one too. You can help me with this bloody case. Make sure I don't fuck it up.'

Wasn't much of a way around it. McCoy nodded, went over to the kitchen cupboard. 'Can for the smartarse?'

Wattie nodded and McCoy got two out, opened them with the tin opener. 'So how did it go?' he asked, handing Wattie a can of pale ale.

'Okay, I think,' said Wattie. The beer bubbled up and he put his mouth over it, sucked up the foam. 'Miss Gilroy took the body away with her, said she'd do the autopsy tomorrow.'

'Next of kin?' asked McCoy.

'Lived with his grandfather if you can believe it, must be about a hundred. Nasty old bugger, hates the polis as he kept telling us. Said Jamsie was as regular as clockwork. Went to the pub every night. Came home at closing time with a pint of Guinness for him. He wasn't lying. We found a flat pint of it on top of the brick midden house thing. Must have gone out the back for a pish or a smoke before he went upstairs. The idea is he puts the pint down and someone must have come up behind him and battered him with –' he dug out his notebook – 'a heavy blunt instrument, likely a brick or hammer of some sort.'

'Nasty,' said McCoy, wondering which of his lads Cooper had got to do the dirty deed. 'So the guy followed him from the pub?'

'That's the theory. Just about to go there now. Fancy chumming me along?'

'Nope.'

'Hard luck,' said Wattie. 'Deal's a deal.'

'Which pub is it?' asked McCoy.

Notebook again. 'The Edrom. Just across the street from his flat.'

'Fuck,' said McCoy. 'Trust that to be his bloody local. You know what? I better come with you anyway.'

'Why?' asked Wattie.

'Because if I don't, the chances of you getting out alive are about fifty-fifty.'

CHAPTER 15

Lots of pubs in Glasgow had the nickname 'The Stab Inn'. Normally it just meant they were rough, not somewhere you'd go for a pint unless you had to. Not the Edrom though. In its case, the name fitted perfectly. People got stabbed in there all the time. And worse. McCoy was never out the place when he was on the beat around here, sometimes twice a night.

Wattie parked across the road from the pub and they got out. Jamsie Dixon's flat was directly across the road, RIP JAMSIE chalked on the wall by the close.

'Somebody must miss him,' said Wattie.

'Fuck knows who,' said McCoy. 'Best rid.'

Wattie locked the car and they stood there for a minute looking over. The Edrom was a low white building, row of wee windows along the top. An old man on crutches was standing outside the entrance, bunnet in his hand with a few coins in it.

'Doesn't look that bad,' said Wattie.

'It is,' said McCoy. 'Let me do the talking.'

They crossed over and McCoy put a fifty-pence piece in the man's hat.

'You see Jamsie last night?' he asked.

The man shook his head. 'Wasn't here last night. Had a room in the Great Eastern. Not got enough tonight.'

McCoy sighed, dug in his pocket, put a couple of quid in the hat.

'Get a room,' he said. 'Not a bottle of Red Biddie.'

The man nodded. 'Will do, son.'

McCoy pulled the pub door open and revealed the Edrom in all its splendour. It looked much like any other pub, long bar at the back, tables lining the walls, carpet darkened by spills and stains, but as soon as you stepped in you could tell you weren't likely to get a warm welcome. Cigarette smoke was thick in the air, Country and Western music on in the background. Radiators and strip lights in wire cages.

Couple of guys turned round to look at who'd walked in, a few others checked them out in the mirrors behind the bar. They headed for the bar and just as McCoy turned to Wattie to ask if he wanted a pint a guy got up from one of the tables, walked over to them.

'Here we go,' said McCoy under his breath.

The guy stood in front of them, small, wiry, his grin showing a gold tooth.

'It is, isn't it?' he said. 'Harry McCoy?'

Took McCoy a minute to place him. Couldn't believe it.

'Patsy? Patsy Hearne? No way!'

The guy nodded. 'Christ, I haven't seen you for, God, must be almost twenty years. Know how I recognised you? You still walk the same, like you've got the weight of the world on your shoulders.'

McCoy thought for a second, worked it out. 'It's twenty-one years,' he said. 'Quarriers Home in Kilbarchan. That's the last place I saw you.'

Hearne nodded. 'And what a shitehole that was. Ran away twice. Do you still see that Stevie Cooper? Hear he's a big man now, no to be messed with.'

McCoy nodded. 'For my sins.'

Hearne nodded over at a table with two other similar-looking guys sitting at it. 'Come on and have a drink, still can't believe it.'

'Cheers,' said McCoy. He dug in his pocket, gave Wattie a tenner. 'You go up to the bar. Anyone starts talking to you, just ignore them.'

Wattie nodded, took the orders and walked to the far end of the bar, well away from the crowd of locals. McCoy sat down and was introduced to Johnny and Mal. They were dressed like Patsy. Suit and white shirt with no tie, gold rings on most fingers, faces lined and weatherbeaten.

'So how you been, Patsy?' asked McCoy.

'Lot better than the last time you saw me. Trying to sit down after that bastard McLean had whipped me senseless with that leather belt of his. Think that decided it for me. That Quarriers

123

was the last home they ever managed to put me in. Wasn't going to get battered like that again.'

'Used to round us up like bloody animals,' said Johnny. 'That's what they did.'

McCoy had to listen hard. His accent was hard to place, sounded a bit Irish, bit something else he couldn't identify.

'They'd turn up at the camp, load half the kids in a van for the crime of being gypsies, or missing school to do the berry picking, that was all the excuse they needed. Took me and my wee brother away from my mum and dad. Took them a year to get me back. And all for our own good.'

He finished talking and took a big gulp of his pint. Hands shaking. Looked like the memories were still fresh.

'Think you gypsy boys were the only ones that got it worse than us,' said McCoy. 'And God knows we got it bad enough.'

'They'll pay,' said Johnny. 'One day they'll pay. I swear on my brother's grave. Six years gone this summer he is. Hung himself from a tree. His mind was scrambled with it all. Still woke up crying every night. I swear—'

Patsy leant over, put his hand on Johnny's. 'Come on, Johnny, you're just upsetting yourself now.'

Johnny looked at him, eyes full. Nodded. Took another drink from his pint.

'Here we go,' said Wattie, appearing with a tray with pints on it. He handed them out and sat down. Smiled at everyone. 'Managed to get a round in without getting my head kicked in,' he said.

'Don't think you need to worry about that,' said Patsy. 'You're a big fucker right enough. Look like a bloody polis!' He laughed. Then realised that neither McCoy nor Wattie were joining in.

'Christ! You're having me on,' he said. 'McCoy, a polis?'

'Yep,' said McCoy, taking a sip of his pint. 'Detective, in fact.'

'How did that happen?' asked Patsy. 'Wonders'll never cease, right enough.'

'Should we be worried?' said Mal.

'No,' said McCoy. 'Just in for a pint, like you. Which brings me to my next question. Why on earth are you lads drinking in this godforsaken shithole?'

He meant it to be funny but it fell flat. Johnny and Mal looked down at their drinks. Patsy looked a bit embarrassed.

'No choice. This and the Bowlers over at Glasgow Green are the only pubs we're welcome in.' He smiled. 'It is a shithole but we're staying at the site over at Westmuir Street, five minutes up the road, so it's local and we don't get any trouble in here.'

'Always been a good pub for us,' added Johnny. 'Landlord's a good man. Always been fair. Our money's as good as anyone's in here.'

'Christ,' said McCoy. 'Sorry about that, I never knew it was so bad.'

'Och, we'll survive,' said Patsy. 'Got good birk today from the shows on the Green so we're having a bit of a night.'

Wattie looked at him like he was talking Chinese.

'Show people,' said Johnny. 'That's what we are. We run the fairs and the rides on Glasgow Green, we're there for the Easter holidays, and birk's a good day's takings.'

'Ah,' said Wattie. 'Got you.'

'Now I'm going to ask you the same question, McCoy,' said Patsy. 'What are you doing in this shithole?' Realised. Pointed over the road. 'Let me guess. Jamsie Dixon?'

McCoy nodded. 'You know him?'

Patsy nodded. 'God, aye, couldn't not if you drink in here. He's in here every night. Landlady even makes him his tea some nights. He's a mad bugger so I hear, but he's always been all right with us.'

'He in Saturday night?' asked McCoy.

Patsy nodded. 'Was all agitated about something, God knows what. Tried to pick a fight with one of the guys from the forge, shouting and bawling at him. Guy made a run for it. A good idea, you wouldn't want to mess with Jamsie, especially when he was riled up.'

'Do you think the guy was angry enough to go after him later?' asked Wattie. 'Sneak up on him?'

Patsy looked at McCoy.

'Don't worry. You're not telling tales. He knows,' said McCoy.

'No, son, it wasn't him. Christ, even the dogs on the street know who did for Jamsie. Was Stevie Cooper.'

'Not in person though,' said McCoy. 'Farmed out the job. Anyone strange in here that night? That you didn't recognise?'

'Hard to tell,' said Patsy. 'Saturday night. The place was mobbed. Normally I only notice the other gypsy lads, don't pay much attention to the rest. Jamsie left as usual, just before closing time, pint of Guinness for his granddad. Didn't see anyone follow him out or anything like that. Tell you something though, whoever Cooper got to do it would have to be some man, you'd have to be to take Jamsie Dixon down.'

'Unless you sneaked up behind him with a dirty big brick,' said McCoy.

'That what happened?' asked Patsy.

'Think so,' said McCoy. 'Can't see how else you'd do it.'

McCoy and Wattie left after another round, Patsy insisting on buying. McCoy promised Patsy to come back another night for a proper drink, said he'd bring Cooper. Talk about old times. They stepped out into the evening air. The old man with the cap was now slumped by the wall, bottle in hand. Pissed.

'I've never met a gypsy,' said Wattie.

'Well, you have now,' said McCoy.

'Always told they were robbing bastards, not to trust them. They seem nice enough though.'

McCoy shook his head, got in the car.

They drove west through the city, stopped at the traffic lights at the Royal. Rain was coming on. Wattie switched the wipers on. 'I'm going to have to interview him, you know.'

'Yep,' said McCoy. 'If Lomax will let you near him, that is. Which I doubt. That's why Cooper pays him what he does. As we know, Cooper's got a cast-iron alibi. Lomax will say it's harassment. Which with the evidence you've got just now it probably is. You're going to need to come up with a good reason if you want to get him in.'

'Shite,' said Wattie. 'What do I do next? Even if we catch the guy that actually did it he's never going to say anything. He'll be too scared of Cooper.'

'Welcome to the wonderful world of Glasgow policing,' said McCoy, pointing at the windscreen. 'Lights.'

Wattie put the car into gear. 'Murray's not going to be happy.'

'No, he's not,' said McCoy. 'But he's done this longer than you and I put together. He knows the score. Just make sure you've covered all the bases, done all you can and he'll be all right.'

Wattie nodded, didn't look sure at all.

'I'm starving, my tea was bloody horrible,' said McCoy. 'Just drop me off in Great Western Road, I'm going to get some chips and walk back.'

Wattie nodded, seemed miles away.

CHAPTER 16

McCoy watched Wattie drive off, lit up, and started walking up towards Hamilton Park Avenue. The night wasn't cold, smir of rain had brought out the smell of tree blossom. Could hear some drunken shouts and laughter from the pubs coming out. Promise of summer and better times in the air. And here was he heading towards a conversation he really didn't want to have.

Cooper had done what he'd done and, unless McCoy was extremely lucky, dragged him into it as his alibi. Wasn't sure if he was more disappointed than angry. He thought that no matter what happened, Cooper was a pal, didn't expect him to fuck him over like that. Still, way he'd been acting and what Billy had told him, he shouldn't be too surprised, he supposed. Things change. Looked like Cooper had changed too.

He opened the gate, walked up the path to the big house, and rang the bell. Still couldn't believe Cooper owned a big house in the West End, but as he said, the money was pouring in, he had to do something. Had to spend it or the accountant had to try and hide it so the taxman wouldn't find it. Mind you, of all the big houses in the West End, he had to have bought the ugliest one.

The front door opened and Iris appeared, fag in hand. Didn't look pleased to see him, never did. Her move from running one of Cooper's shebeens to being his housekeeper hadn't made her any cheerier. She looked him up and down.

'He's no here.' she said. 'You've missed him.'

'Where is he?' asked McCoy.

'Memen Road,' said Iris.

McCoy couldn't believe it. Memen Road was Cooper's old flat, a two-bedroom dump up a close in one of the worst streets in Glasgow.

'What's he doing there?' asked McCoy.

Iris sniffed, decided to lower herself sufficiently to have a conversation. 'Left today, said he'd never liked this place, was going back to where he came from.'

'Christ,' said McCoy. 'He's mad. Memen Road's a dump, hasn't even got hot water.'

She shrugged. 'Up to him, I suppose.'

'What's up with him, Iris?' he asked. 'He all right?'

She snorted. 'You think he'd tell me? All he did was shout the odds at me like a bear with a bloody sore head. Just told me to pack some of his clothes, bring them over tomorrow. Billy's no happy about it.'

Could tell by her face she wished she hadn't said the last bit.

'That right?' asked McCoy. 'Billy got a bit too used to the high life, has he? Staying here in the big house with you making his dinner every night, no boss to tell him what to do. Life of Riley. No way he'll be happy if it all moves back to Memen Road.'

Iris went to close the door. Not before McCoy stuck his foot in it.

'Watch it, Iris. If Cooper moves back there's no more you pretending you're a West Ender, no more Billy as king of the castle. Don't think he'll be keeping this big house just to keep you two happy. You'll be back to washing spunk-covered sheets and arranging back-street abortions in the shebeen.'

She peered at him through the crack in the door. Took a deep inhale of her Capstan. Blew the smoke in his face. 'Think you're something, don't you, McCoy? Think you're a big polis but you're just like the rest of us, all of us living off the back of Stevie Cooper. Dancing to his tune. The only difference is, you won't admit it.'

'Fuck off Iris. I—'

But he was talking to a closed door, she'd slammed it in his face. He walked back down the street, stinging from what Iris had said. Stinging because it might just be true. Saw a taxi coming down Great Western Road, hailed it. He settled back in the cab, stared out the window at the lights of Glasgow passing by. Had a strange feeling like everything was going backwards. Cooper back to

Memen Road and his old unpredictable self, and him? He was getting tired of it all. He was thirty-odd, living in a shitty flat by himself, career didn't seem to be going anywhere, already marked as a loner. Drinking too much. Even had a bloody ulcer now for his trouble. Maybe he needed a change too. Something big before he got too old and stuck where he was. Just had to figure out what. Promised himself he'd think about it properly when this was all done.

Cab turned up towards Springburn. Night wasn't so rosy up this way. No smell of tree blossom here. They passed the Bells, man standing outside holding a hanky up to what looked like a bleeding and broken nose, group of kids, couldn't have been more than ten or so, standing across the street, laughing and pointing. He hadn't been to Memen Road for a year or so and he hadn't missed it a bit. Not least because the last time he was there he had to beg Cooper not to kill one of his boys in front of him. And now he was going back, back to the shithole flat and back to the Stevie that lived there and did things like that. Suddenly wasn't as confident about accusing him of arranging Jamsie's death and dragging him into it. If Cooper was back to being Cooper, he wasn't sure about accusing him of anything.

The cab pulled over on Hawthorn Street, driver wouldn't go any further. McCoy didn't blame him, just paid him and got out. Memen Road was a no-go area for the police, never mind some elderly taxi driver with a hearing aid. The row of run-down tenements had become a dumping ground for people the council couldn't deal with. The problem families and the alkies. Stevie had slowly colonised the whole of the end close and was now the only occupant. His boys billeted next door, keeping guard.

As usual, there was a scattering of kids and teenagers hanging around a fire in a dustbin in one of the front gardens. One of them put a crisp packet full of glue behind his back as McCoy walked up to them. Didn't make any difference, he looked so spangled he could hardly stand. Something comical about a bunch of twelve-year-olds trying to look hard, but he knew these kids. Give them another couple of years and you'd cross the street to avoid them.

'He in?' he asked.

A tall boy with a scar on his face and a torn star jumper nodded.

'Tell him McCoy's here, eh?'

The boy nodded and a wee boy of about eight in shorts and wellies ran towards the last close. McCoy warmed his hands at the fire, waited. Wasn't long until the wee boy appeared out the close and ran back.

'Okay,' he said, panting. 'You can go up.'

McCoy lit up and walked down to Cooper's close, wondering what exactly he was going to say. He started climbing the stairs, got to the first-floor landing and had to stand to the side to let two good-looking girls, all mini-skirts and platforms and the stink of menthol cigarettes, pass. Cooper'd been busy then.

He got to the top landing, saw the door was wide open. He got his breath back and stepped in. Cooper was standing at the kitchen sink, back to him, vest and jeans on, braces hanging down. He was drinking a pint glass of water, head tilted back. He set the empty glass down on the draining board. Turned. 'You just gonna stand there?' he asked. 'Come in if you're coming.'

McCoy walked into the kitchen, sat down at the table. 'Didn't think I'd ever end up back here.'

The kitchen was just a scarred and marked wooden table, a pulley with nothing hanging from it, couple of chairs and a picture of James Dean torn from a magazine sellotaped above the fireplace. It was cold, smelt damp. Tried not to think about the guy that had been handcuffed to the range when he'd been here once. Nose already broken, just waiting to get taken into the back room for more.

Cooper pulled one of the chairs out, sat down opposite him. Yawned.

'Sometimes think I should never have left,' he said. 'I was happy here. Was moving to the West End that made everything turn to shite.' He smiled. 'And before you ask me, McCoy, Jamsie Dixon had nothing to do with me.'

'You expect me to believe that?' asked McCoy.

'You expect me to give a fuck?' said Cooper.

'Can't say I'm all torn up about it, but I didn't do it. I was with you and then your pal the captain all night. Ask him.'

'Yes, thanks for that, getting me as your alibi, really going to go down well with Murray. Thought you were better than that.'

'I am,' said Cooper. 'And as I said, I had nothing to do with Jamsie Dixon so I don't need you as an alibi.'

'So who did kill him then?' asked McCoy.

Cooper shrugged. 'No idea.'

McCoy wished he could believe him. 'Where did Billy go that night? Saw him leaving the boxing with somebody.'

Cooper sighed. 'What? This the big theory? Do you think I sent him off to take care of Jamsie Dixon? Billy's good for a lot of things but not something like that. Too scared for his good looks. Besides, Jamsie Dixon would have spread him across the nearest wall.'

'So where did he go?' asked McCoy.

'You see they two lassies leaving just now? That's what Billy does. Greases the wheels. I'd been in prison for six months, just got out. What do you think he was fixing up for later that night?'

'Dirty bugger,' said McCoy.

'I've had enough of my right hand to last a lifetime. Nothing else to do in prison. I ran out of wanks.'

'They'll pull you in though,' said McCoy. 'Interview you.'

'They'll try, you mean, and they'll fail. Lomax'll deal with that,' said Cooper evenly. 'That's what I pay him for.'

McCoy tried another tack. 'What are you doing back here, Stevie?'

'Thinking,' he said. 'That okay with you?'

McCoy nodded. 'You okay?'

Cooper smiled. 'Fine and dandy. For the first time in a long time. Don't you worry about me, McCoy.'

And the funny thing was, he seemed like he was. He was calm, in control, none of the screaming and shouting he'd expected. He was more like the Cooper that reminded McCoy why he was still a pal after all these years. Cooper yawned again, scratched his chest.

'I'm not daft, McCoy. There's a reason I had nothing to do with Jamsie. Do you really think I wanted Desy Dixon coming after me? That guy's mental.'

'Everyone thinks you did it though,' said McCoy. 'And unfortunately, that'll probably include Desy Dixon.'

'Yep. So now I need to have a think. Decide how I'm going to handle it. You done?'

McCoy nodded. Stood up. 'Look after yourself, Stevie,' he said.

Cooper smiled again. 'As I said, McCoy, don't worry about me.' Touched his finger to his temple. 'Almost forgot. Here's my good deed of the day. There's someone you do need to worry about though. Your pal Hughie Faulds.'

'What?' said McCoy, surprised. 'Why?'

'He's no back here by accident,' said Cooper. 'Needed to get out of Ireland before the boys got him. They already tried to blow up his car in Belfast.'

'Faulds? He's a polis, why would they do that?' asked McCoy.

'Stay away from him,' said Cooper. 'I mean it. He's a dead man walking. Don't get caught in the crossfire.'

'What did he do?' asked McCoy.

'You really want to know?' asked Cooper.

McCoy nodded, suddenly not sure if he did.

'Next time you and Hughie Faulds are having a nice wee chat, you ask him about Paul McVeigh,' said Cooper. 'Ask him what happened to him. Now beat it.'

McCoy stepped out the close and walked up the street, nodded at the group by the fire. Was more confused now than he was before. Cooper wasn't the ranting and raving loony Billy had described and he didn't seem to be lying about Jamsie, but it didn't make sense. Who else would be interested in killing Jamsie Dixon? Wasn't sure he trusted Wattie enough to be able to find out. Might have to keep helping him longer than he'd thought.

He got to Hawthorn Street, lit up, looked up and down for a cab. And Hughie Faulds? What was that about? Far as McCoy knew he'd come back because his wife didn't want the kids growing up in the middle of a war zone. Knew Cooper had connections with the IRA, cousins and uncles back in Belfast. Maybe he knew what he was talking about. Cab appeared and McCoy whistled at it. Got in. Sat back. Wondered who Paul McVeigh was. Wondered if it was worth finding out.

15TH APRIL 1974

'How's Watson getting on?' asked Murray, settling down in his chair. The chief inspector's new life with Phyllis Gilroy was treating him well, so well he could hardly fit in it. Too many dinner parties and too much wine from Phyllis's father's cellar.

McCoy nodded at the buff-coloured file sitting on Murray's desk. 'Did you read his report?'

'No,' said Murray. 'I'm asking you, smartarse.'

'What is all this?' asked McCoy. 'I don't get it. You were the one that picked Wattie out the pile, said he was worth it so could he shadow me. And all I hear now is complaints and doubts. Why have you got it in for him?'

'I don't have it in for him, as you put it. I'm just worried he's not coming up to par. Thought he'd get a bit more maturity about him, a bit more of a grasp of what the job's about.'

'Paired him with the wrong guy then, didn't you?' said McCoy, smiling.

Murray didn't look happy. 'I'm serious, McCoy. He still acts like a teenager half the bloody time. It has to change.'

McCoy sighed. 'He's doing fine, done all the stuff he's meant to do, but it's a difficult one. Jamsie Dixon was muscle for hire and he was a nasty bastard as well. Must be a lot of people who wanted him dead.'

'Including Stevie Cooper,' said Murray.

'Including Stevie Cooper,' said McCoy evenly. 'Who has a cast-iron alibi. Doesn't mean he didn't organise it though, but that's not going to be easy to prove.'

Murray started patting his tweed jacket looking for his pipe. Found it and started banging it on the edge of his desk. 'Can't say I'll be shedding any tears about the demise of Jamsie Dixon. Glasgow's a better place without him.' Starting scraping at the bowl with his penknife. 'Where's the mental brother again?'

'Gateshead,' said McCoy. 'Although he'll probably come up here for the funeral.'

'And to avenge his brother?' asked Murray, disappearing in a cloud of bluish tobacco smoke.

'Let's hope not, but I wouldn't be surprised,' said McCoy.

'Just what we need,' said Murray, waving his arms at the cloud. 'If he does anything it'll be an excuse for the clowns at the *Record* to do another one of their "Glasgow's Violent Streets" numbers and Pitt Street'll be calling me in for a roasting.'

'I'll ask around, see if anyone knows what Desy's up to,' said McCoy.

Murray nodded, picked up a file from the pile

in front of him, handed it over. 'Special Branch report on the bomb casualty. Or, as I call it, an exercise in hand-washing. Bloody disgrace. Have a look, follow it up, make sure he didn't make any other bombs before he splattered himself all over his flat.'

'Bomb in the Cathedral not make any difference?' asked McCoy.

Murray shook his head. 'No injuries, no significant damage. Not enough to make them get involved. Even had the cheek to suggest it was a prank.'

'Maybe it was,' said McCoy. 'Hard to see what other motivation there was.'

'Think that's the end of it?' asked Murray.

McCoy shrugged. 'I hope so. One boy dead, another injured. Maybe whoever is involved has come to their senses.' He took the file and stood up. 'You want me to keep checking on Wattie?'

'What do you think?' asked Murray. 'Do you need to?'

'Might be a good idea,' said McCoy.

Murray nodded, went back to his pipe and his files. Remembered. 'How'd you get on at the doctor's?' he asked.

'Fine,' said McCoy. 'Indigestion, apparently.'

McCoy stepped back into the main office, sat down at his desk. Life with Phyllis Gilroy seemed to be suiting Murray's personality as well as his waistline. He was a lot calmer, not so much screaming and shouting. Maybe that was the kind

143

of change McCoy needed, to shack up with someone, come home every night to his tea on the table and a night sitting on the couch watching rubbish on the TV. Life could be worse. He needed to do something, that was for sure, even his love life was grinding to a halt. Apart from a one-off lumber at the Victoria a couple of weeks ago he was in a real barren stretch. Mind you, the woman from the Victoria had been quite something, right enough. Almost made up for it.

'What you smiling at?' asked Wattie.

'Sorry, was miles away,' said McCoy, looking up at him. 'You've got baby sick on your shoulder.'

'Fuck!' said Wattie twisting his neck round trying to look at the shoulder of his shirt. 'Wee bugger must have done it this morning.'

'Do you mean your beloved first-born son, Douglas Watson Junior?' asked McCoy.

'No, I mean the wee bugger,' said Wattie.

'Away and wash it off,' said McCoy. 'Then you can come with me in the car, tell me how you're getting on.'

Wattie nodded, hurried off to the bathroom. McCoy wondered if he should have mentioned the egg on his tie too.

McCoy sat in the car, turning the knob of the radio, trying to find the news. Every station seemed to be playing that bloody 'Waterloo' song. Gave up, switched it off as Wattie eased himself into the passenger seat, shoulder now wet, egg stain intact.

'Next of kin?' asked McCoy as he drove towards Charing Cross.

'Christ, don't ask,' said Wattie. 'Paul Watt was an only child, mum and dad killed in some car crash five years ago. So next of kin is some old uncle in Durham. I called him up but he didn't seem to know what I was talking about. Think he was a bit gaga. Asked if I was going to do anything about the kids playing in the street and could I get him a loaf and some milk.'

'Nasty,' said McCoy.

'Where are we going?' asked Wattie.

'Maryhill,' said McCoy. 'Chapel Street, just behind the Viking. We can go for a pint afterwards.'

'There?' asked Wattie. 'Do we have to?'

'What's up with the Viking?' asked McCoy. Then he remembered. Last time they'd been there Stevie Cooper was in the process of battering some guy tied to a chair into next week.

'Maybe not,' he said. 'Could try the Munns Vaults along the road.'

Didn't take them long to get there, pulled in by a warehouse, a big sign saying THOMSON'S WHOLESALE PRODUCE above the entrance. Painted apples and oranges surrounding the letters. Yard was full of towers of wooden crates, ground strewn with old fruit and vegetables. A van was parked by the big doors, two lads loading sacks of potatoes onto it while the driver sat in his seat, smoking and reading the paper.

'How's Mary?' asked McCoy as they got out of the car. 'Speaking to you yet?'

'Yep. I've done my penance. Changed enough nappies to be forgiven. Now she's talking about going back to work,' said Wattie.

'That was quick,' said McCoy. 'What'll happen to the wee bugger? Her mum take him during the day?'

'If by the wee bugger you mean my beloved first-born son Douglas Watson Junior, then that's the plan. That's where she is now,' said Wattie. 'In Knightswood, asking her.'

'Need the boss, son,' said McCoy as a teenager with a remarkable amount of acne, box of bananas in his arms, appeared from behind a wall of crates. He nodded over at a wee office by the back door.

'I wondered what had happened to him,' said the boss, who turned out to be a middle-aged man with a red birthmark over his left eye. 'He was normally good at calling in if he was sick. Never occurred to me that he could have died. That's a nasty bloody surprise.'

He looked like the wind had just gone out his sails, sat back in his chair, reached for his cigarettes.

'He was only young,' he said. 'That's terrible.' He looked up at them. 'What happened?'

'Rather not say just now,' said McCoy. 'What was he like?'

'Paul?' he asked. 'Bit dreamy but a good worker.

Just a normal warehouseman. Been here for over a year.' He lit his cigarette with trembling hands, dropped the match into an overflowing ashtray. 'Still can't believe it.'

'Any pals here?' asked McCoy. 'Anyone we should talk to?'

The boss shook his head. 'He didn't mix much. The boys here can be a bit lairy, if you know what I mean. Paul wasn't like that, was quiet.'

'Girlfriends?' asked McCoy.

'Never mentioned anyone. Mind you, I doubt if he would have. The only thing he ever talked about was the Terrys. Loved it.'

'The Territorial Army?' asked McCoy. 'He was in that?'

The boss nodded. 'Aye, had the uniform and everything, went away for weekends, camps and that. It's just down the road, his base, or platoon, or whatever they call it. Hotspur Street.'

They left the boss sitting at his desk looking glum and walked back towards the car.

'A toy soldier,' said Wattie. 'Aren't they all bit weird?'

'Yep,' said McCoy. 'Worse than special constables, and that's saying something. Suppose we should go and have a word.'

'So what's happening with Jamsie Dixon?' asked McCoy as they pulled out the yard, drove over the bridge, and waited at the lights by the Viking.

'Not much,' said Wattie. 'I've organised a proper search of the back courts today, see if they can

147

turn up a weapon. Medical report is back today, see what that says.'

'Other than someone battered fuck out the back of his head?' asked McCoy.

Wattie shrugged. 'I'm hoping it'll say more than that.'

'Cooper said he didn't have anything to do with it,' said McCoy, pressing down the accelerator as the lights changed.

'That's not exactly a surprise, is it?' said Wattie. 'You believe him?'

'Nope,' said McCoy. 'But if nothing else develops and he sticks to that story with Lomax fending off any questions I'm not sure how we're ever going to get any further.'

'Great,' said Wattie gloomily. 'My first big case over before it began.'

'Might be,' said McCoy. 'It happens more than you'd think. Everyone knows who did it and nobody can do anything about it. Keeps guys like Lomax in pinstripe suits and Jaguar cars.'

CHAPTER 18

The Territorial Army Base of The Royal Highland Fusiliers was a big white building with a yard down at the bottom of Hostspur Street. The reason it was gleaming in the sunshine soon became apparent as Wattie and McCoy drew up. There were about twenty lads in army trousers and bare chests armed with paintbrushes white-washing it. The lads seemed to be having a good laugh doing it, lots of shouts, and not very convincing accidental spatters of paint across each other's faces. One with a shock of ginger hair looked like he'd painted a vest on himself. They looked a bit young to be in the Terrys to McCoy – fifteen, sixteen. Maybe army cadets. A man of about thirty dressed in PE kit was standing off to the side trying to keep them in order with shouts and blasts from the whistle around his neck.

'You in charge?' asked McCoy.

'Of this sorry attempt at painting or in general?' asked the man. Posh Scottish accent, slight Highland burr. 'Both, I'm afraid.' He held his hand out to shake. 'Lieutenant Meiklejohn. How can I help you?'

'Paul Watt,' said McCoy, holding out his police card.

'Ah,' said Meiklejohn. 'Thought you'd be calling. Why don't we go inside?'

He led them through an open back door and into the building. They crossed a gym, ropes and weights laid out on the floor, bars up the walls, walked down a corridor lined with maps, and into a room that looked like a staffroom. Couple of couches, a table with a checked tablecloth on it, bookcase, long photos of seated soldiers, a couple of crossed swords over a coat of arms on the wall. Smell reminded McCoy of a children's home. Floor cleaner, cigarettes, sweat and paint.

Meiklejohn pointed at the couch. 'Please, have a seat.'

They sat down and he flicked the switch on the electric kettle. 'Tea?' he asked.

'We're okay,' said McCoy. 'Just need to ask you some questions.'

'Sorry. Of course,' said Meiklejohn. He pulled a chair over, sat opposite them.

'What was he like?' asked McCoy. 'Paul Watt?'

'He was a good lad,' said Meiklejohn. 'He was trying to decide whether to join up properly. The Regular Army, I mean. I had the sense he didn't have much going on in his life but the Territorials. Never absent, always here, sometimes when he wasn't supposed to be. I don't know his family situation, but he never really mentioned anyone. Apart from that, he was pretty quiet, not the most physical of the lads, or the most boisterous.'

'So how did someone like that end up blowing himself up building a bomb?' asked McCoy.

'Is that really what happened?' asked Meiklejohn. 'I heard that but it just didn't seem possible.' He shook his head. 'The answer is, I have absolutely no idea. There was nothing in his behaviour or manner to suggest he was either capable of or interested in doing such a thing.'

The switch of the kettle clicked out and they all turned to look at it.

'Do we know who or what the bomb was destined for?' asked Meiklejohn.

'Not yet,' said McCoy. 'He ever mention a Donny Stewart?'

Meiklejohn shook his head. 'Not that I remember. He's not one of the lads here either.'

'Place like this,' said Wattie. 'Do you have stuff that could be used in building a bomb?'

'No,' said Meiklejohn, smiling. 'Our ordnance is restricted to rifles, mostly inactive and used for drill practice. No grenades or bombs. There's a locked gun cabinet with some pistols and live ammunition in it, but that hasn't been opened for years, I don't think.'

'Anything else you can tell us about him?' asked McCoy.

Meiklejohn thought, shook his head. 'He was an ordinary lad, not the brightest and best, but a good heart.'

McCoy was getting a bit tired of all this good lads and good heart stuff. The smell was making him unsettled, making him think of things he didn't want to. He wanted to leave. Needed to accelerate things. Wasn't going to get anything out Meiklejohn the normal way. Time to push his buttons.

'Were you fond of him, Mr Meiklejohn?' asked McCoy. 'Paul, I mean?'

Meiklejohn looked taken aback. Ears started to go red. 'It's Lieutenant Meiklejohn and no, not particularly. I'm not sure what you mean.'

'Really?' asked McCoy. 'I was just wondering. Buy all the lads here birthday presents, do you?'

Meiklejohn's ears were scarlet now.

'*The Life and Death of St Kilda*. Happy birthday from Henry. Found it in his flat.' McCoy pointed back at the door. 'Sign outside says Lieutenant H. Meiklejohn. Henry, isn't it?'

Meiklejohn looked at him. Looked at him the way a scared dog looks at his master. Then he settled himself. Straightened his back. 'Watt was interested in Scottish history, as I am. I saw a second-hand paperback in a bookshop so I bought it for him. That's all.'

'Is it?' asked McCoy. 'Buy any of the other boys gifts, did you?'

'I have no idea what you are implying,' said Meiklejohn.

'Yes, you do,' said McCoy with venom. 'You know exactly what I'm implying. Lonely lad, no

152

family, not the brightest, suddenly an authority figure shows an interest in him, starts buying him presents. Believe me, Meiklejohn, I know exactly what I'm implying and I know exactly how it's done. Boys like that are the easiest to get drunk, the easiest to show scud mags to, and boys like that tend to do what they're told.'

Nothing. No one spoke. Just the ticking of the clock on the wall. Distant shouts and laughter from the boys outside.

'I think you'd better leave,' said Meiklejohn. 'Now.'

Outside McCoy lit up, tried to calm down a bit. The ginger lad with the painted vest had made it into a T-shirt now, was chasing one of the others with a loaded brush.

'You okay?' asked Wattie, appearing behind his shoulder.

McCoy nodded.

'How did you know the book was from him?' he asked.

'I didn't,' said McCoy. 'Lucky guess. H for Henry.'

'You think Meiklejohn and him were, you know . . .?' asked Wattie.

McCoy shrugged. 'Don't know if that's what it was, but there was definitely something going on between them. Something more than Meiklejohn is admitting.'

Wattie shook his head. 'An army officer? A poof? Are you sure?'

That was enough. All the pent-up anger came out. 'Fuck sake, Wattie! Murray is right. You are like a bloody big kid! Wake up! This is the big bad world. You really want to be a detective, then smarten up, stop wandering about like fucking Pollyanna. You're a grown man, a father, a polis. Need to grow up and quick!'

Walked back to the car, left Wattie trailing behind him.

'What's up with you?' he asked, getting in the car.

'Nothing,' said McCoy. 'But you're going to have to start seeing through people like Meiklejohn, stop believing everything anybody tells you.'

'That's me told,' said Wattie, starting the engine.

'Aye, and think yourself lucky it's me telling you, not Murray. If it was him he'd—'

The radio crackled into life.

'Watson? Need you back at the station ASAP.'

CHAPTER 19

One of the uniforms on the fingertip search had found it, hidden behind a bin in the middens of the next back court up.

'Fuck me,' said Wattie.

They were standing in the station looking at a tagged plastic bag on Murray's desk. A plastic bag that contained a hammer, the head of which was covered in sticky blood, blonde hairs clinging to it.

'Looks like you're off and running,' said Murray. 'Better get it over to the lab, see what they make of it.'

Wattie nodded, picked the bag up gingerly, hurried off.

'Boy's got lucky,' said Murray.

McCoy nodded. 'Very. If some bugger's been stupid enough to leave his fingerprints on it, he'll be laughing.'

'Anything on the bomber?' asked Murray, sitting down.

McCoy shrugged, 'For a guy who was building bombs in his flat he seems to have been leading a very dull life.'

155

'Maybe that's the point,' said Murray. 'Hide in plain sight.'

'Maybe, but it's weird. Special Branch are saying it's not paramilitary, but what is it then? Doesn't seem like the kind of guy who would have a major grudge against anyone. Was liked at work, enjoyed the Terrys. No employer that had sacked him, no nothing. How'd he learn to make a bomb? Who was the target?'

'He's not one of those German, what do you call them? Badder whatevers?' asked Murray.

'Don't think so. They were hardcore revolutionaries, trying to overthrow the system. All this poor bugger wanted to do was join the army.'

'Not exactly radical,' said Murray. 'The opposite.'

'I'm going to go down to Dunoon. See if I can find anything out about the other lad involved.'

'The American sailor?' asked Murray.

McCoy nodded.

'It's not going to turn into some diplomatic thing, is it?' said Murray, looking worried. 'American Navy? That's the last bloody thing we need.'

'Hope not,' said McCoy. 'He was AWOL when it happened. Hoping they'll just wash their hands of him.'

Murray nodded. 'Keep an eye on Watson as well, eh? This hammer is a big step forward, make sure he deals with it properly. Now, a question for you. What do I buy Phyllis for her fiftieth birthday?'

156

'What?' McCoy had been blindsided, too fast a switch.

'Phyllis. Fiftieth birthday.'

'What are you asking me for?' asked McCoy.

'Because you're in front of me and I've got to buy it this afternoon and I've no bloody idea.'

'Christ, I don't know,' said McCoy. 'Jewellery?'

'She's rich as bloody Croesus. Don't think I can compete in that department.'

'A painting? She likes paintings, doesn't she?'

A big smile crossed Murray's face. 'House is full of them. Good idea. Where do I buy one?'

'Murray, give us a break.'

Murray held his hands up. 'Fine. I'll have a think.'

'All getting very serious, you and Phyllis. Be buying her a ring next.'

McCoy left Murray worrying about rings and paintings and sat back down at his desk. Tried to work out what was going on with Paul Watt. Even if he was involved with Meiklejohn somehow, what did that have to do with making bombs? And how the fuck did he meet up with an American sailor? And then it struck him. Seemed obvious now. Time for a wee visit before he headed to Dunoon.

Bobby Thorne hadn't lasted long in exile in Spain. The heat was too much so he'd come back a couple of months ago, bought a wee pub at the top of Hope Street. The Backstage Bar. Covered the walls

157

in pictures of himself with various other turns from the Scottish Variety scene. Bobby and Moira Anderson, Bobby and Jack Milroy, Bobby and The One O'Clock Gang. The only real surprise was the one of Bobby and The Beatles. Winter of 1963 at the Beach Ballroom, Aberdeen. All four of them and Bobby grinning at the camera, each with a bottle of whisky in their hand. The pub had done well, punters going in before or after visiting the Theatre Royal, the Metropole, the Apollo.

McCoy pulled the door open and stepped into the darkness and the familiar smell of cigarettes and beer. Wasn't busy yet, just one couple sat up the back. Too early. The man himself was behind the bar, hairpiece in place, short-sleeved white shirt, pencil in hand, filling out what looked like a sales register. He looked up. Slowly looked McCoy up and down.

'Well, well, look what the cat dragged in. Harry McCoy. To what do I owe this dubious pleasure?'

'Need to ask you a few questions,' said McCoy, pulling a stool out at the bar and sitting down.

Bobby and McCoy had run into each other a couple of years ago when Bobby's long-time partner had been murdered. He wouldn't say they were friends exactly but he'd been in the bar a few times, had a few chats. Bobby always seemed to know what was going on in the less upfront parts of town. He pulled a pint, set it down in front of McCoy, pushed a glass to the whisky bottle in the gantry for himself, and sat down.

'I'm all ears,' said Bobby. 'Better than doing the bloody accounts.'

'American sailors,' said McCoy.

Bobby raised his eyebrows. 'Chance would be a fine thing.'

'If they were in Glasgow, looking for . . . y'know . . . where would they go?'

Bobby looked wide-eyed and innocent. 'I don't know what you mean, Mr McCoy. Looking for what? Could you explain exactly?'

'Yes, you bloody do,' said McCoy, smiling.

Bobby brushed some imaginary lint from his shirt. 'Although you wouldn't know it to look at me, my days of chasing after trade are long gone. I'm too old and too tired after working here every night. However . . .' He held up a finger, leaned back and hollered, 'Barry!' down into the open cellar hatch.

Couple of seconds later a head popped up.

'What?' it asked.

Bobby nodded at McCoy. 'Polis. They want a word with you.'

Barry's face went white and he climbed the rest of the stairs, stood behind the bar looking nervous. He was a big lad, white cap sleeve T-shirt, tight jeans, Rod Stewart-style hair.

'Mr McCoy here wants to know where to pick up an American sailor,' said Bobby. 'Thought you could let him know.'

'Don't worry, son,' said McCoy quickly before the guy made a run for it. 'Just need some information. Nothing else.'

Colour started to return to Barry's face. 'Young?' he asked. 'From the Holy Loch, you mean?'

McCoy nodded.

'Don't get that many of them, more's the pity. The only place I've ever met any was in the Duke of Wellington.'

Bobby rolled his eyes. 'Might have known. That place is dog rough.'

Barry ignored him. 'They're always jumpy though, usually say they're here on holiday, visiting family, something like that. Don't want you knowing they're in the navy.' He grinned. 'Only find out when things get going and you see the dog tags they've forgotten to take off.'

McCoy dug in his pocket, got out one of the pictures of Donny Stewart, handed it over. 'You ever see him?' he asked.

Barry looked at it and shook his head. 'No, but he's not the type I'd notice, to be honest. Not big enough. I'm six foot one and fifteen stone, want someone who can throw me about a bit, know what I mean?'

'No, Mr McCoy does not, thank you very much,' said Bobby. 'Begone. Away back down to your pit.'

Barry nodded, disappeared back into the cellar.

'Any help?' asked Bobby.

'Don't know,' said McCoy. 'Not quite sure what it is I'm looking for. Don't even know if the boy's a –' was about to say poof, changed quickly – 'a gay.'

'Gay, not *a* gay.'

'Ah,' said McCoy.

'Tell you what,' said Bobby. 'I'll send the monster from the deep down there tonight. Get him to ask around. Think he's more likely to get on in there than you. No offence.'

'Cheers,' said McCoy. 'I owe you.'

Bobby nodded. 'I know. That's why I'm doing it. Never know when I might need a favour from the boys in blue. Speaking of which, what happened to your pal? The big blond dish?'

'Wattie?' asked McCoy. 'Just had a wee baby.'

Bobby sighed again. 'Always the good-looking ones that turn out to be straight. Story of my life.'

McCoy left him to go back to his sales register, stepped out the pub into the early evening sunshine. Quarter to seven. If he got going he should get to Dunoon by half eight. The Paul Jones should be busy enough by then.

CHAPTER 20

A lorry had broken down just outside Port Glasgow, blocked the road for a good half an hour so it was almost nine by the time McCoy got to the Paul Jones in Dunoon. The bar was halfway along the main street, opposite the church. Inside it was a square with a bar along the side, tables dotted about, menu on the wall featuring burgers. Was full of young guys who McCoy assumed were American sailors. They had the usual denims, cords and T-shirts, but none of them had hair past their collars. A dead giveaway.

He made his way to the bar, not easy, the place was packed. Two girls were working, both young, both good-looking and both dressed up, no doubt part of the bar's attraction. Looked well in control of the situation, trading jokes and insults with the lads. He managed to catch the eye of the blonde one and she came over. He showed his police card, asked her if she had ten minutes. She said she'd check, asked the brunette one, and came back nodding. One of the sailors put some money in the jukebox in the corner. Drums and a twanging guitar blasted out and suddenly the place went

162

nuts. Crowd all singing along at the top of their voices '*It ain't me, it ain't me, I ain't no fortunate son*', jumping up and down, punching the air.

McCoy looked at the barmaid and she shrugged, shouted in his ear. 'They always go mental to this one.'

McCoy pointed to the door, wasn't any point trying to talk above thirty lads singing along with Creedence Clearwater Revival.

They stood on the pavement outside the pub, shouts and singing a dull rumble as the door closed behind them. The last of the families were making their way back to their B&Bs and hotels. Sleeping kids holding kites and fishing rods in their hands slumped in their dads' arms. McCoy took his cigarettes out, offered her one, and they lit up.

'I only started on these to keep the midges away,' she said, waving her cigarette in the air. 'And now I'm on twenty a day.' She held her hand out. 'Catrina.'

'McCoy,' said McCoy. 'You all right to answer a few questions?'

She nodded. 'Was due a break.'

He got the picture of Donny Stewart out his wallet, showed her it. 'You know him?' he asked.

'That the lad that's gone missing?'

McCoy nodded.

She shook her head. 'I recognise him, he's been in a few times, but I don't know him. Just another one of the boys. If they're not annoying me or asking me out they tend to all blur together. Big short-haired lads with good teeth.'

'You get locals in there as well?' McCoy asked, glancing back towards the pub.

'Not really. The occasional girl looking for an American boyfriend. No guys. They tend to stick to different pubs. American Navy boys in here, locals up the road in the Ingram, never the twain shall meet. Unless they're fighting, that is.' She thought for a minute. 'Although we did get a few in a year or so ago. A couple of long-haired hippy types started coming in. Started talking loud, saying things like baby-killers and Impee . . .?'

'Imperialists?' asked McCoy.

'That's it. Imperialists. Talking about Vietnam at the top of their voices. Think they were just trying to wind the boys up. After coming in a few times and them not taking the bait they stopped coming.'

'Do you know who they were, these guys?' asked McCoy.

She shook her head. 'But I'll bet they're from the Zoo.'

'The Zoo?' asked McCoy, puzzled.

She smiled. 'That's what we call it. It's a commune up by Knockland, a farm. All sorts of hippies and God knows what staying there. All Free Love and no washing your hair. Not for me.'

McCoy remembered what Donny's pal Saunders had told him about which way the gold car had gone. 'Is that the same way as Innellan?'

She nodded, pointed to the left down towards the ferry pier. 'Yes, you just keep going another six or so miles.'

'Don't know anything about a big gold car, do you?' asked McCoy.

'Me? No.' She smiled again. 'But my dad does. We were walking down Argyll Street the other day and a big gold car stopped by the Co-op and these two guys came out of it. Afghan coats, beards. Not even wearing shoes. Just about sent my dad apoplectic. Said if they were all about peace and love they should sell the bloody car and give the money to the poor, that the car was worth a fortune.'

'He say what kind it was?' asked McCoy. 'Your dad?'

'He said it was a Daimler? A something or other Daimler, I think.'

A blast of 'Bad Moon Rising' and a head popped out the pub door. Blond crew cut, American accent.

'Catrina? Susan says she needs you back. Pronto.'

Disappeared back inside.

Catrina dropped her cigarette onto the pavement and ground it out with her red platform sandal. 'I better go back,' she said. 'Susan'll be having a shit fit.'

'And you think this car is from the Zoo?' McCoy asked. 'The commune?'

She nodded. 'Good chance, not that many other hippies about here.'

She said goodbye, another blast of Creedence as she pulled the door open and went in. McCoy stood for a minute listening to the muffled music. Seemed like the Zoo was the place he needed to go. Not tonight though, he'd never find it in the dark. He'd passed a big hotel on the way to the pub. The Argyll. Decided to stay there and look for the Zoo in the morning.

He was walking down the street towards it when he saw him. Stewart was standing outside a pub stopping the people coming out and showing them a photo. Didn't seem to be having much luck, people shaking their heads, moving on. He looked a bit defeated, head down. McCoy felt sorry for him, wondered if anyone would care enough to do something like that if he went missing. Not his dad, that was for sure.

He approached Stewart as another couple were telling him they didn't recognise the boy in the photo.

'You look like you could do with a drink,' said McCoy.

Stewart looked up. 'Harry! Boy, am I glad to see you. I'm getting nowhere here. A drink would be much appreciated.'

McCoy pushed the pub door and they went in.

Stewart sat down and McCoy got them a couple of pints and a couple of whiskies and brought them over to a table by the fireplace. Pub was a comfy mixture of tartan wallpaper and pictures of boats, the clientele seemed to be fifty-fifty locals

166

and holidaymakers. A fire was crackling in the fireplace, Dean Martin playing in the background.

'Any news?' asked Stewart, picking his pint up.

McCoy shook his head. 'Not really. I'm just down here asking around, like you are.'

Stewart nodded, looked resigned. 'I just didn't know what else to do, thought I'd try and make myself useful,' he said. 'Been out there for a few hours, feet are sore, but it's better than sitting in my hotel room staring at the walls.'

'Anybody seen him?' asked McCoy.

He shook his head. 'Not really. The young navy guys recognise him but they don't know anything about what's happened to him. Locals try and be helpful, they look at the picture, say sorry they don't know him. That's about it.'

'What about the navy?' asked McCoy. 'They been any help?'

'I went up to the base this afternoon, had a word. Far as they are concerned he's AWOL. If the shore police find him they'll chuck him in the brig. That's it.'

'Are they looking?'

'Not really,' said Stewart. 'They've asked in a few bars, made an announcement at the base. Standard stuff.' He smiled. 'Guess a former captain doesn't have as much clout as I thought.'

'We'll find him,' said McCoy.

Stewart held up his drink and they clinked glasses. 'I cancelled the return flight. No reason to go back. I should be here. Whatever happens,

I'm not going home until I find out what's happened to Donny.'

The barman rang his bell, bellowed 'Last orders!' and Stewart went up to the bar. McCoy watched him inch in at the bar, twenty-pound note held up in his hand. Really did look like Jack Nicklaus. The more he thought about it, the more he thought there was something a bit strange about all this stuff with Donny Stewart and Paul Watt. A bomb had gone off in their flat, another in the Cathedral, and nobody seemed to care that much. The navy didn't care about Donny Stewart and Special Branch really didn't care about Paul Watt. Seemed like the only people that cared were him and Stewart.

'Penny for them?' said Stewart, sitting back down.

'Nothing important,' said McCoy. 'Just having a think.'

Stewart nodded. 'How's your pal Steve?'

'Don't know,' said McCoy. 'He's acting a bit strange, to be honest. Think the stretch in prison might have affected him more than he lets on. He still got your suit?'

'Shit,' said Stewart. 'Forgot about that. Not sure I'm going to see that again. Seemed very taken with it. Got a lot of compliments at the casino. So pleased he even went off to show it to some tailor guy he knows.'

McCoy was about to finish his pint but he put it back down on the table. 'He did what?'

'Said he knew a guy round the corner in some square, wanted to show him the suit, see if he could copy it.'

'St Enoch Square?' asked McCoy.

'Yeah, think that was it,' said Stewart. 'Why?'

'How long was he away for?' asked McCoy.

Stewart sat back, looked doubtful. 'I'm not sure, I was a few sheets to the wind by then. He said he was going and I went to the bar to get a drink and got talking to some guys at the bar about Vietnam. Next time I looked round he was back, sitting at the table.'

'Ten minutes?' asked McCoy.

Stewart shook his head. 'No, longer than that. More like half an hour, maybe forty minutes.'

Another shout from the barman. 'Gentlemen, please!' Boy was walking around picking the glasses off the table. Time to go.

'Fancy a walk?' asked Stewart. 'I'm still all over the place with this jet lag.'

McCoy nodded. 'Why not?'

They walked along the main street, Stewart talking about Boston and McCoy nodding occasionally. All the while trying to work out if Cooper had had enough time to get from the casino in Hope Street to Shettleston and back. Would be tight, that was for sure, but if he had a car waiting outside he could probably do it. And he knew something else. If he went and asked wee Arthur the tailor he'd tell them Cooper had been in to see him that night whether he had or not. Would he be stupid enough to dump the hammer he used in the next back court? Didn't think so, but you never knew.

They ended up sitting on the sea wall passing a silver flask of whisky Stewart had produced from his jacket pocket. It was a beautiful night, still, lights of Greenock and Gourock twinkling across the river.

'Did you always want to be a sailor?' asked McCoy.

Stewart nodded. 'Since I was a kid. There was something about the sea, don't know what it was, just always drew me. That and the fact I come from generations of sailors. That might have had something to do with it.' He took a swig and passed the flask. 'What about you? You always want to be a cop?'

McCoy took a slug, grimaced. Whisky wasn't helping his stomach one bit. 'Nope. I just kind of fell into it, didn't give it that much thought. I was fostered. The family I lived with came from a long line of polis. Just seemed natural.'

'You good at it?' asked Stewart.

McCoy grinned. 'Depends who you ask.'

'You never want to go somewhere else? See the world?' asked Stewart.

'Maybe one day,' said McCoy. 'Never really thought about it, just always thought I'd be in Glasgow. Suppose I could go anywhere, nothing really keeping me here.'

They sat for a minute watching the lights of the last ferry heading towards Greenock.

'You know I wasn't entirely truthful with you, Harry,' said Stewart.

'That right?' asked McCoy. 'What about?'

'Outside the Central, in the car. You asked me if there was anything about Donny I wanted to say off the record.'

McCoy didn't say anything, let him speak.

'There was an incident at Donny's school. Boarding school. Him and another boy were caught together. They were on a camping trip . . .'

McCoy passed him the flask and he took a long slug. Shook his head.

'The shit I had to pull to make it go away. Donny said it was a one-off. I thought it was just the kind of things boys get up to when they are cooped up together. Christ knows it happens enough in the navy. I thought he'd grow out of it.' He smiled, looked at McCoy. 'I'm not sure he did. That any help?'

McCoy shrugged. 'Don't know. Might be. Thanks for telling me.'

Stewart handed him back the flask. 'What if we don't find him?' he asked. 'What if . . .'

McCoy returned the flask, told him they would. Wished he was as sure of it as he sounded.

16TH APRIL 1974

CHAPTER 21

McCoy was up and at them early, figured it would be the best way to catch the commune dwellers at home, didn't think they would be the type to be up with the rising sun. Managed to stuff down some porridge just like the doctor said. Fact it tasted like wallpaper glue didn't help much but he'd woken up twice in the night with pains in his stomach. Had to do something. Vowed never to drink whisky again. Almost believed himself.

He stepped out of the hotel and into the warm sunshine of a fine spring day. Clyde was a deep blue, hills green, holiday postcard stuff. Were even a few yachts dotted about in the water, white sails catching the light. Didn't have much of a map but he figured since the road to Knockland didn't go anywhere else, just a dead end, he'd find the Zoo without too much trouble.

Radio was still blasting out 'Waterloo' every five minutes so he gave up, turned it off, and rolled down the car windows. Smell of cowshit and earth after the rain as he drove out the town. Dunoon petered out into a row of big houses set back from

175

the road facing the water, then farmland. Sort of remembered being out this way on a day trip from the care home outside Dunoon. Wondered how many other childhood memories he'd lost trying to forget the bad ones. A price he was happy to pay.

Started to think about what Stewart had been saying last night. Maybe he was stuck in a rut, maybe that's what was making him restless. Wasn't really anyone to miss him if he left Glasgow. His ex Angela had moved to New York, started a new life. Maybe he needed to do something like that. Make a big change.

Almost missed it, too busy thinking, miles away. He stopped the car, reversed a couple of hundred yards. There was a hand-painted wooden sign by the side of the road, 'Mason's farm. Take the next left' on it, words surrounded by flowers and peace signs. Had to be it.

The first left turned out to be a rutted farm road leading down towards the shining water. He turned in, car rolling and rocking over the rutted mud. Few minutes later he stopped the car in front of a gate held closed by a bit of rope. Got out, opened it and drove onto the property.

There were a few sheep and cows dotted about the fields. Newborn lambs standing by their mums. The road turned a corner and he saw an old cow barn, big letters on it in white paint.

YOU ARE NOW ENTERING FREE ALBA!

McCoy's idea that he would catch the commune dwellers on the hop didn't play out. As he drove up to the group of farm buildings he could see a few people milling about. The farm buildings themselves were quite something. Murals had been painted on the sides: rainbows, flowers, smiling kids, a big marijuana leaf. Next to them was what looked like an old bus, painted as well, striped material covering the windows as makeshift curtains.

A young bearded guy in a dressing gown and welly boots held up his hands in front of the car, directed him off to the side. McCoy pulled in and cut the engine, rolled down the window. The guy leant in, smell of patchouli and grass coming off him, and smiled.

'Can I help you, mate?' he asked in a cockney accent.

'Hope so,' said McCoy getting out the car. 'Looking for an American guy. Donny Stewart.'

The guy sucked air in through his teeth. 'That's about the only thing we don't have,' he said. 'We've got Germans, couple of Dutch, a Belgian, even a couple of bloody South Africans, but no Americans.'

'That right?' asked McCoy, looking around. Some chickens were scratching the earth, a couple of kids were chasing a Border collie puppy around, two women in long skirts and headscarves with garden forks over their shoulders watching from the door of a barn.

'Who's in charge here?' he asked.

The guy grinned. 'No one's in charge here, mate. It's a commune, that's the point.'

McCoy sighed. 'Okay, whose farm is it, who owns the place?'

'That would be me.'

He turned and a middle-aged woman in dungarees, yellow T-shirt and sandshoes was standing there. Even in the work clothes she was a stunner, long red hair, clear skin, bright green eyes. She stepped forward, spoke in a cut-glass accent.

'I'm Margo,' she said. 'Margo Lindsay.'

Wasn't like she needed to introduce herself. McCoy recognised her straight away. After all, there weren't any other Scottish actresses who had won an Oscar.

'Tea?' she asked.

Ten minutes later McCoy had a chipped tin mug of rosehip tea, whatever that was, in his hand, and was sitting on a kitchen chair in the backyard of the farmhouse, looking out over the water. Was a strange enough situation without Margo Lindsay sitting beside him holding out a plate of homemade biscuits.

'You don't remember me, do you?' asked McCoy, taking one.

'Should I?' she asked, looking amused. 'By the way, watch your teeth on the biscuits. Culinary excellence is not one of our strong points here.'

'I arrested you once,' he said.

She looked him up and down. Shook her head.

'Did you? To be honest, I've been arrested more times than I can remember. When was it?'

'Glasgow Green. The Shipbuilders benefit thing. The Rally.'

'Ah! The one with The Humblebums and Matt, you mean?' she said.

McCoy nodded.

'Definitely no chance of remembering that one. I was completely stoned. I ate a hash cookie by mistake just before I left the flat. What had I done, anyway?' she asked.

'Not much,' said McCoy. 'Think they just wanted rid of you. Causing too much trouble.'

'Sounds about right,' she said, sipping her tea. 'So what brings a Glasgow policeman up here?'

'Looking for someone,' said McCoy. 'American sailor called Donny Stewart. From the base down the road.'

She shook her head, carefully brushed a butterfly off her arm.

'No Americans here. Certainly not any from that bloody base. Not sure our more ideologically minded members would allow it. What's he done, this boy?'

'Nothing,' said McCoy. 'Just need to have a chat with him. How about a lad called Paul Watt? Scottish.'

'No. I'm good with names, and I don't remember him. We get people coming and going, some only stay a few days, but I'm good at remembering them and I don't remember him.'

'What is this place?' asked McCoy.

'It's a place to try and live in a different way. To change the way society is structured.' she said. 'An experiment, I suppose. People come here who have rejected the nuclear family model or who don't fit in anywhere else or are just tired of the capitalist rat race. We run our little society with a different set of values.'

'Does it work?' he asked.

She smiled. 'Does your way?'

'Fair point,' said McCoy.

'We're getting there,' she said. 'Trying to make Scotland a better and kinder place to live.' She looked at the small gold watch on her wrist. 'Daily meeting in ten minutes. One of the few drawbacks of communal living. Anything else I can help you with, Mr Policeman?'

'Just one thing,' said McCoy. 'Have you got a big gold car? Daimler?'

'No,' she said. 'But my brother has. Well, it was my father's, but he pays the insurance and the upkeep so he sees it as his. He grudgingly allows us to use it when he's not in Scotland but he's here just now so he's taken it back. Always complains about the state of it when he gets it. Don't blame him really, the kids here don't treat it with much respect.'

'Who uses it when it's here?' asked McCoy.

'Anyone who wants to. We use it to get supplies in from Dunoon or Glasgow. Stuff we can't grow or make here. Sometimes they just take it for a drive. Picnics, that sort of thing.'

She looked at her watch again.

'Where does your brother live?' asked McCoy.

'Angus? He still lives in the family pile. It's about four miles up the road, outside Invervegain. Can't miss it. Ugliest house in Scotland, overlooks the bay.'

A young woman appeared in the doorway of the farmhouse. 'Margo? You ready?'

'Coming,' said Margo. 'All good, Mr . . .?'

'McCoy,' said McCoy, standing up. He looked back at the run-down farmhouse. 'You ever miss it?' he asked. 'Hollywood, being a film star, all that stuff?'

She shook her head. 'Not a bit. Shouldn't say this, sounds very ungrateful, but I never enjoyed it in the first place. Fell into it. I was young, it seemed an easy life, and it was, but what we are doing here is much more important, trying to work out a new life for the people of Scotland. That's much more important than dressing up as Lady Macbeth or someone's wife to sell a few cinema tickets.'

McCoy drove away from the farm, still not quite believing he'd met Margo Lindsay. 'Mad Margo' as the papers had started to call her when she turned her back on acting and started getting involved in politics. She'd been a fixture at every protest in Scotland for the past couple of years, happy to tell the press about the benefits of communism or Sufism or the plight of the Palestinians, or whatever cause it was that week.

181

McCoy had always liked her despite all the preaching. Least she'd had a bit of a sense of humour about her, unlike most of her fellow protesters. The fact that she was one of the most beautiful women he'd ever seen helped too. Most political people he'd met saw the world in black and white, right and wrong, at least she saw some shades of grey. Wasn't sure about her latest enthusiasm though. Wasn't sure he'd want to be part of a new Scotland that involved living on porridge and eggs on a mucky farm. Lovely view of the sea or not.

CHAPTER 22

McCoy thought he'd missed it, was about to turn back and retrace his steps when he saw a glimpse of pale stone between the trees in the distance. He drove on another half a mile or so until he saw a small unmarked road leading off the one he was on. He dimly remembered reading some article about Margo Lindsay where she'd said her brother was in the army, other than that he didn't have much of a clue.

He had only gone a couple of hundred yards up the side road when he came to an ornate iron gate, the boarded-up stone gatehouse next to it looking like it hadn't been used for years. He got out to open the gate and found it was locked. Looked around, didn't quite know what to do. Then there was a squawk, whine of feedback and a voice emerged from a small speaker mounted on a tree by the gate.

'Can I help you?'

McCoy leant into the speaker, wasn't quite sure if they could hear him.

'Come to see Mr Lindsay,' he said.

183

'Colonel Lindsay,' the speaker corrected. 'Do you have an appointment?'

'No,' said McCoy. 'Detective McCoy. Glasgow Police. Would like to ask him some questions.'

Speaker was silent for a minute. Then: 'I'll ask if he'll see you.'

McCoy was about to tell whoever it was that it was a police investigation and he better fucking see him when the speaker squawked again and went dead. He told it to fuck off, sat down on a fallen log at the side of the road and lit up.

He'd smoked two cigarettes, watched a ladybird crawl up his arm, and was about to give up and go home when he heard a crunching of boots on gravel and a guy in his late teens appeared at the other side of the gate. He was dressed in khaki trousers and one of those green army jumpers with patches on the shoulders and elbows. Polished black boots, short hair.

McCoy waved. Guy didn't wave back. Took a key out his pocket, unlocked the gate, held it open. 'Up the drive,' he said. 'Someone will meet you outside the house.'

McCoy got back in the car, drove through the gate, the guy watching him all the time. Maybe this was some sort of army base, he thought, maybe that's what all the fuss was about. Lindsay could have sold the family home to them, he supposed. He drove on, followed the road as it swung round to the left, and he saw the house for the first time.

Margo was right, it was an ugly house. A huge ugly house. A grey granite box half covered in ivy, small windows peppering the sides, round wings coming off to the side. Roof was a mess of chimney stacks and small turrets. Looked a bit like Colditz, except less welcoming.

Another young bloke was standing by the main entrance as McCoy pulled up. Same boots and khakis but no jumper this time, instead he was wearing a white T-shirt with DEFENS printed on it in light blue. McCoy got out the car, put his suit jacket on, yawned and stretched.

'Been driving too long,' he said amiably. 'Wears you out for some reason. God knows why, you're just sitting on your arse.'

The bloke didn't smile. 'Do you have identification?' he asked.

McCoy dug his police card out, handed it over, nodded at the bloke's T-shirt. 'That's spelt wrong, you know.' Bloke didn't answer. McCoy shrugged. 'This an army base, is it?'

Still didn't reply, just handed the card back.

'Follow me,' he said, and walked off down the drive.

McCoy walked behind him, still not quite sure where he was but wherever it was, he didn't like it. He was in the back arse of nowhere in a place run by silent young men who wouldn't even look at him. If the plan was to make him feel uncomfortable, it was working. The guy suddenly veered off onto a path through the woods, dry leaves and twigs crunching under his feet.

McCoy jogged to keep up. 'Where are we going?' he asked.

No response, the guy just kept walking.

Ten minutes later they stepped out the woods and into a clearing. The sun was shining through the trees, pools of light and dark amongst the grass and small bushes, air full of pollen and clumps of circling midges. More young guys gathered round at the other side of the clearing. All of them were dressed in khaki pants and DEFENS T-shirts. An older man, maybe in his fifties, dressed in an army jumper, boots and a dark green and red kilt was standing at the centre of the group, leaning on a tall walking stick.

He looked up, waved at McCoy to come over. As he walked towards them he realised they were all looking at something on the ground. He couldn't quite make out what it was, whatever it was was hidden by their legs and the long grass. As he got nearer and they parted to let him through it came into focus and his stomach lurched. A dead deer was lying on the ground, neck at a funny angle, blank black eye staring at the sky. A cloud of black flies were buzzing around the blood oozing from a neat hole in its shoulder. The last thing McCoy wanted to do was get any closer, but he made himself.

'Mr Lindsay?' he said to the older man.

The man turned and looked at him. He had the

same colouring as his sister but his ginger hair was close-cropped, pale skin, green eyes in a face that looked like he'd spent most of his time outdoors. He nodded at McCoy.

'Colonel Angus Lindsay. Can you give me a few minutes?' he asked. 'Bit in the middle of things right now. Delicate part of the dressing.'

Accent was as posh as his sister's. Sounded like Prince Philip. McCoy nodded and one of the lads knelt down by the back end of the deer. Long knife in his hand, he looked up at Lindsay.

'Remember what I taught you. First, cut around the anus and remove it,' said Lindsay.

McCoy's stomach lurched again. He looked away but still heard a horrible noise like a pair of scissors cutting through a heavy cloth.

'Okay, now grab the skin in the middle of its stomach and cut from the back to the front.'

More scissor noises.

'Careful now!' said Lindsay. 'Don't nick the stomach.'

McCoy looked up at the sky, birds singing, leaves rustling in the wind, flies buzzing. Tried to ignore the grunting of the young lad and the growing copper-penny smell of blood in the still air.

'Now cut at the top, at the diaphragm,' said Lindsay. 'And release the stomach and the intestines.'

McCoy timed it wrong, dropped his head just in time to see the lad, white T-shirt now red with wet blood, pull what looked like a grey plastic bag followed by a thick bluish rope of intestines out the body cavity of the deer. That was enough.

'I'm just going to stand over there,' he said. 'Have a cigarette.'

McCoy moved off quickly to the other side of the clearing. Tried to breathe deep, not think about what was happening a few yards away. Took out his cigarettes, realised his hands were shaking. Lit up and heard Lindsay say to the lad that he had to 'exsanguinate' the body now. Looked up at the sky as he heard a noise like somebody pouring out a big bucket of water onto the ground.

A couple of minutes later Lindsay wandered over. 'Squeamish are you, Mr McCoy?' he asked, smiling.

McCoy nodded. ''Fraid so.'

'Not the best attribute for a detective, I would imagine. Now, how can I help you?'

'First of all,' asked McCoy, 'what is this place? An army base?'

Lindsay shook his head, laughed. 'No, it's my private residence. Been in the family for generations. Came to me a few years ago when my father passed away.'

'Are you in the army?' McCoy asked.

'Yes, but I'm on leave from the service at the moment.'

McCoy nodded over to the boys standing by the deer. 'And these guys?'

'Friends,' said Lindsay.

McCoy laughed this time. 'Friends? You sure?'

'Perfectly,' said Lindsay, suddenly icy. 'Now, as I can't imagine who my friends are is a police matter, may I ask why you are here?'

McCoy took out the picture of Donny Stewart. Showed it to Lindsay. 'He one of your friends, is he?'

Lindsay barely glanced at it. 'It looks like he serves in the United States Navy by his uniform. No, I don't know anyone in the US Navy.'

McCoy put the picture away.

Lindsay looked at his watch. 'Is that it then?'

'No,' said McCoy. He was starting to get annoyed. Realised he sounded it too. Lindsay raised his eyebrows. 'You own a car, I believe?'

'I own several cars,' said Lindsay.

'One a gold-coloured Daimler, is it?'

'Yes,' said Lindsay. 'A Daimler Majestic. Like this estate, it was my father's. Why do you ask?'

'Can I have a look at it?' asked McCoy.

'No,' said Lindsay. 'Firstly, it's being cleaned and serviced in Glasgow at the moment. My sister's collection of freaks and oddballs have managed to almost run it into the ground, and secondly –' he stopped and smiled – 'not without a warrant. Now if that's all . . .'

McCoy nodded and Lindsay walked back over to the lads, sent one of them over.

'I'll walk you back to the car,' he said.

They started back through the trees.

'What's your name?' asked McCoy.

The lad didn't say anything, just kept walking

ahead of him, boots leading the way. The other lad hadn't told McCoy his name either. McCoy thought he'd go for the hat-trick and asked the one that held the gate on the road open for him. No luck there either.

All of them stayed silent, all looking at him like he was shite on their shoe. Their silence and refusal to answer any questions wasn't the only thing the three of them had in common. They all had the DEFENS T-shirts on, arms bare. And on their bare arms they had something else in common. On each arm, in amongst the freckles and the hairs, there were tiny dots and splatters of dried whitewash catching the sun.

McCoy drove back onto the main road, trying not to think of the sound of the deer's blood pouring onto the grass. He had a couple of hours' drive back to Glasgow. Enough time to try and work out what was going on. So he did what Murray had always taught him to do. Go back to the beginning, find the connections, find the pattern. Didn't always work, but it was worth a try.

It looked as though Donny Stewart and Paul Watt had been building a bomb together. A bomb that had gone off, killing Paul and injuring Donny. According to Faulds, it wasn't that difficult to get the ingredients for that kind of bomb, you could get them in any Co-op, so tracing things that way was going to be a dead end. Real question was: what were they building the bomb for? Who was it meant for before it went off in Paul's

190

face and splattered him all over the living-room wall? And who had planted the bomb in the Cathedral? Donny Stewart, if he was well enough? Someone else? Were they doing all this for a prank? Had to be more than that, but it was hard to see what.

He pulled in behind the row of cars waiting for the ferry at Dunoon pier. Could see the ferry out in the water, was about halfway across, enough time for a cigarette. He got out the car, leant against it, lit up. Could hear the music and the screams from the fair in the park. Wondered if Patsy Hearne was working there or whether he was still at Glasgow Green. He'd liked Patsy when he was a boy. He was a right cheeky bugger, always answering the teachers back, taking no shit. None of them did, the gypsy boys, all as hard as nails. Supposed it was to do with their upbringing. They had to be.

Even Patsy had probably seen more of the world than he had, travelling with the fair. All McCoy had ever seen was Glasgow. One trip to Manchester to visit a girlfriend who didn't really want him there. Never been to London, never been abroad, never been on an aeroplane. Even kids these days went to Spain for their holidays. A car behind him blew its horn and he realised they were boarding. Held his hand up to say sorry, got back in the car.

They set off and he got out the car, made his way to the front of the ferry. Sun was sparkling off the water, nice feel of the spray on his face. Paul

191

Watt and Meiklejohn at the barracks seemed close and the army cadets from his barracks had turned up at Lindsay's holiday camp. The same Lindsay whose car Donny Stewart had last been seen in.

It was like some weird circle – they were all connected but McCoy still had no idea why. Was Lindsay dangerous or just some guy who liked muscly young men hanging about his estate? It was creepy but it wasn't a crime, and Lindsay was right, McCoy couldn't look at the car without a warrant, didn't have enough reason. Besides, he wasn't sure what good looking at the car would do. Maybe Donny Stewart was staying with Lindsay at the big house, hiding out from the navy. But there was no way McCoy was going to get any sort of warrant to search the house without an awful lot more evidence.

He hated to admit it, but he was kind of stuck. Couldn't see how he could move forward. If Donny Stewart had decided he didn't want to be found by the navy or his dad, it wouldn't be that hard for him to disappear. The only way he was going to break cover was if his injury became so bad he needed to go to a hospital. Even then it was probably easy enough to give a false name, say he was just here on holiday and it was an accident. Everything on the investigation seemed to have ground to a halt. Something was going to have to happen for McCoy to pick up the trail again. He just hoped it wasn't another bomb going off.

★   ★   ★

'Back from your holidays?' asked Billy the desk sergeant as McCoy walked into the station. 'Some of us have been working.'

'That'll be a first,' said McCoy. 'Unless you count staring at page three girls all day and filling out betting slips as work.'

'Get it up you, smartarse,' said Billy, handing him a note. 'Some American guy called Stewart phoned for you, says he's at the Central Hotel, the number's there, and Wattie's running about like a blue-arsed fly looking for you.'

'How come?' asked McCoy.

Billy shrugged. Head back down over his paper.

'Where is he?' asked McCoy.

'Just went to get something to eat, be at City Bakeries. Go and get him before he blows a bloody gasket.'

McCoy left the station and walked up towards the shops. Wattie was standing in the queue, big lump amongst all the female office workers and girls from the dress factory. McCoy stuck his fingers in his mouth and whistled. Wattie turned, saw him and came running over.

'Christ, it must be important if you're willing to lose your place in the City Bakeries queue,' said McCoy. 'What's up?'

'The guy from the forensic place phoned, about the hammer . . .'

'And?' asked McCoy.

'And there's a thumbprint on it,' said Wattie. 'And it's Stevie Cooper's.'

CHAPTER 23

McCoy sat at his desk trying to take it in. There was a slim chance Cooper had been stupid enough to dump the hammer nearby but there was no way he was stupid enough to leave a fingerprint in Jamsie Dixon's blood on it. Unless. Unless Billy was right and he really was acting strange, not giving much of a shit what happened to him as long as he got Jamsie Dixon. He looked up at the clock. Archie Lomax was walking Cooper in for an interview at two p.m., twenty minutes' time.

Wattie was at his desk bent over his notes, going over them all, getting them in order. Lips moving as he rehearsed his questions. If there was one thing McCoy knew, it was that Wattie didn't stand a chance against Archie Lomax. A lawyer like Lomax would run rings round him. Last thing McCoy wanted was to sit in on the interview, but Murray would murder him if he didn't. Someone like Cooper was too big a catch to leave to Wattie alone.

He got out his packet of Embassy, lit up. When Cooper walked into the interview room and saw him that would be that. He would see McCoy sitting there as a betrayal, no question. The circumstances wouldn't matter to him. McCoy would become just another polis sitting across from him in an interview room. Another one of the Enemy.

'You ready?' He looked up and Wattie was standing there.

McCoy nodded. 'You all set?' he asked. 'Got all your notes?'

Wattie nodded. Looking anything but confident.

'Look, Wattie, don't expect too much. Lomax isn't going to let Cooper say anything that helps us. That's why he's there, to stop him. Just ask your questions, I'll only chip in if I think you've missed anything, okay?'

Wattie nodded again. He'd another baby sick stain on the shoulder of his shirt, had odd socks on too. Lomax was going to walk all over him.

'Away outside for a minute, Wattie,' said McCoy. 'Take some deep breaths, calm down, eh?'

Wattie nodded, headed for the door. McCoy shook his head. This was going to be a fucking car crash.

'Well, Mr Watson?' asked Archie Lomax, drumming his fingers on the scarred and graffitied tabletop. 'Are you going to interview my client or not?'

The interview room was McCoy's least favourite place in the station. He hated being in it. It wasn't much more than a square box, table and four

195

chairs screwed into the floor. It was always too hot, no window, and it always stank. Stank of cigarettes, unwashed clothes and desperation. Wasn't any different today.

Wattie shuffled his notes a few more times, looked up. 'Mr Cooper, would you care to tell us why a hammer found in the back court next to Mr Dixon's flat came to have both his blood and your fingerprint on it?'

Not a bad opening, to be fair, McCoy thought, could have been a lot worse.

Cooper leant forward, greasy lick of blond hair falling on his forehead. Grinned.

'No comment,' he said.

McCoy sat back in his chair, looked at the study in contrasts. Archie Lomax was fifty-odd, thinning dark hair swept back, gold-rimmed glasses perched on his nose. He'd his usual chalk-stripe suit on, white shirt, blue tie. Cooper was dressed as he always was, jeans, short-sleeved shirt, red Harrington jacket. Just like James Dean, as he always said. Blond quiff ramming the point home. He was a big man, big shoulders, beefy hands. Both looked right for their trades, thought McCoy. Same as him and Wattie. Cheap suits, bri-nylon shirts, striped ties and scuffed shoes. The plainclothes polis uniform.

Wattie looked down at his notes, pulled out a photograph of a hammer with a ruler placed beside it for scale. He spun it round, pushed it in front of Cooper and Lomax.

'Mr Cooper, do you recognise this hammer?' he asked.

Cooper leant forward, looked at the picture. Looked up. 'No.'

'That's funny,' said Wattie. 'Because your fingerprint is on it.'

'Tell me,' said Lomax. 'Is this fingerprint in blood?'

Wattie shook his head.

'In that case, I'm not entirely sure why you are endeavouring to connect the two things? My client's fingerprint on the handle of the hammer made in grease or dirt and the blood and bone matter on the head of the hammer belonging to Mr Dixon? What exactly is the connection?'

Wattie didn't say anything. Lomax kept going.

'My client could have touched that hammer at any point in the past year or so. It certainly doesn't mean he was guilty of using it on the unfortunate Mr Dixon. I'll make it plain, shall I? It simply means both the murderer and my client touched the hammer at some unrelated point. Tell me, were there any other fingerprints on this mysterious hammer?'

'No,' said Wattie. 'Just Mr Cooper's.'

'Really,' said Lomax, smiling. 'How very convenient.'

Wattie was getting rolled and there wasn't much McCoy could do about it. Lomax was the best in the city. Only hoped Wattie would treat it as the to-and-fro show it was, not get too wound up.

Wattie picked up his ballpoint pen, clicked the

end a few times. Wasn't a bad idea, bought himself some time. He put the pen down. Looked at Cooper. 'Had you been involved in a fight with Mr Dixon earlier on the evening of the 13th of April, the night he was killed?'

Cooper looked over at McCoy. McCoy held his stare. Lomax looked extravagantly bored.

'You may wish to amend your question, Mr Watson. My client wasn't involved in a fight. He was attacked in broad daylight by Mr Dixon.' Lomax looked at McCoy. Smiled. 'As any witnesses present will testify, won't they, Mr McCoy?'

McCoy didn't say anything, barely nodded.

'Sorry,' said Lomax. 'I didn't hear your reply.'

'Yes,' said McCoy.

'Excellent,' said Lomax. 'So the scenario is this: my client is having an enjoyable dinner in the Malmaison with Detective Harry McCoy of the Glasgow Police and' – he looked down at his notes, raised his eyebrows – 'former Captain Andrew Stewart of the United States Navy. Esteemed company indeed. So this Dixon appears out of nowhere and attempts to slash him with an open razor. Not really what you would call a fight, is it, Mr Watson? Or maybe we could ask your colleague Mr McCoy to confirm that account. After all, he was there, wasn't he?'

Wattie couldn't have looked more out of his depth if he'd tried. He shuffled his notes again.

'And where were you later that evening, Mr Cooper?' he asked.

Lomax was about to speak when Cooper curled his fists, punched the air a few times.

'At the boxing with your pal sitting there and the navy boy Stewart. Then McCoy fucked off when the blood started flowing and we went on to a casino. Was there all night, got home about two with a girl called Helen, don't know her second name, fucked her brains out, then woke up with a cunt of a hangover about ten the next day. That okay with you, is it?'

McCoy knew he had to say it, didn't want to but knew he had to. 'Not quite all night at the casino,' he said, 'was it?'

Lomax raised his eyebrows. Cooper looked surprised.

McCoy carried on. 'Your esteemed witness says you disappeared for about forty minutes around about nine-thirty. Care to talk us through that one, Mr Lomax? Although going by the look on your face it's all a bit of a surprise to you too, eh?'

Lomax didn't flinch. Been in the game too long to give anything away. Cooper wasn't so good at hiding it, didn't look happy. McCoy knew him like the back of his hand and he was getting angry now. Cheeks were starting to get a bit flushed. Knew if he looked under the desk his boot would be drumming on the dirty lino floor.

Cooper pointed at him. 'Finally decided to open your trap, did you?' he said.

Lomax coughed discreetly into his hand. His usual signal to tell his clients to shut the fuck up.

'Forty minutes unaccounted for,' said McCoy. 'More than enough time to get to Shettleston and settle some scores, eh, Stevie?'

Lomax coughed again. McCoy knew the warning wasn't going to work, could tell by the colour in Cooper's face, by the way his hands were curling into fists.

'Fuck you, McCoy,' he said. 'You better watch yourself.'

'That's not very nice, Stevie,' said McCoy. 'All I did was ask you a question.'

Lomax jumped in. 'Which my client has no intention of answering. Now if we—'

'I went to see wee Arthur Blake the tailor in St Enoch Square,' said Cooper. 'Ask him.' He stood up. 'That us done?' he asked Lomax.

'I believe so,' said Lomax, checking his notes. He looked up.

'Mr Watson, as you are fairly new in this game, may I give you some advice? Don't drag my client in here again with such little reason, and if you do, ask your colleague here' – he nodded at McCoy – 'to learn some manners. Good day.'

He put his papers in his briefcase and they went to walk out. McCoy caught Cooper's eye. He looked furious, really fucking furious. He'd seen that look before, just never directed at him. Had a horrible feeling he'd just crossed a very dangerous line.

*　　*　　*

200

'Well, that got us absolutely nowhere!'

Murray had just delivered his verdict on Wattie's account of the interview.

Wattie's face told the story, couldn't have looked more crushed if he'd tried. Took his file back off Murray's desk, sat it on his lap.

'Well, we always knew how it was going to be,' said McCoy, trying to lessen the blow.

'Did we?' said Murray. 'That our attitude now, is it? Give up before we start?'

'C'mon, Murray, it was a standard to-and-fro,' said McCoy. 'The kind of thing Lomax does in his sleep. We knew exactly what was going to happen.'

'Doesn't help that you were Cooper's bloody alibi,' said Murray. 'How on earth did—'

'I wasn't,' said McCoy. 'That would be the captain.'

'That right is it, smartarse?' said Murray. 'Think it's a big laugh, do you? I've given up telling you to stay away from Cooper, but it's serious this time. This comes to trial, you know fine well Lomax'll get you, Detective Harry McCoy of the Glasgow Police and your wee night out with the chief suspect up on the stand for everyone to hear. The papers will love it. The detective and the criminal. Best pals. And if that doesn't work, you can bet your arse he'll use it as an excuse to go for a mistrial. How do you think that's going to go down at Pitt Street?'

He sat back in his chair, didn't look happy,

started filling the barrel of his pipe with his usual stinking tobacco.

'Don't think you have to worry about me and Cooper any more,' said McCoy.

'Good,' said Murray. 'What, you two fallen out, have you? About bloody time.'

Something in McCoy switched. Was sick of Murray sitting there making Wattie feel like shit, making him feel like shit. He sat forward, looked Murray in the eye. Spat it out.

'Not just fallen out. Now he hates me and he's probably going to come after me. And do you know why? All because you made me sit in on your wee dog and pony show that we both knew was fucking pointless. If that cheers you up, then—'

They both turned as the door burst open. Billy from the front desk standing there, a sheet of paper in his hand.

'There's been another one.'

CHAPTER 24

The Tennent's Caledonian Brewery offices looked like a wrecking ball had hit them. McCoy coughed, got a hanky out his pocket, held it over his mouth. It was hard to breathe with all the dust and smoke in the air. The entrance was just a hole now, stairs that led up to it now led nowhere, stopped in mid-air in a tangle of concrete and steel rods. The bomb had taken a good chunk of the front of the building off, turned it into the rubble and dust that was now covering the street. Medics were carrying a blanket-covered body on a stretcher towards the bank of ambulances parked across the road. One of them looked up at McCoy and shook his head. Was too early to tell how many were dead yet, they were still searching through the rubble of what had been the front offices. There was a big splatter of drying blood on the road next to McCoy's shoe, a purse lying open, coins spilling out of it. He moved off to the side, didn't want to look at it any more. Whatever bombs had blown up Paul Watt and the Cathedral altar were nothing compared to this. This looked like a war zone.

Most of the staff were standing in the yard, a bedraggled, dust-covered group lined up by the shiny metal tanks and pipes. Some of them were crying, some being tended to by ambulance men, some just standing there, dazed. Initial reports from the uniforms first on the scene said about twenty or so injured, including a couple of passersby. So far there were three confirmed dead, looked like it was going to be more. Most of the minor injuries had been caused by flying glass. Easy to believe. McCoy could feel it crunching under his feet as he pulled up the barrier rope and moved closer to the building. The smoke and dust in the air was worse here. Even with the hanky he kept coughing, overwhelming smell of malt wasn't helping either.

The bomb had also brought chaos to the evening rush hour. Duke Street was one of the main eastern routes in and out of the centre of town. Cars and buses were backed up a quarter of a mile each way. Constant noise of horns and shouts. Traffic cops running about trying to set up alternative routes. The rope barriers blocking off the area round the brewery were lined with people, workers who had been on their way home, kids, even the old and downtrodden from the Great Eastern Hotel had turned their attention away from looking for tonight's bottle to take a gawp at what was going on.

McCoy had read it twice but he still couldn't believe what he was holding in his hand. The message that had been phoned in to the station, written out in Billy's copperplate handwriting.

The Sons of the 51 are responsible for bombing the brewery in Duke Street and Glasgow Cathedral. We will free Scotland from the oppression of alcohol and the influence of foreign occupiers. With our help, Scotland will rise again. Today is the first day of the war for liberation.

He read it again. Wondered what the hell they were in for now. Wondered what the Sons of the 51 meant. Looked up as a fire engine reversed towards the office building, men jumping off it with hoses, looking for a standpipe. Looked back at the message. Wasn't going to be long until the papers got a hold of it. Chances were they had probably been sent one already, and when they published it all hell would break loose.

At least they knew what Paul Watt had been building bombs for now. Remembered the sign on the wall of the barn at Margo Lindsay's farm. YOU ARE NOW ENTERING FREE ALBA. Did they have something to do with it? Maybe the commune were some sort of Scottish Angry Brigade-type thing? Couldn't see it himself, the people there all seemed like half-stoned hippies, back-to-the-land types, more likely to sit cross-legged discussing things for hours while passing a joint than the type to do anything about it. Still didn't know why the Cathedral had been bombed. What had that got to do with enemy occupiers? It didn't make sense.

A police car drew up at the other side of the roped-off area and Hughie Faulds got out, ignored the press guys gathered by the rope, waved over. A uniform lifted the rope for him and Faulds ducked under it, picked his way through the debris covering the road, shook McCoy's hand.

'Christ, it's like being back in Belfast,' he said. 'I thought I'd left all this behind.'

McCoy handed him the paper. He read it, looked up.

'This serious?' he said. 'Oppression of alcohol. Are they joking?'

McCoy nodded over at the bombed building. 'Doesn't look like it.'

'Fuck,' said Faulds. 'You get anywhere yet?'

'Just got here myself,' said McCoy. 'This look like the same kind of bomb as West Princes Street?'

Faulds sniffed the air. 'It's Co-op mix again, but it always is. Can just get it under the malt. You smell it at the Cathedral?'

McCoy nodded.

'Casualties?'

'Three dead so far, lots of injuries,' said McCoy.

'So it's going to get serious then?' asked Faulds. 'Might need to bring you in. That okay?'

'If you clear it with my boss.' He looked at McCoy, grinned, and shook his head. 'You've done it already, haven't you?'

'Want to go and have a look around?' McCoy asked.

Faulds dipped back under the rope, headed for the firemen gathered over by the front of the building. McCoy watched him go, realised he'd forgotten to ask him about Paul McVeigh and what Cooper had said. Would have to wait until next time he saw him. Thought of Cooper made him remember what he'd said to Murray in his office. Moment of anger he regretted. What he'd said was all true but he hadn't framed it in the best way, that was for sure. If Billy hadn't come in with the news he was sure Murray would be chewing him out now, or he'd be suspended.

'Twenty-three injured. Seven seriously. Three dead so far.'

McCoy turned and Wattie was standing there, notebook open.

'The security guard at reception, a man delivering new roller towels for the bathrooms and a woman who worked in the accounts department.'

He snapped it shut. 'What a mess. They're taking the worst of them up to the Royal. Treating the rest in the yard in the back of the ambulances, mostly just cuts that need stitches.' He looked around. 'Murray here yet?'

McCoy shook his head. 'Straight to Pitt Street.'

'Lucky for you,' said Wattie. He paused for a minute. 'He thinks I'm an idiot, doesn't he?'

'No, he thinks you're young, which you are, and

207

he thinks you need to step up a bit. He's not that wrong, Wattie.'

Wattie nodded. 'With the baby and everything I've been a bit all over the place. Should settle down now, eh?'

McCoy nodded. He hoped so. 'You know about cars, don't you?'

Wattie nodded. 'A bit.'

'Where would I get a Daimler serviced?' asked McCoy.

'What, you won the pools, have you?' asked Wattie.

'I wish. Where?'

'There's only one Daimler dealer and garage about here. Gauld's. Corner of Mosspark Boulevard and Paisley Road West.'

'You done here?' asked McCoy.

'Think so,' said Wattie.

'Okay,' said McCoy. 'Faulds is taking over the site, least he knows what he's talking about. Forensic guys'll be ages before they've got anything concrete to tell us.'

Could still hear horns being stood on and shouts from the road behind them.

'And the traffic boys are dealing with all those noisy buggers. Not much more I can do here, to be honest.'

'Good. Let's go and look at some posh motors. This dust is driving me up the wall.'

CHAPTER 25

McCoy had no idea who in Glasgow would be in the market for a Rolls-Royce or a Bentley but there they were, all polished and shining, lined up behind the big glass windows.

'That's a Rolls-Royce Silver Phantom,' said Wattie, pointing through the showroom window. 'And that's a Corniche. Don't see many of those anywhere, never mind Glasgow.'

McCoy nodded. No real interest in anything Wattie was saying but he seemed happy, looked like a kid peering in a toy-shop window on Christmas Eve. McCoy hadn't needed Wattie to drive him, could have done it himself, but he felt a bit sorry for him. He'd really tried in the interview and McCoy didn't think he'd done that bad, wasn't sure why Murray had been so rough on him. Tried to remember if Murray had been like that with him when he was starting out. Probably had, but McCoy had never been as naive as Wattie. He'd been the opposite, in fact. Cynical, thinking the worst of everyone.

'How much are these things anyway?' he asked.

Wattie pointed at a discreet sign by a big silver car. 'Thirteen thousand pounds,' he said.

'What?' said McCoy. 'You could buy a bloody house for that!'

'Aye, but you can't drive around in a house,' said Wattie.

Both of them realised how stupid it sounded, started laughing.

'C'mon,' said McCoy. 'Let's take a closer look at the big vroom vrooms.'

McCoy supposed they didn't look very much like prospective Rolls buyers, maybe that was why the salesman walked up to them with a look like he'd a bad smell under his nose the minute they walked in.

'Can I help you, gentlemen?' he asked.

McCoy took his card out, showed him it. 'You got a Daimler in for service? Gold colour, under the name of Lindsay?'

The salesman walked over to the desk, looked at a ledger. McCoy turned to speak to Wattie and realised he was already over the other side of the showroom gawping at some big convertible. Murray was right. He did have to bloody grow up.

'We did,' said the salesman looking up. 'Daimler Majestic, 1968. Gold paintwork, red interior. Beautiful car, not the kind you see every—'

'Did?' asked McCoy.

Salesman didn't look very happy at being interrupted. 'Yes. You've just missed them, drove off about half an hour ago.'

'Shite,' said McCoy. 'Who took it?'

'It was Colonel Lindsay himself this time. He came in with a young friend. He normally just sends a driver. He was charming, told me—'

'What was being done to it?' asked McCoy.

Another interruption. Really wasn't happy this time. 'Nothing yet,' he said. 'It was booked in for a service and a deep clean tomorrow. The colonel said he needed it back urgently. Change of circumstances.'

'Did he now,' said McCoy. 'Can I use your phone? You got the registration there?'

The salesman wrote it down on a bit of paper, handed it to him, pointed at a phone on a desk by the window. 'You can use that one, on the junior's desk,' he said, as if it was all McCoy was good for.

McCoy picked it up and dialled the front desk at the station.

'Billy, it's McCoy. I'm at Fauld's. Need you to send an alert out. Need to pick up a car, a Daimler Majestic. Colour gold. Registration Alpha, November, Papa, three, six, two, Hotel.'

Listened to Billy read it back.

'That's right. And it's to do with the bomb this afternoon, so top priority, eh?'

He put the phone down, walked away and it started ringing again. He walked back, picked it up, listened.

'Got it. On my way.'

Put the phone down. Shouted.

'Wattie! Let's go!'

211

CHAPTER 26

It was getting dark by the time they got there. They could see the lights set up on the road ahead from a mile or so away. A mixture of dim spinning blue and harsh spotlights. Billy had called back immediately because the traffic police were already aware of the gold Daimler ANP 362H. It had been involved in a serious crash on the back road from Lambhill to Milngavie. Ambulances and fire engines had already been despatched.

A traffic cop directed them to pull in to a side road a couple of hundred yards from the site of the crash. Wattie parked behind a police transit and cut the engine. They got out the car just as the traffic cop came over, hand held out to shake.

'Jimmy Reed,' he said.

McCoy shook it, introduced them and they started walking up the road towards the lights.

'Got called in about an hour ago,' said Reed. 'Looks like the driver lost control somehow. They've hit a tree head-on, not a pretty sight.'

'Is he dead?' asked Wattie.

Reed shook his head. 'The driver's alive, trapped

212

in the car. The passenger is though, was thrown through the windscreen, looks like he broke his neck when he landed. Young guy as well, can't be more than twenty.'

Smell of petrol got stronger the closer they got. A loud whine started, the sound of metal on metal.

'Trying to cut the driver out,' said Reed. 'Looks like both his legs are broken. This way.'

He held a rope up, they walked through the parked fire engines and into the ring of light coming from the spotlights set up around the mangled car. McCoy wasn't sure he wanted to get much closer but he needed to make sure it was Lindsay. The whine was coming from a buzzsaw a fireman was holding to the hinge of the bent and bloody car door. He grunted, pushed the blade down harder, the whine got louder and the door dropped off, clanging onto the ground.

Suddenly McCoy could see a leg that was twisted the wrong way, ripped and blood-soaked khaki trousers. He looked away quick.

'Okay, that's him!' shouted the fireman.

A couple of ambulance guys wheeled a stretcher as close to the car as they could.

'After three,' said one of them. 'Slow and steady.'

They gathered round the car, bent over, took a hold of the driver. The fireman looked at each of them in turn. Nodded.

'Three!'

And they slowly hoisted the body out the car.

Both of the driver's legs were crushed, didn't

seem to be hanging properly. Other than that he looked okay. Just wee cuts to his face and hands from the broken windscreen. As he came into the light McCoy could see the familiar short red hair. Was Lindsay all right. He caught sight of the blood dripping off his leg, bright red in the lights, and backed away. He'd seen enough.

He walked away from the circle of light and lit up. Watched them carrying the stretcher towards the back of an ambulance, loading it in.

'Well, I never.'

He turned and Dr Purdie was standing there. Suit, tie and leather bag. McCoy was more used to seeing him at Cooper's flat, coat over pyjamas, called in the middle of the night to sew up another gang casualty to reduce his betting losses, than in a smart suit and tie. His shock must have registered.

'I live over there,' said Purdie, pointing to a driveway leading to a lit-up cottage. 'Had just got out the car when this all happened. Don't have a fag, do you? Wife doesn't let me smoke at home.'

McCoy handed him his packet and he lit up. Light from his match illuminated the dried blood on his hands.

'Thanks,' he said. 'You don't usually do traffic accidents, do you? A bit below you, are they not?'

'Depends who's driving,' said McCoy. 'Speaking of which, will he make it?'

Purdie sucked the air through his teeth. 'Think

so. Lucky I was here, he wouldn't otherwise. The right leg is pretty comprehensively crushed. Blood was pouring out of it. I managed to stop the bleeding, got a tourniquet on it fast, otherwise he would have been dead in ten minutes.' He smiled. 'Was quite exciting actually, I haven't worked in A&E for years. Think it's given me a taste for it again.'

'Can't imagine anything worse,' said McCoy.

'Yes, I know you're not keen on blood and guts. Other than the legs he seems okay. I knocked him out soon as I could before the shock wore off and the pain started. If the ambulance driver steps on it he'll be at the Royal in twenty minutes.'

Just as he said that the ambulance started accelerating up the road to Glasgow, lights and siren going. They watched it disappear round a bend in the road.

'They may have to amputate the right leg, but if that goes okay he should be fine.'

'The passenger?' asked McCoy.

'A different story, sadly,' said Purdie. 'Broken neck. Do you want to see?'

McCoy didn't, but he wanted to see who it was. 'How bad?' he asked.

Purdie smiled. 'No blood, honest. Come on.'

He led McCoy past the crushed car that mechanics were now attaching a hoist to and walked another fifty yards or so up the road. A uniform was standing next to what looked like a bundle of blankets on the road. He nodded as they approached and Purdie squatted down by one end of them.

'Ready?' he asked.

McCoy nodded and Purdie drew back the blanket. The guy who had led him back to the car from the woods on Lindsay's estate was lying there. His head was at a funny angle but other than that and the bluish bump on his forehead he looked normal. Purdie had been right. No blood. He nodded and Purdie covered him over again.

'You recognise him?' he asked.

'I've met him, don't know his name though.'

'Shame,' said Purdie. 'Just a young lad. Funny though, neither of them had any ID on them. Just like commandos in the war.'

'What?' asked McCoy.

'When they dropped them behind enemy lines, parachuted them in. Had to make sure they had no ID or family photos, anything that would help the Germans identify them.' He smiled. 'Too many war comics when I was young.' He looked down at his hands. 'Better get home and get this washed off.'

McCoy watched him walk back towards the lights. The car was on the back of a tow truck now, road would be cleared in half an hour or so, back open, just like nothing had happened. He watched Purdie shake hands with Wattie and point back at where McCoy was standing. Wattie waved and walked over. Time to get going, not much else they could do until the morning.

Soldiers in a war, thought McCoy. God help us.

17TH APRIL 1974

CHAPTER 27

'Wake up, you prick.'

McCoy sat up in bed, heart thumping. Thought he'd imagined it but then he saw the figure sitting in the chair at the end of his bed. Heart sped up even more. Knew who it was even in the dim light of the streetlights coming in through the bedroom window. He would know that heavy shape anywhere. Stevie Cooper.

'Stevie?' he asked. 'What are you doing here? How did you get in?'

'Thought you were smart today, didn't you? Sitting in that interview room, smirk on your face. Saying nothing—'

'Stevie, I—'

'Then dropping your wee bombshell.'

McCoy blinked a few times, tried to get the sleep out his eyes, couldn't see Cooper's face in the shadows, couldn't gauge how much trouble he was in. Could hear the drumming of his boot on the floorboards though. Not a good sign.

'You trying to fuck me, McCoy? Trying to stick the knife in your old pal?'

McCoy shook his head.

219

'No?' said Cooper. 'You sure? Because it feels like it.'

Cooper sat forward. Light from the window now falling on his face. He looked calm, no red in his cheeks.

'I had to do it, Stevie. It's my job. Murray would have killed me if—'

'Good old Murray, eh? What is it they say again? A dog can't serve two masters.'

'I don't serve either one of you,' said McCoy, bristling.

'Maybe so,' said Cooper.

'Look, if you're stupid enough to leave a fingerprint on that hammer what am I supposed to do? Ignore it?'

'I didn't,' said Cooper. 'Billy did.' He stood up. 'Want a cup of tea?'

Ten minutes later, McCoy, suit trousers and vest on, was sitting at his kitchen table sipping a pretty good cup of tea. Cooper opposite doing the same.

'I didn't know you could make good tea.'

'Lots you don't know, McCoy. That's your trouble, you think you know everything about everybody.'

'Billy?' asked McCoy. 'I don't get it.'

'Not yet,' said Cooper. 'Need to know something first. You on my side if I need you?'

McCoy looked at him. 'Stevie, I'm a polis—'

'Yes or no?' asked Cooper.

McCoy didn't really need to think. 'Yes,' he said. 'Happy now?'

And he was. A big grin broke over Cooper's face. It was that simple. He leant backwards, got the half-full bottle of whisky off the kitchen shelf, splashed a good measure into each mug. Held his out.

McCoy knocked it with his. 'Cheers.'

Swallowed back a mouthful of the whisky tea. Wasn't that bad.

'Okay, tell me. Billy?'

'I didn't kill Jamsie Dixon. I'm no that stupid. And I didn't go and see wee Arthur the tailor either.'

'So where did you go?' asked McCoy.

'I went to see Brian Oliver.'

McCoy looked at him blankly.

'Remember when they sent me to the Kibble after I punched Father Hannigan?'

McCoy didn't. Cooper was forever punching whoever was in charge, was hard to keep track, but he nodded anyway.

'Anyway, Brian Oliver was in there as well. Cunts stuck him in there for stealing a packet of fags from a newsagent. He's a good lad, always has been. And now he works for William Norton.'

McCoy knew William Norton well enough but he was still lost.

'When I was in Aberdeen, in the jail, Billy came up to see me.'

'I know,' said McCoy. 'He told me you were mental, ranting and raving about Jamsie Dixon.'

Cooper sat back. 'Did he now? Well, I never even

mentioned Jamsie Dixon to him, and I definitely wasn't ranting and raving. All we did was have a chat about the business, I told him I wanted some boxers, that was it. But that's not the important thing.'

'What is?' asked McCoy.

'Went back to the cell, and a new bloke's been moved in. A Glasgow guy. Malky Arnott.'

'Christ, bad luck. I've arrested him a few times. He still a dodgy wee shitebag?'

'Yep. He's a prick all right, but he says to me, I didn't know you were pals with Willie Norton. So I say I'm not and he says, well, your pal is. Tells me he was in Glasgow a couple of weeks ago, at one of Billy Chan's poker nights and Billy is there with Norton, sitting at his table, big pals.'

'Maybe it was just a night out,' said McCoy. Thought a minute. 'Hang on. Last time I saw William Norton he was walking up the path to your house, all set for a confab. What happened?'

'What happened is after ten minutes I told him to get to fuck. Old fucker thought he was still the big man, talking about what I could do for him. Was looking for a number two, not a partner. And Billy was there all the time, listening in.'

'Shite,' said McCoy. He could see where this was going.

'Dug a bit deeper, seems Norton's been at the house while I was in Aberdeen. Iris told me.'

'She hear anything?'

Cooper shook his head. 'Billy's too fly for that.

Sent her out to get the messages or to take some cash to the accountant every time he was there. So Saturday night I leave the casino and I go and see Brian Oliver. Met him in Dunbar's, no cunt ever goes in there. Tells me Billy and Norton are big pals now, talking about the future, what they're going to do.'

'Without you.'

Cooper nodded. 'Without me.'

'So bye-bye, Jamsie Dixon, you're the prime suspect and here's the hammer for proof.'

'And there's me inside for the next twenty years.'

'Christ,' said McCoy. 'I didn't think Billy had it in him.'

'He doesn't,' said Cooper. 'But Norton does and he's telling Billy he'll be his second, filling his head with all sorts of shite. Stupid cunt couldn't even get the hammer right. Lomax'll get me off.'

'Where did it come from?' asked McCoy.

'Oh, it's my hammer all right. When me and Ellie first moved into the house I used it all the time, hanging up pictures, fixing the floorboards in the wee bedroom, all sorts.'

'And Billy was helping you?'

Cooper nodded. 'Knew where to find it, knew it would have at least one fingerprint on it. Trouble was, it wasn't in blood.'

McCoy nodded. Chances of them charging Cooper with murder using the evidence from the hammer were slim, to say the least. 'So what are you going to do?'

223

'I'm going away for a couple of days,' said Cooper. 'Got some stuff to do.'

'Where are you going to go?' asked McCoy.

'You remember I told you about the Batter Squad at the prison?'

McCoy nodded.

'When they had me down and they were kicking fuck out of me I felt powerless for the first time in a long time – since we were in the basement with Father Kelly and I swore that was never going to happen to me again. That no one or nobody was going to get in my way, turn me over, fuck me about. I was going to fuck them all before they fucked me.'

He stood up.

'So that's where I'm going. To make sure it doesn't happen again.'

McCoy heard the front door shut. He walked over to the window and watched Cooper walk down the street, hands in pockets. He stood there for a while, drinking his whisky tea, watching the sun come up. Wouldn't want to be Billy Weir for all the tea in China.

CHAPTER 28

McCoy yawned. Hadn't been able to get back to sleep after Cooper left. Was too wound up, mind racing. He was regretting the whisky tea, ulcer was killing him, and now he was stuck standing outside the car pound fence watching some arse with a lab coat on taking blood samples from the smashed-up Daimler. He needed to know if Donny Stewart had been in the car after he been injured in the bomb at his flat, and he wanted to know before he went to see Lindsay at the hospital.

The arse with the lab coat hadn't been happy about being dragged out his wee hidey-hole at the labs but McCoy didn't much care. Hadn't really needed to come to the pound and watch him, but he was avoiding the station. Still hadn't spoken to Murray, and he didn't want to until he had something concrete to give him.

If he could link Donny Stewart and the bombs to Lindsay's car, he could probably get a warrant to search the big house. Try and work out what was going on with his wee private army. It was all connected, he could feel it. The boys at the barracks were the same boys at Lindsay's house, Donny Stewart, the Sons of the 51, whoever the fuck they were. He just had to find out how before another bomb went off. He looked at his watch. Half nine. Was supposed to meet Faulds at the brewery at ten.

'You done?' he shouted.

The arse in the lab coat looked up. 'Ten minutes.'

'Good,' said McCoy. 'Results on my desk by lunchtime. Top priority.'

The arse with the lab coat nodded, went back to his wee bottles, packing them in his case. Even at this distance, McCoy could see him mouthing 'wanker' under his breath.

Duke Street was open again but down to one lane. Took McCoy a while to get along it from the High Street. Temporary lights only seemed to let one car through at a time. He sat, drummed his hands on the steering wheel. Wondered where Cooper had gone. Reminded himself to call the Central Hotel if he got the blood result. Let Stewart know.

Temporary lights changed again and McCoy just made it through. Pulled into the brewery yard and parked there. Faulds was leaning against his car, puffing away. He looked up as McCoy drove in, waved. McCoy parked, got out, could still feel the crunch of powdered glass underneath his feet, and walked over.

'So Mr Bomb Expert. What are you going to tell me?'

'Bomb expert, my arse,' said Faulds. 'You're too cheap to get one of them over from Belfast.'

'True,' said McCoy. 'We've got the monkey, not the organ grinder.'

'Cheeky bastard,' said Faulds, grinning. 'Follow me.'

They walked out the yard and onto the side of the street that was still cordoned off, stood in front of the ruined building.

'As predicted, it was Co-op mix, stuff came back from the lab this morning. Quite a bit of it as well, almost five pounds, I would say. The one at the flat was much smaller, a couple of pounds at most. Cathedral even less.'

'Same person make them?' asked McCoy.

Faulds shrugged. 'Hard to say. Either the guy at the flat managed to make a few and distributed them before he accidentally blew himself up, or he taught someone else to make them. Someone less shit at it than him, presumably.'

'Fuck,' said McCoy. 'So there's going to be more?'

'Probably,' said Faulds. 'Cathedral is beginning to look like a test run for the bigger stuff. You saw their wee message? They're setting out their stall. Looks more like the beginning than the end.'

'Anything else you can tell me?' asked McCoy.

'Luckily for most of the people in the building he didn't place it very well. Think it was just on the front step, most of the blast just blew glass all over the place. If he'd put it inside the building, in a stairwell, or near a structural wall, the whole place would probably have come down, casualties would have been huge.'

'Was that deliberate or incompetent?' asked McCoy.

'Can't tell. Could have been on his way inside and panicked, just left it there. Maybe the security guy at the desk stopped him. Not sure we'll ever know.'

'Unless we find the bomber,' said McCoy. 'Or bombers, more like. Need to get them before there's another one.'

'Exactly,' said Faulds. 'How are you getting on with that?'

'Hopefully, things'll be different by the end of the day, might know a lot more. What you doing today?'

'Special Branch want to take another look at all this. Meeting two of them off the plane from London this afternoon.'

'Great,' said McCoy. 'Bastards said it wasn't worth worrying about and now they're here to make us look stupid and save the day.'

Faulds smiled. 'Mr McCoy, I'm saddened and dismayed by your attitude to our fellow officers in law.'

'Aye right,' said McCoy. Remembered. 'Oh, and who's Paul McVeigh?'

Faulds turned and looked at him, no smile on his face now. 'What are you asking me that for?'

'A pal told me to ask.'

'What pal?' asked Faulds. 'Who?'

McCoy didn't like where this was going. 'Can't remember now,' he said.

Both of them knew he was lying.

'And what else did this pal say?' asked Faulds.

'Just said you should watch yourself.'

'Is that a threat?'

'Hang on, Faulds, it wasn't me that said it and I don't even know who Paul McVeigh is, so don't fucking come at me. I thought I was doing you a favour.'

'Funny pals you've got, McCoy,' said Faulds. 'You hanging about with the 'Ra boys? That it?'

'Come on, Faulds—'

Faulds stepped closer to him, shoved his face in McCoy's, poked his finger into his shoulder. Hard. 'You better watch yourself too, McCoy. Remember what fucking side you're on.' He pushed past him, headed for his car.

'Faulds!' McCoy shouted after him. 'Come on! Come back!'

But Faulds ignored him, got in the car, slammed the door and drove off.

CHAPTER 29

Wattie was sitting at his desk when McCoy got to the station. Amongst the ringing phones and Thomson shouting the odds about someone using all the milk and the radio playing 'Waterloo' at top volume, Wattie was silently staring into space, burning cigarette in the ashtray in front of him, pile of files on the floor by his desk.

'Busy?' asked McCoy, sitting down and biting into the Chelsea bun he'd bought at City Bakeries.

Wattie blinked a couple of times. Came to. 'McCoy! Sorry, was miles away.'

'Thinking of your beautiful baby offspring?' asked McCoy, trying not to drop crumbs all over his desk.

'No, he's fine. Cries all night then smiles and giggles all day. Driving us up the bloody wall. Was just trying to think what to do next with this bloody Jamsie Dixon case.'

'Door-to-doors turn anything up?' asked McCoy.

Wattie shook his head. 'Not a sausage. Nobody saw anything, nobody heard anything.'

'Not that much of a surprise in Shettleston,' said

McCoy, rolling up the paper bakery bag and dropping it into the bin. 'Not the most polis-friendly area in Glasgow.'

'And I'm never going to get anywhere with Stevie Cooper and Lomax.'

'Nobody does. That's why Lomax earns the big bucks. He's run rings round better men than you and I,' said McCoy. Thought about saying something about Billy Weir but didn't know how to do it. 'Forensics?' he asked.

'Fuck all that helps,' said Wattie. 'I can tell you what Dixon had for dinner that night but that's not going to help anyone.'

'What was it?' asked McCoy. 'Fillet steak? Caviar? A fish supper?'

'Hang on,' said Wattie scrabbling about in his pile of files. Found one and opened it. 'Here we go. Not quite as luxurious. A hot dog, possibly two, fried onions, bread.'

McCoy sat back, thought for a minute. 'Where would Jamsie Dixon get something like that?' he asked.

'The pictures?' said Wattie. 'They sell hot dogs.'

McCoy shook his head. 'You don't get fried onions at the pictures, would stink the place out.'

'Maybe he made it?' asked Wattie.

'Jamsie Dixon?' said McCoy. 'Doubt he's been in a kitchen in—'

He stopped.

'What?' asked Wattie. 'What's up?'

'The shows,' said McCoy. 'The fair. They sell hot dogs and onions. Off a cart. You can smell it a mile off.'

'Why would Jamsie Dixon be at the shows?' asked Wattie. 'He didn't have any kids.'

'Nope,' said McCoy. 'Maybe Patsy Hearne and his pals weren't telling the whole truth about that night.'

'Your pals at the Edrom?' asked Wattie.

McCoy nodded. 'Maybe we'll go and see them later. Meanwhile, why don't you check the cafes round Jamsie's end of Shettleston. Make sure none of them were doing some hot dog special that night.'

Wattie nodded, walked off to get the Yellow Pages from the cupboard in the corridor. McCoy lit up, started going through the phone messages on his desk. Two from Stewart at the Central. Wee box ticked beside Please Call Back. A message from Pitt Street about some training thing that he was never going to reply to and a message from a Kenny Barnes from Special Branch. Could they meet up? Train was getting in at seven.

Wattie arrived back, Yellow Pages in hand, dumped them on the mess on his desk.

'Anybody looking for me from the labs?' asked McCoy. 'Arse-faced bloke?'

'Shite, sorry,' said Wattie, started searching amongst the debris on his desk. Found it. 'Called about half an hour ago. Type A negative found on back seats. Whatever the fuck that means.'

'Ya dancer!' shouted McCoy, raising his fists above his head. 'Now we're on. Fancy a trip to the hospital?'

The Royal sat at the top of the town next to the Cathedral, and just like the Cathedral it was a monumental building, all towers and grand entrances, its stone black from the centuries of smoke and dust from the factories of the nearby East End.

McCoy seemed to have spent half his working life in the place. From dragging blood-soaked drunks into A&E on a Friday night when he was on the beat to interviewing suspects in guarded rooms handcuffed to an iron bedhead.

Lindsay was in the John Slater ward, on the second floor. They got in the lift with a middle-aged woman holding a bunch of flowers in one hand and a squirming toddler in the other, and pressed the button.

'How's Mary?'

'She's persuaded her mum to take Wee Duggie three days a week. She's away into the *Record* today to see if she can go back part-time.'

'That right? And what do you think about that?' asked McCoy as they stepped out into the long, antiseptic-smelling corridor.

'I think if she wants to go back and it makes her

happy she should go back. Besides, Duggie loves his granny's. She's got a wee dog, he's all over it every time we go there. Not sure the dog'll be that happy about it, mind you.'

They found the ward and were directed to a private room by the far nurse's station. They were just about to open the door when an elderly Indian man in a white coat with a stethoscope around his neck stepped out.

'Can I help you gents?' he asked.

McCoy held out his police card. 'Looking to have a word with Mr Linsday,' he said. Looked at the badge on the man's lapel. 'Dr Basu.'

Dr Basu smiled. 'I'm afraid that is not going to be possible,' he said. 'Mr Lindsay had his leg amputated below the knee an hour ago. He'll barely be out of sedation by this evening and he needs time to recover.'

McCoy nodded. Wasn't much else he could say. If he was out of it, he was out of it. Didn't help him though.

'When can we speak to him then?'

'Tomorrow, late afternoon at the earliest. We need to step lightly.'

'He'll be all right though?' asked McCoy.

The doctor sighed. 'I would say so, but he's in his late fifties, he's been in a horrible automobile accident and he's just had a major operation. We need to keep a close eye on him. Phone tomorrow morning and I'll let you know how he's getting on.'

He said goodbye and wandered off down the corridor.

'What now?' asked Wattie.

McCoy looked at his watch. 'Too early to go and see Patsy Hearne, may as well go and rattle Meiklejohn's cage.'

CHAPTER 30

Meiklejohn was running some sort of keep-fit class when they got there. Asked them to take a seat, told them he wouldn't be long. Wattie and McCoy settled themselves on a bench at the back of the gym, leant back against the wall bars. The class was ten or so teenage boys doing various exercises. Star jumps, press-ups, that kind of thing. Was making McCoy tired just watching them.

'You ever want to join the army?' asked Wattie.

'Nope,' said McCoy. 'Police is bad enough for idiots telling you what to do, the army'd be a thousand times worse. You?'

Wattie nodded. 'Thought about it when I was at school but my dad was having none of it. Told me I wasn't going off to fight some imperialist war for a bunch of capitalist swine.'

McCoy looked at him. 'What? Call Me Ken said that?'

'Oh aye,' said Wattie. 'Card-carrying member of the Communist Party of Great Britain, my dad.'

'Who'd have thought it?' asked McCoy.

'Aye, he's a bit past it now but you should have

seen him when he was younger. Was forever organising marches against South Africa, CND, was a shop steward and all, the full shebang.'

'What did he say when you joined the polis?'

'Wasn't that happy but he said it was better than being cannon fodder for the shipyard owners.'

They watched the boys for a while, McCoy still trying to take in Call Me Ken's past. Supposed you just never knew. Meiklejohn seemed like a good teacher, the boys were laughing and joking with him, enjoying the session. He stopped a couple of them laughing at some fat lad trying to do squats, encouraged the sweating, red-faced boy to keep trying.

Maybe Wattie was right, maybe McCoy had gone too far the other way. Treating everyone as guilty before he even started. Maybe Meiklejohn was a good guy, maybe he really had bought Paul Watt the book because he thought he'd find it interesting. Meiklejohn blew a whistle, told the boys they were done, to hit the showers. McCoy stood up. Time to find out.

Five minutes later they were back in Meiklejohn's wee office. Light streaming in through the window, lighting up the wall of photographs. Meiklejohn was sweating, hair wet at his neck, exertion from the gym. He sat down, offered them tea.

'We're fine,' said McCoy.

Stood up and poured himself a pint glass of water, chugged half of it back at the sink then sat back down.

'Not as young or as fit as I used to be,' he said. 'Now, how can I help you?'

McCoy dug in his pocket, took out a photograph, handed it to him. Meiklejohn took it, looked at it then looked up. 'That's one of your lads,' said McCoy. 'As you can see by the angle, his neck is broken.'

Meiklejohn swallowed. Photo hanging loose in his hand.

'He died in a car accident yesterday afternoon. Car was being driven by Colonel Angus Lindsay. Lindsay's in hospital. Battered and broken but they think he'll live.'

'Why would you show me that photo?' asked Meiklejohn.

'Because things are getting serious,' said McCoy. 'Two young men that you knew, that came to your Terrys group, have ended up dead. Need to know exactly what's going on with you, Lindsay and your young lads.'

Meiklejohn didn't say anything.

'I went up to Knockland House, up by Dunoon. Looks to me like your lads are acting as some sort of private army for Lindsay. I recognised them from the other day, when they were painting. What's that all about?'

Meiklejohn just sat there. Face had gone white, looked like he was going to be sick or pass out.

'Okay,' said McCoy, starting to lose his temper. 'Let me make it easier for you. Are you fucking them, is Lindsay fucking them, or are you both fucking them?'

Could hear Wattie draw in his breath, rumble of traffic outside.

Meiklejohn jumped up suddenly, ran to the sink, threw up his water. Stood there shaking, gasping, waiting for it to happen again.

McCoy pressed hard. 'I'm going to make you an offer, Meiklejohn. You tell me what you know now and I'll see what I can do. If you don't we're going down the station and someone much less sympathetic than me is going to ask you about all the fourteen-year-old boys you've got hanging about.'

Meiklejohn just stood there, hands grasping the sink, face white as a sheet.

'Last chance,' said McCoy. Waited another minute. 'Okay, that's that.' Went to stand up.

Meiklejohn turned, tears in his eyes. 'You're wrong.'

'Am I?' asked McCoy. 'Well, you tell me how.'

Meiklejohn sat down. Kept his head down, staring at his sandshoes, wouldn't look at them. 'I'm not a pervert. I have no interest in teenage boys. Never have done. I'm an army instructor. I'm good at it. Good with the new recruits. I remember what it was like for me. Sent off to the army when I was sixteen. I understand what they are going through. I help them become good soldiers.' He looked up. 'But that is it.'

'Paul Watt,' said McCoy.

Meiklejohn wiped at his eyes. 'Paul Watt was a lost soul. Couldn't find his place anywhere. Wanted to enlist in the army.' He smiled. 'They would never have taken him. He had no coordination, no strength, no skills. Nothing the army was looking for, so I felt sorry for him. I bought him that book after he told me he was getting interested in Scottish history, that's it.'

He pushed his wet hair back.

'I shouldn't have done it. I know that. You have to be careful in the army. People will take one tiny thing and blow it up into something it's not. Especially when you work with youngsters. You have to be scrupulous, and I wasn't. I regret that now. But believe me, it's nothing like what you said, I promise you. Any accusation like that, no matter that it's untrue, and I'm out. I'm asking you, begging you, please don't take this any further.'

McCoy sat back. The funny thing was, he believed him. Wasn't sure why but his story seemed to ring true. And if he was being honest to himself, he had no evidence to point to anything different. Was about to do something that wasn't nice though. He needed to.

'Colonel Angus Lindsay. Tell us everything you know and we walk out of here and you never see us again.'

Meiklejohn looked at him like a whipped dog. Nodded. 'Do you know much about Lindsay?'

McCoy shook his head.

'He's an incredible soldier, served in the Second World War, Malaya, Kenya, all sorts of areas of conflict. Been decorated too many times to remember. The Highlanders was his first regiment, so when I heard he was back living in Scotland I wrote to him, asked him if he would come and give a talk to the boys. He wrote back, said he would be delighted. The boys loved him, he's a great speaker, inspirational. And I thought that was that.'

'Then?' asked McCoy.

'Then I started hearing that he'd been inviting some of the boys up to his estate. Offered to teach them fieldcraft, that sort of thing. Soon most of them were up there most weekends. And at first, I was delighted. A lot of these boys had never been outside Glasgow, I thought it was a good thing for them to be in the countryside, new experiences.' He picked his glass up off the floor, took a few sips. 'Then a few weeks ago Colin Kennedy, one of the boys, was late, missed the van taking them up there. Came here and asked me if I could drive him up, was desperate not to miss his weekend at the estate. So I said I would.'

He stopped. Pushed his hair back again.

'And when I got there I realised what was really going on. You're right. He's running some sort of private army. Different uniforms, a new command structure, total devotion to Lindsay. Was like he had brainwashed them.'

'I saw it,' said McCoy.

241

'You know what I mean then. So I confronted Lindsay, told him I thought this was all going too far.'

'And?'

'And he stood there, one of my boys either side, poker-faced in those bloody DEFENS T-shirts and he told me to get off his property immediately or he would call the police. I told him not to be ridiculous and he just nodded at the two boys and they manhandled me off the property. My lads!' He shook his head. 'I couldn't believe it. They wouldn't even acknowledge me, wouldn't even speak to me. Half of them don't come to cadets or Terrys any more. I tried to talk to my commanding officer but he said I must be exaggerating. Implied that I was just jealous that the boys had close contact with such a great soldier.'

'And was Paul Watt one?' asked McCoy.

Meiklejohn nodded. 'Fell for it hook, line and sinker. Must have felt like he had finally found a home. I tried to talk to him about it and he told me that I was irrelevant, that the British Army was a waste of time.'

'So how did someone like him end up building a bomb?' asked McCoy.

Meiklejohn shook his head. 'I have no idea. I would have thought that was way beyond Paul's abilities. Are you sure it was him?'

McCoy and Wattie left him sitting in his office, promised him things wouldn't go any further and

242

walked back to the car, McCoy thinking over what Meiklejohn had said.

'You believe him?' asked Wattie.

'I think so,' said McCoy. 'Do you?'

Wattie nodded. 'Yep.'

They got in the car and Wattie turned the engine over. McCoy lit up as they drove out the barracks yard and down towards the West End. Had a feeling in the pit of his stomach. Maybe they had all read it wrong. Maybe Paul Watt wasn't the bomb-builder after all, maybe it just went off when he was carrying it or putting it in a bag or something. Maybe they had been looking at the wrong person all along. Maybe Donny Stewart wasn't just an AWOL sailor. Maybe he was an AWOL sailor still building bombs to kill even more people.

CHAPTER 31

The fair was spread out over a good bit of Glasgow Green. Roundabouts, flying saucers, waltzers, dodgems, rows of shooting stalls, hook-a-duck games. Fact the place was mobbed wasn't helping either. Crowds of teenagers milling about eyeing each other up, looking for a fight or a winch. Wee wide-eyed kids being pulled along by their mums and dads, faces all red and sticky from candyfloss and toffee apples, balloons held in chubby hands. Each ride seemed to be playing a different tune. 'Waterloo', 'Metal Guru', 'Billy, Don't Be A Hero'. Jamsie Dixon could definitely have got his last meal here all right. The smell of frying onions and hot fat was everywhere they went, hanging over the whole fair.

McCoy and Wattie wandered around a bit dazed, looking for Patsy amongst the guys on the back of the dodgems jumping from one to another and the guys holding out air rifles telling everyone they could win a prize. Was a while before they saw him. He was on the waltzers, stepping amongst them as they whirled round, grabbing the back of the seats and spinning them, girls screaming and laughing. God knows how he didn't fall and kill himself.

They stood and watched him doing his fancy footwork and waited for the ride to end. The seats started to slow down, finally stopped and the safety bars came up, passengers walking dizzily towards the edge and the steps back to solid ground. McCoy managed to shout 'Patsy!' in the space between 'Drive-In Saturday' ending and 'Billy, Don't Be A Hero' beginning again and Patsy waved at them.

'Break's in ten, Harry!' he shouted as the new people sat down and he pushed the safety bars down.

McCoy nodded and they sat down on the edge of a closed-up kiddies' roundabout. Lit up.

'Fancy your chances?' asked Wattie, nodding over at a shooting range.

McCoy shook his head. 'No point. They're all fixed.'

'That right?' said Wattie. Sat for a second then started making clucking noises, waving his arms up and down.

McCoy shook his head. 'If you think that calling me a chicken is going to make me take you on at the shooting then you're dead right,' he said, standing up. 'Get your money out, Watson.'

By the time Patsy had finished his break and come to find them, they were a couple of quid down each and Wattie had a bright yellow teddy bear stuck under his arm and a big grin on his face.

Patsy nodded at the bear. 'Don't tell me you lads are here to play at being cowboys?'

McCoy shook his head. 'Need a word, Patsy. Somewhere we can go?'

Patsy led them round the back of the shows, down by the river. There were ten or so caravans parked in a sort of circle. They walked into it and Patsy pulled the door on a white and silver caravan and held it open.

'This is Tommy's, he'll no mind us using it for a wee while. His missus is on the ducks, be empty.'

Wattie and McCoy stepped inside and looked around. If ever the expression 'it was like a wee palace' was to be used, this was the time. The caravan was immaculate. Brown plush seating, carpets and curtains to match, animal ornaments lining the windowsills. A coffee table in the middle with a big vase of artificial flowers in the middle. Not a thing out of place.

'Sit down, lads,' said Patsy, pointing at one of the padded benches. They did and Patsy sat on the one opposite, leant forward and opened a drawer in the coffee table, pulled out an onyx ashtray.

'What can I do you for?' he asked, lighting up.

'You don't seem that surprised to see us,' said McCoy.

Patsy smiled. 'People like us get used to the polis coming to visit.'

'That what we are now? The polis?' said McCoy.

Patsy shrugged. 'Well, it doesn't feel like you're here to have that wee drink we were talking about, does it?'

'Okay,' said McCoy. 'Jamsie Dixon. You didn't just see him at the pub the night he got killed, did you? He was here that night.'

'How do you know that?' asked Patsy, looking surprised.

'Like you said,' said McCoy. 'We're the polis. What was he doing here?'

Patsy sighed. 'He was here to collect.'

'Collect what?'

'What do you think? Money.'

'What for?' asked McCoy.

'To make sure these caravans don't mysteriously go up in flames in the middle of the night or the rides get vandalised. I'd done the collection from everyone, gathered up the money. This is a good time for us, we make good money this time of the year. Couldn't afford to close down if the rides got nobbled, so we decide to pay.'

'Who was he collecting for?' asked McCoy.

Patsy shrugged. 'Don't know. Just told us what would happen if we didn't pay.'

'And you believed him?' asked McCoy.

'Course I believed him,' said Patsy. 'You know what Jamsie Dixon was like. He made his money hurting people, smashing things up. Plus, just in case we weren't sure, the kiddies' roundabout, the one you were sitting on earlier on, got done over the night he asked us. Power cables cut. Sugar in the tank.'

'Why didn't you tell me?' asked McCoy.

Patsy laughed. 'You're okay, McCoy, but every other polis I've ever dealt with has treated us like scum. Lying, thieving gypsies, that's us. We're first in the line to blame. Steal the sweets from your kid's mouth. Was easier to not tell you.' He nodded over at Wattie. 'I don't know him. Less he knows about our business the better.'

'Thanks,' said Wattie.

'No offence but that's the way it is, pal. Can't be too careful.'

'You sure you had nothing to do with his death?' asked McCoy.

Patsy crossed himself. 'As I live and breathe.'

'If you're lying, Patsy, I'll find out and I'll be back,' said McCoy. 'And I won't be friendly.'

Patsy nodded, and Wattie and McCoy stood up to go.

'You got a young one?' asked Patsy, pointing to the teddy under Wattie's arm.

Wattie nodded. 'Wee boy.'

'Well, for fuck sake don't give him that. We get them from China, twenty for a quid. It's got staples and pins holding it together, bloody dangerous.'

They stepped out the caravan back into the noise and the smells of the shows. Wattie dropped the teddy in the first bin they passed.

'Glad he told me,' he said. 'Mary would have killed me. Where we off to now?'

'Think you're done for the day. Away home and see the baby.'

'What you going to do?' asked Wattie.

'You can drop me in town. Got to see some guy from Special Branch. Lucky me.'

CHAPTER 32

Kenny Barnes was small for a polis, wiry. Curly brown hair. Had a brown pinstripe suit on, brown shirt and a dark green tie. McCoy had assumed he would be coming from London but he'd come off the Manchester train, Adidas sports bag in one hand, wee cigar in the other.

'All right, mate?' he asked, walking up to McCoy. He was London through and through. 'Bloody cafe on the train was closed, I'm dying for a drink. Mouth's like the bottom of a bloody budgie's cage. Where we off to?'

McCoy pointed along Waterloo Street. 'Place along here, the Admiral, does a decent pint.'

Barnes nodded and they walked along the street, Barnes puffing on his cigar.

'You in Manchester?' asked McCoy.

Barnes nodded. 'For my sins. You ever been there? Fucking shithole. Full of Mancs apart from anything else.'

Funny that, thought McCoy. 'Just here,' he said and pulled the door of the Admiral open.

The familiar smell of beer and cigarette smoke

hit them, chatter of drinkers. As always, the Admiral was a mixture of office workers having a drink before heading home, train passengers, the occasional regular.

Barnes found a table by the side wall and McCoy went up to the bar. Wasn't looking forward to the night at all. In his experience, Special Branch really did think they were something special, a cut above a normal polis, and they weren't afraid to let you know it. Barnes didn't seem likely to be any different. A know-it-all wide boy, all mouth and trousers. The barman put the pints on the counter and McCoy took them over to the table, wondered how little time he could get away with spending with Barnes and his stinking cigar.

'Cheers, mate,' said Barnes, taking a sip. 'Needed that.'

'What were you doing in Manchester?' asked McCoy, trying to make conversation.

'This and that,' said Barnes.

Fair enough, thought McCoy. If Barnes thought his work was too important to discuss with someone like him, it meant he would be out of here quicker.

Barnes got the packet of Hamlet out his pocket, took one out, and started to unwrap the cellophane around the wee cigar.

'So,' said McCoy. 'Sure you know most of this already but I'll go over it. There's been three bombs so far. One that went off in a flat, killing the presumed bomb-maker, and one that was put inside the Cathedral. Biggest was planted at the entrance of the Tennent's Caledonian Brewery. Killed three people and injured many more. We got a message from a group calling—'

He stopped. Realised Barnes was sitting back in his chair, grinning at him.

'What is it?' asked McCoy.

Barnes took a drag on his cigar, blew out thick heavy smoke and fanned it away from his face. 'I don't give a fuck about some nutter blowing up a brewery. Couldn't give a shit, mate. The more of you jocks blowing each other up the better.' He sat forward, looked McCoy in the eye. 'What I really want to know is why you are passing threatening messages from the IRA to a fellow police officer.'

McCoy sat back in his chair. Hadn't been expecting that. And no way was he rolling over for this wee shite. Decided to take the offensive.

'Who is Paul McVeigh?' he asked.

'Paul McVeigh was a nasty little IRA cunt.'

'Was?'

'Yep,' said Barnes. 'Dead as a doornail now. Fucker got what was coming to him. Although you might not see it that way, eh, mate?'

'What are you doing here, Barnes?' asked McCoy.

'I thought I'd covered that, made it plain. Maybe not, so I'll say it again. I'm here to ask you why the fuck you're delivering the IRA's threats for them. And you still haven't told me.'

'I never delivered anything for anybody,' said McCoy.

'Not what Faulds says. Says you told him to watch himself.' Another cloud of cigar smoke. 'Now how would you know to tell him that?'

McCoy suddenly had the feeling he was in trouble, proper trouble.

Barnes sighed. 'You've got previous, mate, this isn't the first time we've had a wee look at you and your Taig pals. Last year you went all the way to Belfast to attend the funeral of Seamus Cooper, a well-known member of the provisional IRA West Belfast Division. The Big Boys. Even went to the wake to show your respects. Joined in with a nice rendition of "The Men Behind The Wire", I heard. Now, why would you be at a thing like that?'

'Family friend,' said McCoy. 'Nothing more. And I didn't.'

'No, he wasn't,' said Barnes. 'You're a fucking liar. You don't even have a family, just a doolally mum in the nuthouse. Mind you, you're quite fond of telling porkies, aren't you, McCoy? Told Faulds you couldn't remember who told you about Paul McVeigh, didn't you?'

McCoy didn't say anything.

Barnes leant forward. 'Didn't you?'

McCoy nodded.

'So that's you then, McCoy. Call yourself a policeman, a copper, but all you are is a lying IRA-supporting traitor. And now you're taking the piss, aren't you?'

McCoy took a swig of his pint. His mouth had gone dry with fear.

'What?' said Barnes. 'You think I don't know who told you?' He shook his head. 'I've got your number all right, McCoy. Now go and get me another drink before I decide to liven up the evening by beating the shit out of you.'

McCoy got up, headed for the bar. Realised his hands were shaking. Ordered two pints and a double whisky. Chucked the whisky over before he went back to the table. Barnes was sitting there, grin on his face, when he put the pints down.

'You're fucked, McCoy,' he said. 'I could turn you inside out. Maybe I'll fly you into Aldergrove, turn you over to the Special Boat Service, let them take you a wee trip in an unmarked helicopter to Black Rock, let them do what they do best. Break traitor cunts like you. Because that's all you deserve.'

'You've got this all wrong,' said McCoy. 'I don't know anything about the IRA and Paul McVeigh. Faulds is a pal. I was only trying to help, tell him to watch out for himself.'

Realised how stupid he sounded. He wouldn't believe him if he was Barnes. Didn't know what else to do.

'You know what I think about that?' asked Barnes. 'I think it's a load of shit. There's only one way out of this for you, McCoy.'

'What's that?' he asked.

Barnes smiled. 'It's simple. You go back to your

pal Cooper and you find out everything he knows about Paul McVeigh and you come and tell me.'

'I don't think Cooper knows anything, he's not—'

Stopped. Realised Barnes was holding his finger up to his mouth. 'Ssh . . . I don't want to hear your fucking excuses. Get information out of Cooper or you're finished. You not read the paper? You and your friends are setting off bombs in London and Birmingham. Not nice, you've got people scared. The judiciary take a very dim view of the IRA these days, and chances are they'll take an even dimmer view of a police officer who's doing their dirty work for them. They'll put you away for years. Years. Do you understand exactly what I'm telling you?'

McCoy nodded.

'Yes, Mr Barnes. I understand,' said Barnes. 'Say it.'

'Yes, Mr Barnes. I understand,' said McCoy, feeling helpless.

Barnes stood up. 'Don't know what it is but threatening people always makes me fucking randy. You're lucky you're not my type. So where do I go to find some tart with big tits that likes it up the shitter?'

'Blythswood Square,' said McCoy. 'Up the hill.'

Barnes walked out of the pub, smell of cheap cigar smoke trailing behind him.

McCoy sat there for half an hour or so, drinking, trying to calm down. Of all the things he'd done that could have got him in trouble, speaking to Faulds was the last thing he'd expected would. He'd thought he was doing Faulds a favour, not condemning himself to a life as a tout. Wasn't going to work anyway. Cooper had no interest in the IRA, wasn't his thing. He didn't know anything about what the IRA was up to, and he didn't care.

Whatever way he looked at it he was fucked. Barnes was bad enough and smart enough to make a couple of coincidences seem like something a lot more sinister, and he had no doubt he would do it if he didn't come up with the goods.

Maybe he should talk to Faulds. Though maybe Faulds wouldn't even talk to him if he thought he was some sort of IRA sympathiser. He couldn't go to Murray. Maybe he could ask Cooper to ask his uncles about something, find something out that he could hand over. But he knew that wouldn't be the end of it, that wasn't how it worked. Once they had you they just made you do more and more.

More he thought about it he realised he had to speak to Faulds somehow. He'd obviously told some contact in Special Branch just after McCoy had spoken to him. How come Faulds had a hotline to Special Branch? Maybe Cooper was right, maybe Faulds had been more than just an ordinary copper in Belfast. McCoy knew one thing: his only hope was to try and find out.

18TH APRIL 1974

CHAPTER 33

McCoy didn't sleep much. Faulds and Barnes going round in his head all night. He gave up about six and made a cup of tea, watched the sun rising over the cranes at the bottom of the street. Decided to make a list of what he had to do that day.

> Find Faulds and get that out the way.
> <u>BOMBS!</u>
> Speak to Stewart, check if Lindsay is awake.
> Possible next targets? Other breweries in town?

He put the pen down, sat at the kitchen table staring into space. He didn't know what was going on with Lindsay and Donny Stewart. Didn't know what was going on with the bombs. Didn't know what Cooper was up to either, whether he'd killed Jamsie Dixon or not. And his stomach hurt.

And then it struck him. If Patsy and the showpeople had paid Jamsie Dixon that night, where was the money? He didn't have it on him when they found him, had a wallet but no money in it. Maybe Patsy still wasn't telling the whole truth, maybe they'd paid him then waited for him in the back court, killed him and taken it back. Made some sort of sense, but if that was what had happened how come Cooper was so sure Billy had done it? Still wasn't quite sure that Cooper hadn't done it himself. For a murder that had no suspects to start with, there seemed to be an awful lot of them now.

He was going to have to leave Wattie to it for the next couple of days. No one involved with Jamsie Dixon was going anywhere and he needed to deal with Faulds and Lindsay, and quick. He finished his tea, rinsed the mug at the sink, put his shirt and shoes on. Put the bottle of Pepto-Bismol he'd bought in his pocket and headed out.

Gardner Street was quiet, not many people up and about yet. He walked down the hill. The sun had some heat in it these days. Definitely spring now. He bought a packet of Embassy from the wee shop on the corner of Dumbarton Road, managed to get a taxi that was dropping someone off at Partick Station. Asked the driver to take him to Tobago Street.

He'd been stationed at Eastern when he'd first started. Hated it. Station was full of backhanders and look-the-other-way types, worst of all being his assigned partner, Bernie Raeburn. Was a private eye now. No doubt he was as useless at that as he was at being a polis. He lit up, sat back in his seat, watching Glasgow go by in the sunshine, wondering what he was going to say to Faulds. They'd been quite good pals before he'd moved to Belfast, thought they still were. Thought he'd have talked to him if there was a problem rather than go running to Special Branch. Just showed how wrong you could be, he supposed.

Taxi stopped in Tobago Street and he stepped out, looked up at his old station. The building was starting to look like it was on its last legs, been rumours it was going to be shut down for years. He for one wouldn't be sad to see it go. He was just about to open the door when it swung open and Callum his old desk sergeant was standing there.

'All right, Callum?' asked McCoy.

He wasn't expecting much but an answer would have been nice. None was forthcoming. Callum just looked at him with contempt.

'You've got a cheek showing your face here, McCoy,' he said. 'What do you want?'

'Just looking for Faulds,' he said. Couldn't even be bothered rising to the bait. Callum was one of the worst of them, had a nice big house in Bishopbriggs that he couldn't have afforded on a polis salary in a million years.

'He went down to London Road ten minutes ago,' said Callum. 'Said he was going to get something to eat.'

McCoy was about to say thanks but Callum had already pulled the door shut.

Seemed like everyone had it in for him just now, thought McCoy as he walked down to London Road. Callum wasn't even in the running. If he knew Faulds, he'd be looking for a fry-up, which meant one place round here. The Milk Churn. As far as McCoy was concerned the Milk Churn had been the only good thing about serving at Eastern. It was a wee cafe that used to be a dairy, now it served soup, sandwiches and a great fry-up. Run by two sisters, open all day, every day.

Turned out McCoy was right. As he approached he could see Faulds sitting at the table in the window. He'd the *Daily Record* sports pages in front of him propped up on the sauce bottles, half-eaten plate of all-day breakfast in front of him. He was lifting a bit of toast up to his mouth when he looked out and saw McCoy across the street. McCoy waved but Faulds didn't wave back. Just put the toast down and waited for him to come in.

'Need a word, Hughie,' said McCoy, sitting down.

Faulds just looked at him. 'I've got nothing to say to you,' he said, went back to his paper.

'Harry! No seen you for ages.' McCoy turned and Lena, one of the sisters, was standing by the table. 'Cup of tea, milk, two sugars?' she asked.

McCoy nodded, waited until she walked back behind the counter before he started again.

'Just listen to me, Faulds. Your pal Barnes seems to think I'm some sort of fucking IRA boy and he's threatened me with everything under the sun if I don't get him info on what they're up to. I've got as much chance of doing that as I have of flapping my arms and flying to the fucking moon. So do you want to tell me what the fuck is going on?'

Faulds looked at him.

'Hughie, for fuck sake!' said McCoy. 'Help me. Please.'

Faulds thought for a few seconds. Nodded. 'Not here. Have your cup of tea, meet me down on Glasgow Green, on the wee suspension bridge in ten minutes.'

McCoy was about to ask him who he thought he was – James bloody Bond? But Faulds had already gone. His tea arrived and he picked a rasher of bacon off Faulds's plate and put it in his mouth. Wondered what he'd got himself into this time.

Faulds was standing in the middle of the bridge, leaning on the rail, looking down at the water. Behind him, the last few Gorbals tenements still standing were marooned in a sea of dusty ground and rubble.

'Sorry about this,' he said as McCoy approached. 'Didn't want anyone from the station turning up.'

Held out his hand to shake. McCoy took it, not quite sure what was going on.

'I'm sorry about the other day,' said Faulds. 'You gave me a shock, I didn't react too well.'

263

'That's okay,' said McCoy. 'I was only trying to warn you to watch out for yourself.'

Faulds nodded. Closer McCoy looked at him he realised he'd lost weight, had dark circles under his eyes. Didn't look good. Looked like a worried man.

'So who was Paul McVeigh?' he asked.

Faulds took a breath. Started.

'Paul McVeigh was a bastard, a right dangerous bastard. High up in the Belfast Brigade. Was internal security. Decided who hadn't been toeing the line, who was an informer and what'd get done to them. He was a one-man judge and jury and he enjoyed his work a bit too much. Always happy to batter someone, or arrange a kneecapping or worse.'

He got his fags out, offered McCoy one, lit up.

'When I was still in Belfast I got told by a tout that he was going to see some young lad they'd accused of passing info on to the army. Was going to tell him when and where to turn up for the kangaroo court.'

'What?' asked McCoy.

'That's the way they do it,' said Faulds. 'Tell you when and where it's going to happen, make sure it's a week or so ahead so you worry yourself to death before the actual thing.'

'Nice,' said McCoy.

'Anyway, the army were looking to pick McVeigh up, hadn't been able to find him, so I told them what the tout had told me. That he was going to be in Beechmount Drive at eight o'clock. Thought that was the end of it.'

'But it wasn't,' said McCoy.

Faulds shook his head. 'That night I got called to a domestic in Clowney Street just around the corner. Usual couple screaming at each other, both of them pissed. I finished there about ten to eight so I thought I'd walk around the corner, see what happened. I get there and there's no army presence, no pigs, no soldiers on the street. Must all be hiding, I think, waiting for the big moment. So I stand at the end of the street, in by the lane that goes behind the houses and I wait. It's just about eight now and I'm wondering what's going on. Still nobody. Then I see McVeigh coming down the street, bold as brass. Just as he does, a white Granada comes screaming round the corner and stops, a guy jumps out, plainclothes, long hair, and he braces, takes a two-handed grip on a revolver and shoots McVeigh in the head. Then he runs over, takes another gun out his jacket, puts it in McVeigh's hand and fires it at the ground. Leaves it there in McVeigh's hand, runs back to the car and they're off, scream round the corner and they're gone. Whole thing took maybe a minute at most. Next thing the street's full of pigs drawing up and army boys getting out all round McVeigh. I don't know what the fuck's going on so I just turn and go.'

He stopped, watched the rowers getting into the boats outside the boathouse for a minute, dropped the last of his fag in the river.

'Funny thing is, the guy that shot him? I heard him shouting at the guys in the car to get going. He was English, posh. Sounded like one of the Sandhurst boys they send over every so often. And sure enough the next day I get a visit from another posh bloke. Says he's British Security. Tells me I was seen at Beechmount Drive. Won't tell me by who. Asks me what I saw so I tell him and he says I'm mistaken. Tells me McVeigh shot at an army patrol first and they returned fire. Looks at me. Asks me again what I saw so I tell him I saw McVeigh shoot at an army patrol and they returned fire. And he smiles and he pats my back and he says as long as that's what I saw I have nothing to worry about.'

'Who was he?' asked McCoy.

Faulds shrugged. 'Don't know who he was but I have my suspicions.'

'And?'

'Been rumours for a while that there's a secret army division in Northern Ireland. Top army blokes but all plainclothes, living off the base. Doing stuff they don't have to account for or explain.' Faulds smiled. 'You ask anyone official though and they don't exist. Never have done, never will do.'

'Christ,' said McCoy.

'Two days later my car blows up while I'm still in the house, tilt switch must have been faulty they said. Turns out the IRA think I led the army unit to McVeigh. And I'm enemy number one. So

I put in a request to come back here and I got a Special Branch contact to check in with.'

'Barnes?'

'Barnes,' said Faulds.

'So when I told you that—'

'I lost it. Called him. I was terrified. Wish I hadn't.'

'And now we're both fucked,' said McCoy.

'I'm sorry, Harry, I just panicked. I'm scared all the time. I'm a witness to a cold-blooded murder and the boys that did it won't like that. Suddenly your car brakes don't work, you get knocked down crossing the road. I've got a wife, two kids . . .' Faulds was shaking now, had tears in his eyes. He wiped them away, lit up again. 'I don't know what to do. Either the IRA are going to kill me for setting up McVeigh or the army boys are going to find a way to make sure I don't ever tell anyone what I saw.' He tried to smile. 'So now both of us are fucked.'

McCoy shook his head. 'No, we're not. We're going to sort it out,' he said. 'Fuck knows how but we will, okay?'

Faulds nodded. 'Okay.'

McCoy left him and walked back along the bridge towards Glasgow Green. The Green was packed. Kids were running about, people walking dogs, some wee girls playing ropes. Patsy and his pals were starting to set up the shows for the night. Everything as normal.

He walked around the fair, stopped by the obelisk and lit up. Tried not to think about the fact he had absolutely no idea how he was going to get Faulds, never mind himself, out of the shit they were in.

CHAPTER 34

Lindsay was next on his list. Twenty-minute walk up the High Street and he was at the Royal. Dr Basu smiled when he saw McCoy walking towards him along the hospital corridor. Waved.

'Mr McCoy! I was just about to call you,' he said. 'Mr Lindsay is awake.'

'Great,' said McCoy. 'How is he?'

Basu smiled again. 'Surprisingly chipper given his circumstances, was eating a bowl of cornflakes when I left him. Excellent recovery.'

'So I can interview him?' asked McCoy.

'I don't see why not,' said Basu, taking the stethoscope off his neck and stuffing it into his pocket. 'Good luck!'

McCoy pushed the door of the private room open and went in. Lindsay was sitting up in bed, empty cornflakes bowl on the locker beside him. He had little metal-rimmed specs on, was reading a copy of *The Times*. He wasn't the only person there. There was a young guy, looked about eighteen, sitting in a chair by the window. Muscles, short hair, army boots, khaki trousers,

DEFENS T-shirt. Lindsay looked up, took his glasses off.

'McCoy, wasn't it?' he said.

McCoy nodded, pulled a chair towards the bed, and sat down. The young guy didn't even acknowledge his presence. Just stared at him.

'Who's your pal?' asked McCoy, nodding at the young man.

'Crawford,' said Lindsay. 'Keeping me company.'

'Looks like a bodyguard,' said McCoy.

Lindsay smiled. 'He's an army cadet. They emphasise physical fitness.'

'How are you feeling?' McCoy asked.

'Well, apart from the fact they've taken most of my right leg off, I'm fine,' said Lindsay. 'Car's a write-off, I'm afraid.'

'So was the passenger,' said McCoy.

'Yes, of course, extremely unfortunate. I lost control. A fox ran across the road and startled me.'

'I thought your car was in to get serviced?' asked McCoy. 'Deep cleaned as well. Why were you so anxious to get it back before they'd even done the job?'

Lindsay didn't say anything, for the first time he seemed less than in control.

'Circumstances changed,' he said. 'I needed the car.'

'For what?' asked McCoy.

'To drive,' he said. 'Is there a particular reason for this visit?'

'Donny Stewart. You sure he's not one of your boys?'

'Who?' asked Lindsay. 'Ah, the boy you showed me the photograph of, the American. As I told you the other day, I don't know anything about him.'

'That's funny,' said McCoy. 'Because his blood was all over the back seat of your car. The car you were so anxious to get back. If only you hadn't crashed it you could have cleaned it back at the house before anyone could take a look at it.'

'Really?' said Lindsay. 'Maybe you should talk to my sister then, she and her waifs and strays have been using the car for months. Maybe they know this, what was it again, Donny Stewart?'

McCoy sat back in his chair, could hear the traffic on Castle Street below the open window. The trouble was, Lindsay had a point. Or a get-out clause at least. Was nothing to prove the blood in the car happened when Lindsay was driving it. Time to try a different tack.

'Why would a man like you need a private army?' he asked.

'A what?' asked Lindsay, looking incredulous.

McCoy nodded over at the lad sitting in the chair. 'All those lads you surround yourself with up at the big house, all dressed the same, all doing what you tell them. What would you call it then?'

'I'd call it teaching fieldcraft,' said Lindsay. 'And the uniforms are because the uniforms they have at the cadets are army property and are not meant to be taken off army property. Why don't you ask Crawford?'

'He speaks, does he?' asked McCoy.

Lindsay nodded.

McCoy turned to Crawford. 'Okay then, why don't you tell me what this is all about?'

Crawford smiled, no warmth in it. 'Colonel Lindsay has been kind enough to teach us field-craft on his grounds. How to make bivouacs, survive on what you can forage and hunt.'

'Very useful in Maryhill, I'm sure,' said McCoy.

Crawford smiled again. Even less warmth. 'Meiklejohn won't allow us to take the uniforms up there so Colonel Lindsay has been kind enough to supply appropriate clothing.'

'And you do everything he says, that it?'

'Colonel Lindsay has never asked me to do anything,' said Crawford. 'I've no idea why you think it's some kind of army.'

'Well, I'll say something for you, Lindsay,' said McCoy. 'You've got him well trained, I'll give you that. If you said jump in the river I think he'd do it.'

'If that's all . . .' said Lindsay, picking up his paper. 'I'm feeling a bit tired.'

McCoy stood up, left the room. In the corridor he cursed under his breath. Couldn't lie to himself. Round one had gone to Lindsay.

CHAPTER 35

The trip to Memen Road was a waste of time. Cooper wasn't there. His boys in the street hadn't seen him, didn't know where he was. Hadn't seen Jumbo either, or Billy. Nobody seemed to know anything. McCoy left them to it, walked back towards his car parked on Ashgill Road. Got in. There was one person who always seemed to know what was going on. Worth a try.

McCoy walked up the path of Cooper's big house in West End. He rang the bell and waited, was just about to turn and go when it opened and Iris was standing there. Usual smart suit and blood-red lipstick. For once she didn't just keep him standing on the doorstep. Held the door wide. 'You coming in?'

Things must be bad, thought McCoy as he followed her down the stairs into the kitchen. Iris being nice to him was practically unheard of. Normally she took every opportunity to look down her nose at him.

McCoy sat down at the kitchen table and Iris started making tea. The French doors were open, the garden looked immaculate, as usual.

'Jumbo still doing his green fingers act?' he asked.

'You just missed him,' she said. 'Came round to make sure the clematis was doing okay.'

'Which one is the clematis?' asked McCoy.

'God knows,' said Iris. 'I just let him blabber on and nod occasionally. Keeps him happy.'

'So he's not here then, I take it?' said McCoy. 'Cooper?'

'Nope. He's gone to that boxing gym place off Duke Street with some American fella. They only stopped by here so he could pick up some clothes.'

'Andy Stewart?' asked McCoy.

Iris nodded, put the mugs down on the table. 'That's him, he's in the army or something. Nice big fella, very polite.'

'Oh aye,' said McCoy. 'Got your eye on him, have you?'

Iris didn't rise to it, didn't say anything, just stirred her tea then looked up at him. 'You know what's going on?'

McCoy wasn't quite sure if it was a question or a statement. 'With Cooper?'

'No, with the bloody King of Siam. Aye, with Cooper. He's no staying here, disappeared from Memen Road for a couple of days, Billy looking everywhere for him. Then he waltzes in this morning with that American fella, all smiles and jokes, says he's going to go and have a look at his boxers. Told him Billy was looking for him, didn't seem to care. Tells me to get Jumbo to come and see him at Memen Road.'

McCoy decided to tread carefully. 'Maybe he's just having a hard time getting used to being out. What's Billy saying to it?'

'Hardly seen him either,' said Iris.

'Why not?' asked McCoy.

Iris didn't say anything. Seemed like both of them half knew something, both of them too scared to say it in case it gave them away.

'Something you want to tell me?' asked McCoy. 'Anybody been here that shouldn't?'

She looked at him. Could sense her deciding whether to speak or not.

''Cause if there is, now would be a good time to do it,' said McCoy.

'And what would I have to say to you?' she asked.

'You tell me,' said McCoy evenly. 'But you know as well as I do that Stevie Cooper only cares about one thing. Loyalty. That's all he's ever cared about, even since we were wee boys.'

Iris went to speak, then stopped herself. She stood up, picked up a denim jacket hanging over one of the kitchen chairs, handed it to McCoy.

'He forgot this. If you're going to the boxing place you can give it to him.'

McCoy stood up, took the jacket from her. 'That it?'

Iris nodded.

McCoy walked back up the stairs and back out

onto the sunny street. Was more puzzled now than he was before. That dance with Iris hadn't got him anywhere. Was she in cahoots with Billy? Did Iris care that much at her age? Did she want to hitch her wagon to Billy? Maybe she just saw which way the wind was blowing and made her decision. After all, was a good chance her and Billy thought Cooper would be in jail by now. What were they going to do now? Someone like William Norton would be anxious to seal the deal, get rid of Cooper another way.

He'd known Iris for years, knew her back when she was still working the hotels, before she started working for Cooper, and the funny thing was that in all that time he'd never seen her look like she did when he'd asked her if she had anything to say to him. She'd looked scared.

CHAPTER 36

Was just about the last thing McCoy expected to see when he walked into Morrison's gym. Andy Stewart was dancing about the ring, dressed in shorts and a vest, practice gloves on, sandy hair sticking to his head with sweat. He was huffing and puffing a bit but he was moving fast, jabbing and diving around some young guy with a head guard on. You could see the remains of a boxer's body on him. Heavy shoulders, big arms. Looked like he could still take care of himself all right.

McCoy watched them for a while. Wondered if he'd have made much of a boxer himself. Doubted it. Too clumsy, not athletic enough. Besides, he'd never seen the great attraction in getting punched in the face for a living. And he'd seen too many ex-boxers down by the grates, noses flattened against their faces, brains scrambled from the pain of too many punches, and all the red biddy drunk to try and take it away.

He was just wondering where Cooper was when his head appeared between two old guys watching the bout from on the other side of the ring, big

277

grin on his face. Cupped his hands to his mouth. Shouted.

'Batter him, Chris!' followed by 'Wallop the big bastard!'

McCoy couldn't believe it. Him and Stewart were like big kids in the playground. He walked round the ring, squeezed in next to Cooper. Shouted in his ear to make himself heard above the shouts and slaps.

'Are you out your mind?' he shouted. 'He's going to have a bloody heart attack, he's forty-odd.'

'McCoy!' shouted Cooper, looking happy to see him, grabbing him in a bear hug. 'We've been talking about you.'

He put the whistle hanging around his neck into his mouth and blew it hard. The boxers stopped, hugged each other. Stewart stood for a minute hands on knees, breathing heavy, big smile on his face.

'Any news about Donny?' he asked, rubbing at his head with a towel.

'Maybe,' said McCoy. 'Need to ask you a few questions.'

'Great,' said Stewart. 'Knew you'd come through. Give me five minutes to take a shower.'

McCoy nodded and Stewart hurried off towards the dressing rooms. He turned to Cooper. 'Need to talk to you too.'

'Sounds serious,' said Cooper.

'It is,' said McCoy.

They sat on a bench at the back of the gym

under a big poster advertising Watt vs Riley. The ring was full of wee boys now, an elderly man taking them through their stances, all of them following him, trying their best. McCoy still couldn't get used to the stink of the place, all old sweat, bleach and Ralgex. Got his fags out and lit one to cover it up.

'Where'd you go on your travels?' asked McCoy, waving his match out.

'Away,' said Cooper.

'That it?'

'You don't need to know everything I do, McCoy,' said Cooper. 'You're no my mammy.'

'No, but she told me to give you this,' said McCoy, handing over the jacket.

'Christ, imagine Iris as your maw,' said Cooper. 'Think I'd rather be in the home.'

'She's fond of you, you know.'

'Fond of the money I pay her, more like.'

'You think she'd give it all up, you, the money, pretending she lives in a big house in the West End, to throw her lot in with Billy?' asked McCoy.

Cooper shrugged. 'Soon find out. Her choice to make.'

'Speaking of Billy, where's he got to? I've not seen him and neither had Iris.'

'A wee birdie told me he's lying low at Norton's. No doubt the both of them wondering what to do about me now that I'm no in the jail and their wee plan has gone off the rails.'

'You worried?'

Cooper laughed. 'Minute I'm worried about those two pricks is the minute I give it all up and retire to a wee caravan at Girvan.'

McCoy wasn't sure how much was bluff, but Cooper seemed like he knew what he was doing, had a plan.

'So what did you want to talk to me about?' asked Cooper.

'Paul McVeigh,' said McCoy. 'Who told you about him and Faulds?'

Cooper looked at him, eyebrows raised. 'Why'd you want to know that? It's bugger all to do with you, McCoy.'

'Aye, well, turns out it is. I've got some wee Special Branch prick thinking I'm the big IRA man because I asked Faulds. That one I'll need to work out myself, but Faulds didn't have anything to do with Paul McVeigh being killed. Your pals are after the wrong man. Need you to call them off.'

Cooper laughed.

'What, Faulds told you that, did he? Now there's a surprise. Mind you, I'd do the same thing if I had the Belfast Brigade coming after me. I'd tell anyone anything. Those boys don't fuck about, believe me.'

'I believe him,' said McCoy.

'Oh, well, that's okay then. I'll just tell the 'Ra boys to back off because Harry McCoy's decided his pal Faulds is innocent. Easy. Consider it done. Anything else I can do for you, Mr McCoy?'

McCoy sighed. 'I mean it, Cooper. I really don't think he had anything to do with it. It was the army.'

'What?' asked Cooper.

'British bad boys. Some kind of rogue army guys. Your pals back in Belfast'll know who they are all right. Will you tell them?'

Cooper sat back, dug his fags out his denim jacket pocket, pulled them out and a train ticket fell to the floor. He put his foot over it, picked it up and stuffed it back in his pocket. 'I might,' he said. 'And if I do I'll need you to do something for me.'

'What's that then?' asked McCoy warily.

'Need you to arrest Jumbo,' said Cooper.

McCoy hadn't been expecting that. 'What?' he asked. 'Jumbo? What for?'

'Because I said,' said Cooper. 'Okay?' Flash of anger in his eyes. 'Need you to get him off the streets for a night. That's the deal, take it or leave it.'

'You going to tell me why?' asked McCoy.

Cooper lit up. Said nothing. Watched the wee boys throwing punches into the air.

McCoy sighed. 'If I pick him up for drunk and disorderly, he'll get a night in the cells at Stewart Street. That do?' he asked.

Cooper grinned. 'Yep. And don't charge him with anything serious, I need him back with me quick. Right?'

McCoy saluted. 'Anything else I can do for you, Mr Cooper?'

'Aye,' said Cooper. 'Stop being a cheeky bugger and get it sorted. I'm relying on you.'

He nodded over in the direction of the changing rooms. 'Here's Andy coming, so not a word.'

McCoy wondered for the umpteenth time why he'd ever got caught up with Stevie Cooper.

Andy Stewart was flushed, wet hair combed into a side shed. He'd a pale blue shirt on, sleeves rolled up, sweat marks round the armpits already.

'You want to get out of here?' he asked McCoy. 'I need some air.'

'Definitely,' said McCoy, standing up. 'You coming, Cooper?'

He shook his head. 'Got some stuff to do here with the boys. Contracts. Need them to sign their lives away. I'll catch up with you later.'

McCoy nodded and they walked towards the door. Stewart started telling him about handing out more photos in Dunoon, asking after Donny in all the local hotels. McCoy nodded occasionally but he wasn't listening. He was thinking. Cooper's foot had been quick but not quick enough. McCoy had seen where the train ticket had been for. A return to Newcastle. Cooper never went anywhere. Only really felt safe in Glasgow. So what the fuck was he doing going to Newcastle?

CHAPTER 37

'**Y**our hotel's not too far,' said McCoy. 'D'you want to walk there?'

'Sure,' said Stewart. 'It'll help me cool down. Been a long time since I worked so hard.'

'When were you last in the ring?' asked McCoy.

Stewart thought for a minute. 'Geez, you're asking now, probably early sixties? Kept my hand in for a while but the weight started piling on and I got too lazy to get it off. This way?'

McCoy nodded and they started along Duke Street heading for the city centre. Tennent's Brewery was just a couple of hundred yards the other way, smell of burnt wood and ash still in the air. It was a mild spring evening, perfect for a walk. Not so perfect for the shabby group of men standing outside the Great Eastern. Most had roll-ups in shaky hands, bottle of Lanliq being passed around.

McCoy had been in there a few times, called to break up fights. Wasn't a place he ever wanted to go into again. The Great Eastern was a vast building full of tiny wooden cells that were rented out to people with nowhere else to go. It got them all, elderly alcoholics, young guys who'd come out of care or prison and didn't know how to cope. Men who saw angels and demons and secret messages on the front of newspapers. No place for anyone to end up.

'Can you help me out, son?' asked an old man with a torn suit, grimy hand held out.

McCoy dug in his pocket, found a couple of fifty pences, handed them over.

The old man took them and smiled a toothless smile. 'That's good of you, son. I'll say a prayer for you. Mind you, I think God stopped listening to me a long time ago. Wouldn't be living in this hellhole if he was.'

McCoy thanked him and they walked on.

'Sure are a lot of bums in Glasgow,' said Stewart. 'Bad as Boston, and that's saying something. Drink?'

McCoy nodded. 'Mostly. Takes its toll. Did Donny ever mention a guy called Lindsay? Older? In the army?'

Stewart shook his head. 'Not that I remember. Why?'

'He ever mention going to some big house in the country? Few miles from the navy base?'

Stewart shook his head. 'He didn't call home that often and when he did he just talked about the job, the boys on the ship, what they'd been up to. That was about it.'

They turned into the High Street and walked down by the train station. Stewart's face had got a bit less red, was breathing easier. Was still rubbing the sweat from his forehead with a hanky every so often though.

'Did he ever mention going to a commune? Sort of a hippy place?'

Stewart stopped walking. Stood there. 'Geez, Harry, what's this all about? You're worrying me now. What have you found out?'

McCoy looked across the street. The Strathduie was just up Blackfriars, and it was a decent enough pub. 'Come on,' he said. 'I'll buy you a drink.'

McCoy left Stewart to find a table and went up to the bar, ordered two pints. He wasn't sure he should be telling Stewart what he was about to, but he didn't see how it could do any harm. And there was an argument he had a right to know what they thought was going on with his son.

He picked up their pints and carried them over. Stewart was sitting at a wee table under six or seven pictures of shields and tartans. He looked worried, fiddling with a beer mat. He took his pint, took a good draught. McCoy sat down. In for a penny.

'So, your Donny's blood and clothes were in Paul Watt's flat, the flat where the bomb went off. Thought is, he was injured but made a run for it.'

Stewart nodded over his pint.

'Some blood of the same type as your son's turned up in a car belonging to Colonel Angus Lindsay. Military type, has a big house not far from Dunoon. His pal from the ship said he'd seen Donny in his car – there aren't many of them. But Lindsay has denied knowing Donny, insists he's never met him.'

'He's lying?' asked Stewart.

'He might be,' said McCoy. 'But he might not. This is where it gets complicated. The car was also being used by the people living in a commune a couple of miles from the base. The blood or Donny could be connected to them.'

'Not sure I can see Donny hanging around a commune with a bunch of hippies, he wasn't that type.'

McCoy nodded but he wasn't sure either he or his dad had a clear idea of what Donny Stewart was like and what he'd been up to.

A boy came in, bundle of *Evening Times* papers under his arm, wandered around the pub, sold a few. McCoy could make out the headline.

TENNENT'S BOMB CLAIMS ANOTHER VICTIM

One of the workers who had been badly injured must have died. He turned back to Stewart.

'So, firstly, it might or might not be Donny's blood at all. It's a rare type but it's not unique. Secondly, if it was Donny's blood we still don't know who else was in the car with him or where they were going. The people at the commune said they'd never met him either—'

286

McCoy stopped mid-sentence, put his pint down.

'Harry? You okay?' asked Stewart.

McCoy didn't answer, just sat there wondering how he could have been so stupid. He stood up and took a closer look at the picture hanging on the wall above Stewart's head. It was a colour print of a coat of arms. He looked at the title written on the frame.

The Scottish Coat of Arms

There was a banner running above the shield in the middle. One word on it.

DEFENS

'Fuck!'

McCoy shouted it so loud the whole pub turned to look at him.

'Harry? What's going on?' asked Stewart.

'Got to go,' he said. 'I'll see you later. Central Hotel bar!'

Ran out the pub, Stewart calling after him.

CHAPTER 38

McCoy hurried back up the hill towards the hospital. Out of breath when he got there, too many bloody cigarettes. Should have called the station and got Murray or Wattie but he was too hyped up, didn't want to waste the time. It had all slotted into place the minute he'd seen the coat of arms. Lindsay, the boys, the bombing.

He let an ambulance pull into the A&E and crossed the driveway, walked into the big main entrance. Scanned the board trying to remember what ward he was in. Saw it. The John Slater. Second floor. He joined the crowd waiting by the lifts, willed it to hurry up.

Wee woman next to him was carrying a box of Milk Tray. She smiled at him. 'The old bugger's favourite. Only ones he can eat without his teeth in.'

McCoy smiled back, wondered why it was always him they spoke to.

The lift arrived and they shuffled in. He watched the flashing lights, got out on the fifth floor. Recognised the ward, walked to Lindsay's room.

288

Lindsay was sitting up in bed, pen in hand, *Times* open at the crossword in front of him. The bodyguard lad stood up from his chair, went to confront him.

'It's fine, Crawford. Sit down,' said Lindsay.

The bodyguard lad sat down. Looked disappointed, like he would have quite enjoyed taking McCoy on.

Lindsay put the paper to the side, smoothed out his covers. 'Back again. And to what do I owe the pleasure this time?'

'I know,' said McCoy. 'I know who you are.'

Lindsay looked puzzled. 'Yes . . .' he said. 'You do.'

'And I know what you've done,' said McCoy.

Lindsay was looking at McCoy like he was mad. He sat up in the bed, took his glasses off. 'What on earth are you talking about?' he asked.

'All these soldier boys. The bombs. It's all you, isn't it?'

Lindsay looked lost. 'You're going to have to help me out,' he said. 'I have the feeling we're at some sort of cross-purposes here.'

McCoy nodded over at the bodyguard lad. 'The thing written on your boy's T-shirt, DEFENS. It's on the coat of arms of Scotland.'

The bodyguard lad looked down at the blue word on his T-shirt as if it was news to him that it was on there.

'That thing, as you call it,' said Lindsay, 'is a Latin word meaning "defend". And for once you

289

are right, it does appear on the coat of arms of Scotland. Quite what that has got to—'

'You and your lads are the Sons of the 51 or whatever stupid name it is you sent to the papers. Donny Stewart and Paul Watt were building bombs for you, weren't they?'

Lindsay didn't answer, was just looking at him like you would look at a particularly dim child who couldn't understand a simple maths problem. A mixture of disappointment and pity. He shook his head.

'For what feels like the hundredth time, I don't know anyone called Donny Stewart,' he said. 'How many more times am I going to have to tell you that before it goes into your thick skull? And as for being in some kind of Scottish terrorist army, you couldn't be more off the mark if you tried. I am a colonel in the British Army – an organisation I have been part of since I was a teenager, an organisation to which I have devoted my life.'

'That doesn't mean anything,' said McCoy. 'Can't think of a better training for what you're doing than being in the army.'

Lindsay shook his head, was getting angry now. 'Jesus Christ, man! I'm in the bloody Highlanders! The motto of The Highlanders is *Cuidich 'n Righ* which means "Defend the King", not defend some stupid idea of bombing a brewery!'

McCoy was starting to feel like he was losing round two as well. Lindsay seemed full of righteous indignation, was acting nothing like a man would when confronted with his guilt.

'And as for DEFENS,' said Lindsay, 'and I can't believe I'm even taking the time to explain this, it's on the coat of arms of the United Kingdom. That's why it's on the boys' shirts. A tribute to our current monarch, Elizabeth the Second. A woman whom I respect more than any other and am honoured and bound to serve.'

McCoy just stood there. If Lindsay had intended to make him feel like a fucking idiot, he had succeeded. Wasn't sure what to say next. Hadn't gone anything like he'd planned. He was about to have another go when Lindsay sank back into his pillows. He looked tired, pale, like the fire in him had suddenly gone out. He winced in pain as he tried to get the words out.

'Now I suggest you leave us, McCoy, and take your slanderous accusations with you. Mark my words. If I hear you have repeated them to anyone I will contact one of your hopefully less simple-minded superior officers and have you dismissed, and then I will sue you until you don't have a pot to piss in.'

Then he gasped, suddenly grabbed at a cardboard bowl on the locker and knocked it to the floor. The bodyguard lad rushed over, quickly picked it up, held it under Lindsay's chin as he vomited up watery greenish bile. The boy wiped at Lindsay's mouth, told him it was going to pass, that it was going to be okay. Lindsay nodded, looked up at McCoy.

'Now get going before I let Crawford here knock seven bells out of you.'

McCoy stepped out the room and back into the corridor, closed the door on the sound of Lindsay being sick again. He fumbled in his pockets for his cigarettes. Felt like he did when he was a wee boy and the priest or one of the brothers shouted at him. Stupid and ashamed. Lit up and took a long drag, tried to calm himself down.

He'd thought he'd worked the whole thing out, but Lindsay had an explanation for everything. Trouble was, it was a plausible explanation as well.

He turned and Dr Basu was standing there.

'You were miles away,' he said, smiling. 'Didn't want to disturb the train of thought. Have you been in to see Mr Lindsay?'

McCoy nodded. 'Wasn't very pleased to see me. Sent me away with a flea in my ear.'

Basu smiled. 'Yes, he did that with one of the nurses this morning. The poor girl was almost in tears. Still, hard to blame him, being in that amount of pain.'

'I can imagine. Must be bloody sore getting your leg off,' said McCoy.

'It isn't pleasant, to say the least. And it's the last thing he needed at this point, but to be honest, it pales into insignificance given his circumstances.'

'What circumstances?' asked McCoy.

'Ah,' said the doctor. 'I thought you knew.'

'Knew what?'

Basu looked a bit sheepish. 'I shouldn't really be telling you about Mr Lindsay's medical condition. It's not appropriate. Sorry.'

'I'm investigating the bombings, bombings that have already killed four people and injured a lot more. I need to know as much as I can about Mr Lindsay.'

'Is he a suspect?' asked Dr Basu.

McCoy nodded. 'And I'm not supposed to tell you that, so we're even.'

'He has cancer,' said Dr Basu. 'Inoperable liver cancer. We are in the final stages. He's been coming here for a few months, I've been trying to do what I can. It's been a hard road, but to his credit, his son has been marvellous, sits with him through all the treatments. Always with him.'

'His son?' asked McCoy.

Dr Basu nodded at the door. 'Crawford Lindsay.'

'I didn't realise he was his son,' said McCoy, thinking of the care the boy had taken with Lindsay as he was sick. Made sense now. 'How long has Lindsay got?'

Dr Basu smiled. 'The question that all doctors hate.' He thought for a minute. 'I would say a month or so. He stopped all the aggressive medical treatment a couple of weeks ago. To be honest, it wasn't doing any good. Strictly palliative care now. He's surviving on morphine and breakfast cereal.'

'Christ,' said McCoy. 'I saw him a couple of days ago and he seemed fine.'

'Yes,' said Basu. 'He's a remarkable man. If it wasn't for his leg he wouldn't be in here, be living life as normal I expect, well as normally as he could. I've no idea how he did it up to now. Sheer willpower, I think. The leg operation seems to have set him back though, taken what strength he had left. I think he's finally resigned to what's happening to him.'

Dr Basu said goodbye and walked off down the corridor. McCoy watched him go. Didn't seem much doubt now. Lindsay was dying, suffering, in great pain. No way he was going to try and orchestrate a series of bombings through that. He almost felt sorry for him. Liver cancer was the last thing you would wish on anyone.

He headed towards the lifts. Trouble was, if the bombings weren't anything to do with Lindsay and his boys then he was back at square one. Back at square one with no real idea what to do next. He pressed the lift button. Waited. Ran his tongue round his dry mouth. Boy, did he need a drink.

CHAPTER 39

'Here he is!' Stewart was sitting at a table in the busy Central Hotel bar, waved as McCoy walked in. The bar was all wooden panels and black and white tiles on the floor. Windows out to Hope Street covered in slatted wooden blinds. Full of a mixture of travelling businessmen and people dressed in their finest waiting for a table at the restaurant next door.

'Sit down, Harry,' he said, looking round the bar. Saw what he was looking for. A young waiter with a ginger beard and freckles was delivering drinks to two women sitting at a nearby table.

'Jackie! My man!' shouted Stewart. 'Two more pints.'

Jackie nodded obligingly, gave a thumbs-up and headed off to the bar.

'You okay?' asked Stewart. 'You ran off in a hurry. Looked like you'd seen a ghost.'

McCoy nodded. 'I'm fine. Thought I was onto something, decided to strike while the iron was hot.'

'Something about Donny?' asked Stewart.

295

'Donny and a lot of other stuff, not so sure now. Might just have made a complete arse of myself. Not for the first time.'

The pints arrived, Jackie arranging them carefully on the beer mats, wiping the table, emptying the ashtray. Short of licking Stewart's arse, couldn't have been more after his tip if he'd tried. McCoy and Stewart waited until he'd gone.

'Where did you go?' asked Stewart. 'You set off like a bat out of hell.'

'Went to see that guy Lindsay in the hospital, up at the Royal. Still not a hundred per cent sure he's got anything to do with Donny or not. He explained it all away but I still think there's something fishy about him.'

'You think he knows what happened to Donny?'

'I just don't know,' said McCoy. 'Normally I'm pretty good at telling when people are lying but that guy's a strange one. I think he's probably telling the truth, just an odd duck. Would need some reason to take it further, but no idea where I'm going to get that.'

He looked up at Stewart. 'Sorry, pal, this isn't helping you much, is it?'

Stewart tried to smile. 'You're working on it. I can't ask for more than that.' He held his pint out and McCoy clinked it with his. 'What you doing tonight? Steve's coming here and we're going to a boxing match. Like the sound of that?'

'Stevie?' he asked. 'My Stevie?'

Stewart laughed. 'Yep. He's got me working as

a scout, going to see some middleweight at the Kelvin Hall, I think it is. Promised me dinner as a reward later. An Indian meal. Never had one. Should be fun, come with us.'

McCoy shook his head. 'Boxing's not really my cup of tea.'

'That's 'cause he hates the sight of blood.'

They looked up and Stevie Cooper was standing there. Usual denims, red jacket and blond quiff.

'Cannae whack it, can you?' he said. 'Never could, not since we were wee boys.'

'Nope,' said McCoy. 'He's right. Gives me the willies. See enough of it at work as it is. Don't need to be seeing any more if I can help it.'

Cooper took his seat with Stewart and sat down. Had just picked up McCoy's cigarettes when Jackie appeared.

'Another round, gents? And for you, sir?' he asked.

Cooper told him yes and he'd have a pint. Jackie practically bowed, scuttled off.

'You sure we can't persuade you, Harry?' said Stewart.

McCoy shook his head. 'Not this time. Got some dirty dishes at home with my name on them. I live an exciting life.'

Stewart stood up. 'Okey-doke. Just going to get my coat from the room, be five minutes.'

Cooper took his seat and they watched Stewart weave his way through the bar, press a note into Jackie's hand. A big one, going by the smile on his freckled face.

'Didn't know you were such big pals,' said McCoy.

Cooper took the matches off the table, lit up. 'There's a lot you don't know about me, McCoy, as I keep telling you. I'm a man of mystery.'

'What's put you in such a good mood?' asked McCoy as Jackie put the drinks down.

'Let's just say things are falling into place.' Took a big draught of his pint, wiped the foam off his mouth. 'What you going to do tonight, you miserable bugger? Come along, I'm even buying us an Indian.'

McCoy shook his head. 'I'm going home. Need to try and work out what the fuck is going on with these bombs before Murray chucks me off the case.'

'Reminds me,' said Cooper, lowering his voice, leaning forward. 'I spoke to my uncle.'

'And?' asked McCoy.

'And he says they'll hold off, look into it. As a favour to me.'

'Great,' said McCoy. 'I'll tell Faulds.'

'Aye, well, he's not off the hook yet, not by a long shot. Make sure and tell him that. Far as they're concerned he's still in the frame.'

McCoy nodded. 'You seen Billy?' he asked.

Cooper shook his head. 'The last person I want to see is that wee cunt. He'll get what's coming to him.'

McCoy was about to ask him what that meant when Stewart appeared, raincoat over his arm.

'Ready?' he asked.

Cooper stood up, finished the last of McCoy's whisky. 'Remember Jumbo,' he said. 'A night in the cells.'

McCoy nodded, and Cooper and Stewart left.

McCoy sat for a while, finished his pint, ordered another one. Watched the comings and goings in the bar. A good-looking woman around his age arrived, sat at a table by herself. For a moment he entertained the idea of sending a drink over, trying his arm. His heart wasn't in it though. Couldn't get rid of the funny feeling in his stomach. Only really got that feeling when he thought something bad was about to happen. Something bad that he couldn't do anything to stop.

19TH APRIL 1974

CHAPTER 40

D awn was just breaking as they drove through the deserted city. McCoy liked Glasgow like this, missed it from his beat days, feeling of being part of the city that most people never see. The occasional car on the streets. Empty pavements, seagulls on last night's bins, miserable-looking people at bus stops waiting for the first bus of the morning. McCoy lit up, coughed for a couple of minutes, always did with the first of the morning. Tried to pretend the cigarette wasn't hurting his stomach. Was still trying to get his head around what had happened.

'That's all you know?' he asked as they drove through a George Square deserted but for starlings. 'That's it?'

Wattie nodded, looked exasperated. 'Don't blame me, that's all I got told. Got a call from the night shift at half four. Seems two people got into Lindsay's room last night, a nurse came to check on him and discovered them. They made a run for it. Left Lindsay half pulled out the bed, two black eyes, nose broken, poor bugger was in some state.'

'I don't get it,' said McCoy. 'Who would beat someone up in a hospital bed?'

'Don't ask me!' said Wattie. 'How am I supposed to know? You're the one working this case while I fanny about getting nowhere with Jamsie Dixon.' He pulled up at the lights at the High Street Station. 'And by the way I got another roasting from Murray yesterday. Wanted to know what progress I'd made. Couldn't really say fuck all, but that's what it amounts to. Luckily he had to take a call from Pitt Street before he got into his stride.'

'You tell him about Patsy and the money?' asked McCoy.

Wattie nodded, grimaced as he pulled some toilet paper off his neck. Inspected the blood on it then threw it out the window.

'He wants me to go back and interview him again, press him harder this time. You know Murray and showpeople. All of them are thieving bastards as far as he's concerned. He was about to start his usual rant about gypsies stealing red diesel when the call came.'

They turned into the hospital car park and Wattie parked at the entrance, stopped the engine, took the key out. Looked at McCoy. Didn't look happy. 'I need to do well, Harry. I don't think Murray's got any faith in me. Got the feeling I'm in the last chance saloon.'

McCoy got out of the car without saying anything. Trouble was, he didn't think Wattie was

304

far wrong. He did need a result, and fast. No point in him telling him that though. Better to try and keep his spirits up.

'C'mon, maybe you'll solve the great hospital attack case of 1974. Murray'll give you a medal.'

Wattie nodded, didn't look convinced, or any happier.

Whoever they were, they had done quite a job on Lindsay. He looked terrible, really terrible. Two black eyes surrounded by yellow bruises, stitches on his nose. Bandage around his left hand. He was crumpled against his pillows, literally looked like a broken man. Even his skin had gone a sickly blueish-white colour. His eyes were closed, his breathing sounded difficult, scratchy.

'Jesus Christ,' said McCoy.

Lindsay's less swollen eye opened, tongue licked at his lips.

'Happy now?' he said in a voice that was barely more than a whisper.

'What?' said McCoy. 'Why would I be happy?'

Lindsay just lay there, kept staring at McCoy. Was a couple of minutes before he gathered enough strength to speak again. McCoy stepped closer to the bed to hear.

'The thugs that did this kept asking me where Donny Stewart was. I presume you sent them? A little work off the books . . .'

He coughed and a watery red liquid ran down his chin.

McCoy went to speak and Lindsay lifted his hand to stop him.

'I don't have much time so I want you to listen to me.'

His body seemed to spasm and he cried out in pain. He pointed to a small glass jar with a straw coming out of the top sitting on the locker. Wattie picked it up, held it up to his mouth, and he took a couple of sips.

'Mr Lindsay, I didn't send any thugs, I promise you.'

McCoy wasn't sure if it was him or the room that was very warm. Maybe they'd put the heating up because he was ill. He tugged at his tie, undid his top button. The feeling in his stomach was back, worse than ever. Dread.

'Yes, you did,' said Lindsay. 'You're the only person interested in Donny Stewart.' He coughed again, wiped at the fluid on his chin with his pyjama sleeve, closed his eyes for a minute. When he opened them they looked brighter, like he was more alive. Something had changed. Whatever he had sipped must have done the trick.

'Mr Lindsay, I—'

'It's Colonel Lindsay,' hissed Lindsay. 'Have some fucking respect.'

McCoy nodded, was going to have to tread carefully. 'Colonel Lindsay. I understand what has happened here is unacceptable but—'

Lindsay was smiling at him now, thin red lips

stretched across his pale face. 'That didn't take long, did it? Gone from throwing your weight about like some sort of Glasgow hardman to a snivelling apologist.' His head swivelled. 'What about you?' he asked, looking at Wattie. 'What have you got to say for yourself?'

Wattie looked like a rabbit in the headlights. Didn't say anything.

'Just as well it's all done,' he said. 'Even if you knew how, it's too late to stop us now. You'll see soon enough. A little entertainment before I shuffle off this mortal coil. Monday was only the beginning. It's going to happen again and again until this country is rid of the pestilence that feeds on it like fleas on a rat.'

'What do you mean?' asked McCoy, starting to feel scared, very scared. 'There's going to be more bombs?'

Lindsay's eyes were starting to lose their sparkle. His body seemed to be relaxing, sinking back into the bed.

Suddenly struck McCoy. 'Where's your son?' he asked. 'Where is he?'

'What? Do you think Crawford is the only one? You underestimate me, McCoy. There's an army out there primed and ready to go. My boys are going to light fires in the rotten cities of this godforsaken country. You have no idea . . .'

McCoy turned to Wattie. 'Get a hold of Murray, tell him what's happening. Quick!'

Wattie nodded, ran out of the room.

Lindsay watched him go. Smiled again. 'Run, rabbit, run,' he said. 'I'd skin him like a deer.'

That was enough. Remembered the deer in the woods. Couldn't stop the anger and the panic. McCoy moved in to the bed, face to face with Lindsay. 'Listen to me, you—'

Stopped. Lindsay eyes were suddenly miles away. McCoy walked over to the locker, picked up the glass jar. Morphine. 'Fucker.'

Lindsay's eyes were closing now.

McCoy bent over him. Grabbed at the collar of his pyjamas, pulled Lindsay up to his face. Body weighed nothing.

'Don't you fucking black out on me now!' he shouted. Slapped his face.

Lindsay's head lolled.

'Where's Donny Stewart?' asked McCoy. 'Is he one of them? Is he?'

Lindsay laughed. 'No, Donny was destined for better things. He was going to be one of the April Dead . . .'

'He was what?'

Lindsay looked at him, managed to focus his eyes for a few seconds. 'Twelve noon.'

'What?' asked McCoy. 'What happens at twelve noon?'

Lindsay's eyes closed over, wasn't much more than a whisper. 'Boom!'

'What? Where? Where do you mean?' asked McCoy. 'Tell me!'

No response. McCoy shook him but it was no use, he was out cold.

He dropped him back onto the pillows, sat down on the edge of the bed, put his head in his hands. Stomach was killing him. Another bomb, maybe more of them. He knew what the bad thing coming was. Mayhem. And it looked like he had helped bring it.

CHAPTER 41

McCoy stepped out Lindsay's room, walked up to the nurses' station. Mind was racing. Knew the bomb was coming and the only person who could tell him where was dead to the world. A nurse was filling out a form on a clipboard when he approached. Showed her his card.

'Lindsay,' he said. 'I need to know the minute he wakes up. Call Stewart Street, ask for me, Detective McCoy. If I'm not there, Watson or Murray. Got it?'

The nurse nodded, looked scared.

'Going to get two uniformed police up here as well. They'll sit outside his door. Nobody goes in except medical staff. Anyone else turns up to see him, call me. Got it?'

She nodded again. 'What has he done?' she asked. 'He's just an old man.'

'He's much more than that, believe me. Who was on duty when he was attacked?'

'Ellen Teirney,' she said. 'She's down in the canteen.'

McCoy thanked her, started walking back towards the stairs.

The staff canteen was a long, windowless room in the basement, strip lights illuminating long tables crowded with nurses in uniform, doctors at a separate table, stethoscopes around their necks, burly porters at another. There was a hum of conversation, smell of frying bacon and toast, radio playing 'Waterloo'. He asked one of the porters to point Ellen out and he pointed to a nurse sitting in one of the armchairs surrounding a wee coffee table by the back. She was young, blonde hair trying to escape from her cap. She was also fast asleep.

McCoy didn't have the time to wait. He shook her arm gently and she woke with a start, blinked her eyes a couple of times, sat up.

'Ellen?' asked McCoy. 'I'm Detective McCoy. Can I have a word about last night?'

She nodded, seemed a bit dazed. He sat down on the armchair next to her. Armchair stank so much of smoke you wouldn't need to bother lighting up, you could just sit in it and inhale.

'Sorry, must have fallen asleep,' she said. 'Was going to have a cup of tea then head home.'

'Not surprised after last night,' said McCoy. 'Can you tell me what happened?'

She picked up her mug of tea, sipped it and

grimaced. 'Stone cold,' she said. 'Must have slept longer than I thought.'

McCoy nodded, just wanting her to get on with it.

'So I went in to check on Mr Lindsay about two. We have to check on all the patients every couple of hours. Anyway, I opened the door and the first thing I saw was he was half out of the bed. At first I thought he'd got up to go to the toilet and fallen or something, then I realised there were two men in the room.'

'Can you describe them?' asked McCoy.

'Not really,' she said. 'It was dark, was just the nightlight that was on. They just pushed past me and ran. I didn't see their faces but they were both big guys. Think one of them might have had a red jacket on.'

McCoy's heart sank a bit more. Had to be Cooper and Stewart. 'Did they say anything?'

'One said "Run" to the other and that was it.'

'What kind of accent?' asked McCoy.

'Just Glasgow,' she said. 'Like you or me.'

'What happened then?'

She yawned again. 'Sorry. I pushed the alarm and tried to get Mr Lindsay back in the bed, then the sister appeared and I told her what had happened and she went back to the station to call the police and I waited for the doctor to come for poor Mr Lindsay.'

McCoy nodded. Had to ask. 'Do you think you would recognise them again?'

She shook her head.

'Okay. Thanks for that,' said McCoy and left her sitting there, eyes already starting to close again. Chances were she'd be back to sleep in minutes.

He walked back along the corridor to the lift. He was going to kill Cooper and Stewart. He could see it now. The two of them going drinking after the boxing. Stewart telling Cooper there was someone who might know about his son. Cooper acting the big man, telling Stewart he could sort it out, suggesting they go and beat it out of him. More drinks, then they decide to do it. Hadn't realised how desperate Stewart was. Was surprised he'd got involved in something as stupid as this. Still, people would do anything when it came to their kids.

He pressed the lift button. At least the nurse couldn't identify them, that was the one good thing in this shitty mess. A shitty mess that he had created. He shouldn't have told Stewart about Lindsay, should have kept his mouth shut for once. The lift arrived and he stepped in. Pressed Ground. Looked at his watch. Was still only half six. This was going to be a long day.

CHAPTER 42

'Tell me again. Exactly what did he say?' asked Murray.

They were sitting in a cafe on the High Street, table by the window, towers of the Royal visible over the tenements. McCoy couldn't face anything but a cup of tea. Had sat and watched as Wattie and Murray demolished two rounds of toast each.

'He said "Twelve noon. Boom!"'

'Christ,' said Murray pulling a serviette out the silver dispenser, wiping melted butter off his fingers. 'Anything else?'

McCoy shook his head. 'There's going to be a bomb at twelve. He said his plan was all in place and his boys were going to carry it out.'

Murray balled the serviette up, dropped it on his plate. 'Any chance he's bluffing?'

'Don't think so. Doesn't seem the type. It's going to happen,' said McCoy. 'I was there. He meant it, Murray. He wasn't messing about.'

'So what the fuck are we supposed to do?' asked Murray, face starting to go red. 'Evacuate the whole of Glasgow?'

'I don't know,' said McCoy. 'I'm just telling you what he said. He said there would be one today at noon and there would be more.'

'And he definitely organised the last one?'

'I think so,' said McCoy, taking a fag out Wattie's packet of Number 6 lying on the table. 'Sure as I can be.'

Murray found his matches, lit his pipe. 'Any bright ideas?'

'We need to get a hold of one of his boys and try to turn him,' said McCoy. 'Wattie and I'll go and speak to Meiklejohn, see which one he thinks is the most likely to crack.'

Murray puffed away, waving the smoke away from the front of his face, and ignoring the tuts from the two women at the next table as the smoke surrounded them.

'You sure he won't tell us anything when he comes round?' he asked. 'Lindsay?'

'He's in the last stages of liver cancer,' said McCoy. 'He took two sips of liquid morphine while I was there. He's out for the count until at least this afternoon, according to the doctor.'

Murray didn't look happy. 'And who bloody beat him up? Was it you?'

'No! Jesus. Come on, Murray, I'm not that bad,' said McCoy.

'So who was it then?'

'No idea,' said McCoy, lying through his teeth.

'Well, what is he going to blow up then?' asked Murray. Realised Wattie had been sitting there all

315

this time saying nothing. 'Well, Watson? You got anything to add or are you just going to sit there on your fat arse shovelling toast into your mouth?'

Wattie looked like he'd been caught out doing something he shouldn't have.

'A pub?' he said. 'An off-sales maybe? Something to do with England?'

'Great,' said Murray. 'That'll narrow it down then. Thanks for your insight.' He turned to McCoy. 'You're sure about this bomb thing?'

McCoy nodded.

Murray sighed. 'I'll go to Pitt Street. See if I can get them to organise a call-around of the likely targets, tell the staff to keep an eye out for bags being left, that sort of thing. How they are going to do it without causing panic stations God only knows, but thankfully that's their problem.' He stood up. 'They're not going to be happy about it and I'm going to have to persuade them. This is Glasgow, city's full of bloody pubs and off-licences. Doubt we'll get through to them all before midday. And no matter what happens, we lose either way. No bomb and they'll think I'm an idiot, one goes off and people lose their lives. It's a mess, McCoy, a fucking mess. Any other ideas?'

McCoy shook his head.

'Get going then, find Meiklejohn,' said Murray. 'Let's just hope we're lucky.'

CHAPTER 43

There was no answer at the Maryhill Barracks. McCoy looked at his watch, was only quarter to eight. Maybe they were still asleep. Didn't seem very military though. He was just about to ring the bell again when Wattie tapped his shoulder.

'That's him, isn't it?' he said.

McCoy turned and a figure in running shorts and a vest was limping along Shakespeare Street towards them. Meiklejohn held his hand up in recognition. Tried to up his pace but the grimace on his face told the story.

'Thought these army blokes were supposed to be fit?' asked Wattie.

Soon as he got a bit closer the reason for his limping was obvious. Meiklejohn's left leg was a mess. Looked like someone had hacked a couple of lumps out of it just below his knee, rest of the leg burns and scar tissue.

'Sorry, gents,' he said as he approached them. 'Tried to go faster but the leg was having none of it.'

'Christ, that looks bad,' said Wattie. 'What happened?'

'Northern Ireland,' said Meiklejohn. 'Hence I'm back here teaching boys to march. Still, could be worse. The other fellow that was in the pig with me is a quadriplegic, still in the hospital.'

He leant against the wall of the barracks, raised his left leg off the ground. 'Not supposed to run on it.' He smiled. 'Should have learnt my lesson by now. Still, enough of my troubles. I assume this isn't a social call?'

McCoy shook his head. ''Fraid not.'

Ten minutes later Meiklejohn was showered, dressed in a tracksuit, sitting across from them in his office.

'I'm all ears,' he said.

McCoy couldn't think of an easy way to say it. 'We think Lindsay was behind the bomb at the Tennent's Brewery. Think him and his lads are about to plant some more, one of which might well go off at twelve noon today.'

Meiklejohn sat back in his chair. 'Are you sure?' he asked. 'About Lindsay?'

McCoy nodded. 'You don't seem that surprised about it.'

Meiklejohn shrugged. 'I thought there was something wrong going on up there. But not for a minute did I think that it would be something like this.'

'What did you think it was then?' asked McCoy.

'I thought one of the boys was going to get killed

318

or injured doing Lindsay's bloody fieldcraft exercises. He's used to working with experienced soldiers, the cream of the British Army. These boys are just kids really. Part-timers in for a laugh and some adventure.'

'That's all you thought?' asked McCoy.

Meiklejohn looked him in the eye. 'That's all.'

'If we're going to put a stop to it we need you to help us out. Which one of his lads would be easiest to turn? Need to know what they have planned soon as.'

'George Orr,' said Meiklejohn immediately. 'Always had the feeling he was less enthusiastic than the rest. Bit older psychologically, bit more interested in girls and drinking than spending a rainy night in an improvised shelter in the woods.'

'Can you phone him?' asked McCoy. 'Say it's some administration thing. If he's in we'll go over there – don't want to tip him off.'

Meiklejohn nodded. Got a file out the drawer, looked up a number, dialled.

'Where does he live?' asked McCoy.

Meiklejohn put his hand over the receiver. 'Lives in Ruchill with his mum, think the dad left a couple— Mrs Orr? It's Meiklejohn at the barracks here. I wonder if George is there, need a word if I could.' Listened. 'Yes, that is a bit worrying. Still, I'm sure he's come to no harm, probably just staying with a pal. Will you get him to call me when he comes in? Nothing desperate, just need to check some dates with him. You too. Bye.'

He put the phone down. A dull click.

'George Orr didn't come home last night, hasn't been in touch. He's never done that before.'

'Fuck,' said McCoy. 'Can you try another one of them?'

Meiklejohn nodded. Dialled. Same story. Bobby Slater hadn't come home last night. Dialled another. Neither had Thomas Ross. Or Henry Robb.

Each time Meiklejohn told them another boy hadn't come home the feeling in McCoy's stomach got worse and worse.

'They've all disappeared,' said Meiklejohn, a look of fear on his face. 'Robb was the last one. Where have they gone?'

McCoy shook his head. Suddenly this was getting very serious. Four of Lindsay's boys missing plus Crawford. What was it he had said again? 'My boys will light fires in your cities.' Looked like whatever mission the lunatic had sent them on had already begun.

Meiklejohn looked as worried as McCoy felt. He was sitting behind the desk, pencil in his mouth, eyes miles away.

'Can you stay here today in case any of them phone in or turn up?' asked McCoy.

Meiklejohn nodded. Sat up.

'You got any photos of them you can give us?' asked McCoy.

'Yes, there are photo booth ones in each of their files.'

Meiklejohn started pulling off the wee photos stapled at the top of each file. Stopped. 'Fuck it. Not regulation but you may as well take the whole files,' he said. 'They've got phone numbers, addresses, that sort of thing. Could come in useful.'

'Wattie, you take them,' said McCoy. 'Get on the car radio. Get a car up to each address, interview the parents, see if any of the boys let something slip about what was going on.'

Wattie nodded. 'Will do.' Picked up the files, headed for the door.

Meiklejohn still looked blindsided. 'You really think they're going to start planting bombs?' he asked. 'I know those boys. I can hardly imagine it.'

'Don't know,' said McCoy. 'But we have to start acting as if they will. If something goes up at noon then we know for sure.'

'And what happens if it does?' asked Meiklejohn.

'Then all hell breaks loose.'

McCoy stood up to go. Meiklejohn stood too. Grimaced again, held onto the desk for support.

'You served in Northern Ireland,' said McCoy. 'Know anything about plainclothes army officers, do what they want?'

Meiklejohn looked like he'd seen a ghost, colour drained from his face. 'What are you asking me that for?'

'Just interested,' said McCoy. 'Heard of them, have you?'

Meiklejohn shook his head.

'How about Paul McVeigh?'

Meiklejohn thought about it a moment too long. 'No, never heard of him. Why do you ask?'

'Doesn't matter,' said McCoy. 'Any of the boys or the parents get in touch phone me at Stewart Street straight away, okay?'

Meiklejohn nodded.

McCoy left him there, standing behind the desk, face still white. Wasn't sure if it was from the pain in his leg or because of what he'd asked him.

He walked across the barracks yard wondering what they could do next. Probably not much but wait until twelve noon and see if anything happened. Try and find the boys in the meantime.

Wondered if it was worth talking to Lindsay's sister. She might know something about what had been going on up at the big house. She seemed nice enough but he wasn't sure how keen she'd be on helping the police against her brother.

He was almost at the car, could see Wattie talking into the radio, reading out from the file he was holding, when he heard a shuffling noise behind him. He turned and Meiklejohn was limping towards him, look of pain on his face.

'McCoy! Wait a minute.'

McCoy stood, waited on Meiklejohn catching up. He got to him, leant his hand on the wall for support.

'I don't know why you're asking me those questions,' he said. 'But you should be careful.' His leg was shaking, sweat across his forehead. 'They're

322

called the Det. Bad boys. Unaccountable to anyone. Pretty much allowed to do what they want, no matter what it is.'

'I thought they were army?' said McCoy.

'Nominally they are,' said Meiklejohn. 'But the normal rules don't apply to them. Be careful who you mention them to. They don't like to be talked about, don't even like people to know they exist.' He frowned. 'Because officially they don't.'

'How come you know so much about them?' asked McCoy. 'Do you know what happened with Paul McVeigh?'

Meiklejohn shook his head. 'I've said too much. Just be careful, McCoy. Very careful.'

McCoy watched as he turned and limped back towards the barracks.

CHAPTER 44

McCoy had never felt more useless or more frustrated in his life. They'd done all they could do. Pitt Street were still phoning off-licences and bars, not even halfway through the list. Meiklejohn hadn't heard anything from any of the boys or their parents. According to Dr Basu, Lindsay was still out for the count and would be until late afternoon. So here they were, sitting in the station watching the clock, waiting until twelve noon. Only half an hour to go and nothing they could do about it. He got the bottle of Pepto-Bismol out his desk drawer, swigged some. Didn't help.

Despite getting up at five a.m., he wasn't tired. He was like everyone else, alert, jumpy, smoking for Scotland. He stubbed his cigarette out in the full ashtray on his desk, needed to do something, think about something else. Saw Wattie coming in the office, bottle of Irn-Bru in one hand, a packet of crisps in the other. He got up and walked over to Wattie's desk, pulled up a chair and sat opposite him.

'You speak to Patsy Hearne again?' he asked.

Wattie nodded. 'Just came from him.' Unscrewed the top of the bottle, took a long slug. 'Exact same story as last time, wasn't budging from it. Last time they saw Jamsie Dixon was at the shows when they gave him the money.'

'So what now?' asked McCoy.

Wattie sighed. Opened his crisps. Held them out. McCoy stuck his hand in, grabbed a handful, shoved them in his mouth.

'Fuck knows. I'm stuck,' said Wattie. 'Sure you've got enough?'

'You eat too much,' said McCoy, chomping away. 'You need to tell Murray.'

'I know. But I'm going to wait until after twelve. If nothing happens he might be in a good mood, go easy. If not he's going to go through me like a hot knife through butter. Any ideas?'

What could he tell him? That it was Billy who'd killed Jamsie Dixon but he had no evidence for that other than Cooper telling him?

He shook his head. 'We'll think of something.'

'Better hurry up. By the way, she's going back to work. Starts next week.'

'That's good,' said McCoy. 'She'll be happy about that.'

'She is. Was practically dancing about the room when she told me. I think Duggie's getting a tooth. His face is all red and he keeps girning and gumming at my hand. You think that's what—'

'You two! Now!'

They turned and Murray was standing outside his office pointing at them. Walked back in.

'Christ, what does he want now?' said Wattie as they stood up.

'Soon find out,' said McCoy.

Murray was down to his shirt and tie, sleeves rolled up over his meaty arms. Looked like an expensive shirt as well. Living with Phyllis Gilroy was definitely changing him. She hadn't managed to do anything about the pipe though. Must have just finished a smoke, the wee office was still sinking of Newton's Gold Flake. They sat down and waited until he'd finished his phone call. He put the receiver down, looked at them.

'That was Pitt Street. Done about three-quarters of the calls. Some of the shops starting to ask questions, press'll be on it soon.'

They all glanced up at the clock on the wall. Ten to twelve. McCoy's stomach tightened again. Tried not to think about whatever innocent people going about their business were going to be dead in ten minutes.

'You with us?'

He turned and Murray was looking at him. He nodded.

'Watson, need you to get your Mary to do us a favour. See if she can discreetly find out if the *Record* received any more press releases from the Sons of the 51 or whatever the fuck they are.'

Wattie nodded.

Murray looked at him. 'Now! You fucking clown!'

326

Wattie got up, scrambled out the office. Murray shook his head. 'I can't tell if that boy's stupid or not.'

'He's not,' said McCoy. 'But he thinks you think he is so he gets flustered.'

'Jesus, this is a police station, not a bloody psychiatric ward,' said Murray. 'He needs to get a grip. He's a grown man with a child, not some teenager. How's he getting on with Jamsie Dixon anyway?'

'Not very well,' said McCoy. 'But nobody would. It's one gangster knocking another one off. Chances of us finding anything useful about it are slim. You know that as well as I do. Look, I'll help him out when this bomb stuff is out the way. I think he's surviving on three hours' sleep a night with the baby. I remember what it was like. I was a zombie for six months.'

'Up to you,' said Murray. 'But whatever happens, we need a result.'

McCoy looked up at the clock. One minute to twelve. Second hand clicked and hit the twelve. He looked at Murray. Didn't know what he was expecting, to hear some distant explosion? Wasn't one, just the sound of the clock ticking and some drunk guy shouting the odds at the front desk.

'Twelve now,' he said.

Murray nodded, drummed his fountain pen on the desk.

'Maybe the whole thing was just a false alarm,' said McCoy with more conviction than he felt.

327

'Let's hope so,' said Murray. 'Soon find out. Forgot to ask. What was that stuff about Donny Stewart meant to mean? He was going to be one of the April Dead?'

'Your guess is as good as mine,' said McCoy. 'He was pretty far gone by that point, maybe he was just talking nonsense. That amount of morphine will—'

Murray's phone was ringing. They both looked at it for a minute. Murray picked it up. Listened. McCoy watched him, only took a few seconds to see by the look on his face that Lindsay wasn't talking nonsense.

Another bomb had gone off.

CHAPTER 45

Wattie pressed harder on the accelerator and the car lurched round the corner and into Woodlands Road. They'd the siren and the lights going. McCoy in the back trying to light up as he got flung from side to side.

'There,' said Murray, pointing out the windscreen.

There was a tower of grey smoke a few hundred yards ahead, smell of burning in the air. Traffic was backed up in front of them, beat cops trying to get them to reverse back down the street.

Wattie pressed on the horn. 'Hang on,' he said and bumped the car half up on the pavement.

The car lurched again and McCoy held onto the seat in front of him. 'Doesn't look as big as the brewery one,' he said. 'That's something.'

Wattie kept sounding the horn but it was no use, the crowd of bystanders was too big.

'Just pull over,' said Murray. 'Leave the car here.'

Five minutes later McCoy, Murray and Wattie were standing looking at the dark, smoking hole that used to be an Agnew's off-licence. There was glass everywhere, from the windows of the shops either side and from the bottles that had been on the shelves of the shop. Couldn't move without it crunching under your feet. Smell of alcohol was so strong you could taste it each time you breathed in. There was another smell underneath it, fainter but definitely there. Almonds.

'Can you get drunk from just smelling drink?' asked Wattie.

Murray rolled his eyes. 'Away and make sure the uniforms are setting up the cordon. Make yourself useful.'

Wattie hurried off towards the police vans parked to block the road each side of the bomb site.

Murray nodded over at the teenage boy sitting on the kerb, wrists handcuffed behind his back. 'Is he all right?'

'Think so,' said McCoy. 'No obvious cuts or wounds. He's no saying much, mind you.'

'Not surprised. The stupid bugger picked the wrong shop to bomb. Should have known not to tangle with Victor Wilkie. How's he doing?'

'I'll find out,' said McCoy. 'You staying around?'

Murray shook his head. 'Going to Pitt Street. Calm the baying hounds. Try and work out what the fuck we're going to say to the press. I'll see you back at the station.'

McCoy watched him walk up to the vans shouting at Wattie to 'bloody hurry up' as he went. Although the off-licence was destroyed, the casualties were nowhere near as bad as at the brewery. One dead, an old man who had been walking past. One serious injury to a woman who worked in the baker's next door. People in the flats above the shops seemed to be fine. Sandstone building had big scorch marks going up it and half the windows were gone, but that was it.

Woodlands Road wasn't that far from West Princes Street, where the bomb that had killed Paul Watt had gone off. Only five minutes or so up the road. McCoy still had no idea why they were targeting this area. Wasn't like it was anything special. Flats full of students from the university, some Asian families further along. Low-rent flats. Not exactly the seat of the establishment.

Could hear reporters shouting to him from behind the cordon, bright flashes from cameras as he walked up the road towards the recovery area the emergency services had set up. Could even see an STV van coming down Gibson Street towards them. Hoped Wattie was managing to keep the cordon tight.

Victor Wilkie was sitting on a fold-up chair by the back doors of an ambulance. Young female nurse cutting the sleeve off his shirt. Eased it off and started picking the glass out his arm with a pair of tweezers. Looked painful but Wilkie didn't seem to be bothered, just sat there as she dropped the bloody shards into a kidney-shaped tray. He was an old beat cop, Wilkie. Still looked like it. Tall, heavy, black moustache and a buzz cut.

'You remember me?' asked McCoy, getting

another fold-up chair from the back of the ambulance and sitting down.

Wilkie peered at him. Shook his head.

'Think you retired about a month after I started. Went to the party in the Glen Douglas. Some night.'

Wilkie grinned. 'Not a night I remember very well.'

'You okay?' asked McCoy, nodding at the nurse attending his arm. 'Happy to answer some questions?'

'I'm fine,' said Wilkie. 'Best do it now, while I remember. Memory isn't what it was.'

'Okay. Just tell me what happened, starting from this morning.'

The nurse rolled his arm over, started picking glass out the other side of it.

'Got a call from Pitt Street this morning. Be on the lookout for any suspicious bags or packages, anybody acting strangely. Didn't think much about it. Never think these things are going to happen to you, do you?'

McCoy shook his head.

'So I goes into the shop, open up. Same as every other day.'

'How long you been working here?' asked McCoy.

Wilkie thought. ''Bout six years, started a couple of years after I retired. Hanging about the house all day was driving me mad, never mind the missus. So I got a wee job, keeps me busy.'

'And . . .'

'And I open the shop. The usual crowd waiting outside. I serve them, put their money in the water bucket. Get—'

'Eh?' said McCoy. 'Water bucket?'

'The money they have is minging. They've been begging all morning, dirty coins all stuck together with God knows what. Goes straight in the bucket.'

'Ah, got you. Sorry.'

'So I get the early boys out the road,' continued Wilkie. 'Start restocking the shelves. I'm doing that and I see the wee bugger outside, got a bag, one of those sport things. Adi? Adis?'

'Adidas,' said McCoy.

'That's it. Written on the side. Anyways, he walks back and forwards a few times, thinks I can't see him, but we have mirrors set up to stop shoplifting so I keep watching him. Another few walks up and down and then he comes in. So I'm thinking, oh aye. I get down from the ladder, get behind the counter, ask him what he wants. Shite.'

The nurse dropped a big shard in the tray and tried to stop the spray of blood coming out of Wilkie's arm. McCoy handed her a big pack of cotton wool, tried not to look. She managed to get it under control and Wilkie started again.

'So he asks for a packet of crisps, pays for them and heads towards the door. Without the bag. I say, "You've forgotten the bag," and he runs. Wee fucker. So I jump over the counter and chase him. He's running up the pavement towards town. I realise there's no way I'm going to catch him, not at my bloody age, so I shout at these guys digging up the road. Tell them to stop him. And fuck me, they did all right. Three of them grab him, get him down on the ground. I turn to go back in the shop and phone it in and boom! The next thing I remember is lying on the pavement like a bloody pin cushion. Glass sticking out me.'

'You did a great job, Mr Wilkie.'

'Tell you what, son, it's made me miss the old days. Got the heart pumping again.'

The nurse was looking at a big bit of green glass with a bit of a torn wine label still pasted to it sticking out Wilkie's wrist. 'Sorry, Mr Wilkie, this one's too deep for me to do here. Need to get you up to the Western. Okay?'

Wilkie nodded, let himself be helped into the back of the ambulance. McCoy said cheerio, thanked him again, and walked back to the young man sitting on the pavement.

'I've seen you before,' he said, recognising the boy's red hair. 'You were messing about with whitewash up at the barracks.'

The boy looked up at him, couldn't be older than sixteen, seventeen.

'How the fuck did you get yourself mixed up in this? You have any idea how much trouble you're in?'

The boy didn't say anything, eyes started tearing up.

'Too late for that now, son,' said McCoy. 'It's

334

way beyond crying and saying sorry. If you don't help us they're going to nail you to the fucking wall. Have a think about that in the van, eh?'

He watched them load the boy in to the back of the police van. Knew he'd been a bastard but he needed the boy to talk – and he was going to have to be even more of one to make him do it.

CHAPTER 46

'It's not going to work,' said McCoy. 'Three of us in there, it's too much. He's scared, but three people's like a wall. He'll just clam up.'

Murray looked across the desk at him. Wattie just looked relieved. They were in Murray's office, boy waiting in the interview room. According to the pictures and files Meiklejohn had given them he was one Thomas Ross. Turned out he looked younger than he was. Had turned eighteen last month. Lived in Partick with his mum. Peel Street, just around the corner from McCoy. Worked in Galbraith's, learning to be a butcher.

'What? Now you think you're the only person that's ever interviewed a suspect?' said Murray.

'No,' said McCoy patiently. 'But I think it'll work best this time if I do it alone.'

'We need information fast, you can't fuck this up, McCoy,' said Murray

'I wasn't intending to,' said McCoy. 'That's the point.'

Murray drummed his fingers on his desk. 'We're up against the clock. Twenty minutes. Then if there's nothing we're coming in.'

336

McCoy nodded. 'I'll get it done.'

He opened the door of the interview room. They'd purposely put him in the smallest and shittiest one. Was the furthest from the office too. He put a glass of water down on the table in front of Ross.

'Thought you might be thirsty,' he said. 'Go ahead.'

Ross took it, drank half at once. He wasn't looking good. Eyes were darting everywhere. Looked like the workers who'd stopped him running away had given him a bit of a doing. He had the beginning of a black eye, a cut on his cheek. His light blue shirt was dirty, torn at the shoulder.

He put the glass down, looked at McCoy. 'Can I see my dad?' he asked. 'I want to see my dad.'

McCoy put his pile of files on the table, sat down. 'Nope,' he said. 'You're an adult. Have been for two years.'

Ross blinked a few times. Even his eyelashes were reddish blonde.

McCoy took a picture out of his file, put it down in front of Ross. A middle-aged woman was smiling up at them, paper Christmas hat on, a glass of something in her hand.

Ross looked at it. Looked back at McCoy.

'That's Una Pollock,' he said. 'Worked at Tennent's.'

He took another photograph from his file, put that in front of Ross.

'And that's what you did to her.'

Ross looked at the picture, his face went white, he leant over, threw up the water into the rubbish bin. Acrid smell suddenly filling the tiny interview room.

McCoy didn't blame him. He could hardly look at the photo himself. 'You'll see both her legs have become detached from her body. Her head is almost totally gone. Her husband had to identify her by her wedding ring. So, Thomas, here's the thing you need to think about. What do you think is going to happen to you when they show that picture to a jury?'

Ross was wiping at his mouth with the cuff of his shirt. Didn't speak.

'Ah! I get it,' said McCoy. 'Good old Lindsay's training. Tell them your name, rank and serial number if captured, nothing else. Well, fuck that. This isn't some sort of war film, this is real, son, and it's about to get realer. You don't get it, do you? I can do anything I want in here. Kick you to fuck, break your ribs. Anything.'

Ross was starting to cry, tears rolling down his cheeks.

McCoy felt like a bastard but he had to keep going. Reminded himself more people were going to die if he didn't get the boy to speak. Needed to press hard.

'Nobody cares about you and nobody's going to save you. Una had four kids, three grandchildren, another one on the way. She's what matters, not what happens to you.'

Ross wiped at his eyes with the sleeve of his shirt. Looked terrified, looked like the kid he was.

McCoy sat back in his chair. 'You know what? You don't seem that stupid so you might have realised by now that Lindsay's wee toy soldiers plan is over. This is it now, this here, me and you. And if you don't start talking it's only going to get worse. A lot worse.'

He got his Regals out his pocket, lit up. Pushed the packet and matches towards Ross. He took them, lit up with shaking hands.

'I didn't kill her,' he said. 'It wasn't me.'

'Doesn't matter,' said McCoy. 'Bomb at Tennent's Brewery was made with Co-op mix. The bomb you had at the off-licence was made with Co-op mix. You're in the organisation. There's a chain of causality. Know what that is?'

Ross shook his head.

'Means you get charged with exactly the same thing as your pal who left the bomb in the Tennent's reception. Murder. They'll find you guilty. How can they not when you were caught red-handed? People don't like the idea of bombs in their city. The judge will be under pressure to go for the maximum possible sentence. Want to know what that is?'

Ross just looked at him, bottom lip trembling.

'That's going to be twenty to twenty-five years in jail. And if you think what I'm doing to you in this wee room is bad, you have no fucking idea what they are going to do to a good-looking young lad like you in jail. They'll turn your arse inside out.'

He let that sink in for a minute.

'So you tell me. Are you going to throw away your life, the whole of your life, to stay loyal to some posh army cunt who gets his kicks wanking off teenagers in the woods or whatever it is he does?'

Ross was looking down, tears and a line of snot falling into his lap. McCoy looked away for a minute, didn't want to be here doing this but he had to. He reached over, patted Ross on the back, got a hanky out his pocket and handed it to him.

'You get one chance to tell me everything you know about Lindsay and his bombing campaign, and one chance only. You do that and everything changes. I tell everyone you cooperated. Meiklejohn writes you a nice character reference. You tell everyone how sorry you are and how you were led astray by Lindsay, and things get better.'

McCoy stood up walked towards the door. 'I'll be back in five minutes. Make the right decision.'

McCoy leant against the corridor wall. Lit up another fag. Was just about chain-smoking these days. Took the Pepto-Bismol out his jacket pocket and had a swig. Tasted like chalk dissolved in water. Had been a long time since he'd hit a suspect. Wasn't going to start again now. Only ones he'd ever hit were the ones that could take it, grown-up villains, hard men. Told himself at the time that the end justified the means but he still felt shitty so he stopped. Wasn't sure scaring the living daylights out an eighteen-year-old boy instead of hitting him was any kinder. Either way, he was left feeling like the kind of bully he hated, chucking his weight about just because he could. Needed to get this over with quick. He dropped the cigarette on the floor and stamped on it. Opened the door.

Ross was sitting in the chair, swollen eye, tear-stained face, stinking of sick, fear coming off him in waves. Foot was drumming on the floor, was pulling the filter of his cigarette apart, teasing the fibres out, putting them in the wee foil ashtray.

McCoy sat down. 'Ready?'

Ross nodded.

'That's the right decision, son. When and where's the next bomb?' he asked.

'I don't know,' said Ross.

McCoy went to stand up. Ross grabbed at him, tried to stop him.

'I'm not lying! Please! It's the way Lindsay organised it. Honest.'

McCoy sat back down.

'He called it a cell structure. You know what that is?'

McCoy shook his head. 'Enlighten me.'

'The idea is that no one knows more than they need to so if they get caught or security gets breached you can't give any information away because you don't know it. He called us cells. All

341

I knew was my assignment. The off-licence. I don't know what anyone else's is.'

'You sure?' he asked.

Ross nodded again. 'The only people that knew the whole plan were Lindsay and Crawford. They gave out the assignments, Did it all face to face, nothing was written down.'

'How many of you are there?'

'Four. George, Bobby, Henry and me. Plus Crawford and Lindsay.'

'What about Donny Stewart?'

Ross shook his head.

'Why not?'

'After the bomb went off in the flat he called Lindsay from Glasgow, needed to be picked up. So me and Lindsay went in the car.'

'The Daimler?'

'Yes. Picked him up round the back of the barracks, he'd been hiding in the back storage room.'

'Did Meiklejohn know?'

Ross shook his head again.

'No. Lindsay thought he was one of the enemy. We were told to keep away from him, not tell him anything. So we picked Donny up and it was weird. He'd a big gash down his leg, blood seeping out of it, thought he'd been hit by the glass from a picture above the fireplace in the flat.'

'So what was weird about it?'

'Lindsay. He couldn't take his eyes off Donny's leg. Made him take his trousers off before he got in the car. Said he wanted to see the extent of the damage. So Donny strips off by the side of the car, stands there in his Y-fronts, and it's like Lindsay's hypnotised, just staring at him, at the gash in his leg.'

Ross swallowed, looked like he wanted to say something but he was scared.

'What else?' asked McCoy. 'Come on, Tom, you're almost there.'

Ross wiped at his nose. Kept his head down, wouldn't look at McCoy. 'The whole time he was looking at him, at his leg, he'd a hard-on. You could see it through his trousers.' And he started to cry.

McCoy got another hanky out his pocket, handed it over. Realised it was his good one, one of the ones Susan had got him for Christmas. Had *H McC* embroidered in the corner. Ross took it, blew his nose a couple of times, wiped at his eyes.

'What happened then?'

'We got back to Knockdow and in the morning Donny was gone. He'd gone back to the navy.'

'He'd what?' asked McCoy.

'Gone back to the ship. Lindsay told me, said it was the best place to get his leg treated, better than going to the hospital in case they started asking questions.'

McCoy sat back in his chair. Wondered what the fuck had really happened to Donny Stewart. He hadn't gone back to his ship. That was for sure.

'Detective Watson is going to come in. Go over

343

everything again, see if you can remember any more. Don't worry, he's a nice guy, not like me. You tell him everything you can. Okay?'

Ross nodded.

'You sure you don't know where we can find the other lads?'

Ross shook his head. 'All I know is what Crawford told me. Saw us at half-hour intervals, made sure we couldn't talk to each other.'

McCoy nodded, turned to go.

'How did Lindsay persuade you all? Get you to believe all that Scotland stuff, the stuff about the drink?'

'Have you met him?' asked Ross, suddenly alive. McCoy nodded.

'Then you'll know what he's like. He's brilliant. And out of all the cadets he chose the five of us. Said we were the boys he'd been looking for for a long time. Told us we were a band of brothers, together for life.'

'And you believed him?' asked McCoy.

Ross nodded, looked down at his lap again. 'I've never really had any friends before, not at school or at the work. Now I had Lindsay and I had the other lads. I was part of something. I was somebody.' He looked up. Smiled. 'I'd follow Colonel Lindsay to the ends of the earth.'

After what Ross had said, Lindsay's house was looking more and more like the place the missing lads had disappeared to. Out the way, secure, not too far from Glasgow. A perfect hiding place. The lads had been out there learning fieldcraft, must know their way around. Hence McCoy and Faulds were sitting in the back of a squad car, lights and siren going, heading towards Gourock and the ferry over to Dunoon.

McCoy had told Murray and Wattie what Ross had said and that he was sure he was telling the truth. Murray swore and ranted but to McCoy it made sense. The cell idea seemed like a good one to him, exactly what a smart military man would do. They'd sent a search party up to the barracks just in case Meiklejohn was lying about Donny Stewart hiding there and to see if any of the other lads were.

Wattie was going to interview Ross again. Take in clean clothes, a cup of tea, something to eat, and see if he could get anything further out of him by playing nice. A quick look at Meiklejohn's files showed that the missing lads were all of a

345

type with Thomas Ross and Paul Watt. Under-achievers, only children, missing fathers, dreamers just looking for something to change their lives. Lindsay had picked them carefully. McCoy had told Wattie to act like the big brother Ross had never had, to be his pal.

The news that it wasn't just Ross, that there were four bombers still out there – including Crawford – made everything go up a gear. With the clock ticking down, everything was being done at double speed. Car they were in was being driven by Colin Nish, the best driver in the station, had been on some advanced course down in England. Seemed a good idea but now McCoy wasn't so sure. Speed he was going was making McCoy feel a bit sick, weaving the car across lanes, sometimes using the other side of the road. If he kept it up there was a good chance they'd die in a car crash before they even got there. Meanwhile, Murray was headed back up to Pitt Street to tell them about the four and to ask for as many resources as they needed. Didn't envy him that one.

'This is bloody hellish,' said Faulds, hands gripping the seat. 'Should we ask him to slow down?'

'Don't think he can,' said McCoy, wincing as they screamed round a bend and the Clyde and the Dumbarton Rock appeared. 'Just going to have to trust him.'

On top of driving at God knows how many miles an hour Nish was also holding the car radio receiver up to his mouth, trying to make himself heard above the engine and the squeal of the tyres.

'Just coming into Port Glasgow now, sir,' he shouted into it. A pause as he listened. 'Okay, all good.'

Put the receiver back. Looked back over to McCoy, shouted in his ear. 'Change of plan. Police boat'll meet us at the dock in Greenock, just by the Custom House Quay. You know it?'

McCoy nodded.

Nish pushed the car into fifth gear, overtook an MG. 'We'll be there in five minutes.'

'Christ,' said Faulds. 'This is like a bloody James Bond film.'

'Blame Murray,' said McCoy. 'I thought we'd just send the locals but he was having none of it. Don't know their arse from their elbow.'

'Probably true,' said Faulds. 'Christ! What now?'

Nish pushed the car across two lanes, hand-brake-turned into the road leading down to the quay at the Customs House and stopped the car scarily near the edge.

'All right, gents,' he said. 'This is where you get out.'

They made their way down the steps and into the police launch. Looked like a kind of speedboat painted blue, a tiny windscreen the only protection against the elements. Young guy in a River Police uniform shook their hands, told them he was Archie Clegg. Then he put his foot on the accelerator and the boat lurched forward, front of it came up out the water, and they were off.

McCoy normally didn't like boats but he was quite enjoying this one. Fact it was bumping over the water at high speed meant it didn't wobble about too much, didn't make you feel sick. He sat down beside Clegg while Faulds cowered in the back, face paler than ever.

'Don't need to go into Dunoon,' shouted McCoy. 'Can you take us up Loch Striven? Drop us near Glenstriven?'

Clegg nodded. 'No problem. Be there in fifteen minutes.'

McCoy sat beside him the whole way, enjoying the speed and the feel of the spray coming off the river. They came up past Gourock and McCoy could see the big ships at the dock at the Holy Loch. Couldn't see any submarines though. Wondered about Donny Stewart, had a feeling that whatever had happened to him wasn't going to be good. Tried to think again what the April Dead could mean. Turned round to see Faulds bent over the side, wiping at his mouth with a pale blue hanky. He turned and looked up at McCoy, looked so miserable that McCoy couldn't help but laugh.

'All right for you, you wanker,' said Faulds. 'I'm dying here, so I am.'

Clegg slowed the boat down, curved it around and brought them into the shore at Glenstriven. They jumped onto the wee landing jetty and started walking up towards the village.

'House is about ten minutes up the road,' said McCoy.

Faulds nodded, still looked a bit green. 'Least we're back on dry land,' he said.

The narrow road was bordered by hedges. It was quiet out here, only noise was birdsong, occasional low moo of a cow. Could see the hills across the loch, snow still dusting the tops. Sun had broken through the clouds, was warm on their shoulders. Was hard to believe they were in a place as nice as this to try and stop some maniac blowing up Glasgow.

'You like the countryside?' asked Faulds.

'Nope,' said McCoy. 'You?'

Faulds shook his head. 'Spent my life in Glasgow and Belfast. City boy. All this nature makes me nervous. Can just about stick a day or so but—'

'Fuck!' said McCoy. 'Forgot to tell you in all this rush. Cooper spoke to his uncle.'

'And?' asked Faulds, looking wary.

'And the boys back in Belfast are going to lay off for a while, have another look at what happened. You're off the hook for a bit.'

Faulds stopped. 'Honest?'

McCoy nodded.

'Thank God for that,' said Faulds.

McCoy pointed through the trees at the house. 'There it is. Knockland.'

Two uniforms were standing by the gate when they got there. Boys from Argyll and Bute Police. Taller one stood forward.

'Danny Finch,' he said. 'Here to help.'

McCoy nodded, shook his hand. Looked about twenty. Other one was Jackson. Looked even younger.

'Okay,' said McCoy. 'Let's go.'

'Got a problem,' said Finch. 'Gate is padlocked. We tried the speaker thing but nobody answered.'

McCoy could hear Faulds mutter 'fuck sake' under his breath.

'What equipment have you got with you?' McCoy asked. 'Bolt cutters? They should do it.'

Finch at least had the decency to go red. 'None,' he said. 'Nobody told us we needed it.'

McCoy resisted the temptation to shout 'How the fuck did you think we were going to get in!' and tried to stay calm.

'The nearest place we could get them is the station in Greenock,' said Finch. 'Take a couple of hours.'

McCoy got out his packet of Regal, pushed it open, took out a fag and lit up. Tried to give himself some time to calm down. Suddenly thought. 'You got a car here?'

Finch nodded, pointed at a navy blue Cortina down the road.

'Let's go,' said McCoy. Turned to Faulds. 'Be back in half an hour.'

CHAPTER 48

McCoy tuned out of listening to Finch's fulsome apologies and just enjoyed the view of the water out the window as they drove towards Dunoon. Didn't like to say it but he should have listened to Murray and double-checked everything. Never trust anyone but the Glasgow Police he always said. The rest are incompetent chancers. McCoy didn't normally agree with him but there was a good chance he'd change his tune now.

'Pull in at the shows,' said McCoy as they drove into Dunoon.

'The shows?' asked Finch. 'Why?'

'Just pull in,' said McCoy. Didn't trust himself to say much else.

Finch drove into the car park in the field beside the fair. McCoy got out, told him he'd be back in ten minutes. Slammed the car door behind him. Needed to let off steam somehow.

The fair was just setting up for the day, canvas covers coming off the stalls, guys checking the rides. Someone had started frying burgers and onions though, smell of that and candy floss was

351

already everywhere. McCoy walked towards a young guy in a Black Sabbath T-shirt and denim shorts.

'All right, pal,' he said. 'Anyone here related to Patsy Hearne?'

The guy looked at him suspiciously. 'Who wants to know?'

'Me. Harry McCoy. Friend of Patsy's from Barnardo's. Saw him the other night in the Edrom. Need a favour.'

McCoy's qualifications seemed to pass muster. Was glad he hadn't mentioned he was a polis.

The guy pointed over at the waltzer. 'See the guy with the black vest? That's Tommy, Patsy's cousin.'

McCoy thanked him. Hoped his plan was going to work out. If it didn't they'd have to wait and get the ferry back to Gourock. Caught sight of Finch hovering about at the edge of the fair. Needed to get the deal done before he decided to come up and join them. Hurried over to the ride.

'Tommy?' he asked. 'Can I have a word?'

Tommy put his spanner down, looked at him.

'Name's Harry McCoy. I'm a pal of your cousin Patsy's from when we were boys in Barnardo's. Can I ask you a favour? You got any tools that would cut through a padlock?'

Tommy nodded. Seemed to be a man of few words.

'Great. There's a fiver in it for you. Got a car, take ten minutes to get there. Okay?'

Tommy nodded again. Was like trying to hold a conversation with a statue.

'Car's over by the entrance, blue Cortina. See you there in five?'

McCoy jogged off before Finch arrived, or God forbid Tommy could suddenly ask a question.

They were waiting in the car, Finch asking various questions about working in Glasgow, when Tommy appeared over the hill, heavy canvas bag over his shoulder. He was small but strong-looking, well-used to physical work. He was just about ten or so yards away, McCoy was about to open the door to let him in, when he stopped, put the bag down, stood there staring.

'What's he doing?' asked Finch.

'Fuck knows,' said McCoy, opening the car door. 'Hold on.'

He walked up to Tommy, trying to look friendly. 'All okay, Tommy?' he asked.

'No,' said Tommy in a broad Donegal accent. 'I'm not getting in a car with a fucking guard.'

Ten minutes later, a lot of persuasion and with a new fee of ten pounds agreed they pulled up at the gates of Knockland. Tommy still didn't seem very happy. Unsurprisingly, hadn't said a word the whole way there. Just sat on the back seat looking glum, canvas bag on his lap.

Faulds was sitting on the same log McCoy had sat on last time he was here, jacket off, batting away midges with his hands.

'Got a bit of help,' said McCoy.

Faulds stood up. 'Good. I'm getting bitten alive out here.'

Tommy walked up to the gates, had a look at the padlock. 'Want it off, do you?' he asked.

McCoy nodded and Tommy got a huge pair of bolt cutters out the bag.

'Where'd you find him?' asked Faulds.

'I'm a friend of his cousin's,' said McCoy.

Tommy grasped the bridge of the padlock between the massive jaws of the bolt cutters, pressed down hard, grunted and pressed down even harder. His face went red under the strain and then there was a ping, a bit of the padlock flew past McCoy's head, and the gate swung open.

'Better take the car,' said McCoy. 'House is a good way up the drive.'

'I'll walk,' said Tommy. Obviously, the thought of getting back in a car with a guard was more than he could bear.

McCoy wasn't sure what he was expecting as they drove up towards the house. Guard dogs? A bunch of lads with guns? Best he could hope for was four teenagers who'd realised that their leader was nowhere to be found and the dream of a drink-free Scotland was over. Had the feeling it wasn't going to be that easy. The expression Lindsay had used about Donny Stewart was still rattling around in his head. 'One of the April Dead.' Did that mean he was dead already? Or maybe he was going to go on some sort of suicide mission with a bomb, like a kamikaze pilot. Christ, that was the last thing they needed.

They pulled up beside the entrance and everyone got out.

'What do we do now?' asked Faulds, looking up at the building.

McCoy stepped forward. 'This,' he said. And rang the bell.

CHAPTER 49

McCoy hadn't expected the door to be answered and he really wasn't expecting the person who answered it. There were footsteps, turn of a lock and the door was opened to reveal Margo Lindsay. She was dressed in a baggy men's boiler suit, famous auburn hair in a loose ponytail. She was holding a half-empty bottle of red wine in one hand and a crystal wine glass in the other.

'I know you,' she said, swaying slightly. 'McCoy.'

'That's it,' he said.

She held up the bottle, tipped a good measure into the glass and sank it. Wiped her mouth. 'Last of my father's cellar. Chateau Marquis de Terme 1952. Old fucker started off with six crates and this and another two bottles is all that's left.' She looked at him. 'What are you doing here anyway?'

'Need to have a look around the house,' said McCoy.

She smiled. 'And do you have a warrant?' Held up her hand. 'Actually, I don't much care if you do or don't. Haven't spoken to my swine of a

356

brother in years.' She bowed, held the door open. 'Be my guest.'

She pushed past McCoy and started walking down the long drive in a less than straight line.

'Was that Margo Lindsay?' asked Faulds as they watched her taking another swig as she walked.

'Yep,' said McCoy. Turned to the two uniforms. 'You two search the grounds, any outbuildings, garages, stables, things like that.'

Finch nodded and the two of them headed for the back of the house.

'I didn't know they were related,' said Faulds.

'She lives at some farm commune down the road,' said McCoy. 'Bunch of hippies.'

He pushed the door open and they went in. Wasn't sure what he thought Lindsay's house would be like, like an army barracks maybe, but it was anything but. The hall was carpeted in pale blue, walls hung with hunting prints and landscapes, enormous gold mirror on one wall. On the other, a table stood, an open book on it like a restaurant reservations book.

McCoy looked at the cover. VISITORS spelled out in gold leaf. Couldn't resist flicking through it.

Thanks for the glorious weekend! Duff and Diana, August 1924

Brendan Behan 21/2/54

Two trout! Boothby September 1965

The list went on and on. McCoy knew who some of the people were. Rest seemed a never-ending list of sirs and lords and dames. He closed it. Above the bureau was a collection of framed photos. Hunting parties. Fishing parties. People in tennis whites. People swimming in the loch.

They walked on down the hallway to a door. Opened it.

'Fuck me,' said Faulds. 'This is quite something.'

It was. The high-ceilinged room in front of them was positively luxurious. Patterned wallpaper, pale green carpet covered in oriental rugs, couches surrounding a coffee table laid out with books and wee Japanese-looking ornaments. There were standard lamps everywhere, paintings lining the walls, armchairs with embroidered cushions. A huge window at the far end of the room framed a view of the loch and the hills behind.

Tommy appeared, sat down on one of the armchairs facing the view. Looked very happy.

'You see anything, hear anything, you give us a shout. Okay?' said McCoy.

Tommy nodded, snuggling further into the velvet comfort.

Faulds and McCoy walked around the rest of the house. Was easy to forget what they were doing there and just be amazed at it all.

'How do you get to live in a place like this?' asked Faulds as they stood in a library, wall-to-wall gilt-edged books, desks, a mahogany ladder on runners.

'It's easy,' said McCoy. 'You get born into the right family.'

Next door was Lindsay's bedroom. Another view over the bay. Paintings of stern-looking men and beautiful women on the walls. A row of well-polished boots and shoes on the floor by a sofa. McCoy sat down on the four-poster bed.

'Think we're barking up the wrong tree here. Can't see Lindsay letting a bunch of Glasgow teenagers run about daft in here.'

'Nope,' said Faulds. 'Maybe there's a bunk-house, something like that? They must have stayed somewhere when they came up here for the weekend.'

'You're right,' said McCoy, standing up. 'What's the chances of those two clowns finding it?'

'Slim,' said Faulds. 'Let's go and have a look.'

They left Tommy snoozing in his armchair and walked back out into the sunshine. There was a gravel path by the side of the house. Had to lead somewhere. Started walking.

'Been thinking about what Ross said, about the cell structure. I know we thought this was the obvious hiding place, but if what Ross said is true,' said McCoy, 'it's more likely that they'll all be in separate places. Lindsay wouldn't allow them to be together. Chances are they're in Glasgow in different flats or boarding houses, not up here waiting for us to find them.'

'Probably,' said Faulds. 'But if that's true, how do we find them? We've got no chance.'

'Maybe we should just go back to Glasgow and organise a call-around all the—'

A whistle. Then another.

'God help us,' said Faulds. 'The Boy Scouts must have found something.'

They had. They'd found the bunkhouse. It was a long log cabin, wee windows punched into the side, black tiled roof. Inside were two rows of camp beds, some of them unmade. It looked like whoever had been there had left in a hurry. There were tin mugs on the table half full of tea. A worn copy of *Playbirds* on the floor. Lockers hanging open, gym stuff bundled up on the floor of one. There was a big saltire on one wall, a cloth banner spelling DEFENS on the other.

'You find anything?' McCoy asked Finch.

He shook his head. 'Just this place. Doesn't look like there's been anyone here for a few days. Food dumped in the bin, flies everywhere. The door was wide open.'

McCoy looked over and saw Faulds had emptied the bin by the door onto the floor. A mess of crisp packets, sweetie wrappers, what looked like a half-eaten fish supper in a newspaper. A hanky stuck together with what McCoy hoped was snot. Faulds didn't seem too bothered, was poking about in it all. He picked up a tiny balled-up piece of paper. Unravelled it. Looked up at McCoy.

'What?' asked McCoy. 'What is it?'

Faulds stood up, walked over to McCoy.

Showed him. Looked like it had been ripped from a bigger piece.

ros Ba

'What does that mean?' asked McCoy.

'God knows,' said Faulds. 'Nothing probably.'

'Might though, why else would you rip it up into wee pieces?'

'Somebody's name?' asked Faulds. 'The B's a capital.'

'What first name ends in ros?' asked McCoy, trying to think. 'Carlos? No, that's not right. Fuck it, we could be here all day trying to think of one.'

He sat on one of the beds, could see a sandshoe under the one opposite. Realised Finch was hovering beside him. Looked up.

'There's a chippy in Greenock,' he said, 'called Coia's, but it's run by Greeks not Italians now, they bought it over.'

McCoy nodded, had no idea why Finch was talking to him about a chippy. 'That right?' he said.

'Anyway,' said Finch. 'There's a guy that works in it and he's called Stav. Stavros. Could that be it?'

'Stavros Ba . . .' said Faulds. 'Fits but it doesn't make much sense.'

'Ba,' said McCoy. Stood up. 'Fuck!'

'What?' said Faulds.

'It's not a name at all,' said McCoy. 'Bar, it's a bar. The Andros Bar.'

'Christ, you could be right,' said Faulds. 'It's not that far from West Princes Street and the off-licence. Shithole, mind you, but it's Great Western Road. Same area. You think it's a target?'

'Could be,' said McCoy.

Faulds went back to the rubbish pile, went through it all carefully, unwrapped every wee bit of paper. Looked up and shook his head.

'Fuck it,' said McCoy. 'It's the best clue we have.' He turned to the two uniforms. 'Which of you can run faster?'

'Me,' said Finch.

'Right, run back to the big house. Call Stewart Street and ask for Watson or Murray. Tell them what we've found, get them to evacuate the Andros Bar on Great Western Road, and let them know there might be a bomb there already. Got it?'

Finch nodded.

'Go!' said McCoy. 'Quick!'

CHAPTER 50

McCoy and Faulds were standing in the main reception room, both staring at the phone, both waiting for it to ring. McCoy was tapping the ash from his cigarette into his palm, couldn't decide if any of the wee bowls dotted around were ashtrays or precious antiques so he'd gone for the safer option. Walked over to the fireplace, emptied the ash into it, took one last draw, and dropped his cigarette in there too. Suddenly struck him.

'Where's Tommy gone?' he asked.

'Must have gone for a wander,' said Faulds. 'His bag's still here.'

'What's keeping them?' asked McCoy. 'Should have heard back by now.'

'Did you give them the number?'

'No, Hughie, I thought I'd just let them try and guess it. What do you—'

'You two are looking for something, that right?'

They turned to see Tommy standing in the doorway.

McCoy nodded. 'Trying to find a young lad that's gone missing. Think he might be injured, or worse.'

Tommy thought for a minute, seemed to approve. 'Bring my bag,' he said, turned, and started walking up the stairs. Stopped halfway up, turned around. 'Those guards aren't here, are they?'

McCoy shook his head. 'Out in the grounds having another look. Tommy, you do know we're the police, don't you?'

'I'm aware of that,' he said. 'But you have suits, not uniforms. That means you're the bosses so I'm hoping you might not be entirely stupid.'

'Thanks,' said McCoy, not quite sure if he was being complimented or insulted.

Tommy nodded, walked up the stairs.

Faulds looked at McCoy. McCoy shrugged, picked up the bag, followed Tommy.

The first floor of the house was all carpeted corridors and bedrooms. Walls dotted with stags' antlers and pictures of Highland landscapes. Through the windows you could see the green of the trees gently swaying in the wind. Tommy led them along a corridor towards the back of the house and stopped at the end of the corridor.

McCoy put the bag down, weighed a ton. Looked at the wall, looked at Faulds, looked at Tommy. Had no idea why they were standing there.

'Tommy? What are we—'

'Never thought I'd be helping the guards but I think there's something not right here.' He tapped along the wall, even McCoy could hear the different sounds. He dug into his bag, brought out a long thin screwdriver, and ran it down the wall. It burst through the wallpaper easily, seemed to be running down a groove. He kept going, traced a big rectangle on the wallpaper. Stood back looking triumphant.

'I had a look outside, at the building,' said Tommy. 'There's the space for a room but no windows. Thought it might be some sort of secure cupboard at first but the space is too big. It's a room all right.'

McCoy watched in amazement as he prised the wallpaper rectangle off. It came away easily, just a thin bit of woodchip covered in floral wallpaper. Behind it was a door.

'Fuck me,' said Faulds.

'Crafty bugger,' said Tommy under his breath. 'Military man owns this place, you said?'

McCoy nodded.

'That explains that then,' said Tommy, pointing at the door lock. 'That's a Mersey lock.'

'What's that when it's at home?' asked Faulds.

'Military design,' said Tommy. 'Used to secure armouries, that sort of thing. Not the kind of lock you would have on a bedroom door – in fact, I've never seen one outside an army base. You'd only have one of those if you really didn't want anyone getting in.'

'Shit,' said McCoy.

'I don't get it. How come you know so much about all this?' asked McCoy.

Tommy looked a bit sheepish. 'Let's just say I

don't always work on the shows. Just helping Patsy out between jobs.'

McCoy stepped past him, hammered on the door. Shouted.

'Donny! You in there?'

Listened. No response. Tried again.

'Stop!' said Tommy, pushing him aside. He looked the door up and down. Knocked softly where McCoy had been knocking then stood back, looked at the door again. Muttered 'you crafty bugger' again under his breath then started knocking all over the door in a grid pattern.

'Thought I heard it,' he said after a minute, turning to McCoy and Faulds. 'The wood's only about an inch thick, like a cover. The real door's underneath it. Sounds like it's iron.'

'Christ,' said McCoy. 'He really doesn't want us to get in there, does he? What are we going to do? We'll never get through that. Need to get the engineers out from Glasgow, going to take hours.'

'Not necessarily,' said Tommy. 'You boys happy to not tell anyone how we opened it?'

McCoy nodded.

'No trouble from the guards?'

McCoy crossed his finger across his chest. 'On my mother's grave.'

Tommy looked at him. 'I'm a man of honour, I don't take that promise lightly. You the same, are you?'

McCoy nodded. No need to tell Tommy his mum

was still alive and his sense of honour had gone missing a good few years ago.

'Right,' said Tommy, digging in his pocket and taking out a set of thin iron picks on a ring. 'Let's give it a go.'

McCoy and Faulds sat on the corridor floor watching Tommy work. He'd been at it for twenty minutes or so. Far as McCoy could make out, picking a lock seemed to consist of sticking the pick in the lock, shaking it about, then swearing. Had no idea what was going to be in that room, what sort of state Donny would be in, whether he would still be alive or not. All he was sure of was that if Lindsay had gone to this much trouble to keep them out, whatever he was hiding in there was going to be grim.

'How you getting on, Tommy?' he asked.

'Getting there,' he said. 'These locks are a bugger though, takes for ever to . . .' He stopped. Turned the pick. There was a soft click. Big grin on his face. 'There we go. Over to you.'

McCoy and Faulds stood up. Waited until Tommy picked up all his stuff, cleared it into his bag, and stepped aside.

McCoy stepped forward and pushed the door open.

CHAPTER 51

The room wasn't large, maybe ten feet square or so. No windows, like Tommy had said, and dark. McCoy felt for the light switch, clicked it. Bright light. Heard Faulds say 'fuck me' behind him and stepped in.

The entire floor of the room was covered in photos, three or four deep, some ripped, some in piles. They were everywhere, only an occasional glimpse of the floorboards through them. There was nothing to do but stand on them. McCoy looked down. His right foot was on a photo of a young black man tied over what looked like a pommel horse, back a mess of cuts and blood. His left one was on a contact sheet, lots of slightly different close-ups or ropes binding someone's arm, tied so tight they were cutting into the flesh.

He looked up quickly, heart was pounding, starting to feel dizzy, but there was no escape. The photos covered the walls too. All images of young men in pain, bound, tortured, bleeding. McCoy tried to breathe slowly, keep calm. There were black men, what looked like Chinese men and lots of young white men, some in uniform, some in

368

what was left of it, or could be discerned through the bloodstains.

McCoy could feel his stomach churning, desperately didn't want to be sick. Cardboard boxes of contact sheets lined the walls, half spilling out. More pain, more blood. There were two dining chairs, one covered in Super-8 reels, little round yellow cases. On the other chair was a projector. There was something written in what McCoy hoped was red paint on the far wall.

VATER! HILF MIR!

McCoy pushed past Faulds, ran out the room, managed to find a bathroom before he threw up. Cleaned himself up, splashed his face with cold water, came back out and stood beside Tommy in the corridor. Got his fags out and lit up. Could hear Faulds walking about in the room then the whirr of a projector and white light streamed out through the bottom of the door.

'What's in there?' asked Tommy.

'Pictures,' said McCoy. 'Pictures of people being tortured.'

'Mother of God,' said Tommy, crossing himself. 'I'm away. Don't want to be seeing any of that.'

McCoy watched him go, wished he could too. Wondered what the fuck they had discovered. Some of the pictures had looked old, starting to fade and go brown. How long had all this been going on? The whirring stopped, the light went out, and Faulds emerged from the room, face ashen, a couple of pictures in his hand.

He stepped forwards and started kicking the corridor wall, plaster started falling away, but he kept kicking on and on until he'd tired himself out. Stopped, sweat on his brow, pushed back his hair. Face looked haunted.

'I need a drink,' he said.

A few minutes later they were sitting at the table in the dining room. Two crystal glasses of whisky and a decanter in front of them. Faulds drank half his in one. His face was still white, hand trembling.

'I've never seen anything like that, Harry,' he said. 'Not in all my years. Jesus Christ.'

McCoy had to ask, although he wasn't sure he wanted to hear the answer. 'What was on the film?'

Faulds shook his head. 'Christ knows. Looks like it was shot years ago. It's a room, you can see through the window, it looks like Africa or somewhere.' Took another drink of the whisky. 'All you can see is a young black guy in some state, looks like he's been punched or kicked, his face is all swollen up. He's tied up to a cross thing, like a wooden X. No clothes on and a soldier, young guy, British uniform, appears with what looks like a huge pair of pliers in his hand.'

Faulds looked down at the table.

'And he puts the guy's balls in them and he pulls them down. There's no sound but you can see the guy screaming and he keeps pulling them together and then he pulls the pliers away and there's just this gush of blood . . .' Faulds looked up at him. 'I couldn't watch any more.'

'Fucking hell,' said McCoy. 'British Army? You sure?'

Faulds nodded. Pushed a picture towards him. McCoy didn't want to look at it but he knew he had to. Was another black man, older this time, collapsed in a heap on the floor of what looked like a cell, blood all over the floor. Two men in uniform, young, smiling, standing either side of him, one had his foot on his head. Smiling for the camera, short whips in hand. McCoy turned it over, writing on the back.

Manyani April 1956

'Manyani?' said McCoy. 'Where's that?'

Faulds shrugged. 'Africa somewhere?' He handed McCoy another photo.

It was hard to make out. Was a bit out of focus, looked like a small village, huts. There was a pile of something at the edge of the picture. McCoy thought it was firewood at first, looked closer. Was a jumble of arms and legs.

He put it down, tried to slow his breathing, gulped his whisky. Turned the picture over.

Batang Kali April 1948

371

'What is all this stuff?' asked McCoy. 'Why has Lindsay got it?'

'That's not the weirdest thing,' said Faulds. 'I found this as well.'

He held out another picture. Looked much more recent. A man was standing spread-eagled against a brick wall, up on his toes. He'd long hair, bruises on his body, only had underpants on, big head-phones covering his ears. McCoy turned it over.

Brendan Shaughnessy. Sixteen hours of stress position. White noise. No food or drink.

McCoy looked up at Faulds.

'I know Brendan Shaughnessy,' Faulds said. 'He's in the Armagh brigade. Arrested him once for drink driving of all things.' He tapped the picture. 'What the fuck is a picture of Brendan Shaughnessy doing here? And what are they doing to him?'

McCoy shook his head. 'I don't know what any of this is or what it's got to do with Lindsay. Need someone who knows about the British Army or military history to come and look at it.'

'Do you think Lindsay is the one who took the pictures?' asked Faulds.

McCoy tried to work it out. 'He could be. He'd need to be at least late fifties by now.'

The phone rang.

They looked at each other, had forgotten they were waiting for a call back. Hurried through to the reception room and McCoy picked it up. Listened.

'Really?' He looked at Faulds, grinned, lifted his arms above his head in triumph. 'That's brilliant. Well done. Listen, Wattie, need you to get someone at the university that knows about the army or recent military history, and I need them up here soon as. Nish, the patrol boat, everything, okay?' Listened again. 'Great.'

Put the phone down.

'That's why it took them a while to phone back. The bastard had put the bomb in a bag. Hidden it in a wee cupboard in the toilets they keep the floor cleaner in. Was timed to go off at eight o'clock tonight. Friday night. At the busiest time. They just managed to defuse it. All clear.'

'Ya dancer!' said Faulds.

McCoy nodded. 'Can you do me a favour? Go and find those two local clowns and tell them to wait at the quay at Glenstriven, bring the university guy up?'

Faulds nodded. 'No worries, they'll be outside somewhere smoking and scratching their arses. Talking about how the Glasgow force kept them out of things.'

McCoy watched him go. Could have gone with him but there was something he needed to do. He needed to go back in that room and see if he could find anything that would help him find out what had happened to Donny Stewart, and he wanted to do it alone. Didn't want Faulds seeing him fainting or being sick again. He climbed up the stairs, stomach already turning over. The last thing in the world he wanted to do was go back to that room but he had to. Just hoped for Donny Stewart's sake that he wouldn't find anything.

CHAPTER 52

McCoy was sitting on the floor amongst all the photos and bits of paper. He'd started by the door and was working his way towards the back of the room. He'd only had to stand up and go outside twice. Once when he found a photo of a hand with two of the fingers chopped off and once when he picked up a photo of a black man's head being submerged in what looked like a latrine bucket.

Still hadn't found anything that connected to Donny Stewart. Most of the photos seemed old, had taken place in foreign countries. He picked up a cardboard box, started flicking through. Stopped. Picked out a photo of a young guy, the same age as the cadets. He was sitting on the big couch in what looked like the reception room downstairs, laughing, bare-chested, bottle of beer in his hand. Kept flicking. Found another one, same guy, but this time he was passed out on the carpet in front of a fireplace. Was definitely downstairs, McCoy recognised the mirror and the pictures on the wall. Looked unconscious. Kept flicking. Stopped. Swore under his breath.

This time he was naked, whole body tied up with ropes. He was lying on a stone floor and he wasn't unconscious or sleeping this time. He was screaming. He looked at the back.

N.H. April 1973.

Was he one of the cadets? Needed to ask Meiklejohn. He stood up, realised there was a piece of paper sticking to his shoe. He peeled it off. It looked old, brownish, ink was faded. Some of it had got wet at some point, words now indistinct.

APRIL FIFTEENTH 1945
. . . . it can't even be described.
I saw things I didn't think could exist on this earth. The smell of human excrement was . . .
. . . . . . I saw hell in the shade of pine trees
. . . . .
and that afternoon . . . . caught one, a young soldier, blond hair, blue eyes . . .
. . . . that were strong enough took their turns with knives and he shouted Vater! Hilf mir!

McCoy looked up at the red painted letters on the wall. Looked back.

and he was crying and . . . . everybody looked away everyone except me

376

I watched. And I suddenly knew what I was here to . . .

Couldn't make any more of it out. Tried to think. What had happened in April '45 in the war? Must have been winding down by then. He put the paper on the pile with the photos he'd picked out and walked down to phone Meiklejohn. Why did it all seem to be about April? Was that when all this had started? April 1945? Felt like he was trying to make sense out of a puzzle with only half the information he needed. Really hoped Wattie had managed to find someone. Maybe they'd be able to make sense of it all.

'You have anybody with the initials NH?' asked McCoy.

'Let me think,' said Meiklejohn.

McCoy waited, tipped his ash into a vase. Could see himself in the mirror hanging over the fireplace. Didn't look good. Old. Tired. Could hear Meiklejohn rustling papers on the other end of the phone. He came back.

'Had to look it up. Two. Neil Harrison and Norman Hall. Why?'

'Any of them missing?'

'No. Saw Norman Hall the other day actually, he's a window cleaner now. Neil Harrison moved to London.'

'Who told you'd he'd gone to London?' asked McCoy.

'Crawford – said he'd been getting off the train from Greenock, met him in Glasgow Central with his suitcase, just about to get on the train. Said he'd had enough of Glasgow and his dad.'

Crawford. That little shit. McCoy was sure now. 'Can you remember when he went?'

'Yes. Last April. I remember because he'd put himself down for the trip to Aldershot and he went the week before. Had to change all the train stuff. Pain in the arse.'

More April, thought McCoy. What if it was April every year?

'Can you have a look in your files, see if anyone else went missing in April? Can you try the proper army too, anyone missing from a Scottish base in April?'

'What's this about?' asked Meiklejohn. 'Just April?'

'Just April. I don't think they just went missing,' said McCoy. 'Think something might have happened to them, something bad.'

'Christ,' said Meiklejohn. 'I'll get on it now.'

He hung up and McCoy put the phone down, then dialled the station. Got put through to Murray.

'Well done on the Andros Bar,' he said. 'Saved a lot of people's lives. That bomb was more than twice the size of the other one. How did you know?'

'We got lucky,' said McCoy. 'Very lucky.'

'What the fuck's going on up there anyway?

Watson's been phoning the university every five minutes.'

'Need an expert here,' said McCoy. 'Are they coming?'

'Should be there any minute,' said Murray. 'Some professor who specialises in twentieth-century military history apparently. Had to bundle him out of some lecture on Suez.'

'That's great. Need you to do something else, Murray. We need a proper search of this house and its grounds. Will probably need Argyll and Bute, and some from Glasgow.'

'Why?' asked Murray. 'What are we looking for?'

'Bodies,' said McCoy. 'There's a good chance it's more than one. Just need to get this professor bloke started here and I'll come back to the station, explain it all.'

Could hear Murray breathe out, could picture the pipe smoke.

'You sure about this, McCoy? It's a big ask, an operation like that.'

McCoy looked down at the picture of Neil Harrison screaming.

'I'm sure,' he said. 'Get them out here as soon as you can. Get Wattie up here to organise them. He was good in the park search for Alice Kelly last year.'

Murray said he would and McCoy put the phone down. Sat down on one of the armchairs. Needed a bit of time by himself. Try to understand what was going on. There was a painting on the wall opposite. Colonel Angus Lindsay. Man with a moustache and a dress uniform looking out. He looked hard, cold. Baton under his arm.

Vater! Hilf mir!

CHAPTER 53

McCoy was sitting on the steps at the entrance to the house watching the goings-on. They'd sent twenty or so uniforms up from Argyll and Bute. They were standing on the lawn, smoking, joking with each other. Vans that had brought them lining the driveway. All he needed now was Wattie to arrive and sort them out. Hoped he'd come with the professor, would save them some time. He lit a cigarette, waved the midges away from his face.

Had the feeling Crawford Lindsay was the key. He'd helped organise the bombings and now that Lindsay was fading, young Crawford would surely be in charge of what happened next. He'd lied about Neil Harrison going to London. Question was whether he knew what he was lying for. Had his dad just told him to do it or was he more involved?

Movement at the turn of the driveway caught his eye. It was Faulds with Wattie and a man who couldn't have looked more like a professor if he'd tried. He'd a tweedy suit, shirt coming out his trousers, wee round glasses. He was looking around, trying to keep up with the other two. Must have been difficult for him, had a bad limp, dragged his left leg.

Wattie waved and McCoy waved back. Happy to see him and not just because he could organise the search. That big daft face of his always managed to cheer McCoy up somehow. He stood up, brushed the grit from the bum of his trousers, and waited for them to get there.

'All right, Harry,' said Wattie. 'Got the troops here, I see.'

'Need you to organise a search,' said McCoy. 'Grounds and any outbuildings. We're looking for recently disturbed earth, under fallen trees, cellars, basements, that sort of thing.'

'For a body, you mean?' asked Wattie.

'Maybe more than one.'

Wattie nodded, walked off, shouted at the group of uniforms to gather round.

'This is Professor Burns,' said Faulds.

McCoy held his hand out and Burns shook it. Nodded up at the house.

'It's a David Bryce,' he said, smiling.

'A what?' said McCoy.

'The architect. I know because I grew up in one. Inzievar House. Near Dunfermline.'

'That right?' said McCoy, wondering why he was always dealing with Scotsmen with posh English accents. 'Come in, need you to have a look at some stuff for us.'

McCoy led him into the dining room. Poured him a glass of whisky, handed it to him. Burns looked puzzled.

'Just drink it,' said McCoy. 'You'll need it.'

Burns took a sip, grimaced. 'Not a big whisky drinker. More of a red wine man.'

'Sure we can find you some of that,' said McCoy. 'Hughie, will you get us a bottle of red wine from the basement?'

Faulds nodded, hurried off.

'The man Watson?' said Burns. 'He didn't really explain why I was needed here. Something about military history?'

McCoy nodded. 'There's a mountain of pictures upstairs, need you to try and identify where they were taken and what's going on in them. Seem to be from the war until Northern Ireland. That your area?'

Burns nodded. 'I specialise in colonial conflict. Remnants of Empire, how it's liberated, becomes independent. Bit shakier on World War Two if I'm being honest.'

Faulds returned and handed Burns a dusty bottle. 'Got the same one Margo was drinking,' he said. 'I don't know anything about wine.'

Burns took it. His eyebrows raised. 'Chateau Marquis de Terme? 1952? That's quite a bottle. Seems a pity to open it without food or without more of a ceremony.'

'Open it,' said McCoy. 'You're going to need it.'

CHAPTER 54

McCoy had walked Burns up to the room, now with a full glass of wine in his hand. Told him that he was about to see some terrible things. Burns looked scared.

'Sorry,' said McCoy. 'But I need you to go in there. Okay?'

Burns nodded and pushed the door open. No way was McCoy going back in. He'd told Burns to come back downstairs when he'd finished and that he was sorry to put him through it. Faulds went in with him. He was the only one who knew how to work the projector.

McCoy stood in the reception room, glanced at the clock on the mantelpiece. They'd been up there for just over an hour. Could see Wattie and a long line of uniforms moving across the grounds through the big window. A beautiful house, malt whisky and expensive red wine, antiques everywhere, and what were they doing? Trying to work out what was happening in the worst photos McCoy had ever seen. Times like this he regretted becoming a policeman. Took out his Pepto-Bismol and had another swig.

Wasn't sure it was doing any good, stomach still hurt most of the time.

He heard footsteps on the stairs and Faulds appeared, pile of photos in his arms, Burns following behind, empty wine glass in hand. McCoy watched as Burns walked over to the sideboard, filled the glass up to the brim, swallowed half of it, and filled it up again. Sat down on the couch and put his head in his hands.

McCoy looked at Faulds, mouthed, 'Is he okay?'

Faulds shrugged. Mouthed 'fuck knows' and put the photographs on the table.

Burns looked up. 'You could have warned me.'

'I did,' said McCoy.

'Not sure anything could have prepared me for that, but you could have tried.'

'I'm sorry,' said McCoy. 'But I couldn't risk putting you off.'

'I broke my leg in a skiing accident when I was fourteen,' said Burns. 'Broke it badly. The plan had been I would join the army.' He smiled. 'When that was off the table I decided to study it. It's been my life's work, something I have enjoyed immensely. Until today, that is. Today I wished I'd never been interested in military history, wished I'd studied ancient Greek, anything that meant I didn't have to go into that room.'

He took another slug of his wine.

'But I did,' he said. 'So what do you want to know?'

'What the pictures are of,' said McCoy. 'Are they

official? Is it all Lindsay or is there a bigger reason they are there? And what has April got to do with it?'

'Let's start with Lindsay,' said Burns. 'After that, it gets more complicated. Lindsay was . . . is?' He looked up.

'Colonel Angus Lindsay. This is his house.'

'He was in The Highlanders it seems,' said Burns. 'First things I found date from April 1945. When they liberated Buchenwald.'

'Christ,' said McCoy.

'There are several official photographs. From what I remember, the plan was to record what had happened in the camps to show the German people, make them realise the horror of what they had done. That was hurriedly shelved when the Russians became the enemy.' He smiled. 'But that's another story. Some other pictures look like snapshots, amateur stuff, presumably taken by Lindsay. And unfortunately there is a bit of film as well. Looks like it's been refilmed off a larger format so it can be shown on an 8mm film projector. For domestic use, the kind you use to bore your relatives with films of your family on holiday.'

He took another large swig of his wine.

'Both the photos and the film show the same thing. As the camps were liberated, and it happened in many of them, feelings were understandably very high. More often than not the authorities looked the other way while the prisoners, those

386

who were able, that is, took revenge on any of the guards who were unlucky enough to be caught.' He got up, flicked through the piles of photos, found the one he was looking for. Handed it to McCoy. 'And that's what Lindsay's photos show.'

McCoy steeled himself, looked down.

A young blond man, uniform half ripped off, was tied to a tree, hands behind his back. He looked healthy but his torso was a mess of dark blood. An emaciated man, half-skeleton, was stabbing him in the chest while others lined up behind him, knives or bits of glass in their hands.

'The prisoners were very weak,' said Burns. 'His cuts and injuries aren't very deep. If you watch the film, which I wouldn't advise, you can see it's the accumulation that kills him. He takes a long time to die.' Another swig of wine. 'This seems to have been the first and the most important event Lindsay was interested in. Hence the writing on the wall. *Vater! Hilf mir!*'

'What does it mean?' asked McCoy.

'It means "Father, help me". That's probably what the man was saying as he was killed.'

Burns drained his glass. 'Can we open another bottle?' he asked.

Faulds nodded, went off to get one.

'Then things get muddy,' said Burns.

'What do you mean?'

'There is a military history that we don't really talk about. The history of things done wrong, illegally. The torture, the abuse. It seems to happen

387

particularly in colonial conflict. The question is whether Lindsay was just there recording it or whether he was instigating it. Are you aware of Amnesty International?'

McCoy shook his head.

'It's a relatively new charity, more of a protest group. They investigate human rights abuses. Treatment of Russian political prisoners in the gulag, that sort of thing.' He stood up, went to the pile again, and took out the photo of Brendan Shaughnessy. 'This is the most recent photograph. Appears to be some sort of detention centre in Northern Ireland.'

Faulds appeared with another bottle in his hand. 'This do?' he asked. Burns didn't even look at it, nodded. Faulds got the corkscrew started and opened it.

'Amnesty International published a report a couple of years ago, 1971, I think. Claimed IRA prisoners were being tortured. British Establishment said it was nonsense. Trashed it. Said it was all Republican propaganda.' He held up the photo of Brendan Shaughnessy. 'Forgive the melodrama, but this would appear to be the smoking gun.'

Faulds handed him another glass. 'That'll cause World War Three back in Ireland.'

Burns nodded. 'One of my PhD students is researching the collapse of colonial power and how it falls into abuse in its last days.' He pointed at the photos. 'Aden, Malaya, Kenya, Ireland, even Korea. They are all there, all photographed by Lindsay.'

Burns swallowed the wine. Smiled. 'Seems rather a coincidence that one man was present at all those occasions.'

'You mean he was there deliberately?' asked McCoy.

Burns nodded. 'Britain used its colonial powers for many things, but one of them was to perfect its torture and interrogation techniques. What was learnt in the Mau Mau camps in Kenya helped inform what seems to be happening in the outskirts of Belfast as we speak.'

'So that's what Lindsay really did in the army? Refined torture techniques?' asked McCoy.

Burns shrugged. 'It's certainly possible.'

'And he got a taste for it,' said Faulds. 'Kept it up when he retired.'

'The missing cadets,' said McCoy. 'For fuck sake.'

He thought of the picture of Neil Harrison screaming. Wondered how many more there had been. Was like Burns had read his mind.

'There are six or seven photos there that don't seem to have a military angle.' He went over to the sideboard to fill his glass again. Stopped. Looked at a worn red leather armchair. Turned to McCoy. 'Christ. One of the photos was taken there. That's the chair.'

His knees buckled and he sank down on the carpet like a little kid. Started to sob.

McCoy handed him his drink. Told him thank you. Headed for the door.

CHAPTER 55

McCoy's head was resting on the car window. He was watching the world go by, trying to think. If Burns was right, Christ knows what had happened to Donny Stewart. He didn't want to think. And it wasn't just Donny. Who knew how many other missing lads there were. Needed Lindsay to start talking about the bombs and the missing boys. Needed to work out how to get him to do that. Had thought of going straight to the hospital but he'd called Dr Basu from Greenock and Lindsay was out of it again, said the best idea was to try in the morning. If he got a good night's sleep he might be compos mentis when he woke up. Wondered if Lindsay was well aware of what he was doing, making himself too drugged up to make any sense, wouldn't have to answer any questions that way.

Wattie was driving. They'd left Faulds at the house. He was going to keep the search going, stay there tonight, and start it again first thing in the morning. McCoy was exhausted, worn out. Images from the room kept coming into his head. Looked at his watch. Coming up for seven. Fancied

390

another drink and something to eat. Maybe he'd go to the Central. If Stewart was there then fine, he could tell him how stupid he and Cooper had been. If not, fine. Had more things on his mind than giving them a row. Besides, what was the point? It was done now, couldn't be undone.

'You asleep?' asked Wattie.

'Nope,' said McCoy. He sat up in his seat. Started looking for his fags.

'Where do you want dropped?' asked Wattie. 'Gardner Street?'

McCoy shook his head. 'Anywhere in the town's fine. Going to go for a drink. What about you?'

'Back home to see the wee man,' said Wattie. 'See what Mary's making for tea. Probably be sending me out for a chippy.'

McCoy lit up. Dropped his match into the ashtray in the door handle. 'Sounds good to me,' he said. And it did. Remembered the weeks after Wee Bobby was born. Flat was chaos, nappies and bottles everywhere, too tired to cook, takeaway most nights. Happy to just sit in the chaos and watch the baby sleeping.

'You want to come round and see him?' asked Wattie.

McCoy shook his head. Felt fragile enough after today, the last thing he needed was to hold a baby and remember what that was like.

'I'll come and see him next weekend,' he said. 'Push him around the park, give you and Mary a few hours off.'

'You're on,' said Wattie as he pulled in at the Jamaica Street lights.

'Meet me at the Royal at eight tomorrow morning,' said McCoy. 'Let's see if we can get any sense out of that bastard Lindsay.'

Wattie sighed. 'Want me to pick you up?'

'Thought you'd never ask,' said McCoy, getting out the car. 'See you tomorrow.'

The hotel bar was mobbed, as usual. Tourists and businessmen in suits getting a few in before they went for their train. McCoy was looking around when Jackie materialised beside him.

'Mr Stewart's in the restaurant,' he said.

McCoy nodded. Wondered how much Jackie's tips income would go down when Stewart went back to America. He walked through the bar heading for the restaurant. Knew Stewart was going to ask him if there was any news about Donny and he was going to say no. Not entirely a lie. They really didn't know what had happened to him yet. McCoy had a fair idea that whatever it was, it wasn't good and it involved Lindsay, but he wasn't telling Stewart that. Today had been bad enough. He pushed the door open, could see Stewart in the corner, *New York Times* open in front of him. Stewart looked up and saw him as he weaved through the tables. At least he had the decency to look guilty.

'Harry,' he said. 'Good to see you. You hungry? Have dinner with me?'

McCoy nodded, realised he was. Hadn't eaten all day. Sat down. Noticed scratches and a bluish bruise on the knuckles of Stewart's hands.

'Get those from boxing practice, did you?' he asked.

Stewart nodded. 'Gloves weren't tight enough.'

'That right?' asked McCoy. 'You went all the way up to the Royal wearing boxing gloves? Stevie have them on too, did he?'

Stewart looked mortified. 'Harry, I'm sorry. We'd had a few too many drinks and—'

McCoy held his hand up. 'It's done. You know how stupid it was. I don't need to tell you.'

Stewart nodded. 'Any news?'

'Nothing concrete,' said McCoy. 'Sorry.'

'You'll find him.'

McCoy nodded, less sure than Stewart was. Was worried that Stewart's faith in him was more hopeful than deserved.

Dinner was the same as last time. Steak and red wine. McCoy wasn't complaining, it was better than the fish fingers he had at home. He polished it off. Said he didn't want any cheese then ate half of Stewart's. The ulcer could go and fuck itself.

'So what else you been doing?' he asked, sipping wine.

'Think I've shown a picture of Donny to everyone in Dunoon,' said Stewart. 'Just got back this afternoon.'

'Any luck?' asked McCoy, digging in his pocket for his fags, deciding to christen the fresh ashtray.

Stewart shook his head. 'Was wondering if I should try throwing my weight about with the navy again. See if they'll get off their asses and do something.'

'How long can you stay here?' asked McCoy.

'Long as it takes,' said Stewart, looking determined. 'I'm not going back without finding Donny. He's my son, I can't—'

And then he started crying. McCoy wasn't sure what to do. He was bad enough with women crying, never mind a big bruiser like Stewart. He sat forward, patted him on the back as Stewart dug a hanky out his pocket, started wiping at his eyes.

'I'm sorry,' he said. 'Sometimes it's just too much. Not knowing, that's the worst thing.' He blew his nose, wiped at his eyes, put his hanky back in his pocket. 'Sorry, Harry. Done more crying this week than I've done in my whole life, I think.'

'That's okay,' said McCoy. 'You've got every right.'

'I don't know why, but I've always worried about Donny. Always been scared for him.'

'Why?' asked McCoy.

Stewart hesitated for a minute. Then started. 'Ever since he was a little guy, it always seemed he was the one kid nobody wanted to play ball with, the one who got his eye blacked, who got made fun of, who didn't get invited to the other kid's houses for a sleepover. Used to come home crying, asking me what was wrong with him, why people made fun of him. And then with the boy at the school . . .'

He shrugged.

'I just thought another world of trouble was opening up for him. That whatever his life was like, he'd just made it a hundred times harder for himself.'

'And you knew how he felt,' said McCoy.

'Yes,' said Stewart.

'And you didn't want it happening all over again.'

Stewart looked at him. Swallowed. 'How did you know?'

'I didn't. Not until now. I was asking around, trying to find out where an American sailor would go to meet someone who was that way inclined. The guy I asked said, "A young one?" Like there had been older ones too.' McCoy smiled. 'I guessed there weren't that many older American sailors in Glasgow just now.'

'Barry,' he said. 'At the Backstage Bar.'

McCoy nodded.

'You want to hear the story?' asked Stewart.

'Only if you want to tell me,' said McCoy. 'It's none of my business.'

Stewart looked up and the waiter appeared out of nowhere. 'Two Johnnie Walkers,' said Stewart. 'Doubles.' He looked at McCoy. 'After all these years I may as well tell someone.'

The drinks arrived and Stewart told his story. How his father had sensed something in him when he was young, made him go to military school, take up boxing, go into the navy. All the stuff a real man did.

'And I did it,' said Stewart. 'Because I was scared. Thought if I did all those things there was no way I could be, you know . . .'

He took a drink of his whisky.

'So I got married, had a kid, just like I was supposed to. Kept everything screwed down tight.' He smiled. 'And when you do that? All you do is increase the pressure and eventually that pressure has to give. And that's how I end up meeting someone like Barry. I'm always away from home, always discreet, always careful.'

'Is that enough?' asked McCoy.

'It is for me,' said Stewart. 'But Donny's a different generation. Maybe it'll be easier for him, I don't know. Maybe I just did the same as my dad, got scared and pushed him into military life. But when I find him I'm going to tell him I know, tell him it's okay. Tell him it's his life to lead.'

'Will you tell him about you?' ask McCoy.

Stewart shook his head, smiled. 'I'm too old for that. Things are what they are.'

McCoy raised his glass. 'Here's to you. And fuck 'em all.'

'Fuck 'em all!' said Stewart and drank his whisky back.

CHAPTER 56

McCoy left Stewart back in the bar being waited on hand and foot by Jackie. Suddenly occurred to him that there might be more to it than someone looking for tips. Not his business really. Was funny, he used to think people like himself with messed-up lives were the exception. Was beginning to think that if you scratched the surface it applied to anyone. Even stinking rich ex-captains in the US Navy. He stepped out the taxi in Dumbarton Road. Plan was to walk up the hill to the flat and get some fresh air. At least that was what he was telling himself. Looked at his watch, just past nine. More than enough time for a couple in the Victoria and straight to bed. With what he'd seen today in that room his only hope of getting to sleep was to go to bed drunk.

He pulled the door open. The Central it was not. The usual old guys propping up the bar, the usual smell of cigarettes and wet jackets. He dug his hand in his pocket for change and headed to the bar, asked for a pint. The barman poured it, handed it to him.

'Someone was in here looking for you,' he said.

'The man from Littlewoods?' asked McCoy. 'Have I won the pools?'

'Have you fuck. A young guy. Said he'd come back.' He nodded over at the door. 'That's him now.'

McCoy turned and Billy was hovering by the door. He raised a hand in hello. Looked jittery, not his usual self.

'Looks like I'm buying another pint,' said McCoy and handed a quid over.

Billy had sat down right at the back of the pub. Back against the wall. Usual uniform of jeans and a denim jacket, feather-cut hair.

McCoy put the pints on the table and sat down. 'Long time no see.'

'Cooper's not coming here is he?' asked Billy.

'Not as far as I know.'

Billy looked relieved, took a sip of his pint.

McCoy couldn't think of any easier way to say it. 'Fuck sake. What happened, Billy? What's going on?'

Billy shrugged. Looked up at the TV on the wall. Fuzzy black-and-white football with the sound turned down. Looked back.

'I tried to make my move.' He smiled. 'Didn't work out.'

'How come?' asked McCoy. 'You had it cushy with Cooper far as I could see.'

'Can see that now but I had William Norton in my ear promising me the world. And I was

398

stupid. I believed him. Thought this was my big chance. Thought I was heading for the big time, didn't I?'

'I still don't get it,' said McCoy. 'Cooper likes you. You're smart. He listened to you. I thought you two were stuck together for life.'

Billy sighed. Watched the paperboy make his way around the tables, bundle of tomorrow's *Daily Record* under his arm. LATEST BOMB PLOT FOILED across the front page.

'It's different for you,' he said.

'How?' asked McCoy.

'Because you're a polis. You don't know what it's like to work with him, be around him every day. Cooper's Cooper. Some days he's your big pal and some days you're scared he's going to kick fuck out of you. Even after all these years I still don't know what mood he's going to be in each day. You're living on your nerves all the time. You don't work for him, Harry, you don't know what it's like. You can't.'

'That's true,' said McCoy. 'But was it that bad?'

'It doesn't really matter now. It's done.'

'What are you going to do?' asked McCoy.

'That's why I'm here,' said Billy, sitting forward. 'I need to ask you a favour.'

'Sure,' said McCoy, hoping that he wasn't going to ask him what he thought he was.

'Can you talk to him?' asked Billy.

McCoy's heart sank. 'About you?'

Billy nodded. 'Tell him I'm sorry?'

McCoy stubbed his cigarette out in the ashtray. 'Think it's a bit beyond that, Billy. Don't you?'

Billy couldn't have looked more miserable. Put his head in his hands. 'What am I going to do?'

'Thought you'd teamed up with Norton?' asked McCoy. 'Was that not the big idea?'

'So did I, but it turns out I'm just another employee – do this, do that, jump when I say jump.' He looked up. Smiled. 'Think I was sold a pup.'

McCoy wanted to help but he couldn't lie. It would only give him false hope and make things worse in the long run. 'Think you've crossed the line with Cooper. You know what he's like. You're either with him or against him.'

Billy nodded.

'I don't want to say this to you, Billy, but I think you better run. Get out of Glasgow. I don't know what else you can do.'

'Thought you might say that,' said Billy. 'Think that's what I'll do.' He stood up. 'Thanks, Harry. You always were a pal.'

McCoy stood up. Suddenly felt scared for Billy. He hugged him. 'Take care of yourself, eh?'

Billy nodded. Headed for the door. Stepped out into the darkness of Dumbarton Road and the door closed behind him.

McCoy sat back down. Felt like shit. Felt for Billy. Had a feeling that was the last time he would see him. He was getting tired of all this. The threats and the violence and the consequences. People's lives ruined. Felt like he was coming to the end of his tether. Just didn't want to live like this any more, to be part of it. Didn't want to see tied-up boys screaming in fear, men getting glass picked out their face. Parents' lives destroyed when he had to tell them what had happened to their son. All the shit that had been thrown at him lately was getting too much. No wonder he had a fucking ulcer.

He sank the rest of his pint.

Headed for home.

20TH APRIL 1974

CHAPTER 57

'H'e's managed some breakfast,' said Dr
Basu. 'That's always a good sign. No
morphine yet this morning so now might
be your best bet to get some sense out of him.'

'His son Crawford hasn't been around, has he?'
asked McCoy.

Dr Basu shook his head. 'Haven't seen him.'

McCoy nodded, pushed the door to Lindsay's
room open, Wattie following behind. Smell of
bleach and floor cleaner, same as every hospital,
but there was something else under it: a faint smell
of decay. Lindsay was sitting up in bed, a copy of
The Times in front of him. Empty cornflakes bowl
on his locker. His face looked a bit less battered
and swollen than it had yesterday. Amputated leg
protected by a wire cage under the covers.

McCoy sat down on one of the chairs by the
bed. Wattie stayed standing at the door, closed it
behind him.

Lindsay took his glasses off, pushed the paper
to the side. Looked at them with an expression of
boredom and contempt.

McCoy could hardly look at him. He was so sick

405

of men like Lindsay, men who damaged people and damaged them again and enjoyed doing it. Then looked at people like him as if they were in the wrong for trying to stop them.

'Neil Harrison,' he said.

Lindsay looked surprised. Smiled. Started to clap slowly. 'Well, it seems like I underestimated you, McCoy. Well done.'

'Is that all you've got to say?' asked McCoy.

'What would you like me to say?' asked Lindsay. 'Seems obvious. You found my room and managed to get in. Not an easy task. May I ask how you managed it?'

'No,' said McCoy. 'What I want you to say is this. Tell us where Crawford and the rest of the lads are. What the plan is.'

Lindsay sank back on his pillows. 'Now why on earth would I tell you that?'

'Because you can come clean before the end. Call the bombs off too. You've still got time.'

Lindsay laughed. 'McCoy. Going by your name, I assume you are a Roman Catholic, yet you don't strike me as the type that believes in atonement. Well, I don't believe in it either. I'm perfectly happy to meet my maker as I am. Were there one, that is. Trouble is, it's just us venal humans. Ugly, stupid and riddled with deceit. No one to answer to but ourselves. I'm happy to live with what I've done and I certainly won't be giving you some cheap deathbed confession. Give me some respect.'

He stopped, grimaced. Took a few deep breaths, started again.

'But you're right about one thing. I've only a little time left. Days maybe. So, let's make it interesting, shall we? Why don't we have a little parlour game to pass the time? What do you say?'

McCoy nodded. Had to sit on his hands to stop himself getting up and smashing Lindsay in the face with his fists.

'Good,' said Lindsay. 'So in the spirit of magnanimity, I'll go first. Private Michael Martyn. There's an abandoned smallholding a few miles up the coast from the house. Two trees behind it. He's buried between them. I trust that's the kind of thing you're looking for?'

'Jesus Christ,' said McCoy. 'You're really going to treat this as a game?'

'Why wouldn't I?' said Lindsay. 'I'm stuck in this bed, view of Glasgow out the window, not a city I was ever fond of. More drunks per capita than anywhere else. Papist cathedrals everywhere. Swilling in its own mess, people on their knees, heritage sold out for a few coins thrown into a begging bowl by the English.' He breathed again. Smiled. 'Consequently, I need to amuse myself somehow. And taunting fools like you is too easy to resist.'

'Where's the next bomb?' asked McCoy evenly.

'Nope,' said Lindsay. 'It's your turn. What are you going to give me to tell you that? What's it worth to stop some more of the alcohol-swilling trash of Glasgow being blown to pieces?'

Could hardly bring himself to say it but he did. 'What do you want?' asked McCoy.

'Now, now, don't be like that. Where's your sense of humour, eh?' said Lindsay. He smiled again. 'I'll make it easy for you. All I want is something simple. It's easy to arrange. In fact, it's something we can take care of right now in this very room. Sound good, Mr McCoy?'

'What is it?' asked McCoy, sitting firmer on his hands.

Lindsay nodded over his head. 'That big fellow behind you. What I want is for him to take his shirt off and let me open the skin on his back with a Stanley knife. Or a scalpel would do. Easier to get a hold of in here.'

'What?' said McCoy. 'Are you fucking joking?'

'Do I sound like I'm joking to you, McCoy?' asked Lindsay. 'Obviously, it would make more sense if I were to ask you, would have a certain symmetry, I suppose, but you're too old, too scrawny. The one behind you. Watson, was it? He reminds me of a certain young man I watched die in the shadow of the pines. A glorious time.'

The shadow of the pines. McCoy knew exactly what he was talking about. The paper he'd found on the floor. The film of the young guard tied to a tree, skeleton-like men lined up to have a go at him with their knives.

Wattie was looking at him, fear on his face.

'Not in a million fucking years,' said McCoy.

'Pity,' said Lindsay. Picked up his paper.

McCoy leant over, struck it out his hands and the pages went flying across the room. 'Listen to me, you piece of garbage. You start talking or—'

'Or what?' snarled Lindsay, suddenly angry. 'What can you possibly do to me, McCoy? I'm the one in charge here. I'm the one who's got the information you want, and there's only one way you're going to get it and that's if you start playing ball. The offer stands for twenty-four hours.'

He leaned across the bed, picked up the glass vial from the locker, and took a few sips from the straw. Pressed the alarm button.

'Where's Donny Stewart?' asked McCoy. 'Is he still alive?'

Lindsay settled back into his pillows.

McCoy grabbed him, sat him up again. He was shouting now, couldn't help himself. 'Where the fuck is he? Tell me!'

Lindsay just smiled. Eyes already starting to go glassy.

McCoy dropped him back onto the pillows.

'I imagine he's still where I left him,' said Lindsay. 'Such a shame I won't get to finish the job I started.'

McCoy got up from his seat, had to get away from Lindsay. Wasn't sure how much longer he would be able to stop himself hitting him.

'I swear, you evil old fucker, I'm going to—'

He stopped as the door opened and a nurse stepped in.

'You okay, Mr Lindsay? Are you comfortable?'

'I'm fine, my dear,' he said. 'But I'm very tired. I need to rest. Could you escort these gentlemen out? Thank you.'

McCoy slammed the door behind him, kicked at a bucket and mop leaning on the corridor wall, and they went flying, clattering on the lino.

'That fucking cunt!' he shouted.

The nurse at the station down the corridor looked up in disapproval. Tutted. Looked back down when she saw the anger on McCoy's face. He got his cigarettes out, lit up. Took a deep drag.

'I swear nothing would give me greater pleasure than beating the information out of him.'

'Think someone already tried that,' said Watson. He leaned against the wall of the corridor. Looked at McCoy. 'Lindsay's going to blow up God knows how many people, Donny Stewart is probably tied up in some cellar, probably dying of starvation or of whatever that cunt has done to him. Families, mums and dads with no idea what happened to their kids, no way of burying them or mourning them properly. Unless . . .'

'Unless what?' asked McCoy.

'Unless we play ball.' He hesitated. 'He can slash me or whatever the fuck he wants to do. I don't care. It's a few minutes' pain against all that. It's worth it. I'll do it.'

'Christ, Wattie, you can't do that. There is no fucking way I'm letting that happen. You hear me?'

Wattie just looked at him.

'No games, no pandering to that bastard. We're going to get him and his pack of wee boys somehow, I swear it. Okay?'

Wattie nodded. Didn't look sure at all.

'Let's go and see what his sister has got to say for herself. If I stay in this hospital any longer I'm going to do something I regret.'

CHAPTER 58

Scotland's only Oscar-winning actress wasn't looking her best. Hard to when you're tied to a radiator in a bedroom next to a bucket full of sick and piss. Margo Lindsay was sleeping, snoring to wake the dead.

'How often does this happen?' asked McCoy.

The long-haired girl in dungarees beside him sighed. 'Couple of times a year. She says, "I'll just have a few drinks," and three days later here she is. Don't worry, she asks us to tie her up when she passes out. It's not us keeping her prisoner.'

McCoy nodded. Didn't doubt it. Had enough experience with alcoholics to believe it.

'When do you think she'll wake up?' asked Wattie.

'Hard to tell,' said the girl. 'Once she gets going she doesn't really sleep, just keeps drinking and drinking until she passes out.'

'Who would you say she's closest to in here?' asked McCoy.

'She's a loner really. Hard to believe for someone who started a commune but it's true.'

'She ever mention her brother? Anywhere they

used to go when they were small? Somewhere secret they had together?'

The girl shook her head. 'Only mentions him when she's swearing about him. That's about it.'

McCoy and Wattie left her there. Asked the girl to call them at the big house the minute Margo woke up. Walked back to the car parked by the cow byre. Had to start facing the inevitable.

'Donny Stewart's probably dead by now,' said McCoy.

'Faulds and the lads not find anything?' asked Wattie.

McCoy shook his head. 'Spoke to him earlier. He's away supervising the Michael Martyn site now. They searched the house, every outhouse, the cellars, everywhere they could think of.'

They got in the car, started driving.

'What are we going to do up at the house?' asked Wattie.

'I don't know,' said McCoy, feeling useless. 'Have another look about, see if we can find any clues as to where Lindsay has hidden him?'

'He's stinking rich, Lindsay,' said Wattie. 'Big house, Daimler.'

McCoy nodded, stuck the car cigarette lighter in, and got his fags out his pocket. Had had enough of fresh country air.

'Yep. Generations of money. All inherited. Your dad would have something to say about that.'

'More of a rant, I think,' said Wattie. 'Same one he does every time one of the royals comes on the telly. Could probably recite it from memory.' Coughed. Put on an angry voice with a thick Greenock accent. 'Bloody leeches! And who pays for it all? The working man, that's who!'

McCoy started laughing, lit his cigarette on the lighter.

'All the jewels! All the cars and the bloody train and the bloody boat and don't get me started on the big houses. How can any family need more than one bloody house? You can't live in two at once! It's a bloody dis—'

McCoy held his hand out. Stopped him. 'The fucker,' he said.

'What?' asked Wattie. 'What you on about?'

'He's got another property. That's why he's so bloody calm and collected. Knows we're searching all around this house and he doesn't give a shit.'

Wattie turned the car into the driveway of Knockland. 'Where is it then?'

'Fuck knows. Need to go through his papers in the house, see if we can find any record or bills. There must be a paper trail. The lads are probably there, hidden away, waiting their turn to plant a bomb.'

'Who's here now?' asked Wattie, nodding at a black Mercedes sitting in front of the house.

'No idea,' said McCoy as Wattie parked the car behind it. 'Soon find out.'

CHAPTER 59

Kenny Barnes was sitting in an armchair in the reception room, an open copy of *Mayfair* in his lap. Looked up as McCoy and Wattie walked in.

'Well, well, if it isn't our Paddy-loving friend,' he said. 'What are you doing here?'

'I'm the detective assigned to the case,' said McCoy. 'What the fuck are you doing here?'

'Now, now,' said Barnes. 'Don't be like that. We're all on the same side.' He looked around the room. 'I didn't realise some of you jocks had dosh. Very nice gaff, this.'

The sight of Barnes sitting there in his dodgy suit, platform shoes, acting like he was in charge was more than McCoy could deal with. But he had to stop himself inflaming the situation and telling the greasy wee bastard to get going.

'Meant to thank you,' said Barnes. 'Blythswood Square. Good advice. Found a wee bird up there. Cheap as chips, took it up the arse like a good 'un. Might go back there tonight if we get out of here in time.'

'We?' asked McCoy. 'Who's we?'

Barnes smiled. 'That's why I'm here. Got a call last night. Hire a smart motor, pick someone up from Glasgow Airport, drive him here.'

'Who?' asked McCoy.

Barnes shrugged. 'All hush hush. Didn't offer his name and I didn't ask. Was told to keep it shut and just do what he says.'

'Where is he?' asked McCoy.

Barnes pointed upwards. 'Upstairs. Told me to stay down here.'

McCoy left Wattie with him and headed for the stairs. Was about time Special Branch got involved. Should have been from the beginning. Just hoped Barnes's boss was less of an arse than he was. Big Mercedes outside, must be high up, might have a brain in his head.

He walked along the corridor towards Lindsay's secret room. Maybe Special Branch had special access to land registries, tax records, things like that. Could help, make finding Lindsay's second property a lot easier.

He pushed the door open.

A man was sitting in one of the chairs, back to him, peering at a photograph in his hand. Pinstripe suit. Briefcase on the floor beside him. Must have heard the door opening. He turned and looked at McCoy. Shook his head.

'How did I know it was going to be you?' he said. 'Just my luck.'

If McCoy had been surprised by Barnes

downstairs he was dumbstruck by who he was looking at now. 'Cavendish?'

'They said a Glasgow detective was in charge. Had a certain inevitability to it.' He stood up. 'Let's go for a stroll, shall we? We need to talk.'

CHAPTER 60

They walked along the side of the loch. Sun was out, high in the sky. Couple of boats out in the loch tethered to a buoy bobbing in the breeze, an ocean liner in the distance speeding away from Greenock. Could hear some of Faulds's boys shouting to each other in the woods, search was still going on. Hadn't found anything yet.

'When was it we last met?' asked Cavendish. 'Remind me.'

'Couple of years ago,' said McCoy. 'You told me what a bent piece of shit I was and how I turned your stomach.'

Cavendish smiled. 'A difficult situation that I needed to be closed down immediately. You understand, I'm sure.'

All McCoy understood was that Cavendish had been sent up by London to shut down a case that was leading back to some of the great and good of British society. Innocent or guilty, it didn't matter: all that mattered was that certain individuals were protected.

'That what you're here for now?' asked McCoy.

'No,' said Cavendish. 'This time it's different. This time I need your help.'

McCoy shook his head. 'Never thought I'd hear you say that.'

'Yes, a bit of a surprise to me too. But we've played it rather badly here, got ourselves in a bit of a mess. Called it wrong.'

'What do you mean?' asked McCoy.

'We knew about Lindsay's little "Free Scotland" hobby. Let him run with it. Seemed harmless. You know what a false flag is?'

McCoy shook his head.

'We used Lindsay as a kind of lightning rod to attract other fanatics. To be honest, they mostly turned out to be grubby little men in Edinburgh pubs talking nonsense about private armies and the Stone of Destiny. Scottish Freedom lot, 1320 Club. Clowns. Not worth worrying about.'

'And you thought Lindsay wasn't worth worrying about either?' asked McCoy.

'Precisely,' said Cavendish. 'It worked for a while. We managed to discover a pretty serious plot to assassinate Prince Charles last year. A lone wolf got pretty near to him. So Lindsay was useful and we thought we had him under control, that fundamentally he was one of us. He has unusual talents, talents that he's been developing for years. And those talents were very useful to us. Seemed like a decent enough trade-off.'

'Torture techniques,' said McCoy.

Cavendish looked surprised. Then realised. 'Ah.

419

Your chat with Professor Burns. Interesting young man. Yes, Lindsay has been very useful in the past.'

'The past?'

'Yes. Obviously, we have to separate ourselves as completely and as quickly as possible. The last thing we need is the British Army involved in this.'

McCoy laughed. 'Isn't that going to be a bit difficult? He's in the bloody army!'

'Actually, he's retired,' said Cavendish. 'As of this morning. It'll be news to him but there you go.'

Cavendish bent down, picked up a stone, threw it into the water. 'It happens. A rogue bad apple infiltrates an organisation. Of course, we knew nothing of his extremist views about Scotland, least of all his building of a private army or his intention to start letting bombs off. A complete and horrible surprise. A good man gone off the rails. Impossible to predict.'

McCoy stopped, sat on an overturned rowing boat, and lit up. 'How are you going to do that?' he asked. 'Make people believe that load of shite?'

Cavendish smiled. 'That's where you come in,' he said. 'Firstly, we need the bombing campaign shut down as soon as possible. You've done a good job so far. We'll give you all the help and resources you need. More help than you can imagine.' Smiled again. 'Much to my surprise, you seem to be our best bet.'

'Okay,' said McCoy. 'But I have some conditions.'

Cavendish rolled his eyes. 'I don't think you quite understand, McCoy. This is an instruction, not a negotiation.'

'Burns saw the picture of Brendan Shaughnessy,' said McCoy. 'Saw everything. Knows all about your grubby little tricks in Belfast.'

Cavendish tried to cover his surprise. 'Burns is containable. He's an established left-wing agitator, Troops Out marches, Socialist Workers Party. Not too difficult to smear, make what he says sound ridiculous.'

'You sure?' asked McCoy. 'How do you know he hasn't told Amnesty International already? How do you know I haven't?'

Cavendish took out a silver cigarette case and lit up. Thought for a minute. Watched some birds fly overhead. 'What do you want?'

'I want your clown Barnes off my back. He seems to think I'm some sort of IRA connection, thinks I'm his big spy.'

Cavendish nodded. 'Rather a liability, Barnes, I always thought. Not the brightest. Done.'

'And there's something else.'

Cavendish nodded again.

'The IRA think Hughie Faulds had something to do with the murder of Paul McVeigh. And they've already tried to blow him up once. Need you to get them to back off.'

Cavendish shook his head. 'Think you overestimate us. The IRA is a terrorist organisation, we don't speak to people like that.'

421

'Yes you do,' said McCoy. 'Trade something for it. Or Faulds might remember who actually did it.'

'And who would that be?' asked Cavendish.

'The Det,' said McCoy.

This time Cavendish couldn't cover it up in time. Looked genuinely surprised. 'Slippery fish, aren't you, McCoy? Know too much for your own good.'

'Are we agreed?' asked McCoy.

Cavendish flicked his cigarette towards the loch. 'I was right. You are a piece of shit. But a useful one. Done. Now just stop these bloody bombings and let me get on with the rest.'

They started walking back towards the house.

'What about the people Lindsay's killed?' asked McCoy. 'The army boys.'

'That needs to be shut down too. But let's get the bombing out the road first, shall we?'

McCoy nodded, wondered what was going on in Cavendish's mind. How he was going to get around what Lindsay had done. That was his problem to think about, he supposed. Knew one thing though. Things like that don't stay buried. And he was going to do everything he could to make sure they didn't. The parents of boys like Neil Harrison had a right to know what had happened to their kids, no matter how horrible it was. Stewart had a right to know what had happened to Donny. No matter what he had promised Cavendish.

CHAPTER 61

Murray sat back in his office chair, held up a sheet of paper.

'This came through from Pitt Street an hour ago.' He started reading. *'All resources are to be mobilised in the hunt for the bombers. All overtime, call-back from holidays covered. Other forces on stand-by if needed. Extraordinary access to Home Office information for the duration of the hunt.'*

Looked up at McCoy. 'Friends in high places? Something you're not telling me, McCoy?'

'If only. Nothing to do with me. Probably just desperate to get it fixed before any more "Glasgow in Bomb Terror" headlines.'

Murray put the paper down. Didn't look a hundred per cent convinced.

'Not sure it'll do us much good,' said McCoy. 'The Land Registry stuff might be useful, this Home Office thing should speed it up, but it'll still take a while. We just need a decent break, not another bunch of people running about like blue-arsed flies.'

'And how are we going to get that?' asked Murray.

423

'Need to find Donny Stewart, if he's still alive that is. I think he's our best bet. He's either hidden on the grounds somewhere, or wherever Lindsay has another property. Faulds is up at the big house now organising all the new arrivals into a proper search. Still like looking for a needle in a haystack though. Lindsay's land goes on for miles.'

'How about the sister?'

'I'm going to see her after this. Hopefully, she'll have slept it off by now. Might be able to tell us if Lindsay's dad left him anywhere else.'

'Margo Lindsay, still can't believe you met her,' said Murray, looking a bit starry-eyed. 'She was a good-looking woman.'

'Still is,' said McCoy. 'When she's not pissed, that is.'

A knock on the door. PC Walker's head appeared.

'Someone here for you, Mr McCoy,' she said. 'Mr Meiklejohn.'

'Great,' said McCoy. 'Do you want to show him in?'

Walker nodded, disappeared.

'Bloke from the barracks,' said McCoy. 'Been looking for other missing soldiers.'

'Christ,' said Murray. 'Let's hope he's no found any. By the way, bought a Joan Eardley for Phyllis. Good idea.'

'A what?' asked McCoy.

'She's an artist. Glasgow. Phyllis has already got one, she likes her. In the kitchen, the big painting of kids with words on it.'

424

'Ah,' said McCoy, pretending to remember.

'Not bloody cheap, I'll tell you that. Still, should go down well.'

Meiklejohn appeared at the door. Looked a bit strange out of his uniform. Pair of cords and a checked shirt with the sleeves rolled up. Bag over his shoulder.

'Come in,' said McCoy. 'Have a seat.'

Meiklejohn limped across the room and sat in a chair, stretched his leg out straight in front of him.

'Cheif Inspector Murray,' said McCoy. 'The boss. How did you get on?'

Meiklejohn leaned over and shook Murray's hand then dug in his bag, came out with a hardback notebook. Looked at them.

'Six possibilities,' he said.

'That many?' said McCoy.

'Seven if we count Neil Harrison. All young men, either soldiers or cadets, all went missing in April or just before. The first one was in 1961. A young man called Duncan McNab went AWOL from the barracks in Cupar. Last seen getting on a bus to Glasgow.'

'Some of them could just be runaways,' said Murray, 'still hiding from the army.'

Meiklejohn nodded. 'I hope so.' He put the notebook on Murray's desk. 'As much as I could find out about each one is in there.'

McCoy took the photo of the screaming boy off Murray's desk. 'Sorry about this, but I need you to look at this picture,' he said. 'You recognise him?'

Meiklejohn's face went white. 'It's Neil Harrison.'

'Thanks,' said McCoy. 'Lindsay never mentioned any other property he had, did he?'

Meiklejohn though for a minute, shook his head. 'Not that I can think of, but to be honest I'm probably not the one he would tell. His sister might know?'

McCoy stood up. 'Great minds. Would you mind staying here to go through all the stuff you've found with Thomson?'

'Of course.'

'How much longer have we got before another bomb?' asked Murray.

'Don't know,' said McCoy. 'Up till now there's been a couple of days between each one. We found the one in the pub yesterday, so . . .'

'Tomorrow?' said Murray.

McCoy sighed. 'Could be. Better get going.'

CHAPTER 62

Margo Lindsay was sitting on a kitchen chair on the lawn at the back of the farm, looking out over the loch. The wind was up, little whitecaps, clouds moving quickly across the sky. She'd a mug of tea in her hand, tartan blanket around her shoulders. She looked pale, a bit shaky. Not surprising.

McCoy lit up, waited for her to start talking.

'My brother and I were never close,' she said. 'Typical upper-class childhood. He was sent off to boarding school just after I was born. He was eight years older, a boy. We didn't have much in common. Only really saw him in the holidays and he certainly wasn't interested in me.' She smiled. 'I was a girl. Not very useful for playing soldiers.'

She took a sip of her tea.

'And then he went into the army straight after boarding school. Sandhurst. Then he seemed to be abroad most often time. Funerals and weddings we saw each other. All very cordial but distant.' She looked up as a squawking seagull flew overhead. 'And, as if acting wasn't bad enough, when I got interested in left-wing politics things became significantly less cordial. My brother is, how shall we say, a difficult man.'

She looked at McCoy. 'What's he done? Is it bad?'

McCoy wasn't going to tell her about the suspected murders. 'Think he's organised a group of lads into planting bombs. Wants a new kind of Scotland.'

'Oh God. Not all that no drinking and Declaration of Arbroath nonsense? He's been on about that for years.'

'Declaration of Arbroath?' asked McCoy.

'In 1320, a group of noblemen, fifty-one to be precise, sent a letter declaring an autonomous Scotland. Angus always seemed to think it should happen again. Luckily we no longer live in a feudal society.'

'Fifty-one,' said McCoy. 'The Sons of the Fifty-One. Makes sense now.'

'There's nothing I would like more than an independent Scotland,' Margo continued, looking out at the loch. 'But it wouldn't be anything like my brother's. Independent, socialist, not yoked to England or America, run by the people for the people.' She turned to him. 'And it will come. I know it. Maybe not in my lifetime, but it will.'

McCoy nodded. Seemed the polite thing to do. 'Does your brother have any other property? Anything else he inherited?'

She smiled. 'The answer is, I wouldn't know. Everything was primogeniture, as tradition demands.'

'Primogeniture?' asked McCoy.

'Everything goes to the oldest male heir. All lands, property or titles. So if he inherited anything other than the big house I wouldn't even know, not unless he chose to tell me.'

'He ever mention anywhere secret? Anywhere you used to go as kids?'

'Not really. There's a smallholding about three miles up the road. We used to go there.'

McCoy nodded. Didn't tell her that's where they were currently looking for Michael Martyn's body. 'You think of anywhere you'll let me know?'

'Of course,' said Margo. Hesitated. 'You saw me yesterday?'

McCoy wasn't sure if it was a question or a statement. He nodded again.

'Not nice. But it happens. My mother was a drunk. As was my father. That's where Angus gets this hatred of drink from. Says it is about getting Scotland off its knees. It's not. It's about him having to lock my mother in the attic when she went on yet another binge and about my father knocking the shit out of him when he'd been on the whisky. Which was most nights. Must have been the only eight-year-old desperate to be sent off to school.'

She pulled the blanket around herself, looked McCoy in the eye. 'I don't know what my brother has done, Mr McCoy, and I don't want to know. But I know this. He was a nice wee boy once, same as everyone else. He's not to blame for what he is. My parents are.'

McCoy stood up. 'Have you heard from Crawford?'

Margo looked lost. 'Crawford?'

'His son.'

Margo shook her head. 'My brother doesn't have any children. Let me guess. Early twenties, army, strong?'

McCoy nodded. 'What is he then?' he asked. 'His boyfriend?'

Margo shook her head again. 'He's a disciple, Mr McCoy. There's been a few. And they tend to be even more fanatical than my brother is. Be careful.'

CHAPTER 63

McCoy looked up at the clock on the wall of the office. He'd come back after interviewing Margo. Didn't seem much point waiting around the big house to see if a body turned up. He stood up, stretched. The Land Registry people hoped to have all the information about Lindsay's properties by tomorrow. He'd called Dr Basu too. No sign of Crawford or anyone else and Lindsay was 'comfortable', whatever that meant. Was just about to get going when his phone went again. Picked it up. No greeting. Just Cooper's voice: 'Jumbo's on his way.'

Then a click as the line went dead. Had almost forgotten about giving Jumbo a night in the cells. Still had no idea why.

He stepped out of the station. Glad to be away from the stale air. Was just starting to get dark, pinkish tinge in the clouds. He lit up just as Jumbo walked round the corner. Seemed to have got even broader if that was possible. He ambled up the street, six foot four of muscle and not enough sense to close a door behind him. Jumbo saw McCoy, a big grin broke on his face, and he waved.

431

Really was like a big kid. Jeans, jumper and sand-shoes as always.

'Mr McCoy!' he said. 'Nice to see you!'

'You been weightlifting, Jumbo?' asked McCoy. 'You're bloody massive.'

He smiled, shook his head. 'Just working in the gardens. If Mr Cooper doesn't need me I work with a firm that does gardens for posh people.'

'How's that?' asked McCoy.

'Brilliant,' said Jumbo. His face clouded. 'Don't think I'll be doing it so much now Mr Cooper's out the jail.'

'Right,' said McCoy, still no idea why he was doing it at all. 'I'm going to arrest you for being drunk and disorderly. Any idea why?'

Jumbo shook his head. 'Mr Cooper just told me to do what you say.'

'Well,' said McCoy, 'that means we're going to the pub.'

Ten minutes later they were in Lauder's. Wasn't the closest but McCoy didn't want to run into anyone from the station. He'd bought himself a pint and Jumbo a pint and a double whisky. Never a big drinker, Jumbo. Had the feeling another pint and a double would make him pissed enough that Billy at the front desk wouldn't think anything was amiss.

'I don't like whisky,' said Jumbo miserably.

'Hard luck,' said McCoy. 'Get it drunk.'

Jumbo looked at it doubtfully, tossed it over then grimaced. Exactly like a kid taking his medicine.

432

'You seen Billy?' asked McCoy.

Jumbo shook his head vigorously. 'Not since Mr Cooper came out the jail. I did the garden at his house when he was away and Billy was there sometimes but I don't know what happened. He wasn't very friendly to me so I just kept out his way.'

McCoy wasn't surprised. Billy never had had much time for Jumbo and if he'd been making his move he'd have had even less reason to tolerate him.

'And how about Iris?'

Jumbo took a big swig of his pint and McCoy said 'same again' to the barman.

'Iris lets me stay at the house if Billy isn't there.'

'That's good,' said McCoy. 'It's a nice house. Where do you stay the other times?' he asked, realising he'd no idea.

'Different places,' said Jumbo. 'Sometimes at Memen Road.' Looked a bit ashamed. 'Sometimes at the Great Eastern, places like that.'

'Christ, Jumbo, that's no good. I'll speak to Cooper. We'll get you a permanent room at the house. He owes you for all the work on the garden.'

'What if Billy's there?' asked Jumbo.

McCoy pushed the pint and double towards him. 'Don't think we need to worry about that.'

It took three rounds before Jumbo looked sufficiently pissed to pass muster. McCoy walked him up the road towards the station, Jumbo swaying slightly.

'When we get there don't say anything okay?' said McCoy.

Jumbo nodded. Didn't look like he was capable of saying that much anyway.

Billy the desk sergeant couldn't have looked less happy to see them. Shook his head as McCoy walked Jumbo to the bench by the door and plonked him down.

'I'm about to go off shift, can you no just send this joker home?' he asked.

'Normally I would,' said McCoy, 'but the big bastard kicked me in the balls.'

Billy sighed. 'Bring him over.'

McCoy got Jumbo up, walked him to the desk.

'Name,' said Billy.

'Jumbo,' said Jumbo.

Billy rolled his eyes. 'Real name, ya clown.'

'Mark Munroe,' said Jumbo.

Was a surprise to McCoy. Didn't think he'd ever heard Jumbo's real name.

'Empty your pockets,' said Billy, getting out a belongings form, writing *Mark Munroe* at the top.

Jumbo dug in his jeans. Produced half a packet of polo fruits, twenty pence in change, a rabbit's-foot keyring and a wallet with cowboy scenes embossed on it.

Billy opened it. Let out a low whistle. Started counting the notes. 'Two hundred and seventy quid,' he said. 'Someone's won on the gee-gees.'

This was a surprise to McCoy too. Wouldn't have thought Jumbo had that much money in a million years. Probably his life savings. Jumbo wouldn't be able to deal with a bank account.

'I don't feel well,' said Jumbo looking miserable. 'I feel a bit sick.'

'Oh, for fuck sake,' said Billy. 'Don't you fucking boak!'

'Think I'll leave you to it,' said McCoy, backing off towards the door. The last thing he heard as he stepped outside was Billy shouting 'You owe me, McCoy!' and a splatter that sounded not unlike someone being very sick on a linoleum floor.

21ST APRIL 1974

CHAPTER 64

McCoy yawned, looked out over the bay. Another Sunday working. Only ten o'clock and it was already hot, going to be roasting for the next three days according to the radio. He'd listened to it in the car to Greenock. Was getting like a routine now: picked up at home, patrol boat, walk up to Knockland. Wasn't a bad commute to work, not on a day like this. Water was sparkling, already a hum of insects, sun hot on the back of his neck.

He turned, started walking back towards the big house. Only fly in the ointment was that they weren't getting anywhere. Still no Donny Stewart, still no trace of the bomber lads. Today was the day they were expecting the next bomb and they still had no idea when or where it was going to be. Could see Faulds at the window, a mug of tea in his hand. He'd been staying there, wasn't much point in going home. Searches began in the morning, only stopped when it got dark. They had dogs coming today, trained to smell dead bodies. Maybe they'd find something. Wasn't sure how much longer Murray could justify the costs of the search with no results, even with Cavendish's say-so. Something had to give soon.

'Lovely day,' said Faulds, walking out into the garden. Handed McCoy a mug of tea and they sat down on a bench by the formal rose beds. 'I could get used to this,' he said. 'Staying here.'

'I bet,' said McCoy. 'They take everything?'

Faulds nodded. Cavendish and Barnes had arrived yesterday, started packing all the contents of the room into cardboard boxes. 'Like nothing had ever been here.'

'You think the prof took anything?' asked McCoy.

'Be a fool not to,' said Faulds. 'Leave Cavendish to worry about that one. We found a patch of turned earth last night, out by the boundary fence. Might be something. Might be nothing. Let's see what the hounds of hell make of it today.'

McCoy nodded. Sipped his tea.

'Least we got Barnes off our backs,' said Faulds. 'For a while anyway.'

Faulds stood up, brushed himself down. 'Better go and see what the teams have been up to this morning. When's Wattie due?'

McCoy looked at his watch. 'Any minute.'

'What you two going to do today?'

McCoy shook his head. 'Wait. Wait for the phone call from the station saying a bomb's gone off. Wait until Lindsay's well enough to speak to. Wait until they find Donny Stewart. Driving me round the bend, feel a bit useless to be honest. Might as well head back to Glasgow this afternoon. Not doing much here except admiring the scenery.'

'Ah, well, don't knock it,' said Faulds, 'Know where I'd rather be on a day like this.'

McCoy watched him walk back into the house. Wondered if the Land Registry people had turned up any more property that belonged to Lindsay. Fuck it, Faulds was right, he may as well enjoy himself while he was here. Walked back towards the shore. Sat down, back against a rowing boat that had been pulled up onto the shore. Sun was hot on his face, noise of waves lapping and insects buzzing.

'Working hard?'

McCoy opened his eyes, looked up at Wattie standing over him.

'Shite, must have fallen asleep.' He sat up. 'Just closed my eyes for a minute.'

'Aye right,' said Wattie, sitting down beside him. 'I believe you, thousands wouldn't.'

McCoy got his cigarettes out his jacket pocket, lit up. Two of them sat there looking out at the boats tethered offshore bobbing up and down in the sunshine.

'I'm boiling,' said McCoy. Took his jacket off. 'Must be seventy.'

Wattie nodded. 'Think another one'll go off today?'

'Probably,' said McCoy. 'Just Crawford left, and I have the feeling his'll be the big one.'

'Fuck,' said Wattie.

McCoy brushed a fly off his hand. It flew around, landed on a pebble next to Wattie's hand. A pebble that had a spot of red shiny blood on it. Looked at Wattie's hand, there was blood dripping off it.

'You're bleeding,' said McCoy.

'What?' asked Wattie. Looked at his hand, pulled it away, out of sight.

'What's wrong?' asked McCoy.

No response.

McCoy looked around, could see more specks of blood on the stones.

'Wattie?'

Wattie stood up, walked towards the water. Stood there looking out. Even at the distance, McCoy could see blood dripping off his hand onto the stones below. And then it struck him.

'Wattie, take your jacket off.'

Nothing.

He got up, walked towards him. 'Take your fucking jacket off, Wattie.'

Wattie turned his head, moved awkwardly, slipped his right arm out, and took the jacket off. McCoy looked away quickly, but not before he saw that the back of his pale blue shirt was dark and wet with blood.

'You didn't,' said McCoy. 'Tell me you didn't.'

He had.

McCoy helped him out the shirt. Difficult, blood making it stick to his back. Eventually came away with some long wound dressings sticking to it.

McCoy stood back and looked. Two long cuts crossing each other just above his shoulder blades.

'Christ, Wattie, you shouldn't have gone to see Lindsay on your own. He's a—'

'I know that now but he said he'd tell me where Donny Stewart was,' he grimaced. 'But he didn't.'

'He was never going to, Wattie. That's all part of Lindsay's game.'

Wattie's head dropped. 'I just wanted something to go my way, something I could tell Murray that I had done. Found Donny Stewart. Been a hero. He's going to get rid of me, Harry, put me back in uniform, back on the beat.'

'No, he's not,' said McCoy with more conviction than he believed. 'Did the nurses put those dressings on?'

Wattie nodded. 'Didn't do much good.'

'Does it hurt?' asked McCoy.

'A bit. Was agony at the time. Made sure he did it as slow as he could.'

'Christ,' said McCoy looking away. Could just imagine Lindsay's face as he drew the blade across Wattie's back. He looked back and Wattie was sitting on the pebbles undoing the laces of his shoes.

'What are you doing?' he asked.

'Going to go in,' said Wattie, pulling his socks off and placing them in his shoes. 'Think the salt-water will be good for it, it'll clean it anyway.'

McCoy was about to tell him he wasn't sure if

the loch was saltwater or not then he stopped himself. What was the point? If it was going to make Wattie feel better why not? Besides, he had to get the blood off him somehow.

'Jesus Christ, Wattie, where'd you get them?' asked McCoy nodding at Wattie's Mickey Mouse patterned Y-fronts.

He grinned. 'Mary's catalogue. Good, aren't they?'

'Not the word I'd use,' said McCoy.

He watched Wattie walk into the loch. He let out a groan as the cold water hit the Mickey Mouse Y-fronts then he dived in. Head came up out the water a few yards further in. He winced, must be saltwater after all.

'Should come in, Harry!' he shouted.

'Aye that'll be right,' said McCoy.

Wattie was a great swimmer. He had won medals while McCoy could only manage a few lengths of the baths in Springburn. Still, it was tempting, the sun was getting higher in the sky, definitely had some heat in it. A compromise was in order. McCoy undid his shoes, took his socks off, and went in for a paddle.

He walked up and down the shore, trousers rolled up. Hadn't realised how desperate Wattie was, how scared he was for his job. He had stopped now, was treading water, a couple of yards from the two tethered boats. One was a rowing boat, the other was a bit grander – had a tall mast, cabin with windows, looked like the kind you could sail around the islands or across to France.

Wondered what Murray would say if he could see them now. Probably wouldn't be able to speak, would just spontaneously combust. Supposed they'd better get back up to the house. Land Registry people had said they would call that morning, should see if they had found anything worth investigating. He shouted at Wattie to come out. Didn't hear him, was still treading water, face up to the sun.

He pulled his trousers further up, wandered a bit further in. 'Wattie!'

He heard him this time. Held his hand up. 'Coming!' he shouted back. Started to swim then stopped. Had his head to the side, treading water.

'Now!' shouted McCoy. 'We need to get back!'

Wattie held his hand up to silence him. Moved his head again until he was facing the bigger boat. Started to swim towards it.

'Fuck sake,' muttered McCoy.

Wattie got to the side of the boat. Stopped. Listened. Shouted at McCoy. 'I can hear something.'

He swam to the side, pulled himself up and onto the boat, and disappeared into the cabin.

McCoy shook his head, wondering what on earth he was up to. Was about to shout him again when Wattie appeared on the deck. Put his hands either side of his mouth and shouted, 'Get out here quick, McCoy! Use the rowing boat!'

McCoy managed to get the rowing boat into the water, pushed it further out, jumped in and grabbed the oars. Got near enough to the big boat that he could throw a rope to Wattie. Wattie grabbed it, started pulling him in.

'What is it?' asked McCoy, stepping up onto the bigger boat, trying not to fall in. 'What's going on?'

Wattie's face was grim. 'There's someone in the boat.'

'What? Is he alive?' asked McCoy.

'Just,' said Wattie as he turned and walked down the steps into the cabin. McCoy took a deep breath and followed him.

CHAPTER 65

McCoy stood in the cabin of the boat in the stink of damp and shit, waiting for his eyes to adjust to the darkness. First thing he noticed was that the floor was swimming in reddish water. The second thing he noticed was the young man. He was naked, tied to the wall, body criss-crossed with tight ropes. Lindsay had obviously been interrupted. The man's left arm and leg were a mess of slashes and cuts. Some of the cuts were crusted with dried blood, some still wet with it. McCoy looked down quickly. Steeled himself and looked up.

The man's head was bent forward, chin on chest, blond hair red with caked blood. Couldn't see much of his face but he seemed tall, slight. It had to be him.

'Donny?' said McCoy.

No response. There was a canteen lying at the back of the cabin. He picked it up and shook it, seemed to have liquid in it. He unscrewed the top. Tasted it. Water. Held it to Donny's lips.

'Think he wore himself out shouting,' said Wattie. 'Was like that when I got in.'

447

'Donny?' asked McCoy. 'Can you hear me? Try and take a drink.'

Nothing.

'Donny?'

'Hang on,' said Wattie, easing closer. He held Donny's head back and McCoy poured the water into his mouth. He spluttered and then his eyes opened, widened. McCoy managed to pour most of the water into his mouth, tried to go slowly, didn't want him to choke, but Donny was drinking it down, couldn't get enough. McCoy finished the canteen, put it down.

'Donny?' he asked.

Donny nodded. Managed to get it out. Just more than a whisper. 'What day is it?'

'Sunday,' said McCoy.

Donny looked at him with horror.

McCoy shook his head. 'Nothing's happened. Not yet. Need to get you out these ropes though. Okay?'

Donny nodded.

McCoy went back up to the deck after they got the first one off him. Left Wattie to it. Couldn't stand the screams as he cut through the ropes and the blood flowed back into Donny's damaged flesh.

Hoped Donny would be able to talk when they got him back to the house. He didn't look good at all. Dehydrated, lost a lot of blood, must have been tied up like that for days. God knows how much he'd suffered down in that cabin. Another scream and McCoy's stomach turned over. He'd seen the fear on his face when he'd told him it was Sunday. This was the day for the last bomb. Crawford's. Had to be something big by the look on Donny's face.

He turned and Wattie was standing at the top of the stairs. He was covered in blood. McCoy wasn't sure if it was his or Donny's.

'That's him free,' he said. 'But he's really weak. Not sure he's going to make it.'

'He will,' said McCoy. 'He has to. Let's get him in the boat.'

CHAPTER 66

Two of the search party uniforms had first aid qualifications. They were attending to Donny now, bent over the couch in the big reception room, trying to stop the bleeding. Getting Donny into the rowing boat had almost killed him. He couldn't walk, was hard to find a part of his body that didn't hurt to lift him by. They managed to get him onto the floor of the rowing boat and they'd paddled into the shore. He'd screamed so loud on the way to shore that Faulds had heard it in the woods, was waiting for them on the shore with the two uniforms, blanket stretched out to carry him in.

McCoy, Faulds and Wattie, now dressed in his trousers and a vest he'd found in Lindsay's wardrobe, were standing by the French windows, smoking. Waiting for the verdict. The uniforms had cut up sheets, made bandages out of them. Faulds had found a first aid box in the kitchen. Now all they could do was wait and hope.

'So he was in that boat the whole time?' asked Faulds.

McCoy nodded.

450

'Christ, how many times have I stood here looking out at the water thinking how nice it would be to go for a wee sail.'

'I've called the Central Hotel,' said McCoy. 'His dad's not there. I'll try him again in a minute.'

'The poor bugger could probably hear us in the garden talking about him,' said Wattie.

'And all the while Lindsay's lying in his hospital bed knowing full well what was going on,' said McCoy. 'Laughing.'

He spat on the grass. No way was Cavendish getting to cover this up. Even if Lindsay died before they could charge him, he was going to make sure the papers knew all about it. Turned to Wattie.

'When does Mary start back at the *Record*? Is it—'

'Mr McCoy.' One of the uniforms was standing by the doorway. 'Do you want to come in?'

McCoy dropped his cigarette on the grass and stepped inside.

Luckily for him, they'd wrapped Donny up in a sheet, red tartan rug over him, so he wouldn't have to look at all the cuts again. The young man's face was deathly white, skin drawn over his bones, eyes closed. For a minute McCoy thought he was dead but then his eyes opened and he looked up at him.

'Think you can answer some questions?' asked McCoy. He knelt down on the floor beside him, took his hand in his. 'Just squeeze my hand if the answer's yes. Okay?'

451

A tiny nod.

'Did Lindsay do this to you?'

A squeeze.

'Do you know about the bombings?'

Another squeeze.

'What is supposed to happen today?'

Immediately realised Donny couldn't answer yes or no to that. Started to say sorry when Donny started speaking. Had to lean in to him to hear.

'This is Crawford's day. The biggest one.'

'Do you know where it is?' asked McCoy.

He shook his head slowly. Tried to speak, could hardly get it out. 'He wanted to bomb the naval . . .'

'Take your time,' said McCoy.

He nodded. Tried again. 'Naval base but couldn't work out how to get past security.'

He started coughing, watery blood running down his chin. McCoy wiped it away with the blanket.

'Going to do somewhere else. Somewhere that would shock everyone.'

'Do you know where he is now?'

Another shake. No.

'Can you think of anywhere he would target?'

Tears started to run down his cheeks. McCoy squeezed his hand.

'It's okay. Your dad's here. He came to look for you. He's a good man, understands everything. Everything.' Wondered if Donny knew what he meant. 'They're going to take you to the hospital now, get you fixed up. Your dad'll be there soon, okay?'

Donny nodded again and his eyes closed.

McCoy stood up, took the uniform aside. 'What do you think?' he asked.

The uniform was young, could only have been early twenties. His expression pretty much told McCoy what he thought. 'I'm not a doctor but he's in very bad shape. If he can survive the trip to hospital he might make it.' He shrugged. 'I just don't know.'

McCoy thanked him. Looked back at Donny Stewart. He was just some lonely American kid looking for friends and this was how he'd ended up. Could hear the siren of an ambulance getting louder as it was coming up the drive. Whatever happened to Donny Stewart was out of his hands now. They'd found him. All they could do was wait for Crawford's bomb to go off and pray it didn't do too much damage. But maximum damage would be exactly what that bastard was aiming for.

CHAPTER 67

McCoy left Faulds and Wattie at the house to deal with the crime scene on the boat and the remains of the search. Couldn't just sit there any longer, admiring the view, waiting for the phone to ring to tell them the bomb had gone off. He figured if Andy Stewart wasn't at his hotel in Glasgow he'd be in Dunoon handing out his pictures. He got in the car and headed down the driveway away from the house. Might as well give him the news.

He parked the car up by the fair. Looked like it was moving on. Men were dismantling the rides with huge spanners, stalls being broken down. McCoy got out of the car, started walking towards town. He'd tell Stewart his son was on the way to the hospital in Greenock, then head to Glasgow. Even if he couldn't do anything about the bomb he felt he should be with Murray when the call came in.

He'd just taken his jacket off, folded it over his arm, was about to loosen his shirt button when he heard a shout.

'Mr McCoy!'

He looked round and Patsy Hearne was running down from the fair towards him. Last person he expected to see. Patsy stopped, held out his hand and they shook.

'What you doing here?' asked McCoy.

'Helping with the pulling down. They're down a few hands, got press-ganged into helping out. What are you doing here?'

'Polis business,' said McCoy. 'Just going into Dunoon to find someone then heading to Glasgow. You want a lift?'

Paul shook his head. 'If only. I'll be here until it gets dark. You ever find out what happened to Jamsie Dixon?'

McCoy shook his head. 'Not sure we ever will. Might have to write that one off.'

'Shite,' said Patsy. 'Thought if you caught who did it we might get our money back. You know a guy called Ronnie Naismith?'

McCoy nodded.

'Seems that's who Jamsie was collecting for. Now he says it's no his fault the money went missing and we still have to pay it.'

'That's rough,' said McCoy.

'You're telling me,' said Patsy. 'Two hundred and seventy quid down the Swanee, not sure how we're going to raise that again.'

McCoy looked at him. 'How much did you say?' he asked.

'Two hundred and seventy bloody quid,' said Patsy.

Patsy went on talking about how they were down on takings this year and how the money was going to be hard to get but McCoy wasn't listening. He said cheerio to Patsy, told him he would see what he could do about Ronnie Naismith, and walked into town. Suddenly everything about Jamsie Dixon's death was starting to make sense.

He'd just walked past the big hotel when he saw Andy Stewart. He was standing outside the Paul Jones, printed pictures of Donny in his hand, trying to talk to the young lads going in and out. Made a change for McCoy, for once he was going to deliver good news. He stopped, lit up, watched him for a minute. Could tell most of the sailors going in and out the pub had seen him and his pictures before. They said hello, wished him luck, hurried on.

McCoy was just about to walk up to him when Stewart saw him, waved. He put the papers back in a plastic bag, jogged down the road towards him.

'Harry!' he said. 'Nice to see you.'

He held out his hand to shake and McCoy took it.

'Getting sick of handing out these pictures all day, I'll tell you that for—'

'We found Donny,' said McCoy.

Stewart stopped. Dropped the plastic bag. Looked at him.

'He's alive,' said McCoy. 'But he's in a bad way.'

'Oh Christ,' said Stewart. He was shaking, looked

like he was about to faint. McCoy pointed at a bench down by the pier.

'Come on and sit down,' he said.

They sat on the bench and McCoy told him the story, Stewart listening, wiping at tears every so often with the sleeve of his shirt.

'Where is he?' asked Stewart.

'Should be at the hospital in Greenock by now,' said McCoy. 'Just across the water.'

Stewart lunged at him, held him in his arms. 'Thank you,' he said. 'Thank you.'

McCoy felt a bit emotional himself, patted Stewart's back, told him it would all be okay now. Eventually Stewart let him go. Sat back.

'Next ferry's in half an hour,' said McCoy.

Stewart smiled. 'In that case, there's time enough for me to buy you a drink.' He stood up. 'Mind if we go to the Paul Jones? I'd like to let the boys know he's okay.'

'Sure,' said McCoy. He couldn't think of anywhere he'd less like to be but he didn't want to spoil Stewart's moment.

457

CHAPTER 68

The Paul Jones was heaving, shift change at the base apparently. A sea of lads in their early twenties, all loud, all sweating in the heat. McCoy took the beer Stewart had bought him, tried to avoid it getting spilled in all the jostling. Even if he was having a rotten time, Stewart was happy. Shaking hands, hugging people, even started crying a few times. The jukebox was going. At least that was half decent. 'Purple Haze' into 'Brown Sugar'.

Last notes of 'Brown Sugar' faded away and a big guy with a blond buzz cut shouted 'everybody ready' and the drums of 'Fortunate Son' started. McCoy groaned, knew what that meant. The place went mental. Everyone suddenly singing along at the top of their voices, jumping up and down, drinks going flying. Bedlam. Three boys were trying to lift Stewart up onto their shoulders. Someone had lifted one of the barmaids over the bar, was dancing around her as she giggled. Supposed if he was young he'd be enjoying it too. Not now, was too old for all that. Put the beer back on the bar, stomach hurt too much to drink it. Time for a cigarette and a breath of fresh air.

McCoy pushed the door open just as a young guy was leaving. His head was down, baseball hat, said thanks, dodged under his arm, and started walking down the street. McCoy got his fags out, wondered why a Scottish guy had been in the bar, barmaid had told him they never went in. And then it hit him.

McCoy swore under his breath. Another boy came out the pub, threw up in the gutter. 'Some folks inherit star spangled eyes' blasting out as McCoy pushed the door open. Foreign occupiers and drink. Should have realised before now. The Paul Jones was the perfect target.

He tried to make his way to the bar to get them to turn the music off and clear the place. He couldn't even get past the first group of lads. They were jumping, shouting, one of them grabbed him, spun him around. He tried to shout but no one could hear him over the noise. He pushed a guy out the way and he tumbled over. Shouts of 'hey, man!' and a big guy grabbed him, pulled his arms behind his back. McCoy was trying to shout 'clear the pub' but no one could hear him above the music and the shouting.

He caught sight of Stewart, bellowed his name as loud as he could, tried to get out the young guy's grip but he couldn't, the guy was twice his size. Stewart came over, face red, a big smile on his face.

McCoy shouted as loud as he could. 'Find a bag! There's a bomb in here!'

Stewart's face changed instantly. He turned, burrowed into the crowd. McCoy had had enough, brought his heel down hard on the guy's shin. The guy grunted but didn't let him go, started dragging him towards the door shouting 'you need to calm down, buddy!' in his ear.

McCoy struggled but it was no use, he couldn't get free. The guy pushed him at the door and it swung open and McCoy was launched out into the street. He fell and hit his head on the pavement, looked up to see Stewart running out the pub door, Adidas sports bag in hand.

He scrambled up and started running down the street after him. Stewart was battering through the crowds on the pavement, shouting at them to get out the way. He turned at the hotel, heading for the pier. McCoy kept running, heart pounding, trying to keep up. He ran through the garden of the hotel just as Stewart got onto the pier, ran around the queue of cars and people waiting for the ferry and stopped at the very edge. Stewart drew his arm back, went to hurl the bag into the water, and just as he let it go, the bomb went off. There was a terrific boom, a white light, the sound of shattering glass and a scream from Stewart.

McCoy ran onto the pier, avoiding the screaming kids, feet crunching on the glass from car windows, pier covered in dead seagulls, piles of feathers and blood. He got to Stewart and rolled him over. His eyes were wide open, terrified, blood pumping out what was left of his right arm. McCoy pulled his tie off, wrapped it as close to the end of the arm as possible, and pulled tight. Stewart screamed. The blood was pumping into McCoy's chest and neck, he could taste it in his mouth. Tried to ignore it, stay focused. Couldn't pass out now. He pulled the tourniquet tighter. Stewart screamed again.

'It's okay,' said McCoy. 'You're going to be all right.'

Stewart nodded, face contorted with pain. 'Please, tell Donny I love him.'

'You can tell him yourself,' said McCoy. 'You're not going anywhere.'

Stewart nodded and his eyes closed. McCoy pulled the tourniquet tighter again, pulled Stewart's head into his lap, and shouted for someone to phone a fucking ambulance.

22ND APRIL 1974

CHAPTER 69

There was nowhere in the world McCoy hated more than the morgue. Even as he got out the taxi and caught sight of the long, low building by the side of the Clyde his stomach turned over. The last thing he wanted to do was look at a dead body, but he had to. He owed him that at least.

As soon as he pulled the heavy wooden door back the smell hit him. Bleach and decay, that sweet pickle smell of formaldehyde in the background. He signed in at the booth at the front and walked down the corridor towards the examination room. The call had come that morning. Got him out of bed. He couldn't believe it. Should have been prepared but he wasn't, hit him like a ton of bricks.

He knocked on the frosted glass. Phyllis Gilroy Chief Medical Examiner, in gold paint.

'Come in.'

At least she was familiar with his fear of blood and guts, hopefully she'd make it easy for him.

He pushed the door open and she was standing there in a snow-white lab coat. Gave him a sympathetic smile. 'Sorry about this, Harry, but we needed someone to do the official identification. Know it's not your favourite place to be.'

'Got to be done,' said McCoy. Tried to sound like he was calm and collected.

He stepped forward and Phyllis walked to the head of the shrouded body on the metal bench in the middle of the room. 'Ready?'

He nodded and she pulled the sheet back.

Was the hair he recognised more than anything. Billy's familiar feather cut. His face was harder to recognise. McCoy made himself look, tried to breathe slowly through his nose. Billy's eyes were swollen shut, a long gash down the right cheek. Most of the teeth gone. His nose was flattened against his cheek, broken and smashed, but it was him all right.

He nodded. 'That's Billy Weir.'

Phyllis placed the sheet back over his head and said she'd see him outside.

McCoy sat down on the steps of the High Court and lit up. Every time he came to the morgue he ended up here, waiting for whatever was going on inside to finish. A bus stopped opposite, wee boy breathed on the window, drew a face. Wondered if Billy had tried to run or whether he'd just waited, knowing the inevitable was coming. What was he? Twenty-two? Twenty-three? What a waste. He'd had a bit of life about him, always up for a laugh. All he did was make one mistake. Crossing Stevie Cooper.

Supposed Cooper had to do it. In his world, he had no choice. A failed takeover had to be dealt with as strongly and as quickly as possible. Needed to show everyone the boss was back in control. Still, didn't know why he hadn't just stabbed Billy and got it over with. Why did he have to beat the fuck out of him? Looked like it had taken a while as well. Once Cooper's blood was up, that was it. He'd just keep hitting and hitting until there was no life left in Billy any more.

'I should change my office to out here,' said Phyllis, sitting down on the step beside him. 'Spend more time out here when you're involved. You okay?'

McCoy nodded. 'What happened to him?'

'More of a case of what didn't,' said Phyllis. 'Basically, he was battered then battered some more. His spleen was ruptured at some point. Internal bleeding. Damage to the brain can't have helped much either. All in all a very nasty business indeed.'

McCoy nodded. Didn't want to imagine it. 'When did it happen?'

'About thirty-six hours ago.' she said. 'Body was discovered last night in long weeds by the side of the Clyde near the suspension bridge.'

McCoy tried to work it out in his head. 'So he was killed . . .'

'Sometime the evening before last,' said Phyllis. 'Saturday the 20th.'

'You sure?'

She nodded. 'Yes.'

McCoy stood up. 'I've got to go, Phyllis. I'll see you.' Started walking up the road towards town.

Phyllis shouting after him. 'McCoy! Come back! I need you to sign the statement!'

CHAPTER 70

'Billy's dead,' said McCoy.

Cooper was leaning against the sink in the kitchen in Memen Road. Half-empty bottle of milk in his hand. 'So I heard,' he said, wiping his mouth. 'Pity, that.'

'Got beaten so hard he died of internal bleeding.'

'Nasty,' said Cooper. 'Still, some say he had it coming.'

'Like you?' asked McCoy.

Cooper swallowed the rest of the milk, put the bottle down by the sink. 'Something you want to ask me, McCoy?'

'Why did you make Jumbo kill Jamsie Dixon? He's not right in the head, Cooper, he's a kid. That's out of order.'

'Is it? Do you know where Jumbo would be now if it wasn't for me? On the fucking street. Every cunt that could ripping the piss out of him. He'd end up giving gobbles to old men behind St Enoch to buy something to eat. You're going to take him in, are you? Give him a fucking job? Make sure he eats? Try and stop him crying in the middle of the night when he remembers how his mum used to tie him to a fucking radiator and feed him dog food? Call him a fucking spastic before she burnt him with her fag? You going to do all that, are you?'

McCoy shook his head.

'Thought not. So shut the fuck up.'

Cooper was starting to breathe heavy. A bad sign. 'How'd you know anyway?' he asked.

'Does it matter?' asked McCoy. 'Don't worry, I know you didn't kill Billy. Made sure you were out at the boxing with Stewart. That's why you wanted Jumbo arrested, wasn't it? Couldn't have been him either, not when he was in the cells. No roads leading back to Stevie Cooper. Desy Dixon did it, didn't he? Finally got to avenge his brother. Trouble is, he took it out on the wrong man and now Billy's dead.'

Cooper shrugged, but McCoy could see it in his eyes, hadn't expected him to work it out.

'Newcastle. I saw the train ticket. Nearest station to Gateshead. You went there to tell him Billy Weir had killed his brother, didn't you? Lit the touch paper and sat back while Desy Dixon did your dirty work for you.'

Could see Cooper's hands gripping the edge of the sink. Knuckles going white.

'Tell me. Was Billy really working with William Norton to get you put away or was he just starting to annoy you? Getting too independent, too friendly with Norton while you were up in Peterhead?'

McCoy wondered how far he could push it. Knew by the look on Cooper's face that he might have gone too far already. No point stopping now. 'Iris whispering in your ear, was she? I called Peterhead this morning. She was your only other visitor. And you fell for it, didn't you? She never liked Billy, always wanted rid of him, and looks like she got her wish, eh? Played you like a proper—'

Didn't have time to finish his sentence before Cooper was on him. A couple of sharp punches to the head and McCoy was on the floor, Cooper straddling him, knees on his shoulders.

McCoy couldn't help himself, said it. 'I always knew you were a bastard, Cooper, just didn't realise how fucking stupid you were.'

He felt the first few punches to his head then everything went black.

It was dark when he opened his eyes. He was lying on the floor, could see bloodstains on the floorboards. Put his hand up to his face, felt the dried blood. His eyes were hurting. Everything was a bit out of focus. Realised he was in the back room in Memen Road. The one that people got dragged into screaming. The one that Cooper used to do his worst. He groaned. Sat up.

Could make out a figure sitting against the opposite wall. Knew it was Cooper by the white vest, blond hair. Saw him raise a bottle of whisky to his mouth, take a long draft.

'Still alive then,' he said.

'Just about,' said McCoy.

Cooper handed him the bottle and he took it, took a swig, liquid cold then burning against the cuts in his mouth. Handed it back. Squeezed his eyes half shut, managed to get Cooper into focus. Looked like whatever had come over him, the storm had passed. He was back to his normal self.

'Like always, McCoy. Never quite as smart as you think you are.'

'How's that?' asked McCoy.

'Billy wasn't the nice guy you thought he was. That I thought.' Cooper took another swig. 'I thought he was my pal, that I could tell him anything. We got stoned one night, just before I went into Peterhead, pissed and stoned.' Cooper took another swig from the bottle. 'And I told him what had happened to me in some of the homes. Told him what the night worker in Barnardo's did to me.'

A flare of light as Cooper lit up. Cooper had only told McCoy the story once. Had been drunk enough to let it out. Had cried afterwards. The only time he'd ever seen Cooper cry.

'You're wrong about Iris too, smartarse. She was in the house one night, could hear Billy and Norton talking. Billy boasting how he'd paid the Batter Squad to do me over and to make sure they shoved a baton up my arse because "that would send him mad".'

Another draft of the whisky.

'And they did. And it did. Was in solitary for

two months, suicide watch. Didn't care what happened to me, didn't care what happened to the business. Just like Billy planned. She heard what I was like, came up and told me what had happened.'

'Christ, Stevie, I didn't realise . . .'

'No, you didn't because you're the polis and I'm the thug. You know everything and I know nothing, feel nothing. Just drink and fuck and damage people for a living.'

He wasn't totally wrong. Had forgotten over the years that Cooper had suffered as much as he had, the fact he didn't show it didn't change things.

'So why you up here anyway, McCoy? What is it you want this time?' he asked. 'What else can I do to help Harry McCoy – after all, that's what I'm here for, isn't it?'

'Stevie . . .'

Cooper held up his hand. 'Just tell me.' He smiled. 'Might as well make up for battering you to fuck.'

CHAPTER 71

'What did Mary say when she saw your back?' asked McCoy, sitting down at his desk.

'She hasn't yet. I slept on the couch, said she needed a proper sleep without me snoring, make up for all the sleep she's lost with the wee man.'

Wattie looked up. 'Christ. What happened to your face?'

'Fell over,' said Mc Coy. 'Come on, you can drive me to the hospital. I need to talk to you.'

They got in the car, pulled out the yard and into the traffic.

'Need you to listen to me,' said McCoy. 'I'm not going to tell you this twice. This is what you tell Murray.'

'Okay,' said Wattie, looking wary.

'You tell him you realise you've been a bit preoccupied lately because you've been cultivating a new tout. He's been difficult to pin down, paranoid about being found out, but he's come through. He's told you that Desy Dixon killed Billy Weir. Because Billy killed his brother Jamsie—'

'Billy did what?'

474

'I mean it, Wattie. Listen,' said McCoy. 'Billy Weir killed Desy's brother so Desy killed him. He battered him to fuck so he was covered in blood. He left a shirt and a jacket in the bottom of the bins at the back of the fruit shop on Clyde Street. You want to go and search them. You'll find them. They'll be covered in Billy's blood. It's a done deal. Jamsie Dixon killed by Billy. Murder solved. Billy Weir killed by Desy Dixon. Murder solved. You've bagged two murders. You'll be the golden boy. You got it?'

Wattie nodded. 'I don't get it though, how—'

'You don't need to get it, Wattie. You just need to get it to work. This is the big one you need to get Murray on side. Don't waste it. Now pull the car over.'

He did and McCoy got out, leaving Wattie sitting there looking shell-shocked. Cooper had come through big time. Had been asked to bring new clothes for Desy Dixon to change into when the deed was done. Had dumped the bloody ones in the bins. With any luck they should still be there.

McCoy walked up the steps to the Royal, opened the door. Woman on reception told him Andy Stewart was in ward two.

Stewart was sitting up in bed when McCoy went in. One arm now cut off below the elbow and wrapped in bandages, face peppered with glass cuts, but he looked happy enough.

'Think your boxing career is over,' said McCoy. 'How's Donny?'

'Saw him this morning.' His face clouded. 'The physical wounds will heal but it's not them I'm worried about. Not sure anyone could go through what he did and come out unscathed. Going to be a long road. A long road.'

'When do you get out?'

'Tomorrow,' he said. 'But I'm going to be here every day with Donny until he's better.'

There were tears glistening in his eyes, fingers pulling at a thread on the blanket over him.

'You saved a lot of people, Andy,' said McCoy. 'You should be proud.'

He looked up, wiped his eyes. 'We saved a lot of people,' said Stewart. 'Hope they're giving you a raise.'

'Something like that, I think,' said McCoy. 'Boss wants to talk to me tomorrow.'

'You deserve it,' said Stewart. 'Without you, Donny would be dead.'

'He say anything about the bombs? About Lindsay?' asked McCoy.

Stewart nodded. 'Said he didn't know anything about bombs until he turned up in Paul Watt's apartment. He thought it was a protest group, that they'd go on marches, that sort of thing. Thought Lindsay didn't know anything about the bomb-making, that's why he went back. To warn him.'

Started to cry again. McCoy sat down beside him on the bed, put his arm round his shoulders as he wept. Could hardly blame him. Was fifty-fifty as to whether Donny would make it and, even if he did, it was impossible to say what damage had been done to his mind. An ordeal like he'd been through was enough to send anyone over the edge.

He left Stewart there, told him he'd come in and see him in the morning. Had something he needed to do now. Wasn't much time left. Walked up the stairs to the next floor. Lindsay's floor. Wasn't sure whether he believed Donny Stewart's story or not. Still, wasn't him he had to convince, would be a jury. Sharp pain in his stomach stopped him for a minute. Felt in his pocket. Cursed. Had left the Pepto-Bismol at home. Couldn't remember the last time he'd eaten something solid. Stomach hurt if he did, hurt if he didn't.

He nodded at the uniform on guard, pushed the door open and went into Lindsay's room. Things had changed. The smell of rot was stronger than the smell of bleach now. Lindsay was propped up in bed. Looked more like a skeleton now than anything else but his eyes were alert. Widened as he realised McCoy was in the room.

McCoy sat down in the chair by the bed, looked at him.

'You're going to be erased,' said McCoy. 'The army and MI5 are going to make sure not a trace of you remains. No glorious army record, no bombing campaign, no murders. It will be like you never even existed. An empty space. Nothing.'

Lindsay looked at him, finally had fear on his face. 'They can't do that.'

'They already have,' said McCoy.

'Crawford will carry on my—' Lindsay stopped, was finding it hard to breathe.

'Crawford's dead,' said McCoy. 'Stepped in front of a train in Greenock this morning. Must have realised how you ruined his life. Just like you ruined so many other people's lives. And all for nothing.'

McCoy stood up, took the vial of liquid morphine from the locker, and handed it to Lindsay. 'Drink it,' he said. 'Or I swear I'll kill you anyway and I'll make it fucking hurt.'

Lindsay looked at him. Lifted the vial, put his lips around the glass straw. Cheeks hollowed as he sucked up the liquid.

'All of it,' said McCoy.

He managed three-quarters of it before he dropped the vial onto the bedclothes, his eyes closed, and the last breath seeped out of him.

McCoy left him there, walked along the corridor, heading for the stairs. Another horrible pain in his stomach. He tried to breathe slowly, wait for the wave to pass. Needed to get to a chemist's fast and get some more Pepto-Bismol. He walked down a few stairs and the pain was so strong he couldn't walk any more. He sat on the stair, tried to breathe. And then he was throwing up. Looked

478

like brown mud, streaks of bright red blood. He put his hand to his mouth, blood running down his chin. He leant against the wall, had never felt pain like it. Threw up again. Heard a pair of shoes on the stairs. He looked up to see Dr Basu standing there.

'Mr McCoy! Are you okay?'

McCoy managed to shake his head. 'I don't think so.'

SUTHERLAND

Crawford took his cup of coffee from the kitchen, sat on the front step of the croft and looked out at the forest below. Lindsay had told him about the place two days ago, the day he'd planted the bomb in the American pub. Too dangerous to go to the hospital to see him so Lindsay had reverted to plan B. A small ad in *The Times*. *Isolated croft for rent in Sutherland*. Then a map reference. Apply to A. Lindsay.

Had taken him a while to find it. Wasn't surprised. Sutherland was huge, most of it unoccupied. And the croft was sixty miles from the nearest town. Lindsay's father had won it in a card game thirty years ago, was still registered to the original owner. He'd had to clear it out a bit, nobody had been there for thirty years after all. Now it was clean and warm and dry. Home.

Sipped his coffee. He was sorry about Henry Robb, but it had to be done. Simple enough. He was the one who looked most like him. Six foot one, brown hair, same age. He'd put his wallet into Robb's pocket before he pushed him off the platform. Wasn't much else to identify you after an express train hits you at sixty miles an hour. Police must be happy. The evil bomber overcome with guilt ends it all.

He smiled. How stupid they were, how easy to fool.

He pulled his DEFENS T-shirt over his head, enjoyed the warmth on his back, felt good on his crossed scars. He folded it up neatly and put it into the fire he'd built just outside the croft. Took his army boots and khaki trousers off too. Stood there naked. Threw them into the roaring fire and watched them burn.

He wasn't interested in changing Scotland any more, never really had been, but Lindsay was and that had been enough for him. Now he was interested in the man who had stopped him doing it. The detective. Harry McCoy. But he could wait. McCoy wasn't going anywhere and he needed time to perfect his plan. He wasn't going to fail, not this time.

There were deer on the hill across the way. Wouldn't go hungry up here. Not after all Lindsay had taught him. He poured the remains of his coffee onto the grass and walked back into the croft. He needed to finish what Lindsay had started. Besides, Neil Harrison's screams were beginning to annoy him.

NO PLAN B

Gift

For more information see www.jackreacher.com